I quietly touched the selector switch to ensure my weapon was on full automatic and squinted down the barrel at the sicarios. Abner's command of Spanish was adequate, but he hadn't grown up on the border. I hoped he'd caught the gist of what was said. I need not have worried. His M16 opened up with a deafening noise just as I pulled the trigger on my weapon. Sparks flew when some rounds missed their mark and ricocheted off the steel of the entrance gate's structures.

Abner said, "This was no time for some 'Halt! You're under arrest' bullshit."

I couldn't have agreed more. "Yeah," I said. "But what in the hell have we stepped in this time?

Border Revenge

Todd Blomerth

Dedication

To Wanda, my writing buddy

Kindle: 978-1-7358087-4-1

EPUB: 978-1-7358087-5-8

Print: 978-1-7358087-6-5

Cover design by Karen Phillips / PhillipsCovers.com

Book formatting by RIAH Publishing / RiahPublishing.com

Contents

Chapter 1

A decision, long concealed, has deadly consequences

At the end of his workday, Israel Sifuentes, custodian for the Kickapoo County Courthouse, trudged through the late afternoon heat, set the hose and sprinkler to run all night on a particularly dry spot, and retrieved a hoe and shovel he'd used to break up the hard soil around some of the courthouse's tired rose bushes. He gave a desultory wave when a sheriff's deputy honked when he backed out of the sheriff's office parking area.

Israel was more than ready to go home, drink two beers, and only two beers, fix a bit of supper and watch TV.

He climbed into his decades old Chevy pickup, swung by the Patels' convenience store, bought a six pack of light beer, and headed for home. He aimed his truck south, his elbow jutting out the driver's side window, his gimme cap lowered to shield against the glare of the summer's afternoon sun.

He didn't notice the dark-skinned man holding a cell phone and leaning up against the store's outside bagged ice dispenser.

Almost exclusively populated by Mexican Americans, Santa Rosa's south-side streets were paved, mostly. The few patches of green Bermuda grass on a lawn along the streets signified some housewife's desperate attempt at growing something besides ornamental cactus and cockleburs.

Where the pavement ended, meandering roadways of hard packed caliche and sand petered out into the desert. Some eventually disappeared into the impassably deep sands lined with salt cedars near the Rio Grande's floodplain. Israel's truck's suspension rattled as it left the street's short expanse of pavement and hit caliche. As the town's structures thinned, he gazed out at the sere grassland and sandstone hills and ancient volcanic outcroppings to the east and west.

Israel's clapboard house squatted a mile south of town. He wished it was resting in the caliche hills north of town where the wealthier gringos built their homes and where the winds occasionally relieved the oppressive summer heat. He lived alone. His wife had died of breast cancer twenty years before. He'd taken care of her with a fierce love that despite his best efforts, didn't keep away the malignancy that ate away at her body.

He drove under his carport, killed the engine, let the stirred-up dust settle a bit, and climbed out, six pack in hand. He noticed his children's crayon marks, barely visible after all these years, on the side wall of the house. He smiled sadly, remembering how he'd gotten after the two kids after they messed up his new paint job. Now, the dim yellows and reds reminded him of the few times his now grown children had made the trip to Santa Rosa. He shook his head.

He visited his two grandchildren in Illinois every year or so, but he wasn't much on air travel. His children hated where he lived — the Texas border. The last time they'd returned was for their mother's funeral.

The kitchen window air conditioning unit kicked on with a hum. Drops of condensate dribbled onto his khaki pants when he closed the truck door. The truck's hood was too hot to touch so he walked behind the truck and glanced toward the mailbox perched on its pole just outside the galvanized metal fence. Idly, he considered checking to see if he'd received anything, but decided it was too far to walk in the heat. Opening the small outside refrigerator he used to chill beer, he peeled two beers out of the plastic and put the remaining four on the first shelf.

He climbed up the carport's two concrete steps and pushed open the kitchen door, welcoming the cool air from the air conditioner. Placing his truck keys on a small hook, Israel picked up the remote, plopped into his recliner, and turned on the national news.

The first beer went down quickly, as always. His limit was two, unless there was some *pachanga* at the Knights of Columbus Hall, when he'd indulge in more than two.

Israel pulled the ring tab on the second beer, then paused when he heard a slight noise behind him.

Remembering an infestation of pests in his neat house, he muttered, "Oh, *Madre de Dios,* I hope I don't have rats in here again."

A hard metal object jabbed the back of his head. *"No, no hay ratones, Sifuentes. Solamente alguien que va a matarte."*

The voice was not from someone this side of the border. Israel dropped his beer, its foam spewing over the living room's worn carpet. When he tried to turn, the barrel of a semiautomatic smashed into his right cheek and ear, knocking him sideways.

A pockmarked-faced, short-haired man with tattoos sneaking over the top of a collared long-sleeve shirt gently took the TV remote control and pushed its off button. The only sounds were Israel's wheezing breath and the hum of the window unit.

"Who are you?" Israel asked in Spanish.

The man responded in Spanish. "Paco Carrizales, at your service." The man stood in front of Israel and bowed mockingly. "It's more important you know why I'm here."

Israel Sifuentes already knew why the pockmarked man was there. Carrizales' willingness to give his name confirmed that the intruder was not concerned about Sifuentes telling on him. Israel was about to die. Desperate to prolong his life, he pretended not to know. "I'm just a janitor, *señor.* Why did you hit me? I have no money." He carefully moved his right hand to gesture toward the sparse room. "Take what you want."

Blood from his injured ear dripped onto the recliner's arm. Out of habit, Israel wiped it away with a hand already bloody from clutching the side of his face.

Carrizales' mouth creased into a sneer. He pointed the pistol at Israel's left kneecap and pulled the trigger.

Israel howled, rocking in a rictus of agony. The Mexican, motionless, patiently waited.

The pain from Israel's destroyed knee became a pulsing throb. Carrizales said, "Did you think you could kill one of our *carnales* and get away with it?"

Two years ago, Israel thought. *Two years ago! And nothing since. Only two others know of that night in Lagrimas. They would never talk. We knew that if anyone ever found out what we had done to the Zeta, we would all die.*

As if on cue, Carrizales asked, "*Ahora*. Now that I have your attention, would you please tell me who else helped to kill one of our *soldados*?"

In his mind, Israel prayed, *Thank you, Mother Mary. This bastard doesn't know about the others.*

Israel knew he would not leave his house alive. He prayed that he would not weaken and give this scum, this cartel trash, the names of his two *compadres*.

But how did he learn about me?

A folding knife appeared, and with a snapping motion, the Mexican opened and locked its blade. Rusty red spots blemished the metal cheek. Carrizales absently wiped the blade on a pant leg, and it reappeared with no blemishes.

Those weren't rust spots, Israel realized, as he remembered that there had been a fourth person, the *norteamericano*. He had phoned Purdy Kendricks to come to Lagrimas to the abandoned adobe hut to see the *sicario* who'd tried to kidnap Purdy's *señora* and their son. The conversation before Purdy Kendricks was sent away was still vivid in his mind:

"We brought you here so you could get the answers you need, but this piece of shit isn't going with you," Lilly Pardo had said quietly in that abandoned adobe.

And Purdy Kendricks had objected: "Christ. You can't take justice into your own hands."

Purdy Kendricks believed in his laws, but cartels pay no attention to laws. I understood this when I pointed a rusty revolver at Señor Purdy's head, even though he was a friend.

Lilly pleaded with him. "Please, Señor Purdy. There is nothing more for you to see here. Please leave now."

With tenderness she touched the deputy's arm, pleading with her words. Her eyes were filled with tears and terror.

"Senor Purdy," she pleaded. "If he goes with you, the sicarios *will find out. The people here"* —she had gestured toward the few houses in the village of Lagrimas — *"they will be killed." She pointed at Teofilo Ramirez,* mi compadre *from the other side of the Rio Bravo. "He will be killed."*

Teofilo nodded. He was puro indio, *and quiet, but his hatred of the cartels was clear. Hatred for what had become of his grandson, once a young man from his village.*

Teofilo, who's Spanish was like a foreign language to him, finally spoke. "We cannot let him go. Los Zetas or another cartel — they used Juan Gabriel. Then they spit him out."

Lilly had continued to plead. "Please, Mr. Purdy. Please leave."

"And him?" Purdy Kendricks had asked, pointing at the Zeta piece of trash.

Teofilo shook his head. I lowered the pistol. Purdy Kendricks was not like others who were not from the frontera. *He realized there would be no "justice" in the American courtrooms for the* sicario *we had captured. I had reminded him, again.*

"You know what would happen. No matter what you promised. Los Zetas, they have eyes and ears everywhere." I pointed my pistol at the bleeding, wounded sicario, *tied up with baling wire and tape. "You heard this scum. Someone will tell. We and our families will be killed. You know this."*

Purdy left, his hands not dirty. We did what needed to be done.

And now? Now, I am about to die.

Chapter 2

Purdy Kendricks gets an unwelcome telephone call

Unseasonable rain splashed against my office window in North Austin on a late Friday afternoon. I leaned back in my chair and rubbed my eyes. Too much time in front of a computer screen trying to learn Excel and put together a budget that made some sense.

A flash of lightning followed by thunder less than a second later made me jump, and I pulled a Bluetooth earbud out of my ear and turned hoping to see where the bolt had struck. Someone in the hallway yelled "Whoa!" when the office lights flickered.

Relieved the computer was on an uninterrupted power supply, and I hadn't lost the data I'd sweated blood over, I pulled out my personal cell phone and called my wife, Betty. She didn't pick up. I left a voicemail asking her to call me about the evening's plans. No way Forrest's coach-pitch baseball game was going to happen in this storm. No way Betty and I were going house-hunting in it either.

"Crap," I muttered and put the cellphone on a stack of papers. I minimized the program and pulled up the National Weather Service radar. The front moving through Central Texas was coming up out of Mexico. The forecast indicated heavy rain. Forrest, my seven-year-old son with visions of whacking a ball out of the park was going to be mighty disappointed.

His Little League team, the Wildcats, had their next game two days from now. Maybe the field would be dried out enough by then. In the meantime, Forrest would bemoan the missed chances to "hit a rope." So far, he'd only gotten one hit, a slow roller past a snoozing shortstop, but it had lit a fire. Like most anything Forrest did, it was going to be fun to watch his new interest grow.

I started to click off the National Weather Service and get back to number crunching. Instead, I moved the cursor away from Austin. Like someone commanded by unknown forces while at a Ouija Board, it traveled west, past Del Rio, to a squiggle on the Rio Grande. An angry looking storm cell perched over Kickapoo County, Texas.

Pull your head out, Kendricks. You don't have time to think about how much you love that God-forsaken place. I minimized the screen, stuffed the earbud back in and picked up my new audio player, and clicked *continue.* "Just the way you are," crooned Diana Krall. The simple piano accompaniment and a small combo let her smoky voice set the mood. I focused on the Excel spreadsheet, humming along while I tried to make sense of the numbers.

"Commander," said a voice beyond the door. Two large knocks followed.

I paused the music. *Damn.* "Come in, Miz Trejo."

Alicia Trejo, widow of a slain Department of Public Safety trooper, was my office manager. She gave me a sideways glance. "You need to turn down your music some. You'll ruin your hearing."

"What music?"

"Commander, you'd be more convincing if you didn't have two earbuds protruding from your head." As always, she refused to crack a smile.

"Yes, ma'am." I grinned. "What is it?"

"You've got a message from Lowell Johnson. He said he's tried calling you, but you didn't pick up. Says its urgent."

"Thanks." It was four o'clock. I pointed out the window. "It's slow around here right now. Why don't you and the rest of the crew knock off and beat some of the traffic."

She nodded and closed the door. Moments later, my small staff was turning off lights and yelling farewells through the wall as they tromped out. I picked up my cellphone. Two missed calls. I reminded myself to ask my son how to set the device to vibrate *and* make some noise when I got a call. I hadn't heard a thing.

I punched in Lowell Johnson's number and got his voicemail. "Hey, you said you needed to get ahold of me and said it's urgent. Returning your call."

I disconnected, saved my Excel spreadsheet, stood up, and stretched. It'd been a long week. Rain or no rain, it was time to spend some time with my family.

I locked my office, stepped into the gloominess of the hallway, and grabbed my Stetson. The phone silently vibrated in my breast pocket. Lowell Johnson again.

"What's up?"

"Purdy, can you hear me?"

"Loud and clear. What's up?"

"I'm not sure what I need to do, Purdy. We've got a problem."

"What's this *we* shit, Lowell? Did you drive drunk...again? Or piss off the illustrious sheriff...again?" I was in a good mood. Giving the owner and editor of the *Kickapoo County Register* some grief came naturally.

"Shut the fuck up, Purdy, and listen!" His voice cracked.

Whoa. "Sorry." I shut up. Lowell was usually even keeled. I re-entered my office and sat on the office settee.

"Israel Sifuentes, Purdy. Israel Sifuentes." Lowell began to cry.

I leaned forward, willing him to continue. I interrupted him. "Lowell, get to it. What's going on?"

"I just got back from the country." I knew he was speaking of the Bar LJ Ranch, which had been in his family for generations. "Going to check the cattle, what with this rain and all..." He stopped, and, this time, I didn't urge him on. I knew what was coming was not going to be good.

Lowell blew out a breath. "Got to the main gate. You know, where you and Forrest go in to go fishing."

I closed my eyes. I'd fished in his stock tanks for years. I could see the cattle guard and locked metal utility gate. Welded pipe supports and a horizontal cross piece with an *LJ* for the Bar LJ Ranch. Dirt road. Nothing but wide-open country in each direction. Fifty yards inside and, at forty-five degrees to the gate, a slight uphill slant to the fifteen-foot-high berm holding back the one acre of water of the largest of the cattle watering holes, stocked with catfish and sun perch.

"Someone's stuck Israel's head on top of one the gate's metal supports, Purdy." He began to cry. "They've stuffed his dick and balls in his mouth and stuck his head on my goddamned fence support. Oh, Jesus Christ."

What I was hearing was beyond anything I'd expected. "Oh my god, Lowell."

"I took off my slicker and covered Israel's head so it wouldn't get wetter. But I gotta get law enforcement out here and I wanted to talk to you first, Purdy. I don't know who to trust with something like this."

I stared at strewn magazines lying on the office coffee table. I was aware of a raw anger focused not on whoever had done this horrible thing to Israel, but at Lowell, the messenger with unwelcome news.

"Purdy, who'd do this to Israel? And why?"

I thought I knew who could have done it but lied. "I don't know."

"Why in God's name would the poor bastard's head end up at my place?"

That I didn't know, but knew I had to do something quick.

"Where are you right now?"

"I drove like a banshee back to US 90. I'm on my way into town."

"Have you seen Lilly Pardo, Lowell?"

The question seemed to catch him off guard. "Yeah, she waited on me at the Cenizo Café a couple of hours ago. Why are you asking about her?"

"Get out of there and call the sheriff. Then you get your ass over there and snatch her up and get her to the sheriff's office."

He paused. "Er. Okay, Purdy. But what's with Lilly?"

"Just do it," I screamed. "Now!"

I disconnected. *Had I somehow betrayed three people?* I wanted to parse through the last two years and analyze if anything I had said or done had gotten Israel killed, but there wasn't time right now. Suddenly, I realized that bringing Lowell into any part of this could make things worse.

Chapter 3
Purdy confronts the past

I immediately called Lowell back. He picked up on the first ring. "Have you called the sheriff yet?" I demanded.

"Damned near wrecked my truck trying to dial. Coming into town now. Was going to swing by and try to see if Lilly's working. Then head to the Sheriff's Office like you told me to. Why?"

I breathed in silent relief. "Hold off."

"What the hell?"

"Lowell, this doesn't go anywhere, but I seriously need you to not mention Lilly Pardo's name to anyone."

"But..."

"Please. Don't say a damned thing about Lilly Pardo to anyone, including *anyone* in law enforcement. Do not stop at the S.O." I tried to remember the night two years ago, and my trip to the tiny town of Lagrimas. Who had I told? Certainly not Betty. I'd shared almost everything with her, but what I witnessed that night was a horror she had no business knowing. To tell anyone what I'd seen would have been fatal for Israel, and Lilly Pardo, and an old man from across the border. And probably anyone in their immediate families. If I'd screwed up, it had already been fatal for Israel Sifuentes.

"What about reporting Israel's goddamned head on my fence post?" Lowell's voice pitched up with anger, aggravated by the four or five single malts he habitually partook of in the late afternoon.

I thought for a moment. "Pull over, Lowell, please. I'll make some phone calls and get back with you."

"Wait, dammit," he exclaimed. "Someone may have followed me."

What in hell? "Can you see anyone?"

"No. No one. It's just that..."

"What, goddamit?" I yelled.

"I noticed a set of tire tracks off US 90 onto the road. Didn't think much about it, until, you know..."

"Where are you now?"

"Tucked up against the side of a service station, next to the outside bathrooms. Just a sec."

I could hear a truck door slam shut. Then he continued, "Had to get out. My legs were cramping, I'm so damned scared. That set of tire tracks. It didn't turn off into any other ranch pastures. Went straight to mine." He coughed, then spit. "Aw, shit. Israel's head looked fresh, whatever the hell that means. Or maybe just wet from the rain. I don't know. I'm replaying it in my mind." Lowell began to sob. "Oh, man, I remember now. Those tracks went into my place."

Lowell seemed about ready to crater. I needed some information and asking questions might calm him down a little. "Where'd the tracks go? How far in?"

"Aw heck, I don't know. I didn't notice. I just saw them after seeing Israel's head on my fencepost."

He was beginning to babble. "Ten miles from nowhere, and I treasure my 'nads, underused as they may be. And I sure don't want them stuffed into my detached head."

I couldn't help it. As macabre as it was, I barked a laugh. Lowell was no coward. He'd proven that by what he printed about the DEA, and by what he'd done at the Griffin ranch in the middle of a nasty gunfight with cartel *sicarios*. But he wasn't stupid either. Someone was making a point, not just with Israel's gruesome death, but by the placement of it on the county newspaper owner's gatepost.

"Go to your office and lock the place up behind you. I'll call you as soon as I can."

"What about checking on Lilly?"

If Sifuentes' killers knew of Lilly, there would be nothing Lowell could do for her, and it would probably be too late. I didn't want him walking in on something and getting himself killed. I was carrying enough worries.

"I'll deal with Lilly. You just do what I said. Please."

"You got it, Kemosabe."

"Wait!"

"What the hell now?"

"Did you take any pictures?"

"Of what?"

"Israel's head."

"Aw shit, really? I just about upchucked when I saw it. And you want to know if I was stupid enough to hang around taking fucking pictures?"

"Well, yeah."

"I just backed up, did a yewee and got the hell out of there."

"Get to the office. Lock up." An idea hit me. "Lowell, had it started raining when you pulled off US 90?"

"Yeah, for about an hour. Why?"

"Tire tracks. Truck or car?"

Lowell paused. "Oh, for God's sake, Purdy. I need another drink." His truck door slammed, and the ignition switch dinged. "I didn't get out and measure the goddamned things. I was trying not to pee in my pants."

No telling when Israel's head had been stuck on the pole, but I wondered if whoever did it was still on the Bar LJ Ranch.

Lowell disconnected, and I walked back into my office. I dialed Betty. The call went to voicemail. "Honey, something's come up. I'll call you later, but I'm stuck at the office right now."

I hoped my voice didn't betray how afraid I was.

My heart was thumping like a trip hammer as I punched in the number for Santa Rosa's Cenizo Diner.

"Cenizo Diner. Can I take your order?" came the voice at the diner.

Thankfully, the raspy voice wasn't anyone's I recognized. I tried to keep it casual.

"Is Lilly working tonight?"

I could barely hear over the noise of clanging dishes and crowd noise. "Don't know. Just got on. Let me check." The racket quieted down for a second and I could picture the waitress putting the phone to her chest or putting her hand over the mouthpiece. "Hey, Beulah, Lilly working tonight?"

Then, "Hold on, Beulah's coming."

Shit.

"This is Beulah. Lilly's busy right now." Despite years in the Texas border region, she still sounded like an African American from the Deep South. "Give me your name and I'll tell her to call you."

Relief washed over me, but, as much as I liked Beulah Jackson, I didn't know what I was dealing with. I quickly disconnected.

There was only one person I knew I could trust. My next call was to Abner Selman. "C'mon. C'mon. C'mon. Pick up, dammit," I muttered, counting the rings.

He finally did. "Purdy, I hope you're calling to tell me that you're extending an invitation for some of Betty's cooking next time I'm in the neighborhood."

I started to cough.

"I didn't think so. What's going on, son?"

"I think we're in deep shit in Kickapoo County, Ranger."

"What's this *we* shit? I'm two weeks away from a passel of accumulated leave time and six months away from retirement. Don't tell me our illustrious Sheriff Johnson has stepped on his dick again," he chuckled.

Privately ridiculing Kickapoo County Sheriff Thomas Jefferson— 'TJ'— Johnson was an excuse for a laugh or two, but I didn't respond.

"That bad?"

"Yes." I relayed to him what Lowell had told me. I didn't offer any conjecture as to why the courthouse janitor had been murdered and dismembered.

When I stopped talking, Abner asked, "And why aren't you encouraging Lowell Johnson to call the sheriff's office. to get investigators out there?"

"Ranger, I don't know who I can trust in Kickapoo County. I think I know why Israel was killed. I'm still trying to sort through whether it was something I said that caused it."

"Doesn't sound likely. Purdy, it's been, what? Over two years since you left. Have you even talked to Israel since then?"

I couldn't remember. "Abner, bad things happen to good people near the border with Mexico."

"Really?"

My inane comment deserved Abner's sarcasm. Israel Sifuentes had helped save my life, and my career. I felt shame at my lack of contact with him. I'd avoided Israel after the night in Lagrimas. Mainly for his safety, but also because, despite the necessity of what was done, it didn't sit well. I'd inherited the ranch's seven thousand acres, but somehow, it still didn't feel like it belonged to me. "I've been back to the Griffin ranch a few times," I said, "and we've visited with my in-laws, but I can't remember the last time I've talked to Israel."

"Why'd Mr. Sifuentes' head end up on a gatepost? And that particular one?"

"It'll take some explaining, Abner."

"I'll just bet it will, son. I'll meet you in Kickapoo County. Damn, what ant's nest just got kicked over?"

*****

I drove home to exchange my State of Texas unmarked, an obviously law enforcement sedan, for my fifteen-year-old Chevy three-quarter-ton pickup.

"Daddy!" Forrest ran up, reached for a hug, and then, as if remembering he was now seven, decided a high-five was more appropriate. I didn't want to admit it, but the boy was growing up. I had once needed to brace myself for his fierce hugs. I missed them. I was in a hurry, but Forrest either didn't notice, or probably didn't care. It was time to regale me with his day's activities. Counseling had restored his little boy's luster of innocence – something I wondered about after he and his mother were nearly kidnapped and killed two years before.

I walked with Forrest to his room where he showed me a new game on his iPad. Once he was distracted playing the game, I returned to the kitchen to convince Betty that some inconsequential nonsense had "come up" that I couldn't get out of.

It didn't work.

"It's raining and you've dropped the sedan you've got every right to drive anywhere to take that gas guzzler truck of yours. Do I look dumb, Purdy?"

She didn't. She stood, hands on hips, beautiful even as she reddened with anger. "I realize that I wore out the term 'trust me,' but Honey, right now that's what you've got to do. I'll be back as soon as I can."

"Does this have something to do with Kickapoo County again?"

"Yes." I nodded, hoping there'd be no more questions.

"At least you're not trying to borrow my new SUV," she muttered. She was attempting to keep it light. Betty was no fool. Spooky smart, she had little trouble reading me like a book.

"Hell no, Honey. I may be stupid, but not that stupid."

She hugged me, kissed me fiercely, and pushed me onto the front porch, locking the door behind her. I quickly transferred a short-barreled shotgun, fully automatic M-16, ammunition, and ballistic vest from the trunk of the state sedan into my Chevy's cargo box. I was no longer an investigator, but I kept a digital camera, latex gloves, zip-lock bags, and some other rudimentary tools in a black expandable case. I tossed it onto the passenger side of the bench seat.

When I pulled onto the street, I called Abner. "Lilly's working tonight, but I don't know when she gets off, and I don't know if she's in danger."

"Well, you must be living right."

"Why?"

"Trooper Johnny Bonavita just happens to be in Santa Rosa."

"What the hell, Abner? What's he doing there? I didn't know Kickapoo County was his home station."

"Pulling border duty further west, mostly, but he also patrols almost to Del Rio." He mentioned the adjacent county seat where Bonavita lived. "He's a good'un, as you know. I haven't said anything about why, but I did ask him to have supper at the Cenizo. He'll hang around Santa Rosa and keep an eye on Lilly."

Thank you, Lord. Tears of relief welled in my eyes. Johnny Bonavita had been accepted to the Texas Department of Public Safety's academy mainly because of how he'd performed as a deputy sheriff in Kickapoo County. I could still see him standing over a dead gut-shot *sicario* who'd tried to kidnap Betty and Forrest. Inwardly, I winced, remembering him trying to keep me from crossing the Rio Grande during a gun battle with cartel members, and me belting him in the jaw and running for it. Yes, as Abner said, he was a good'un. Solid, dependable, and hopefully, close-lipped.

Austin and San Antonio outbound traffic on a Friday afternoon was a bitch, even more so because of the wet roads. In light traffic, it was five hours from Austin to Santa Rosa. It took me nearly seven. I stopped for gas and a burger in Hondo. I sat in the truck cab with the defroster and wipers going, replaying in my head the phone call I'd received from Israel Sifuentes:

"I need you to see and hear something," he'd said, almost in a whisper.

"Now? It's almost two in the morning. Can it wait until I get some sleep?"

"Señor Purdy, everyone heard what happened. That is why I want you to meet with me. Please. Trust me. And please, señor. Don't bring nobody with you."

And I hadn't. Then it hit me. I'd called the Kickapoo County Sheriff's Office dispatcher:

"I'm heading to Lágrimas, Jake. Israel Sifuentes called and asked me to come."

Aw, Jeez. My childhood friend, Jake Nichols, was dispatching that night. Well meaning, lonely, troubled Jake Nichols. There was no way Jake would have intentionally harmed Israel. But his poor judgment had been evident in sharing information with the DEA during my investigation of the murders of Otabiano and Raquel Vasquez.

I punched absently at my MP3 player. Benny Goodman's 1939 version of *There'll Be Some Changes Made* started, with Louise Tobin taking the vocals. I hoped the diminutive Texas powerhouse's voice portended something good, but doubted it. She followed with *I Didn't Know What It Was*, and for the run of two 78 rpm sides, my stomach settled down.

An hour out, the rain quit, and I rolled down the driver's side window. The freshly damp greasewood sweetened the air. *Only God can figure it out, but I loved this part of Texas.*

The turnoff from US 90 onto County Road 201 that led toward Lowell Johnson's ranch entrance was eight miles east of Santa Rosa.

I pulled off the tarmac. No way I was going to the Bar LJ alone. As planned, I'd wait on Abner. Either he'd ride with me, or we'd take both vehicles. Israel wasn't going anywhere.

I called Lowell. "I'm on my way out to your place. You okay?"

He assured me that a couple more single malts had "calmed him a bit" and that he'd still be waiting at the newspaper office "assuming you don't get shot in the dark first."

I killed the engine and listened. Nothing. Then, distant yips of coyotes. I called Abner.

"I'm twenty minutes out," he said.

I ended the call, stepped out, and shut the truck door. The engine cooled and pinged, and my eyes slowly adjusted to the darkness. Clouds were thinning. A sliver of moon and a swath of the Milky Way peeked through the overcast. I turned on my flashlight and shined it onto the road's surface.

Then I called Lowell again. "When you left, do you remember any tracks besides your incoming ones and that one set you'd followed in?"

Lowell burped. "Now that I *do* remember. I was so damned scared that someone might have come in behind me that I unracked that .30-30, jacked a round into it, and stuck its barrel down between my legs as I drove toward 90. I was afraid someone'd come and box me in as I was leaving, so I looked extra careful. Just my incoming tracks and whoever was still on my place."

I thought hard. Only three pasture gates existed off County Road 201 between US 90 and Lowell's place.

Lowell kept talking. "No one came up that road. No one tried to box me in. All I saw was muddy tracks, rain, and that poor man's severed head popping back into my head."

I'd fished at one of Lowell's stock tanks many times. I closed my eyes and tried to recall the ranches and the thousands of acres that often comprised Texas ranch "pastures."

"Whose places have fences along County Road 101?"

He gave me the owners' names. "As I recall, all three of those ranches generally use other access they all have off US 90, don't they?" I asked.

"Yessir, they do. Unless they're moving cattle into those areas. And no one's got any cows on either side of the county road right now. Why?"

I grunted.

"What now?"

"Nothing. Be there in a bit."

"You aren't going out there by yourself, are you?"

I admitted that I was waiting on Abner Selman.

"Good. I feel better. You have a knack for getting shot at."

I disconnected. Lowell hadn't offered to back me up.

The flashlight's beam scattered on the ridges and troughs of muddy tire tracks. They confirmed no other vehicle had come up the county road after he'd fled. But neither had they come back down.

I patted the Chevy's hood appreciatively. "I'm glad we waited. Aren't you?" I spoke as if it was a living thing. I opened its toolbox, donned my ballistic vest, removed the M16, loaded it, clicked the selector switch to full-auto and muttered, "C'mon, Ranger."

Chapter 4
A New Life and a Secret

Jack Eddleman got the call late on a Wednesday at four p.m. "You still like working the Canadian border?" A dumbass joke from David Sanchez, one of the many supervising agents at DEA headquarters in Springfield, Virginia.

He bit his tongue. "What can I do for you, sir?"

The Omaha Division of the United States Drug Enforcement Agency stretches from Nebraska to the Canadian border. Jack Eddleman had spent two weeks bouncing between Sioux Falls, South Dakota, Duluth, Minnesota, and Cedar Rapids, Iowa, chasing down leads on fake prescription pills containing fentanyl and methamphetamine. The accounts provided by various snitches confirmed the deadly combination was coming from South or Central America, through Mexico – not from Canada.

He'd stopped in at the Resident Office in Fargo to drop off tagged evidence, then had driven the 190 miles to his small, rented apartment in Bismarck. After unlocking its front door and shoving two small luggage pieces inside with his foot, he'd cursed the summer heat of the Great Plains, and returned to the small DEA station near the State Capitol. After perfunctory hellos to the two secretaries, he closed his office door.

He was tired of dealing with nickel and dime street snitches. He was tired of talking with small-town hick cops. He was tired of Bismarck, North Dakota. How long would he be in exile?

"You've spent two years pushing paper clips around in Bismarck," observed Sanchez. "You want another stab at working interdiction along the Mexican border?"

"Sure." Eddleman didn't want to act too eager. "Why now? What did I do to get out of this icebox?"

"The new president of Mexico isn't doing jack shit. He wants to replace 'guns with hugs.' Stupid, or corrupt, but probably both. Cartel death count below the border is going through the roof. Cops, soldiers, journalists, too. Some of it's bleeding over onto our side. We can move you back south, but you'll have to behave yourself."

Being talked to like a wayward schoolboy didn't set well with Eddleman. He grimaced and walked to the office door and locked it,

"What sector?" he asked. *Please don't send me to the Left Coast. Or Arizona.*

Sanchez shuffled some papers. "Your situation seems to have cooled down. The Agency's bleeding personnel right now, and we need you back where you can do some good. We're putting you in the Houston Division, working out of the San Antonio office. A lot of emphasis on stuff upriver from Laredo, past Del Rio as far as the Big Bend. Intel says the cartels are creating routes through Texas' least populated counties to get drugs across."

Eddleman stepped into the office's small bathroom, muting his phone as he glimpsed at himself in the mirror. *Damn, I'm grinning like a possum eating a sweet potato.*

"Less people, more open spaces, fewer roads," Sanchez continued. "Cartels fighting over the plazas. We've got decent intel and have actually choked off some of the poison coming across." He sounded surprised. "*Zetas* have control in Nuevo Laredo, which means *Familia Norteña* is desperate to find other ways to get their dope across. Ciudad Acuña is under their control, but for how long? And now, *Jalisco New Generation* is pushing their territory east. As usual, it's hard to figure who'll end up on top."

I may be in a cold hell, Eddleman thought, *but I've still got men keeping me up to date on everything.* And Sanchez knew that. The DEA had many secrets, but mostly those were kept against an often-hostile outside world, and not within the Agency.

"Your transfer will get signed tomorrow. Of course, you've got enough seniority you can turn it down and ride your time out where you are."

Eddleman snorted. "When do I need to report?"

'We need you in San Antonio within two weeks. Any questions?"

Eddleman had many questions, but they didn't need asking to his supervisor. As far as Eddleman was concerned, he could close his apartment, and be there in two days. "I'll do my best to get there, but there are some loose ends up here I'd like to clean up." Which wasn't true. Dealing with drug interdiction near the Canadian border was as boring as looking at the North Dakota prairie.

Sanchez wasn't fooled. "Yeah, sure. Just be there," he retorted, and disconnected.

Eddleman looked out his office window over the neat, orderly, and generally law-abiding, North Dakota capital city. Absently, he reached into his breast pocket, pulling out a circular tin of Kodiak snuff. He tapped it, then opened the lid and placed a pinch inside his front gumline, releasing the wintergreen scent. Eddleman glanced at the ten-point mule deer mounted on the wall. He thought, *If truth be told, this exile to Bismarck hasn't been all bad. The bird hunting has been good, and I've stocked my freezer with plenty of good-sized mule deer venison. But this place is a dead-end assignment. Damned few Canucks are smuggling fentanyl, meth, and cocaine through the open prairies of the Dakotas.*

Twice divorced and with little contact with his grown son, Eddleman considered his casual relationship with a pretty bookkeeper for a construction and oil field supply company. Unfortunately, she had hinted at something permanent — like marriage.

No thanks. I'll miss the hunting.

He'd come within an inch of getting terminated from the Agency after the *Kickapoo County Courier's* editor had all but accused him of killing a Laredo plumbing company owner during a night gun battle.

The bullet that killed Pete Vasquez when he crossed the Rio Grande was never recovered — the rifle's power and river mud where the round ended up ensured that.

Eddleman replayed the frantic phone call from one of his best DEA agents trying desperately to escape from a cartel attack:

"Had to put a gun to Vasquez' head to get him to unlock the office door," Luke said. *"The snitch took precious time wiping a computer program,"* What was he talking about? I'd wondered, as my agent and our informant fled from Laredo and cartel killers. *"Don't know,"* Luke barked angrily, nearly blotted out by the roar of his truck engine. *"But I've got a thumb drive he was leaving with."*

He gritted his teeth remembering what came next. *On a lonely South Texas highway, some fucking* sicario *had put a bullet through Luke's head. Blood and brains all over the roadway. I leaned over, looking at what was left of Luke's head when I spotted something in Luke's clenched left hand. I palmed the device and slipped it into my pocket. No way was that thumb drive going to be inventoried as crime scene evidence until I knew what it contained.*

Eddleman turned to the office's gun safe. His thumbprint identified on the pad, and the safe's door clicked open. He reached around the long guns and slid his hand toward the back of the safe, touching a small leather coin purse. For what seemed like the ten thousandth time, he unzipped the purse, pooched it open and confirmed its only content – a thumb drive. And for the ten thousandth time, he inwardly recited its contents from memory:

Hackamore tree - 375kEe

Diablo chico - 1.2

Oto's bench - 823k

East vega notch - 228k

Sunset Y - 1.7

And so many more. Thirty-five lines of words and numbers.

No one else, or at least no one living, was sure of the thumb drive's existence. To most, the contents would be gibberish. But Eddleman was damned sure he knew what the gibberish meant. To prove it, he needed to be where he could operate legally in Kickapoo County, Texas. Showing up down there while being stationed near the Canadian border had not been an option. No way could he have explained that away.

Eddleman opened his phone and pulled up the photo of the front page of the *Kickapoo County Courier*, its two-year-old headlines all but calling him a murderer: AUTOPSY SHOWS SHOT THROUGH THE CHEST. WHO KILLED PETE VASQUEZ?

He did a mental rundown of what he knew of many of those involved when he was down at the border. *Vasquez, that lying bastard, and his damned thumb drive had caused the death of a damned good agent. Vasquez was dirty, and, in the end, few lost much sleep over his demise.*

That is, except for that self-righteous whiskey drinking son of a bitch, Lowell Johnson, who won national newspaper reporting prizes for "responsible and courageous journalism," and preened like a peacock. Hopefully, he'll die of cirrhosis.

And Ranger Abner Selman. But he's retiring in a matter of months and will probably end up fishing at his place on the Pecos River and put law enforcement worries behind him.

Oh, yeah. And Purdy Kendricks. Somehow, Kendricks ended up in Austin, Texas, with a goddamned promotion instead of drunk, or divorced, or dead. He moved there to keep his wife and brat kid from getting snatched by the Mexicans. There was no way in hell his wife will let Kendricks live anywhere closer to the border than the state capital after she and the boy had escaped death — or worse — when she'd killed a would-be kidnapper.

There isn't much chance Kendricks will spend any time near the seven thousand acres he inherited from Laura Griffin Saenz after she'd got herself killed by cartel sicarios in that running gun battle on San Antonio's interstate system. Not pretty.

"Dammit," Eddleman said aloud, thinking of the ranch's erstwhile owner. "I wish that woman was still alive. It'd make figuring out where Pete Vasquez' money is buried a whole lot easier."

Pete Vasquez hadn't upped everything to the DEA about his plumbing supply company's foray into the darker business of transporting cartel cocaine. No sir. He *sure as hell hadn't. The thumb drive was proof that the sneaky bastard had failed to disclose he'd been stashing a shit-pot full of drug money all over Laura Griffin Saenz's hardscrabble Rio Grande-hugging ranch. All I have to do is find it. All $17,375,850. And not get caught or killed doing it.*

Chapter 5
Unwelcome and deadly visitors

I moved away from the truck. In the moonlight, its white surface offered a perfect target backstop for anyone wanting to take a shot at me. I walked the fifty or so yards back to US 90. At two in the morning, I saw no traffic in either direction. Hunkering down in the highway's shallow bar ditch, I called the Ranger.

"I'm about ten miles out."

"Which is why I'm calling you," I replied. "From what I can tell, no one's come back down County Road 201 after Lowell." I quietly told him what I had discovered, scanning the darkness as I spoke.

Minutes later, headlights off, Abner rolled to a stop behind my pickup. Dome light also disengaged, he stepped out and joined me in the darkness. "What's up?"

I took a chance, turned on my flashlight, and showed him Lowell's tracks in and out, someone else's only going in.

Abner walked back to his sedan, popped his trunk, then grabbed several items. A metallic clack told me one was a rifle — no doubt something like what I was holding. Then, the sound of a zipper. Abner had uncased something. He tapped my arm and handed me a bulky oddly shaped object. "You need to get you one of these."

I made out the shape of some sort of monocular.

"Let's check out the area," Abner whispered when I raised the thing to my eye. Suddenly, I was seeing an entire countryside, bathed in green light.

"Wow," I muttered. I did a quick 360. Small clumps of bushes, eerily eel-like grass, fenceposts, and barbed wire, but no threat. "What is this beauty?"

"Zeiss sold some of these to the State. They're not cheap, but they do come in handy."

Using the monocular, I scoped back eastward down US 90. In the distance, an approaching tractor-trailer's headlights were on bright. Their intensity flashed white, overwhelming the monocular's green tone, and I winced.

I handed Abner the Zeiss.

"Keep it. I brought two."

Abner unsnapped the holster strap on the traditional Ranger 1911 Colt .45, and I slung the Zeiss' strap over my neck.

"Lowell likes his whisky," Abner opined. "You sure he's being accurate about this extra set of tracks?"

"Enough to be worried."

Abner shined his flashlight toward the tire tracks. "Good enough."

The drizzle quit when we started walking north off US 90 on the county road. A few hundred yards in, there was no sign of an ambush.

"Purdy, I'd just as soon not get my ass shot off tonight out here," Abner said. We turned back toward US 90, Abner on one side, me on the other, both close to fence lines to avoid County Road 201's muddy ruts.

"Me either." I wasn't all that anxious to take a *pasear* down a lonely county road in the middle of the night either, but Israel's head was evidence, and I had doubts about whether it'd be there in the morning. The likelihood of a wild animal absconding with a fresh meal was likely if it hadn't happened already. Lowell's attempt at protecting Israel's head wasn't going to be much of an obstacle to a hungry coyote.

When we reach the vehicles, Abner asked, "Why didn't whoever's out there just go ahead and kill Lowell?"

"This whole situation has me totally confused."

Israel's death was a warning — clearly. But to whom? It made some sort of sense that Israel's part in the killing of a *sicario*, if discovered, would, in the twisted minds of the Mexican cartels, merit vengeance. But Lowell Johnson had had nothing to do with the events in a deserted adobe in Lagrimas. Hell, he didn't even know about them.

And now, someone might be hiding in ambush for whomever Lowell called to investigate. There was no way in hell even the most insightful cartel boss would surmise that I'd drive all the way from Austin, Texas, in the middle of the night.

The whole situation was just plain weird, and it struck me. "I'm not the target. Or at least, not the only one. Maybe Lowell's the stalking horse, or whatever you call it. It doesn't matter who shows up, as long as they're wearing badges. If what I'm thinking is correct, someone's waiting inside the Bar LJ fences, and they've been sent to kill cops."

"Killing a few cops near the border would definitely send a message," Abner grunted. "Your call. We ought to wait 'til daylight and come in with an army."

He didn't mean it. We had been together in enough scrapes that I felt sure he wasn't going to walk away from this that easily.

"Do we walk the two miles to Lowell's or ride?" Abner asked. He donned a windbreaker. The rain had brought with it a cool front and a brisk northerly wind.

Nervously, I peeled open my ballistic vest, then closed it more snugly. "Long way on foot."

"Your county, Purdy. You know it. Me, not so well. Can we be seen, even if we're not heard?"

"Lights off, and idling, I'd say, with this wind, we can get a mile before we worry about anyone hearing us. That is, if they're still inside Lowell's front gate."

"Let's take your truck. It's old and if it gets shot up, I don't have to explain it to some bean counter at State."

I'd come to think of myself as reasonable. Yet here I was intentionally heading toward an ambush.

Abner climbed into the truck bed, and I could hear and feel his movement when he leaned over the cab. I started the engine, killed the running and dash lights, and, with the monocular to one eye, began a slow crawl toward the entrance gate of the LJ Ranch.

My GPS map signal showed when we got a mile in from the highway. Still nothing. I killed the engine and Abner crawled down off the truck. He grunted in pain, an auditory reminder that he was no longer a young man. Which made me admire him even more. A few weeks from retiring from the dangers of being a lawman, and this Ranger was accompanying me in one seriously questionable action. I knew he and his wife had a little fishing cabin on the headwaters of the Pecos River. If I were him, I wouldn't have accepted this kind of assignment under those circumstances.

Abner muttered, "Make sure when we head inside there's no one boxing us in on this road. I can't climb fence and I'm too fat to scoot under without getting torn to hell by barbed wire."

I quietly shut the passenger door, and bumped it closed with my butt, and we began to walk the remaining mile, each on opposite sides of the road. All I could hear was the crunch and occasional squeak of boots against caliche and loose sand and my heartbeat roaring in my ears. Walking made it hard to focus the Zeiss, so every fifty yards or so, I'd pause and look around.

The approach to the LJ gate was maddeningly slow. I just hoped we would see the truck tracks veer off into an adjoining ranch's pasture. Prove this whole exercise was ridiculous. No such luck.

After an eternity, the Zeiss picked up the high steel posts and cross bar that signaled the entrance of Lowell's family ranch. They looked to be about a football field's length ahead. Faintly behind that, the light green from the moon and stars darkened into a darker hue I recognized as the earthen berm of a large stock tank. The last time I had fished there was with Forrest two years before. It was hard to reconcile the memory of Forrest catching a catfish with the possibility that the mounded banks might conceal men wanting to murder me.

Abner crossed the forty-five feet to my side of the road. "That Lowell's place?" he whispered.

"End of the road," I whispered. I placed Abner's right hand on my left arm and pointed toward the stock tank's berm fifty yards and to the left of the Bar LJ gate. "Tank dam."

He squeezed my forearm to acknowledge he understood.

The north wind gave me a bit of reassurance our muffled conversation couldn't be heard. Hopefully, we were undetected – unless whoever was up there had his own night vision equipment. I pushed that unpleasant thought away.

I indicated to him that I'd move first, then wait for him halfway to the gate. We'd leapfrog toward the yet unseen head of Israel Sifuentes.

He tapped my shoulder, leaned to his right, and rested his M16 on top of a cedar fence post. Awkward, but it gave him a steady sight picture. I moved off at a low crouch. Ten steps up, and an eerie howl broke out. *Shit!* I bent at the waist, trying to get the thumping in my chest under control. The howling turned into several yips, and a distant response. Coyote talk. After several more steps, I crouched and waited on Abner.

When level with me, the ranger stood quietly, glassing the tank dam. I checked the muddy road behind us. Nothing.

Do I move with my automatic weapon aimed, or continue to glass the area with the Zeiss? I couldn't do both at the same time. There were no man-shaped figures near the gate, so I left the M16 slung across my chest and crept forward. Twenty yards from the gate, I began a duck walk to lower my profile if someone was looking our way. The LJ entrance crosspiece had a simple "LJ" welded underneath it. Steel fence posts replaced cedar posts. Directly over me was a bulky object, the slicker-covered, severed, and abased head of Israel Sifuentes. The Zeiss detected the darker evidence of blood and viscera that had dripped onto the light sandy surface below it.

Now, in the semi-light of the night vision monocular, the muddy series of tire tracks seemed a mottled mess. And past the gate, no truck. Just greenish clumps of brush and rock dotting the whiteness of caliche and sand.

Had Lowell been mistaken? Were we chasing ghosts? I edged up to the closed sixteen-foot steel swing gate and felt around. A piece of chain looped around the center crosspiece, seemingly secured by a padlock. Careful not to allow the chain to clang against the gate, I felt the lock's clasps. The chain and lock had been cut, then carefully positioned as if still secured. Someone was on the Bar LJ.

A slight footfall signaled Abner's arrival. We crouched in the mud, the only sound our labored breathing. Who was out there? And where? And why?

Then, I heard it. The gentle click of a vehicle door being opened. The Zeiss flared a bit. Someone was parked just out of view on the west side of Lowell's stock tank. A cough, then soft and indistinct voices. Then, a click as the door closed and the cab light went off. The green in the Zeiss returned.

Dear Lord, I hope there's no more than two people in that truck.

I glanced behind us. Nothing threatening from behind. Abner moved away from the gate and across twenty yards down County Road 201 and lay prone. He'd picked a location where he could shoot toward the sound without hitting me. The gate assembly afforded some cover in the darkness, and I used it to shield me and backed away, then crawled until I was directly across from him. I lay in the mud and pointed my M16 toward the sound. The Zeiss showed a small piece of dark green detach from the earthen tank's form and become two figures. A cigarette lighter flared, revealing two cowboy-hatted men. The tip of a cigarette whitened the green. A cough, and the smoke was handed to the other figure. The Zeiss flared as the second figure took a long pull.

I thought, *Hell, that's not a cigarette. Those two are smoking a joint!* I almost grinned. We hadn't been detected.

The two began to walk toward the gate. I squirmed, trying to get lower in the muck. I needn't have bothered. The two opened the gate and walked the several yards right up to Lowell's slicker. One of the men pulled the slicker from the severed head.

"*Nos asugaremos de que esos pinches vean esto.*"

I understood what he said. *We'll make sure those fuckers see this.*

No need to wonder why, as the other male, shorter, and carrying a rifle, responded. *"Cuando se detengan, mataremos hasta el ultimo."*

When they show up, we'll kill them all.

The Mexicans, who were clearly *sicarios* from some cartel, were going to kill everyone who showed up. The two probably assumed whoever showed would be in a vehicle. In a flash of thought, I pondered the throw-away life of a *sicario*. No way were these underlings assured they could complete the task assigned them. Even in an ambush, unless they succeeded in killing everyone, their lives were forfeit.

I quietly touched the selector switch to ensure my weapon was on full automatic and squinted down the barrel at the *sicarios*. Abner's command of Spanish was adequate, but he hadn't grown up on the border. I hoped he'd caught the gist of what was said.

I need not have worried. His M16 opened up with a deafening noise just as I pulled the trigger on my weapon. Sparks flew when some rounds missed their mark and ricocheted off the steel of the entrance gate's structures. A fiery arc, then another zipped into the slumping bodies. In the madness of the moment, some part of my mind absorbed that Abner had a mixed load with tracers.

The taller Mexican was down and stayed down. The shorter one turned to flee, took two faltering steps, and fell onto his face. It was over in less than five seconds.

"Shit!" The concussive sounds rang in my ears. I ran toward the gate, pushed it open. Now night blind, I stumbled over one body searching for any weapon. I heard, rather than saw, Abner beside me.

"Are they both dead?" he asked.

"Have to be." Although I wasn't taking any chances. My right foot banged against something. I reached and recognized the shape of some sort of machine pistol. I picked up the weapon, cleared it and dropped its magazine onto the ground. "Got one automatic."

Abner wheezed, "Got another. Feels like an AK."

By then I was running toward the base of the tank dam. We had to ensure there was no one else in the bad guys' truck.

There was.

A voice called, *"*Fonso! ¡Paco! *¿Qué está pasando?"* What's happening?

I yelled out, *"Nada. Pinche animales tratando comer la cabeza!"*

As if the guy in the truck hadn't heard voices in English and was going to be fooled by an Anglo voice telling him that all that firepower was because of scavenger animals trying to eat at Israel's head stuck on a post.

"Como?" came his reply.

I rounded the berm. Without the Zeiss monocular, all I could see was the dark shape of a pickup truck. The third man was reaching into the bed of the truck when I pulled the trigger.

Two rounds. Then the breach locked open. No time to eject a magazine and reload. I raced forward and slammed into the man's body and we both fell to the ground. The palm of his hand hit the underside of my nose. The pain was excruciating.

Then wham! Not an M16. A much larger caliber. Gasping for air, Abner pulled me up.

"He's down. He's down." Abner opened the truck's driver's door and the dome light lit the scene. Abner, a .45 automatic still pointing at the inert body of a man whose face had been blown off. Somehow, earbuds remained stuck in his ears, their cord, no longer attached to a device, trailing across the dead man's chest.

"Where's your rifle?" I asked, like that was somehow important.

Abner stepped back and picked his M16 off the ground. I looked inside the truck. A half-smoked joint smoldered in the truck's ashtray. A video display flickered on the floorboard and an MP3 player's tinny speaker emitted loud conjunto music.

Abner said, "This was no time for some 'Halt! You're under arrest' bullshit."

I couldn't have agreed more. "Yeah," I said. "But what in the *hell* have we stepped in this time?

Chapter 6

How to explain three dead men

At four in the morning, Santa Rosa was about as dead as any town can be, for which I was grateful. I drove behind the Ranger's car through town and pulled into a carport behind the small brick building that housed the Kickapoo County Courier. On the seat next to me sat the profaned head of Israel Sifuentes, still covered by Lowell's slicker, the whole bloody mess stuffed in a thirty-nine -gallon kitchen garbage bag, its opening secured by a zip tie. *Bizarre companionship.*

I rapped on the back door. No answer. On the verge of panic, I punched in Lowell's number, thinking something had happened to him.

"Wha?" Lowell croaked.

"Open your door, Lowell."

""Kay." Lowell's efforts with his rarely used back door finally showed results when he yanked it open. "Sorry, thing's stuck."

Abner and I pushed past him and into a short hall with a table with a printer and two desktop computers on top of it.

"What's that?" Lowell pointed at the garbage bag I clutched.

"What do you think?" I asked.

"Oh, shit."

"You got a refrigerator in this place?"

"Aw, shit, man. A bloody head in my refrigerator?"

I wasn't in the mood to deal with Lowell's whining. Exasperated, I walked through the *Courier's* hallway into Lowell's office. An apartment-sized refrigerator stood across from his scratched mahogany desk. Taking out a jar of martini olives and two wire racks, I shoved the black garbage bag inside and shut the door.

"Evidence," I said, and plopped into an upholstered chair. Abner sprawled on the office's ratty sofa and fell asleep within a minute.

Lowell stared at me, then finally pointed at my nose. "What happened?"

"I think I broke my nose." I rose, opened the refrigerator, reached into its small freezer compartment, and grabbed an ice tray.

"Well, don't bleed on my furniture." He quickly retrieved a dirty hand towel from the office bathroom. I wobbled the ice tray until the cubes broke loose, then dumped them into the towel.

Lowell turned to me. "What the hell happened out there?"

The adrenaline rush of combat had run its course in me, and my body and mind were cratering. Then the cold from the ice began to seep through the towel. "Later, Lowell. Just need a couple of hours. Wake me up before seven." I closed my eyes and leaned my head against my wadded-up jacket, hoping sleep would come. No such luck. My nose throbbed, and I spent the next two hours avoiding eye contact with Lowell while the ice cubes melted, and water dripped down my face. In my racing mind, I was second guessing everything Abner and I had done.

I must have drifted off because I woke to Lowell's booming voice, "Well, howdy, Trooper." He was almost shouting into his cell phone, snapping his fingers at the same time, indicating he wanted something to write on.

Groaning, I pushed myself off the chair and stood, wiping moisture off my face, stashing the sodden towel under a chair. Lowell listened on the phone, doing a lot of "uh huhs" as I handed a pad and pen to him. Furiously, with the phone to one ear, he wrote, "He wants to come here. 'Kay ?????"

I looked at Abner, thinking furiously about how to direct the conversation.

Lowell tossed the notepad on the desk and said, "Great." Then disconnected. "He'll be here in about sixty seconds. He know you guys are here?"

Abner shrugged. "He's about to find out."

Moments later, DPS Trooper Johnny Bonavita stood in the *Courier* office foyer. Still the same Johnny Bonavita, but more mature and surer of himself. He glanced from Lowell to the ranger and finally to me, unable to hide his surprise.

"Hey, Trooper," I said. "Good to see you." We exchanged *abrazo*s. "Glad you were in the area last night."

Lowell handed him a cup of coffee from a fresh pot and patted the trooper on the arm. Lowell had had much to do with Bonavita's selection to the Department of Public Safety Academy, and it was obvious he was quite proud of his young friend.

The friendly homecoming was enjoyable, despite the trooper's quizzical glances at my nose, and the bloody towel. Lowell followed through with another cup of black coffee. The ranger looked ragged, and I knew I looked worse.

"Anything happen last night with Lilly Pardo?" Abner asked Bonavita.

"Nothing, Ranger. I hung around the café as long as I could without looking like I was there for a reason besides eating. Got to say hi to a lot of folks. Then followed Lilly home. Looks like she lives with someone else—"

"Lilly's widowed momma," interjected Lowell.

"And sat there until dawn watching the house. No indication of anyone snooping around. Only one car came down her street after her shift ended, and I recognized the car. One of the local drunks probably coming back from the KC Hall with a snootful. He pulled into his driveway, sort of, six or so houses down, stumbled out and slunk into his house."

Trooper Bonavita's expression indicated he expected some sort of explanation of why he'd been called to watch Lilly. And what I had to do with the situation.

Abner nodded and asked, "Where you headed?"

"Down to Laredo. Got some classes there." Bonavita paused, eyeing my nose. "You sure you don't need me around?"

"Trooper," I said, "I'm not going to ask you to lie, but unless someone specifically asks, 'Hey, when you were driving through Santa Rosa did you come upon Texas Ranger Abner Selman and State Officer Purdy Kendricks,' you just plain have no idea we were here."

Bonavita cocked his head. "Did I see Mr. Johnson?" He pointed his chin toward Lowell.

"Rather you didn't," Selman said. "We've got something." —He gestured toward me. "And it's serious, but just how and who's involved we're not sure." He paused. "Will that hold you for a bit?"

"Two years out of the Academy and already in deep shit." His smile belied the seriousness of what we were asking of him. "Not going to ask, but I just have a feeling, Officer Kendricks and Ranger Selman, that there is some business unfinished from two years ago."

Abner thanked Johnny, then promised he'd get an explanation when the time was right. They shook hands, Bonavita stepped outside, and Abner closed the front door behind him. The trooper's sedan backed out onto US 90 and disappeared toward Laredo.

"Can we trust Johnny to say nothing?" I asked.

"Hell, Ranger," blurted Lowell. "If you can't trust that young man to do what he says, the State of Texas is in trouble."

Lowell offered to take us to breakfast.

"Not a good idea, Lowell," I said. We didn't need to be seen by anyone else.

Abner calmly asked, "Lowell, how about you get us some breakfast tacos to eat here?" The Courier's parking area was recessed and invisible from US 90, but eventually someone was going to notice a state sedan and my white pickup. The sooner some sort of decision was made about where we were going with last night's events, the better.

Grudgingly, Lowell took our requests and called in a take-out order at the Cenizo Diner. He pulled a felt Stetson over his disheveled hair and slouched out. I locked the office door behind him.

"We've got a head in his refrigerator," I said, as if that was necessary information.

"And there are three dead bodies no doubt being nibbled on by buzzards as we speak," Abner responded.

"And a truck that doesn't belong there."

I took over Lowell's office chair and propped my boots on his desk. Abner sat back on the sofa. For a moment, we were trapped in our own thoughts.

Finally, the ranger said, "We need to see the inside of Israel's house. And we need to deal with three dead men."

"And no telling what else."

A rap on the back door, and Lowell trudged in with a paper sack full of breakfast tacos.

Two hours later, the sun was up, but the cold front that had blown in kept the air chilly. As we ate, Lowell reached for the scotch bottle. He saw my jaundiced look and defensively asked, "What? I don't deserve this. Just because you've been high and dry for a while doesn't mean I have to follow your sterling example."

He tempered the nastiness of the remark with an apology and an excuse. "Sorry, Purdy. I'm glad you're clean and sober, but I am inclined in the other direction. And last night gave me the heebie jeebies."

The expensive scotch dribbled into a glass. Its amber hue was so damned inviting. I could just about taste the peaty liquid calming me as it moved down my throat. Lowell set the Balvenie on his credenza. The scotch was sherry cask aged and exquisitely beautiful to me. I reminded myself that I hadn't hit an AA meeting in three months.

"Purdy!" Abner barked.

"Huh?" I'd fallen asleep during a blink.

"We need to get moving," he chided.

I stood, reached in the refrigerator, and grabbed the black garbage bag with Israel's severed and abused head.

"Aw crap," Lowell said. "I'm going to throw that refrigerator out. I won't ever be able to put my lunch in there again."

I replaced the two metal racks and thanked Lowell. He had a job to do, and it would mean lying his ass off to the Kickapoo County Sheriff's Office.

"One more time," Abner donned his Stetson. "What're you going to do?"

"Before I repeat it for the umpteenth time," Lowell snorted and turned to me, "you going to tell me why you wanted me to get Lilly Pardo to safety, then didn't."

Abner glanced my way with a nearly imperceptible shake of his head. But Lowell deserved at least some trust. Besides, I wasn't going to give him much. "I thought Lilly may have seen something that could have put her into some trouble. I'm not so sure. And I don't want anyone thinking otherwise."

He had already given us his word that Lilly's name would not be repeated. Lowell was as street smart as any small-town newspaper editor could be, but he didn't have a point of reference on which to hang any suppositions. Until yesterday, I'd prayed that the killing in Lagrimas was unknown to anyone in Kickapoo County except for the three people involved. Now? I was sure I'd been mistaken.

"Just keep an eye out for anyone showing an interest in her. Be subtle."

The sound of truckers jake-braking echoed outside the *Courier* office. I remembered stopping truckers and threatening to issue a citation for that noisy nonsense. Now, I couldn't care less. Traffic violations seemed so pissant since I'd seen the result of cartel killings and had just helped kill three *sicarios*.

Police protocols had to be followed. Investigation procedures. Chain of custody. Documentation. Photographs. Videographers. All those were parts of what I should expect in this type of case. And I was about to do none of those things.

"Let me know when I can start going back to my place," Lowell said.

"Not for a few hours. When you do, there'll be two dead Mexicans near your gate..." I began.

"Two dead Mexicans!" Lowell's voice went up an octave. "What the fuck are you talking about?"

"Actually, three," intoned Abner.

Lowell plopped onto his ratty sofa. "Why am I going to see three dead people?"

"And an unidentified truck," I added.

Lowell grabbed his head with both hands and moaned. "How did they get there?"

Abner responded. "Let's just agree we're glad you got the hell away from there. They were waiting to kill whoever showed up."

It took another fifteen minutes to calm Lowell enough so he'd remember what to say.

"I'll notice the lock broken and two dead Mexicans sprawled next to my gate. Shell casings scattered all over the place. I'll say to myself, 'What the hell?' Then I'll find some cell coverage and call the SO and tell them what I've found. I'll mention some footprints going around the tank dam but won't go there. I won't say a damned thing about Israel. Or tire tracks. Or calling Purdy. Or seeing either one of you two so-and-sos. How'd I do?"

I hugged him. "Lowell, I know this burns in your craw, but until we know what's going on in this county, it's better that the less people know about Israel and any connection with your place."

He nodded, still not totally convinced.

When we stepped outside, I called Betty and left a message that I had been called to a run of the mill investigation way south of San Antonio. I didn't want her to worry why I didn't come home at all. I explained that cell phone signal was minimal, and I would explain later. I was glad I didn't have to lie to her directly.

We left Abner's sedan parked behind Lowell's office, and Abner and I drove the mile or so to Israel's house past the ill-defined edge of town. Going there was a risk, but we had to find out if what had happened to Israel had started at his house. I never understood Israel's penchant for privacy, but now I was thankful there were no neighbors who would notice when I stopped behind Israel's pickup. I grabbed my investigator's kit and rubber gloves, and we quickly pushed our way into the side door and into the kitchen.

The window air conditioner was on, but not running. The cold front had kept it from circulating air, and a sweet, metallic smell of blood caught in my throat.

"Something happened here, for sure, Ranger."

Abner moved gently, making sure not to touch anything. "Look." He pointed. "Blood in the recliner."

I began taking pictures. "Yeah, but not much."

Abner took out a pen from his breast pocket, leaned down and pointed to the old carpet. "Blood here. Hole here, too." I handed him a pair of latex gloves and after donning them, he pulled back the rug. "What I thought. Bullet in the floor."

The misshapen slug was buried a quarter of an inch below the wood floor's surface. After taking measurements and photographs, I thought about gently levering the slug into an evidence bag but decided against it.

"Abner, I'll bet this bullet went through Israel's knee or leg," I said. "A perfect way to get a conversation going with someone with a faulty memory."

Abner shook his head sadly. "Had to hurt like hell."

Lots of pictures, but no scraping of blood spots, nor dusting for prints. That would be an obvious tipoff that law enforcement had been there.

Apart from the blood on and around the recliner, the only other blood was a thin trail on the floor indicating where Israel had been dragged out.

"They didn't cut his head off here," Abner said. "No telling where, but the gorefest didn't start here, thank God."

We spent an hour in Israel's house. It was nine thirty before we got all we could. Some photos, and a good idea of what had happened. When Betty called me back, I let the call go to voicemail.

I thought about how Israel would not show up for work for several days, and someone would come looking for him, then call the sheriff's office. Israel would be presumed dead, but for now, the cause would remain unknown – except to the killer.

Abner and I closed the door, backed out, and looped back into Santa Rosa on another ill-defined dirt road. I dropped Abner off behind the *Courier*.

"You got plans while you're here?" he asked.

What kind of plans would I have, given how I ended up here? I wondered.

"No. Not really." I said.

"You checked your place out lately?"

I knew what he was talking about. And no, I hadn't. Abner had questioned me about the seven thousand acres owned by Laura Griffin when he was trying to figure out where she was getting money for her new and improved lifestyle after Pete Vasquez' death.

"Ranger, I've been out there, maybe two times since Laura got herself killed. With all the issues about her money, I've tried to stay away from the place."

"Just wondering. Can't help it. I still say there's money stashed all over that otherwise worthless tract of land." He laughed to soften the jab. But two years ago, I'd had to answer to him, and others in his chain of command about what I knew about Laura Griffin's property. Then I'd inherited it.

"I'd be lying if I said I haven't thought about what may be hidden out there. But if I start looking, I think it'll take me down a rabbit hole I can't get out of. The neighbor's running a few cows on it. I'm not even charging him 'cause it keeps the ag exemption on the place."

He abruptly changed the subject. "Let me take the poor man's head into San Antonio. I'll drop it with the ME."

I looked at him, about to object.

"Purdy, I'm six months from retirement. If something goes off the tracks, and there is some explaining to do, I'm in a better position than you are." He looked at me as if daring me to refute this.

I didn't argue. I gave him the garbage bag, grateful to get the faint, fetid smell of its ripening contents out of my truck. I reached over and patted the bag for some reason. I felt the rounded top of Israel's head. "Amigo, I don't know who did this to you, but I'm going to make him pay."

Of course, I had no idea how I was going to do that.

Now I had to deal with Lilly Pardo.

Chapter 7
Purdy makes a promise

Trooper Bonavita had ensured nothing happened to Lilly Pardo last night, but there was no assurance that something wouldn't happen today, or the next day.

"I've got to get Lilly out of town," I said when Abner called later.

"Be careful," he responded. "You get spotted, we may have some explaining to do that we aren't ready to do yet, Purdy."

"I know. Still. I think she works late shift. I'll find her cell number and try to set up a visit with her away from folks."

"Good luck with that, but you're right. We can't have another situation like what happened to Israel."

He disconnected, and I wondered how to contact Lilly quietly and away from Santa Rosa. I took a deep breath and called her workplace.

"Cenizo Diner, Beulah speaking. How may we help you?"

"Beulah, it's me. Purdy Kendricks."

"Well, hi..."

"Beulah, please don't say my name right now."

I could hear the clatter of dishes from the diner's kitchen. Then, she said loudly, "Thanks, Mr. Davis. Appreciate the business." A pause, then, "Okay, *sir*. What may I do for *you*?"

Beulah was busting my chops. It wasn't the first time. "Is Lilly working today?"

"Yes, *sir*! Mashed potatoes with that? *Sir?*"

"Jesus, Beulah, cut me some slack. I'm trying to keep the lady safe."

"Well, sir. You sho' have po' ways of showing it, sir. I's gwine to do what eva the massa aks me." Beulah Wilson was African American, perhaps the only one in the county. She only lapsed into this shuck and jive nonsense when she was pissed. She sounded that way now.

"Beulah, give me your cell number. Go outside and I'll call you." I paused. "Please."

She seemed to calm down, told me her number, and disconnected.

I punched in what she'd provided, and after several rings, she picked up. "What's going on? You can't come see me? You don't visit or send cards. Then you call me out of the blue about someone else's problems?"

I muttered an apology. She grunted an acceptance and told me Lilly was off for the day.

"What's going on, Purdy Kendricks? You in trouble again? Hell, more important is whether you've got Lilly in some kind of danger?"

"You'll have to trust me on this, but I need to talk to Lilly – quietly. She may be in some danger. And no, I didn't get her that way. Just trust me and keep quiet for now. It's important. And you haven't heard from me."

"Purdy, trouble seems to show up in Santa Rosa whenever you're here."

"Can't disagree, but I don't have the time right now to explain it."

She snorted disapproval. "I'll text you her number, but you don't let my best waitress get hurt, you hear?" She rang off.

When I had Lilly's number, I called it. It went to voicemail.

"Lilly, Purdy Kendricks here. We need to talk. Soon. About Lagrimas." That was all she needed to know I was serious.

I visualized Santa Rosa's dusty streets in the "Mexican" part of town, wondering how to reach Lilly's small bungalow without people noticing me. I sat in my truck with the engine idling, slumped in the seat, and waited. When my cell phone finally rang, it was Lilly.

"Deputy Kendricks?"

"This is Purdy, Lilly. Thanks for calling me back."

"What about Lagrimas? The fear in her voice was palpable. What's going on?"

"Where are you right now?"

"At home with momma. Why?"

"Is there some place we can visit? Someplace private?"

"You can come to my house. Momma's about half-deaf."

I explained that it would be better if we met elsewhere, and she reluctantly agreed.

Half a mile south of town, I parked on one side of Guadalupe Cemetery and rolled down the window. Hot dusty air and the distant sound of conjunto music washed through the air. Twenty minutes later, Lilly circled the chain linked burial ground, edging her car up behind my truck. She killed the engine, got out, but didn't move away from her car door. She'd aged more than the two years since I'd last seen her. Her head of raven hair had streaks of gray now.

I walked to where she stood. "Lilly, how're you doing?"

Tears welled in her eyes and ran down her cheeks. "How do you think I'm doing? You mentioning Lagrimas? You and I – we two only got one connection to Lagrimas and that's that *pinche puto* we..." She stopped, as if too afraid to verbalize about the bullet exploding the *sicario's* head of, then brushed her tears away with a trembling hand. "Ever since that night I've prayed that I'd never hear anything about that place again. Now..." She began to cry. "What? What's going on? Did someone find his body? We thought the *animales* in the Rio Grande would take care of it."

Now I knew how the three had disposed of the *sicario* after he was killed. No surprise. "Israel," I interrupted. "He's dead."

"How?"

Good question. I had no idea where Israel's headless torso was, although I suspected it would eventually be devoured by wild animals or seen floating in the Rio Grande – like what Lilly had just revealed as a *Zeta* killer's disposal site. "I don't know."

"Then how the hell you know he's dead, Deputy?"

I hadn't been a deputy in Kickapoo County in over two years, but this wasn't the time to correct her on my new title. Lilly suddenly reached for the car door for support, then eased back into the driver's seat, her complexion ashy. This was not the time to tell her about Israel's decapitation. She was hanging on by a thread.

"Lilly, I know." I wasn't going to tell Lilly about Israel's head in a plastic garbage bag. "Can I ask you some questions?"

She slumped onto the front seat, crossed her hands over the steering wheel and put her head in her hands. Teardrops appeared on her skirt as she cried silently.

I asked again. She nodded.

"You, Israel, and the guy from Mexico..."

"Teofilo. Teofilo Ramirez," she muttered.

"Have any of you discussed..."

"No. Not me. Not Israel. And Teofilo – he's a distant cousin – he'd never say anything. What we did, we did for you." She looked up suddenly, anger written on her face. "We did this because of you, Deputy. They'd tried to kill your wife and little boy. No one was to know what we did. Did you tell anyone? Did you?" She was almost screaming. "Did you say something to some fucking cop or DEA agent?"

"No. No one. Not my wife. Not anyone."

"What about that ranger? Your *compadre*?" she demanded.

I had to get control of the conversation. "Lilly! I haven't told anyone. But Israel's dead. And I don't want you to be dead also." I thought of the reality that death for a woman at the hands of an avenging cartel would certainly be preceded by rape, torture, and disfigurement. "That's why I'm in Santa Rosa. To make sure that doesn't happen to you."

Lilly reached into a small purse, pulled out a crumpled pack of cigarettes and a lighter. With the cigarette in her mouth, she couldn't get the small butane lighter to strike. I took it from her shaking hand, spun the striker wheel, and held its flame as she sucked in the smoke. I handed back the lighter.

"Thanks," she murmured.

I knew the answer to the next question but asked it anyway. "Teofilo, he has a cell phone?"

"Yes," she replied, surprising me. "Who doesn't? But there's no cell coverage in the *pueblito*. He only turns it on when he gets near a tower. Aren't many in Mexico, at least this area." She pointed her chin toward the vacant badlands to the south.

"You seen him lately?"

"No. He stays at his *ejido*." Another pause. "Except he's been sick. I think he's gone to Piedras Negras, or Acuña, or maybe Monterrey for some medicine. The government doctor sent him."

I scuffed my boot in the dust trying to make sense of it. If Lilly, and Teofilo, and Israel hadn't talked, who had? I shook my head.

"What? Why are you shaking your head?"

"No, Lilly. I haven't talked to anyone about that night, *senora*. No one." At least that part of my reply was accurate. "Right now, I want to make sure you are safe. Is there someplace you can go – away from Santa Rosa – for a while?"

Lilly blew smoke from the side of her mouth in a long stream. "What? You think I'm living in this fucking town, taking care of my old mother, because I want to? You think I've got money to spend? With Beulah's big paycheck and the nickel and dime tips?"

I persisted. "Where do you have family? San Antonio, or Dallas or Houston? Can you take a week or so? I'll make sure your job is still here when you get back."

She flicked the butt toward the cemetery's chain link fence. "You're scared, aren't you, deputy? I can see it all over your face."

"Yeah," I admitted. "I am. I've got to find out who killed Israel. I have to find out if Israel said anything before he died." She looked up as I leaned over her car door. "And I can't do this while I'm trying to protect you. You may *not* even be in any trouble, Lilly."

She barked a humorless laugh.

"It's possible." And it was.

"Shee-ittt."

Finally, after another fifteen minutes, Lilly agreed to leave Santa Rosa with her mother. "You promise me that I'll have my job when I get back?"

I had no clue but nodded anyway. "When can you leave?"

Lilly promised she'd be gone before nightfall. I opened my wallet and handed her a gas credit card. "Use this," and gave her my zip code for the gas pump. She pulled a pen from behind her ear and wrote the five digits on her palm.

I tucked my truck in behind the Courier's office and rapped on the back door. Lowell peeked out a window, then let me in. I took time to notice the office's stained and scratched walls and gloomy, brindle brown trim.

"When's the last time this place was painted?" I asked. "The 1960s? You'd think that as an award-winning newspaper man you'd have the pride to spruce up the office."

"Thought you were gone back to Austin. What are you hanging around here for?"

"Can I hang out here for a few hours?" I asked.

"Do I have a choice?"

I walked to the front, turned the OPEN sign to CLOSED, pulled down the blinds, watching motes of dust rise from their surfaces. I collapsed on the small sofa. "Please wake me up in a couple of hours."

I closed my eyes, hoping dreams would not torment me. Moments later, someone was pushing on my shoulder. "Hey! Wake up, Purdy. I let you sleep a little more than two hours."

Panicked, I pushed up and peered out the west side window. The sun showed late afternoon. "Shit!"

I raced to my pickup and backed out and drove slowly toward Lilly's house. No car. No lights. I dialed her cell number. She picked up on the third ring.

"You and your mom okay?" The voice of someone, it sounded like an older Hispanic woman, jabbered in the background.

"Just a sec. *¡Callate, Mami!* Jeez, my mom is pissed about this. I'm driving in traffic on a loop around San Antonio." She paused. "Everything okay?"

"Yes." I slumped in the seat, unrealized tension easing.

"You talked to Beulah yet? She okay with what I'm doing?"

"All taken care of," I lied. "Just don't call her, or anyone else in Santa Rosa. Text me where you are. I'll be in touch."

I turned on the truck's radio and picked up an AM station from Del Rio advertising some new and improved tequila, "just available in the United States." Suddenly, I was thirsty, but not for water. I turned off the radio. *Thought I was past that. I haven't made an AA meeting in months.* My gut response to the booze ad told me I was definitely wrong. I felt my breast pocket for the MP3 player. I pushed the play button and jabbed in the earbuds.

Karen Souza's cover of *Every Breath You Take,* piano and bass in support, pulsed gently. Thankful for the gentle voicing, I put the truck in drive.

There were four things I needed to do.

I needed to convince Beulah she'd keep Lilly's job for her and throw in some vacation pay to boot.

I needed to find Teofilo, a wizened indigenous man I'd seen only once in a darkened adobe two years ago, to tell him he might be in danger.

Even sadder, I had to find Jake Nichols, my school chum, dispatcher for the Kickapoo County Sheriff's Office. I suspected Jake, likeable Jake, despite my warning to never mention my phone call, had slipped and told someone of my trip to Lagrimas to meet Israel Sifuentes. And that someone had put two and two together, and got Israel brutally murdered.

And, finally, I had to tell my wife something. I wrote a long text explaining I would be involved in a made-up investigation for quite some time.

Then, I put some distance between me and Santa Rosa. Maybe I just was avoiding talking to Jake.

On the east side of Kickapoo County, I pulled off US 90 and onto the county road that led to the Griffin Place – now mine. I'd worked for Clayton Griffin while in high school and had loved everything about it. Then I fell for Clayton's daughter, Laura Griffin, and been spurned. Two years ago, Otabiano Vasquez, the ranch foreman, and his wife Raquel were murdered near their house on the Rio Grande. Then, good folks had been killed in a gun battle on the property. After Pete Vasquez' death, there was talk of drug money he'd stashed on its acreage. And soon, of Laura Griffin Saenz' renewed her Alamo Heights lifestyle.

I'd called her and confronted her.

"I think I know why you went down there. Both times, I'd said."

She feigned surprise. "I just wanted to put the place in order a bit," she'd explained, unconvincingly.

"Bullshit. You don't give a damn about the ranch. Haven't in years. Pete stashed money on the place while his grandparents were alive?"

I paused, wishing for a denial. When she said nothing. I continued, "And he told you where at least some of it is."

Again, nothing but Laura breathing into the phone.

"You've gotten access to some money, Laura. I suspect quite a bit. It hasn't gone unnoticed."

Finally, she replied, surprising me. "Pete Vasquez put me through hell. I have no doubt that he had a guilty conscience. I'll be careful. Now leave me alone."

And she had disconnected.

Her admission was something, but I was never sure of exactly what. A few weeks after that, she was dead, executed by a cartel member. And shortly afterward, I'd received a phone call from a San Antonio estate lawyer, telling me she'd her seven thousand acres of West Texas to me. His response when I told him I didn't want Laura's ranch had sounded gleeful:

"Her cover letter to the codicil indicated she knew you'd say that. That's why she wanted me to be her executor. She also paid quite a handsome retainer for me to represent her estate in the event of her death. She was quite a character, Mr. Kendricks. She wrote, and I quote, 'If I die, tell Purdy Kendricks that I have no living relatives I'd let touch the place. That it's mine to bestow, and I want the son of a bitch to have it.'"

I had tried to avoid Kickapoo County. My mother, lost in a fog of dementia, lived in the local nursing home, and no longer recognized me. Still, I'd visited, and while in Santa Rosa, felt obligated to drop by and say hello to Betty's sister,

Paula. I'd made one or two cursory visits to the land I'd been gifted. That was it.

I almost lost my wife and son to ruthless murderers in the God-forsaken place.

Yet here I was again.

A new county road sign perched at the entrance to the dirt track turning south off US 90, catching me off guard. Fresh cement anchoring it tenuously into the caliche and sand. The untended ribbon through the badlands toward the Rio Grande now had a designation – Kickapoo County Road 106.

The new title hadn't changed the quality of the dirt track. I started down its washboard surface hoping in a weird way to see my seven thousand acres. Several tracks indented the road's surface. Nothing unusual there – other ranches, most of them substantially larger than mine, had pastures abutting the county road. At the top of a caliche-strewn hill, County Road 106 turned west. At that fork, it was another fifty yards to the Griffin place's locked entrance. One set of tire tracks I'd vaguely noticed didn't turn west, continuing up to the ranch. They appeared too narrow for a typical ranch truck.

The gate chain had accumulated several locks attached to cut links over the years, added by utility companies, game wardens, and others needing access. My lock was a combination. Now, another link had been removed, and in its place was a shiny new standard key lock. Nothing seemed disturbed. But the tires' marks extended past the cattle guard.

Someone had driven onto the Griffin place and maybe was still there.

Chapter 8
Los Zetas make a decision

Guillermo Blanco considered himself a patient man, but he had limits. Standing near a Humvee, he scrolled through the digital photo printouts taken just outside of Ciudad Acuña. They depicted three of his men hung from a highway pedestrian overpass on Federal Highway 29, throats cut, pants pulled down to their ankles, and chests branded with LFN. The LFN signified *La Familia Norteña*, the recently revived scum the *Zetas* had run out of Nuevo Laredo two years earlier.

Blanco wasn't shocked. Business was business, but the LFN's efforts seemed so pedestrian. Half the Mexicans near the American border had witnessed this type of display in the last decade. And the crudely lettered sign dangling from the bodies' feet was almost unreadable because of the blood and gore that dripped down the tan cardboard. *Bush league*, he thought.

"Que dice el letrero?" What's the sign say? he asked his second in command, Arturo Navarrete.

Navarrete responded, "The *culeros* can't spell, but basically, it says *los Zetas* are all pussies, and LFN is coming after us."

Navarrete handed back the cell phone with its images to Blanco. With the help of the *chingasos* in the *Jalisco New Generation* cartel, or CJNC, the LFN thought it could re-take the plazas of Ciudad Acuña and Nuevo Laredo.

"Fuckers, we will kill them all," Navarrete muttered. "They think that the *Zetas* are too weak to fight back. We will destroy them." Unconsciously, he took the stance of a boxer, raising large, scarred knuckles, as if to throw a punch.

The LFN was disrupting the orderly flow of cocaine and fentanyl to the hungry users in *los estados unidos and los Zetas'* cash flow was starting to hurt. If the *Zetas* showed weakness, other cartels would challenge the *Zetas* on the Mexican side. There were always jackals waiting to take a bite out of the *Zetas'* territories.

"The fucking DEA and Border Patrol are all over the main ports of entry, like *pulgas* on a cur dog. A way to circumvent these difficulties needs to be found. We've lost too much product." Blanco said. *There was always something,* he thought, and spat into the brush, then blew his nose into a handkerchief.

When Blanco spoke with such formality, his scarred lieutenant knew his boss didn't want any suggestions.

After a few minutes of silence, Blanco lit a cigarette and said, "Our men are hunting for the LFN and CGNC killers, and with the help of Santa Muerte, revenge will be exacted. We aren't going to fail."

Perhaps, thought Navarrete. *Perhaps. Running a cartel isn't a simple operation. There is so much to consider.* Blanco, Navarrete, and several *Zetas* stood ten kilometers inside Mexico. No sense getting too close to the border, out of respect for border patrols and pressure sensors buried in paths. DEA agents were intent on kidnapping Mexican drug bigwigs and willing to lie about where they nabbed them. And there were the *yanqui* drones. He hated the drones — American eyes in the air.

The Mexican territory where the men stood presented no such problems. The area's police and military knew better than to bother the *Zetas.*

Blanco lifted binoculars and eyed the bleakness of eastern Kickapoo County, Texas, across the narrow ribbon of water the *gringos* called the Rio Grande.

"*Parece lo mismo,*" he said. The desolation was the same on both sides of the ribbon of dirty water also called the Rio Bravo. He fired up a cocaine-laced marijuana cigarette, pulled a lungful, handed the spliff to Navarrete, and peered at the Google Earth printouts of the Texas/Mexico border.

Blanco let out a humorless laugh, recalling grasping Pete Vasquez, the Laredo toilet importer, by the balls when the *Zetas* discovered that man's main income was muling large loads of drugs for the LFN.

"I gave him a choice," he said aloud. "Work for us, or we kill you and your grandparents. Oh, he'd squealed like a pig, but he came around *muy pronto*. And as a bonus, we used the ranch owned by his *gringa puta* girlfriend as the launching point to kill Huerta, sixty kilometers inside the *frontera*. And without anyone the wiser."

Navarrete handed back the spliff and released the smoke from his lungs. He knew the whole story, but he let Blanco talk on. It was never a good idea to interrupt "Cantinflas," as Blanco was dubbed. Always a smile on his face, like the 1960's actor, even when he was cutting someone's throat.

Blanco's hit squad and a *gringo* sniper had crossed into Mexico from the remote Texas county almost three years ago, and killed Venustiano Huerta, Blanco's old nemesis and leader of *La Familia Norteña*. The sniper had blown Huerta's head to pieces from almost a kilometer away, in front of his woman and son at a supposedly impenetrable hacienda fortress.

Navarrete grinned. His left orbital bones had never been repaired after he ended his time in the boxing ring. The smile made the affected eye seem to fall back into his skull.

"What makes you smile, *carnal*?"

"*Jefe*, you remember that LFN guy who came over to us after that happened?"

"*Sí.*" And Blanco, remembering, barked a laugh. "He said Huerta's brains splattered the wall like day old *fideos con salsa*."

The action had stopped LFN's brash move against the *Zetas* – for a time.

"Well, the old couple," interjected Navarrete, recalling that the *Zetas* had hunted down their own sniper to ensure his silence, but the LFN getting there first, the three deaths on the Griffin ranch and the ensuing uproar by the border patrol and the media on the American side of the border. *"Los viejitos perdieron sus vidas..."*

"The cost of doing business," responded Blanco. "Besides, they had shit for a grandson."

Navarrete nodded. But Otabiano and Raquel Vasquez had had nothing to do with Pete Vasquez' misadventures. They had died violently. And, Navarrete thought, *needlessly.* Their deaths had stirred up too much attention and anger.

"Jefe," began Navarrete, carefully neutral in tone. "Is crossing product into and through that *condado"* – he pointed toward Kickapoo County – worth the risk?"

Blanco gave the question some thought. It wasn't going to be as easy as crossing loads in tractor-trailer rigs. There was only one decent crossing upriver at a hamlet dubbed Lagrimas, next to US 90. It was a place where every inhabitant had relatives in Mexico, and thus they would close their eyes when crossings were made – or else. Or perhaps even at the Griffin ranch, or any other ranch abutting the river. Or another place where *norteamericanos* with ranches and police were hungry for cash.

Blanco laughed again. *"Dicen que Kendricks y su familia quedan en Austin ahora. Una buen distancia.* Yes, Kendricks was the only lawman in Kickapoo County who'd had the *cojones* — and the brains —– to challenge them, and he no longer lives there. "Austin is a good place for that bilingual *shit* and his family to be."

He took another toke on the spliff. "Kendricks interrupted our capture of Pete Vasquez, and his *puta amiga,* Laura Griffin. that greedy bitch. Kendricks interfered with us torturing her and doing the same to Pete Vasquez. Kendricks and other *gabachos* interfered too much."

Blanco and Navarrete knew all about the rumors that Pete Vasquez had stashed a lot of money somewhere. Where? An offshore bank account? On the bitch's ranch? Who knew?

Whatever Pete Vasquez had hidden was nothing compared to the profits of supplying the hungry *norteamericanos* with their drugs.

"No Border Patrol headquarters close, eh?" Blanco opined. "No big, tethered balloon with radar near here, either. I think we can do good business here."

Blanco stepped into his Humvee. For a few moments, Navarrete was by himself, gazing northward. "I'm not so sure," he muttered.

Navarrete's nickname, "El Tramposo," – the Cunning One – wasn't given him without a reason. Guillermo Blanco was the *jefe*, yes, but Navarrete knew that if Blanco miscalculated, Blanco's bosses would not look kindly upon him. Navarrete would support "Cantinflas" as long as it was expedient to do so. But if Blanco's decision to use Kickapoo County as a new crossing point for the *Zeta's* drugs failed, he — the Cunning One— would not hesitate to put a bullet in the bastard's ever-smiling face.

*****

Jack Eddleman walked into the DEA office in San Antonio a week after his transfer notice. He didn't expect a warm greeting and wasn't disappointed. The damage his alleged conduct had done to the DEA's relationship with several Texas law enforcement agencies had not healed. Eddleman hadn't been indicted with Vasquez' death, but Lowell Johnson's *Kickapoo County Courier* had all but called him a murderer, and the San Antonio and other Texas news outlets had not been much kinder.

Two years in the Dakotas was a small price to pay in Eddleman's mind for killing Pete Vasquez, although he hadn't felt it at the time. Still smarting from David Sanchez' admonishments before he left Bismarck, he remained stone-faced as he checked in and assigned a desk in an open area. Quite a comedown from Bismarck, space-wise, but he could manage it.

Eddleman unloaded pens and paper into the desk drawers and signed into the intra-agency network on his computer.

"*Que paso, amigo?*" popped up on his screen. He cracked a smile as he recognized the sender – Leroy Breaux, who'd helped him flip Vasquez. The effort had almost resulted in a monster drug haul. But it hadn't, not because of an informer, but because of plain dumb luck.

"*Pues, nada,*" Eddleman typed. "Where are you?"

"One office over," was the response. Eddleman craned his neck, finally spotting Breaux standing in a doorway.

Breaux waved, then typed "You aren't exactly a welcome addition to the office right now, so excuse me if I don't come give you a kiss on the lips. Angela's Café at six?"

Eddleman agreed to meet at an old watering hole on San Antonio's Southside, and turned his attention to business.

*****

Eddleman pulled into Angela's parking lot in his personal vehicle and went inside. With little time to find an apartment, he'd paid for a week-to-week extended stay motel near downtown, but hadn't unloaded anything yet, trusting that Angela's reputation as a police hangout would prevent San Antonio's *cholos* from stealing his car or his possessions, or cutting out the car's catalytic converter. Leroy Breaux occupied a booth at the back of the dimly lit bar. He stood when Eddleman approached.

"Good to see you again. Didn't think it was going to happen." Breaux didn't need to say more. He'd narrowly avoided reassignment after the Vasquez dustup. He still admired his former boss, but he was now wary of him.

The two sat, and Breaux motioned to the barmaid for two beers, without mentioning brands. Seconds later, she appeared with frosted mugs and two Yuenglings.

"Yuengling?" Eddleman asked. "Some kind of Chink beer?"

"Nah, from Pennsylvania. Been around forever, but just now showing up in Texas," replied Breaux.

They settled into a comfortable silence and drained their mugs. Breaux signaled for another round, but Eddleman stopped him. "Only one for me, amigo. If I get stopped by PD and test more than point-oh-two, it'd be an excuse to bounce me."

"That bad?"

"Don't know, but don't want to chance it."

"Glad to have you with us again, Jack. We were doing some good work."

Eddleman nodded appreciatively. "Vasquez could have brought us a motherload of cases."

"Sorry he didn't," Breaux said. "Border has calmed down a bit, as you know, but now..." He pulled off a baseball cap, displaying a bald patch. "Cartels are fractured all to hell. It's always been like nailing Jell-O to a wall figuring out where the dope's coming in. Now, it's even worse. The Jalisco motherfuckers are nastier than the *Zetas*, if that's possible."

Another hour with Breaux and Eddleman felt reasonably sure about which landmines to avoid inside the DEA office structure. "I'm anxious to get back to doing what I think I was good at," he assured Breaux.

"Don't need to tell me that, Jack. There'll be plenty of chances to prove that."

"So, Leroy, what are you hearing? Besides the usual 'cartel A just butchered six of cartel B's *sicarios*?'"

"No surprise" replied Breaux. "We're catching a lot more stuff at the legal crossings. Some snitches, some cooperation with the Mexican Army, at least those in it that haven't stayed bought, and we have better scanners. Talk now is that the latest bloodbath between the groups has gotten some of them thinking, again, about trying to use remote areas."

"Didn't work before," Eddleman said. "Too easy to spot for large hauls."

"Yeah, but they're forcing the illegals to do their dirty work and thinking we're too busy in the cities to look closely enough."

"Uggh," Eddleman laughed. "Sounds like a lot of time in we-no-tell motels."

Breaux nodded. "No Fairmont Inns or Ramadas in most of the *podunk* border towns smaller than Laredo, El Paso, and Del Rio."

Eddleman leaned forward. "Leroy, truth be told, I'm damned excited about being here. It's where I belong, and you and I know it." He reached into his breast pocket for a tin of Kodiak.

"You still dipping that shit?" Breaux laughed, then high-fived him. "Jack, we need you here. The whole fucking border of Texas is becoming a Third-World shithouse."

After sharing a few remembrances, Eddleman shook hands with Breaux and left, assured that Breaux, at least, was still an ally. His chances of working Kickapoo County were looking better.

He drove to his motel, unpacked, and settled in for the night. He didn't give a damn about what the Texas border was becoming. He just needed the time and space to find over seventeen million dollars Pete Vasquez had hidden somewhere on a godforsaken ranch next to the Rio Grande.

Chapter 9

A troubling discovery at the Griffin Ranch

I said aloud, "If anyone's here, he'll be down by the river." I set the numbers on my combination lock to 0-6-2-7 – Forrest's birthday was June 27, and pulled its shackle. I unwrapped the chain securing the gate to the post and walked back to the truck to grab my binoculars. The Griffin Ranch – I still called it that, despite the deed showing me as the sole owner– appeared benign. Its west side was mostly eroded limestone hillocks. To my front, the terrain flattened out for several miles. What vegetation there was would not hide anything of consequence.

I swung open the gate, then moved the shotgun, M16, and extra ammunition to the front seat. After the tires clattered on the cattleguard, the only sound was the truck's engine as the soft sand muted my passage south. A few hundred yards inside the fence, I noticed more tracks, indicating a return passage. "Looks like whoever was here *did* leave," I muttered. I hoped so, recalling the massive gun battle two years ago. I was a long way from Santa Rosa with no cell coverage.

Two miles in, I stopped on a small rise overlooking what was once the ranch's main house, when Laura Griffin's daddy, Clayton Griffin, was alive.

I took cover behind the hood. If someone was in the old ranch house or its outbuildings, I would have some protection. I swept the area through the binoculars. The tire tracks hadn't left the ranch road, so I drove to the ranch house. A padlock securing the back porch door appeared intact. The dilapidated out-building, once used as a welding shop and garage, was buttoned up tight.

The Aermotor windmill rattled and clanged, spinning in the light breeze. The windmill's rods plunged into the well casing, making a small sucking noise as the pump pulled water out of the ground and splashed it into a steel tank. I'd worked on this place as a high school kid. On countless hot afternoons after a day's work under the Texas sun, I'd stripped down to underwear and swam in the tank's chilly water, feeling old man's stocked goldfish nibble on my toes. The thought pulled me back to a simpler time. I set the binoculars down and, for a few minutes, listened and looked, feeling both happy and sad. Clayton Griffin had taken pride in his ranch.

I drove under under the large live oak tree and away from the Griffin house. So far, no surprises. Half a mile further, I braked at the edge of a small swale and turned off the ignition. The wind had died, and all I heard was the ticking of the engine metal as it cooled down. In the distance was a rock and wood house, now in ruins. It had once been the home of Otabiano and Raquel Vasquez. Otabiano, Griffin's *segundo,* stayed on after Clayton Griffin died. She'd let them continue to live on the place.

I shook my head. Too many memories. The two had been murdered in the canebrake next to the Rio Grande, the southern border of the ranch. I didn't need binoculars to confirm the sorry state of what had once been a happy home. Just months after their murders, the structure provided me and others protection in a gun battle with Mexican drug dealers. It had been shot to shit.

Four vultures circled above the river's green flood plain. The tire tracks I'd followed continued toward the Vasquez house, but the vehicle that made them wasn't there. I stopped next to the front door, listening. A puff of wind slapped the screen door against the wall, startling me. I pushed the front door open and looked inside. Empty. I walked around back.

Twenty paces from the clothesline in the back yard, I was on the bluff overlooking the Rio Grande. The heavy growth of cane and salt cedar upriver still showed blackened limbs from the fire that had nearly killed me, Laura, and Pete, two years ago, but was starting to fill out green again. The shallow river swept against the bank on the United States side; the rise of the alluvial plain on the Mexico side more gently sloping.

Tire imprints showed the truck had parked off to my right. No footprints exited the truck. Strange. I'd driven to the ranch six months earlier to meet with a young man from the Dallas area who'd bought a few hundred adjacent acres on the river. I offered to let him use my acreage for grazing so we both could keep the ag exemption. He'd thanked me, and said he'd get back with me but never did. He'd seemed uninterested, and I guessed that with some good high bluffs on the Rio Grande, he bought his land for recreation. A few hundred acres in this part of the world wasn't big enough for anything else. As far as I could tell, the new owner hadn't bothered to stock his small tract or do anything with it.

I hadn't tried to lease my ranch since then. Now, I saw no sign of livestock. No animals grazing. No fresh cow shit. Who trespassed? Why? The most innocent explanation was someone looking for a place to put in the river for catfishing. It was also the most implausible. There were other accessible put-in points. You didn't just go onto someone else's property without permission. The locals knew the rules and honored them.

I'd put it off as long as I could. It was time to have a talk with Jake Nichols, the Kickapoo County Sheriff's Office dispatcher.

I secured the gate chain and ensured the lock's shackle held. I set the four tumblers to 0-6-2-7, wondering again who'd cut the chain and re-secured it with his own keyed lock.

The drive back to US 90 took thirty minutes. Once on the blacktop, I wondered what I was going to say to Jake.

Skirting Santa Rosa's business district, I parked in front of Jake's tiny house he'd inherited from his mother. Jake lived in the poor part of town. Most of his Hispanic neighbors made an effort to keep their properties looking decent. Jake's place reflected badly on them. Broken and missing asbestos siding. Grass burrs multiplying in the yard. The chain link fence on the north side property line was now propped up and retied to the support poles. No doubt by the neighbor next door.

The sun was down, with an afterglow. I collected the contents of the jammed-full mailbox and pushed through the badly hung gate. On the front porch, I brushed the dust off a ladder-back chair and sat.

Six o'clock came and went. I knew Jake was on a day shift, but he didn't have much of a life outside of dispatching, and often agreed to substitute in for a sick dispatcher or one wanting to do something with the family.

I needn't have worried. His old pickup's headlights appeared from the north. The truck slowed, then turned into the driveway on the house's north side.

"Purdy? Is that you?" he called from his pickup.

I waved the bundle in my hand. "Got your mail. You've got some bills in here."

"Geez, Purdy, what brings you here?" In the dark, Jake's acne-scarred face was barely visible. "How long you been waiting?"

I looked around. A couple of neighbors several houses down were talking in a front yard. "Let's go inside."

"Sure, Purdy. Sure." Jake retrieved a sixpack from his truck, then walked to the front door. "I hardly ever go in this door. Mostly use the side door by the truck."

He sounded nervous. Once inside, he switched on a small desk lamp. Old magazines, mostly about computers or the Wild West, lay stacked in chairs and on a small table.

"Can I get you something to drink? Water? That's all I got besides the beer." He gestured toward the Dos Equis cans.

"Thanks, Jake. I'm fine. Can we talk?"

"Sure, Purdy. Sure. Why didn't you just come by the Sheriff's Office?" He gestured to the disarray. "Lot neater than my place, you know." A cloud seemed to pass over his face. I wondered if he was remembering the only other time I'd been inside, and what happened then. It had not been a pleasant conversation.

I moved magazines and sat on a chair beside a green vinyl covered table. Jake stood in the kitchen doorway, looking confused. He walked into the kitchen, and I heard the refrigerator door open and shut. He returned and made space on the threadbare couch, popped a beer open, and drank half of it. He set the beer down on the couch arm and unbuttoned his wrinkled uniform shirt. His belly, covered with a greyish, stained t-shirt, lapped over the uniform pants and belt.

Jake took another swallow. "Purdy, what brings you back to Santa Rosa? You checked on Paula?"

I leaned forward. "Paula doesn't know I'm here. Almost no one knows I'm here." Paula Richardson was Betty's sister and her fierce defender. Right now, I was on good terms with my sister-in-law, but that could change in a heartbeat if Paula suspected I'd been in town without quickly visiting. Given what I'd put Betty through before we left town, anything that Paula thought would upset her sister's new life and her safety would guarantee her hostility. "It needs to stay that way, at least for now."

Jake's rumpled appearance and poorly kept house didn't mean Jake was slow. My boyhood chum was the smartest kid in school. I knew from experience that his sharp mind hadn't atrophied as he'd grown up.

His eyes narrowed. "Okay, amigo. What's going on? Why're you meeting me here, after dark, in Momma's crappy house? Last time, it wasn't pleasant."

It hadn't been. Jake's employer, the County Sheriff, had once humiliated Jake's widowed mother. Jake, fifteen at the time, had witnessed it. Eddleman convinced Jake that the sheriff was possibly corrupt, talking Jake into serving as a pipeline into the sheriff's office. Jake's misguided attempts had nearly ruined my investigation into the death of Pete Vasquez' grandparents.

I'd considered how to broach the subject of Israel Sifuentes. Tiptoeing around wouldn't be appreciated. But Jake might clam up if I outright accused him of something.

"Israel Sifuentes. You seen him lately?"

I could almost see Jake's mind working. "Don't insult my intelligence, Purdy. Or our friendship."

"Sorry."

"All the time, Purdy. All the time. Shit, he works across the street!"

"Jake, someone killed Israel."

He leaned forward. "When? Where? This county? Why haven't we heard about it?"

I'd been Jake's closest friend in school. We were both from Lagrimas. More importantly, I'd become Jake's friend in the simplest way – I'd never made fun of him or bullied him. I'd refused to call him anything but by his Christian name. I later found out how much these small kindnesses were valued. I felt the weight of treading carefully with this fragile man now.

"I need your promise that what we're about to talk about stays here."

He nodded his agreement.

"Jake, someone cut his head off and stuck it on a fencepost at the entrance to Lowell Johnson's ranch."

Jake started to interrupt, but I held up a hand, and he pushed back into the couch cushion. "No one in law enforcement knows about it, and I need for it to stay that way."

He crushed the beer can and set it on the floor. "Why're you telling me? Shit, I'm just a piss-ant dispatcher."

"Because I trust you." Which I did. "You remember a phone call I made to you two years ago?"

"Hell, there were hundreds, Purdy. That was a long time ago."

"Sorry. I called you about heading out to Lagrimas in the middle of the night. Israel had called me. You'd been real worried. Wanted me to take someone with me but I'd insisted I needed to go alone."

Jake leaned forward, and the couch groaned at the weight shift. "Yeah, Purdy. I do remember."

"I was sworn to secrecy back then, and I didn't know why I was told to go there."

"Well, what was it?"

"Can't say. Doesn't matter now. But I did go out to Lagrimas. I was the only one who knew Israel asked me out there. I never told you. I've never told anyone, including Betty, or Selman, or anyone." I paused. "But I might have fucked up, Jake. So, what I'm asking you now is not an accusation. I may not have made it clear enough that it was a secret. I may have caused Israel's death."

Jake wasn't stupid. "But you're here, talking to me. So, you think I've got something to do with what's going on, right?"

"Jake, I don't know.

"Aw geez, Purdy." Jake stood, running fingers through his thinning hair. "Someone's killed Israel, and you and me are the only ones who know about it. That's what's going on, isn't it?"

I nodded. "Did you ever mention that Lagrimas trip to anyone, Jake? Even in passing?"

"I'm thinking. I'm thinking. But if I did, it would have only been to someone at the Sheriff's Office."

Which was why I was there. "And?"

"I gotta think on this, Purdy. I'm not trying to put you off, but I need to sit here a while and try to recall. Is anyone else in trouble because of this?" Jake's voice quavered. "If I did something to cause Israel's death..."

I stood. "Quit it, Jake. We're friends. Always will be." I realized as I said it that I wanted someone besides me to carry this guilty load.

He promised he'd call if he thought of anything. We shook hands, but Jake suddenly reached around my shoulders and put a wrestler's hug on me. "I miss you, Purdy. This place's not the same without you. Please give Betty my love."

Driving away, I wondered if I was any closer to finding out who had divulged my conversation with Israel about Lagrimas that night two years ago.

I pushed in my blue-toothed earbuds and tapped "play." Jessica Molaskey's album *Pentimento* started. Her sultry voice along with Johnny Pizzarelli's guitar loosened the fist in my gut. Endorphins kept me from fretting and helped me stay awake. I was thirty miles from Austin when my cell phone danced on my thigh.

It was Jake Nichols.

"Purdy, I've thought it over. I never said anything to anyone back then. But, about six months ago, I did mention it to someone."

"And..."

"One day, there were about four lawyers in there; and the judge's secretary in his outer office was filling out court reset forms for some others." He named the judge, the elected district attorney, and several defense lawyers. "I think there may have been some defendants standing around near the outside office too. I can't even remember who all people were."

For just a moment, I'd hoped I could pinpoint the cartel's information source. It was too much to expect.

Chapter 10

Drug airplanes and a plaza takeover

"We've got two bogies," a radar operator said as the EPIC staff followed the blips on radar screens. "I'll assign them IDs Tango 1 and Tango 2," she added. The two Tangos were small aircraft, tracking east to west. Because they might turn north and enter US airspace, DEA and Border Protection armed twin-engine aircraft and helicopters were alerted.

It was two a.m., Central Daylight time when she began radar tracking two low flying aircraft one hundred miles inside Mexico. The El Paso Intelligence Center, or EPIC, was created in 1974, in the words of its website, to "identify threats to the Nation, with an emphasis on the Southwest border." EPIC's personnel, mostly employees of the DEA and U.S. Customs and Border Protection, were sequestered in a non-descript structure adjacent to the El Paso International Airport, tasked with providing intelligence and assistance in drug interdictions.

The Tethered Aerostat Radar System, or TARS, a system of balloons strung between Puerto Rico and California, provided real time data on air traffic involved with drug smuggling. Two of the monoliths kept watch near Eagle Pass and Marfa, Texas.

The acronym-rich combination of technological wizardry was part of the United States' mostly futile attempts at narcotics interdiction.

The TARS radar operator provided the narrative. "Tango 1 has just disappeared in ground clutter." Then, "Ditto, Tango 2."

Five minutes later, neither aircraft had reappeared. Two DEA agents sitting in the EPIC command center pored over billions of pixels of northern Mexico's terrain.

A five thousand pound, thirty-six-foot-long Predator B unmanned aerial vehicle called a UAV was directed to the area, illegally flying inside Mexican airspace. Within an hour, the drone sent back images of two low humps in the desert topography. Infrared cameras detected heat sources like aircraft engines. Tango 1 and Tango 2 sat covered with camouflage next to a dirt strip at a small Mexican town dubbed El Mosco.

The DEA office in San Antonio received the intel a day later. On Monday morning at eight a.m., Leroy Breaux called Eddleman on his cell phone, and it went to voicemail. From his office door, he spotted Eddleman at his desk, and let out a low whistle. Eddleman, on the phone with a San Antonio police officer discussing a Southside street dealer, indicated with his fingers to "hold a sec." He disconnected and went to Breaux.

"Shut the door, will you, Jack?" Breaux asked, his Louisiana accent noticeable.

Eddleman shut the door. "What's up?"

"Take a look at this just in from El Paso." He handed Eddleman a sheaf of papers and photos, sat back in his chair, waiting for a response.

Eddleman glanced through the collection. "Two planes, staged for smuggling. Nothing unusual there, except they landed further inside Mexico than I would have expected."

"Jack," Breaux chided, "doesn't El Mosco sound familiar?"

Eddleman pulled a topographic printout from the pile of papers showing the bleakness of northern Coahuila, one of Mexico's northern counties. "I must be getting old. That pissant place is fifty or so miles east of where the *Zetas* assassinated Venustiano Huerta."

"Bingo, my friend."

Eddleman looked up. "Okay, but is there a connection?" He tapped the photograph. "All of northern Mexico is a drug cartel staging area of one kind or another."

"DEA HQ thinks you and I are smart enough to shine some light on this tidbit. Get ready to talk about it, 'cause we're due at a meeting in about..." He checked his wristwatch. "...five minutes."

The conference room filled with DEA agents and analysts. Eddleman was surprised when the Special Agent in Charge (SAC) Victoria Fleming, from Houston, strolled into the meeting. She was five feet and a couple of inches and weighed less than one hundred and twenty pounds. Forty-nine years old, she'd survived the DEA's ingrained sexism and three marriages. Reputedly sleeping only four hours a night, she'd thrived in overseas assignments in Colombia, Peru, and Afghanistan, despite being kidnapped once and shot and wounded twice. Tagged as an up-and-comer, she'd been transferred from Puerto Rico and taken over the Houston Field Division, encompassing much of 118,000 miles of Texas and 645 miles of the Mexican border. This all came in the shakeup that resulted from the gunfight on the Griffin Ranch in Kickapoo County and the unsolved killing of DEA informant, Pete Vasquez.

She took off her blazer, showing a wiry, whip-thin build. Several agents in the mostly male group shot additional surreptitious glances at their boss's gymnast-firm body. "Gentlemen. Ladies." SAC Fleming nodded at the gathering. "Good to see everyone bright and chipper this morning. Except Miller." She pointed to an agent dealing with a newborn baby. "Still up all night?"

Hoots of laughter erupted.

"Agents Breaux and Eddleman have been looking over the new info received from our balloons and EPIC." Fleming turned to Eddleman. "Welcome back into the fold, Jack." She smiled. "Know you miss the Dakotas, but glad you're back where you can do some real work for a change."

Some groans and a few laughs followed at Eddleman's expense. He felt relief at the good-natured ribbing. It was a signal for now that he wasn't going to be treated like a pariah.

The witch could have nixed the transfer. She could make my life here a living hell, he thought, appreciative that she'd chosen not to do so.

"Among our many other challenges in our holy war against drugs..."

More groans and laughter.

"As I was saying, among our many other challenges, we've got new intel that says the *Zetas* are going to try pushing larger than usual loads across the Texas border away from their normal routes. Most of what we can guess comes from our eyes in the sky plus phone and computer intercepts, but we've also got people in Mexico. Let's hope they stay alive and well."

She turned toward the two, sitting together in the back of the room. "Comments, gentlemen?"

Calmly, Breaux stood. "By way of background, the *Zetas* assassinated LFN's Venustiano Huerta about fifty or so miles due west of a village named El Mosco two and a half years ago. *Zetas* now control that part of the Coahuilan landscape, which as you know merely holds the earth together." He gestured to Eddleman, a generous offer to his former partner to share his knowledge of the area.

Jack Eddleman took the handoff. "*Zetas* sent a kill team from a ranch in Kickapoo County." He pointed at a wall map of Texas. "Once the mission was accomplished, they tried to snuff out their own hit squad. They killed one of them. Local law enforcement in Kickapoo County and a Texas Ranger found his body in the Rio Grande. We're not sure who killed Shivelli, the hired sniper, but whoever killed him also killed an old Mexican couple taking care of a small ranch nearby, and on our side of the river."

Eddleman didn't mention the Griffin Ranch by name. Most of his audience knew the ranch in question was where, weeks later, Eddleman's snitch, Pete Vasquez, had been killed. And that Jack Eddleman was suspected of being his killer.

An analyst passed out copied drone photos of topography and infrared pictures. Eddleman elaborated, "Two aircraft were spotted a couple of nights ago. Not sure why they're parked where they are, but that part of Coahuila is *Zeta* territory. At the same time, LFN is pushing back. *Zetas* are supposedly going to try some new - or at least new to the area - tricks. That could mean rural crossings. Any questions?"

"You've been away for a while, Jack," interjected a female agent. "You might want to watch Ciudad Acuña real close. Our sources there say the tension is so thick you can't cut it with a knife. *Zetas* may want to try some new tricks, but they may have more on their plate than they can handle. The Jalisco New Generation, CJNC, has been picking off *Zeta sicarios* left and right."

Eddleman nodded.

SAC Fleming spent ten more minutes describing Kickapoo and surrounding areas on the western part of the Houston Field Division's operational zone. "We'll work with the El Paso Division," she said, "but right now, we're in assessment mode."

No one in the room expressed any surprise. Drug interdictions were occurring in the Pacific Ocean and the Caribbean Sea — capturing submarines ladened with drugs. Drones dropped cocaine over San Diego. Illegals were forced to mule kilos of heroin, cocaine, and fentanyl across the Arizona desert.

One thing Fleming had learned in her years in law enforcement was that efforts at drug enforcement were about as effective as sticking one's finger in a single hole in a badly leaking dam.

SAC Fleming glanced at the agents' jaded looks. Slamming her folder onto the podium, she took a deep breath. "Listen up, goddammit! I'm not expecting miracles, but 100,000 people are dying each year in this country from drug overdoses. Shit is pouring into the country from our enemies to the south. The Chinese are selling the precursors for fentanyl and anything else the communist government will let them get away with. So quit dicking around!"

An older DEA agent, obviously on friendly terms with SAC Fleming, dared ask a question. "Victoria, no offense, but we all know that. What's so important about this particular operation?"

She shook her head in apology. "Truthfully? If you get lucky, we might take some bad guys off the streets for a while. Just before I walked in here this morning, I found out my best friend's nineteen-year-old son, a college kid in San Marcos, died from a fentanyl overdose yesterday. Never used it before in his life.

But he thought he'd try a line of cocaine at a frat party. It was laced." She stared stonily at the assembly before starting for the conference room exit, then turned back. "Like some of you in this room, this poison just hit me too close to home. Sorry for the speech." She left the room.

"She's cold as a witch's tit," muttered one male agent to another.

A female agent overheard it. "Yeah, asshole, but she's got bigger balls than any of you wimps."

"Well, shit. On that note," said Breaux, "I guess we'd better get to work."

****

Guillermo Blanco's *Los Zetas sicarios,* wary of an ambush by LFN or CJNG enemies, lined up fifteen Humvees, all with pedestal-mounted machineguns, and eight to ten armed *Zetas.* They were waiting at a warehouse seventy-five kilometers south of Ciudad Acuña, a city of 300,000. The *Zetas* were locked in an ongoing struggle with the LFN for the border city's plaza. The Jalisco New Generation cartel had infiltrated some of its *sicarios* to help the LFN.

The Jalisco-based cartel operated on the principle that "the enemy of my enemy is my friend." And the *Zetas* were definitely an enemy. Blanco's plan was simple: kill every *sicario* from other cartels who might be inside the city.

Blanco turned to Navarrete. "You know what you have to do tonight, right? We secure the plaza in Acuña, then we start crossing some product further west."

We secure the plaza in Ciudad Acuña, thought Navarrete, *we won't need to cross our product further west.*

"I know what you are thinking," grinned Blanco. "The fucking DEA, they're hurting us at the *frontera.* Sure, those *jotos* — those queers — from Jalisco will be out of the way, but we need to diversify, my friend."

Navarrete waited until Blanco drove off in a heavily armed suburban. The Humvee drivers idled their engines while the *Zeta* killers sat or stood, mimicking calm.

What the fuck does that smiling asshole Cantinflas think he's running? A furniture store? Diversify? Navarrete thought as he lit a Marlboro. He turned toward his men. "Time to go, *muchachos.* Kill every Jalisco and LFN *puto* you find."

Inside Ciudad Acuña, *Zeta* killers formed an invisible ring around LFN strongholds. Three bars, located on Calle Reforma, Calle Benito Juarez, and Calle Victoria were under observation from *sicarios* hidden in nearby apartments or offices. The *Policia Municipal* suddenly disappeared from the streets – warned by the *Zetas* that any members who interfered with the operation would be killed – as would their families.

At nightfall, the Humvees rolled into town. On cue, *Zetas* stormed the three bars. Two fell quickly, and with only one *Zeta* killed. The few LFN and *Jalisco Nueva Generacion* survivors were pulled into the streets, forced to kneel, and *Zetas* cut their throats. The third locale, the closest to the bridge across the Rio Grande into the Texas town of Del Rio, was a tougher nut to crack for Navarrete's men. After six of their own were killed, the *Zetas* set fire to the structure, and burned it down along with seventeen of their enemy.

Navarrete's cellphone buzzed. Blanco spoke tersely, "You took too long. The *gringos* closed the bridge after bullets went across into *los estados unidos*."

Fuck you, thought Navarrete. "I apologize, *jefe*." Navarrete swallowed his anger. "We got the job done as quickly as possible."

The plaza in Ciudad Acuña was now under *Zeta* control.

"I'm a little disappointed but..." Blanco paused, "good job." Before Navarrete could respond, Blanco broke the connection.

Navarrete looked at his phone. *I have other ideas. If you, the smiling clown Cantinflas, continue with this plan to run drugs into desolate Texas locations, it will backfire, and I will put a bullet through your brain and show* todos los pendejos *how a real man leads* los Zetas.

Chapter 11

Purdy's juggling act and an unexpected call for help

Nearing Austin, my phone rang. It was Lowell Johnson.

"Hey, Purdy," he said, "is it clear for me to head out to my ranch in the morning?"

Feeling fuzzy headed from the long drive, I thought for a second before answering. "Yeah." I paused. "Think you can manage it?"

Big sigh. He answered, "God help me, but yes. Just please get this shit cleared up. I'm scared to death now."

I rang off just as I turned into my driveway. It was two a.m.

I parked the truck and transferred my firearms and body armor into the trunk of the state sedan, then quietly unlocked the front door.

Betty was asleep on the sofa. When I shut the door, she woke and yawned. "You're back. I'm glad." She smiled and pulled a blanket up to her shoulders. *God, she is beautiful.*

"Yeah," I whispered. "I'm back, and glad to be home." I hugged her with a fierceness foreign to my usual greetings.

When she lifted her face for a kiss, she wrinkled her nose. Her expression turned dark. "Purdy, you need to strip off those clothes and get in the shower."

Uh oh.

Trying to keep it light, I muttered, "I bet I stink. Haven't had time to bathe." I shrugged off my jean jacket, shirt, and undershirt. Betty's expression told me I was in trouble.

She stood. "Give me your clothes. They're going in the washer, right now."

Betty put my shirt up to her nose. "Gunpowder." She turned on the living room's ceiling light and held my shirt up, inspecting it. "Is this blood?" She pointed to a small spot near the collar.

My plan had been to *not* tell Betty anything about what happened. Which was incredibly stupid. Worse, it was an insult to the woman's intelligence. "Probably," was all I could get out.

"Is it yours?"

"No, hon. It's not. I'm not hurt."

She tweaked my nose. I flinched in pain.

"Well, someone or something smacked you good. Is it broken?"

"Probably, but I'll explain it later, please."

"Get your shower while I put these clothes in the washer. I don't want to smell them and I sure as hell don't want to see any blood." She turned toward the utility room, then paused. "Whatever happened? Did it happen in Kickapoo County?"

I couldn't look her in the face. Sitting on the sofa, I pulled off my boots and socks. "Yes," I finally answered.

"Oh shit, Purdy. Oh, shit. We've been through hell together. Don't tell me I've got to deal with more of that godforsaken place. More importantly, don't you dare put your son in danger."

"I won't. I promise." I had no idea whether I was telling the truth.

Betty shook her head. She turned and walked to the laundry room, looked back and warned, "And don't put me in danger of becoming a widow."

A half-hour later, I crawled onto my side of the bed. Betty was under the covers, her back to me. She was either sound asleep or avoiding learning about whatever I'd been up to.

Morning came too early, evidenced by Forrest yelling, "Get up, Daddy." He launched himself onto the bed and me before I could react. I grabbed him and tickled him until his peals of laughter filled the room. For a few moments, I forgot the pall that hung in the air.

"School time, boys," Betty yelled from the kitchen. "Purdy, you taking your son to school today?" The smell of frying bacon wafted into our bedroom.

I rolled onto Forrest, pinning him down. "Son, do I *have* to take you to school today?"

He giggled, the light dusting of freckles on his cheeks apparent in the pale morning light. "No, Daddy. You can take me fishing!"

"Hah!"

I pulled him off the bed, swatted his butt lightly, and told him to finish dressing. I hoped Forrest's enthusiastic love for his parents would buffer the friction between Betty and me. A full pot of coffee was warming. A jar of honey and a container of heavy cream sat next to my favorite mug.

"Thanks for the coffee, hon."

She gave me a quick peck on the cheek, then placed a platter of scrambled eggs, toast, and bacon on the kitchen table in front of me.

Thirty minutes later, after fending off his questions about my whereabouts the last two days, I dropped Forrest at school,

"Love you, Daddy!"

"Love you too, son. See you after school."

When he grabbed his backpack and ran for the school's entrance, I shuddered, remembering how close he and his mother had come to death at the hands of the Zetas two years ago.

The memory of trying to find Betty and Forrest, after seeing the bullet holes and blood inside our tiny Santa Rosa home triggered a panic attack. I broke into chills and sweat bloomed under my arms. The attack didn't abate until I parked in the gloom of my office building's basement garage. I shut off the engine, taking deep breaths. I didn't want anyone to see me in this state. Ten minutes later, I had enough control to face the day.

"Nice to see you made it in today, Commander," Alicia Trejo greeted me when I arrived at the Drug Interdiction Support Agency. Besides me, the office consisted of Alicia and two researchers. Not much of a fiefdom. "Missed you around here." The widow of a murdered DPS trooper, she ran the place like a drill sergeant.

Her face was questioned my two-day absence. I'd forgotten to check in. Not a good thing, especially since the tiny agency had been created less than two years ago. Its stated task was to "assist other law enforcement and related departments with logistical and informational support in the detection, interdiction, and prosecution of those suspected of importing illegal and harmful controlled substances into the State of Texas." Its lofty title and description belied that it mostly provided research and background information for frontline law enforcement. And that it was created, at least in part, to give a former underpaid Kickapoo County Deputy Sheriff with a law enforcement-related State job, and his family with a safe place to live, away from the border.

"What's wrong with your nose?"

"Ran into a door."

"Uh huh." Alicia Trejo shook her head and went back to whatever she was doing on the computer.

I called Abner an hour later.

"Israel's head has been delivered," he said. "I signed it in as a John Doe for now." He gave me the case number.

I told him, "I've got the flash drive with photos of Israel's house that needs locking up, but we don't have a secure evidence locker at my office. Suggestions?"

"I'll drop by for coffee in about an hour," he replied. "I'll put it in our evidence lockers with the same case number as the John Doe head." He paused. "You doing all right?"

Good question. "Things are a bit frosty with Betty right now. She smelled gun smoke and spotted some blood on my shirt. She knows I've been back to Kickapoo County."

"My wife never understands why I do what I do either," he assured me. "I've slept on the sofa a few nights. But somehow, we've made it. Married forty-one years and counting."

"Sorry," was all I could say.

"Don't be sorry. Doris is as good as they get. Married me when I was fresh out of the Academy and didn't have two nickels to rub together. She's lived with me in cracker box houses in Pecos, Jasper, and Rio Grande City. We finally bought a house when I moved to DPS Headquarters in Austin. Hell, we couldn't afford Austin. We ended up living in Lockhart. Closest place we can afford. I heard you and Betty are having hell trying to buy a house."

Abner never volunteered much information about his personal life, and I hadn't asked. I thought it was interesting he decided to share.

"And now, you've got a fishing camp out in the middle of nowhere," I said. "You going to sell your house and move back out to the boondocks? Where is it? Pandale, south of Ozona?"

Abner laughed. "I'd end up out there by myself. See you in a short." He disconnected.

It was closer to noon when Abner made it in. Rather than coffee, Alicia Trejo ordered takeout from a nearby Chinese restaurant. After thanking her, I closed the office door. I asked him, "Wonder when the shit will hit the fan?"

My cell phone buzzed. The Kickapoo County Sheriff's Office. I glanced at the screen. "Looks like right now. I'll put it on the speaker."

I set the phone where we could both hear it. "Kendricks here. Who have I got on the line?"

"Purdy, it's the sheriff." The raspy voice of Kickapoo County Sheriff TJ Johnson wheezed. "We got us a problem."

Abner and I exchanged glances. "What is it, Sheriff?" I figured it must be hell to have to make this phone call to his former investigator, especially since he couldn't stand me.

"We got a call from Lowell Johnson this morning, around nine o'clock. He'd gone out to his ranch and spotted some dead bodies. Three Mexes, all dead of gunshot wounds. Two by his front gate. One back behind the stock tank next to a pickup truck. Spent ammo everywhere."

"What do you want me to do? You need my help?" I made sure to add the word "help" because the fat bastard was having to swallow his pride to make the call. Not only was he calling me, but he was also referencing the Lowell Johnson, who he also detested.

"Since you left, we ain't got a certified investigator. I know we're supposed to ask you and your office to 'coordinate' – whatever that means. We need help on this one. I tried calling Selman, but I understand he's near retirement, and my call went straight to Message. Haven't heard back yet."

Abner leaned over the table. "Sheriff, Ranger Selman here. Sorry, I just got to the Commander's office." He made air quotes with his hands, just to give me hell. "And I haven't checked my phone."

You could almost smell the relief pouring off TJ as he responded. Probably thought he was on friendly ground now, talking with Abner. "Good to hear your voice, Ranger. Let me tell you what else we saw out at Lowell's Bar LJ ranch. Something spilled blood all over a steel post next to the front gate. We've taken pictures, of course, but there's no body connected to the blood. The ground around that post is a gory mess. Like someone stuck a body or part of a body on top of the pole."

Fifteen minutes later, after assurances from the Ranger that assistance was forthcoming, TJ disconnected.

I leaned back in my chair. "You know what I think about TJ, but I feel sorry for him. For him to ask for help with anything in his bailiwick has never been easy, but asking me? Tough."

Selman snorted. "He's not worth a damn, Purdy, and you know it. You saved his bacon, and then he tried to stick it to you. If it hadn't been for Lowell and his newspaper threatening to tell the world about TJ peeing in his pants during that shootout, he'd have done everything he could to torpedo you from getting this job. Save your pity for someone who deserves it."

"Point taken," I conceded. "But now what? They don't have an investigator. It's just a matter of time until someone starts asking 'where the hell is Israel?'" I took a deep breath. "I'm ready to go back down there, Ranger."

Selman help up his hand. "Oh, you'll get there. No doubts about that. But first, I need to send a forensics man down there. Someone we can trust."

"And?"

"Purdy, this is a bit unusual, but Bexar County ME just hired a fella from Colorado. Formerly with the Denver Medical Examiner's office. Met him on an elk hunt in the San Juan Mountains. He's developed respiratory problems, so he's moved to Texas. He's supposed to be one of the best. More important to you and me right now, I think, is that he's not connected with anyone in law enforcement on the border. Since I'm the one that helped him get the job, I think we can trust him. At least with much of the investigative work."

"He's not going to do crime scene stuff, Abner. He's a cause of death kind of guy."

"Yeah, but he's got some experience in forensics, too. Name's Harris Whittaker. We need someone down there we can trust. He'll have access to Israel's head right now, and if we ever find the rest of his body...." He paused.

I doubted we'd ever find the rest of Israel, but Abner was on a roll.

I said, "It's a start. And since we're talking about who we can trust, it's time I tell you about my talk with Jake Nichols. And about what happened in Lagrimas. Things are getting really interesting."

Abner laughed. "You say that like it's a good thing. We both know better."

Chapter 12

Memories revealed and a visit to the Medical Examiner

The atmosphere at home continued chilly. To escape Betty's dark mood, I retreated to Forrest's bedroom after supper and continued reading to him from C.S. Forester's *Mr. Midshipman Hornblower*. The youthful Horatio's adventures in the British Navy were distracting, and Forrest constantly peppered me with questions about why France and England were so mad at each other in the 1790s. My answers were followed up with more "whys," and I wondered whether my amazing son was serious about the history or just seeing how long he could keep his dad from making him go to sleep on a school night.

"Okay, sport. Enough for tonight." I closed the hardback book my mom had given me when I was Forrest's age. I received a strong neck hug and kiss before I exited and gently closed his door.

Betty had put on a pot of decaf coffee. She poured two mugs, added sugar and cream in hers, and handed me one. We sat on the sofa.

"Can we talk?" she asked.

It was more of a command than a question.

"What are you doing back in Kickapoo County, hon?

I told her, "Someone killed Israel Sifuentes.

A shocked look washed over her. "Who? Why?"

"I don't know." But I was sure I did, which if admitted would lead to acknowledgement I had hidden things from her for over two years.

"Mighty tight-lipped, Cowboy. You going to tell me about it?"

"Nothing to tell."

Betty leaned into the cushions with a thoughtful look.

"You're not shooting straight with me, are you?"

I said nothing, the unsaid denial proof enough to her of my duplicity.

"You refuse to share parts of your life with me, and it cuts me to the quick. I thought we had gotten past that, and now..." She paused. "I married you for better or worse. The drinking, the shitty job, and what I had to do – taking another human being's life, and yet..."

And you saved your life and our son's. And killed someone who needed killing. A wave of emotions swept through me. I was looking at a woman who had shown incredible bravery. I again reached over, and Betty allowed me to draw her to me. My shirt dampened where her face lay, and I became aware of my own tears as I stroked her long auburn hair. The tears were not just from sadness, but also from guilt I carried for allowing horror to come upon the two people I loved most. Horrific consequences had flowed from my investigation on the border.

We sat there quietly. Murmurs emanated from Forrest's room.

"He's dreaming is all." Betty reached for tissues, blew her nose, and let out a slight laugh. "Boy, we're a mess, aren't we?"

She sat on the edge of the couch and put her hand on my knee. "Okay, Honey, I'm through with my cry. Now tell me about why you're developing two black eyes and a swollen nose. And smelled of burned gunpowder, gun oil, and had blood on your shirt?"

I gave a short-hand version of the attempted ambush at Lowell Johnson's Bar LJ Ranch. Whatever Betty was thinking, she kept to herself.

"I want justice for Israel. For what they did to him." As the words tumbled out of me, I realized how ridiculous they sounded.

Betty drove that point home. "Seriously, do you really think you're going to find out who killed Israel? Or even if you do, bring them to justice?"

I didn't answer.

"Jesus, Purdy. You've lived around the border damned near all your life. Get real. Whoever is responsible for Israel's death is *ya se fue* by now, drinking tequila in some shithole bar in the interior of Mexico."

Betty's colorful language, however mild, surprised me. Its usage only happened when she was very, very upset.

I felt myself getting angrier and angrier. Not so much at Betty's verbal assault, but at the accuracy of it. Pete Vasquez' grandparents were never 'avenged' in my version of American justice. I was a fool if I thought Israel's death would have a different result.

Betty reached over and cupped a hand under my chin. "You're getting that pouty look you get when you're mad."

She knew me too well. She was guilty only of being honest.

But if I couldn't find Israel's killer or killers, I was determined to find out who used Jake's information to bring about Israel's death.

*****

I left Austin at ten a.m. The drive to San Antonio took an hour and a half. The Austin-San Antonio Corridor, as it is dubbed, had once been a calming stretch of farm and ranch land. Seemingly overnight, almost the entire corridor had changed to outlet malls, business parks, and truck stops.

The Bexar County Medical Examiner facilities were co-located with the county's Criminal Investigation Laboratory, northwest off Loop 410 amid hospitals and a golf course. No doubt this caused plenty of snide comments about convenience. I was met at the front desk by Assistant Medical Examiner Tim Villarreal.

"Deputy Kendricks, as I live and breathe." Villarreal shook my hand and led me back to his office. The white lab coat hid his short, stocky, boxer's body.

"Doc, I'm surprised to see you, too. Thought you'd be hired away by now by some high dollar practice."

"Naw. No one wants me working around live bodies. Here, my patients don't complain if I operate on the wrong kidney."

I groaned at what was no doubt one of his endless supply of dead body jokes. "Your hair's got some gray in it," I teased.

"You noticed? Got married right after all that brouhaha in, what was that, Kickapoo County?"

He didn't wait for an answer, as he turned into his small office, now adorned with several color photos of a stunningly beautiful African American woman.

"Your wife?"

He grinned proudly.

"She blind, or what?"

Seemingly oblivious to my kidding, he offered me a seat. "Expecting our first child in three months."

"Boy or girl?"

"Girl! Victoria Louise."

I glanced at a frame with Tim and his new bride. She was at least four inches taller. "Hope she takes after her mother."

He hooted a loud laugh. "Hell, even my relatives in Mexico hope so. One of my *tias* told me, *'No quiero que tu hija sea bajita y fornida!'* Imagine, my own blood thinking she'll turn out short and stocky like me!"

I laughed.

"What can I do for you?"

I gave him the identification number, and he typed it onto a keyboard.

Villarreal pulled back theatrically from the computer screen. "Whoa! Haven't had many of these, even in San Antonio. John Doe. Well, we've been thinking about shortening the tag name to J. Doe as he's not all here."

I didn't laugh. He looked up. "Sorry, bad joke. John Doe's still in a cooler." He checked his computer screen again. "He's been assigned to me. You know who he is?"

I gave a terse nod.

"Deputy, I'm thinking from your looks that he may have been a friend of yours."

"Let's just say the man didn't deserve to die."

"Why the John Doe then?"

I leaned forward. "Your office will get his real name once he's 'officially' identified, but for now, it's best he stays a John Doe."

Villarreal fidgeted in his chair. "I keep calling you 'deputy,' but you're not in uniform this time. You still with the SO down in Santa Rosa?"

I explained my new employment, leaving off the 'commander' title that went with the job. It was bad enough being addressed that way by Alicia Trejo. Villarreal offered coffee and poured us two cups.

All this pleasant chitchat started to wind down. "Purdy, what's the real reason for the visit?"

"You all just hired a new investigator. Name's Harris Whittaker. You know him?"

"I'm on the hiring committee, so, yeah, I do." Villarreal tilted his head, leaned forward. "This guy gets a big attaboy from Texas Ranger Abner Selman. You know him?"

I took a sip of coffee. "I know him." I was curious about Selman's connection to Whittaker, too.

"Interesting." He glanced at something on the computer. "Your John Doe was brought here by the same ranger." He paused, and I filled in the silence.

"I hear Whittaker is good at what he does. I also understand he's got additional training in forensic crime scene stuff. I was wondering if your office would see fit to assign him to my John Doe matter."

"Why? You all have the rest of your John Doe somewhere?"

"Sadly, no. But I would appreciate it if you could find out something for me."

"Okay. What?"

I leaned onto Villarreal's desk. "This is personal, but I'd like to know if Isr....er, John Doe died before his head was hacked off his body."

"In other words, whether he died —" He glanced again at the computer screen and clicked onto photographs. —before feeling himself get cut to pieces."

I nodded. It was all I could do.

"Purdy, I don't know what you're carrying around with you about this, but I promise you I'll do my best to give you an answer, and hopefully, the kinder one. Without a body, it's going to be a wild-assed guess, but there may be indications of whether the decapitation was postmortem."

"Thanks."

He stood. "Now let me introduce you to our new ME investigator." He picked up a desk phone and punched on it. "Mr. Whittaker, this is Dr. Villarreal. You got a few minutes?" He nodded, hung up, and said, "Let's go."

I'm not sure what I expected, but the Harris Whittaker I was introduced to wasn't it. When we entered his office, he stood and held out his right hand. At six feet, eight inches tall, he looked like a defensive guard for an NFL football team. Completely bald, I presumed from shaving his scalp, he sported a small salt and pepper goatee. Small silver studs were barely visible in both ears. I extended my hand, Whittaker grasped it, and I felt like I'd slipped my hand into a catcher's mitt. We shook, and he gently squeezed. I was relieved he hadn't crushed any bones.

"Please, sit," Whittaker said, as he settled uncomfortably into a desk chair two sizes too small.

"You probably aren't going to like this, Mr. Whittaker, but I'm about to involve you with cases where former Deputy Sheriff Purdy Kendricks" – Dr. Villarreal waved a hand generally in my direction, and I took it as a cue to affect a bow of fake humility – "has and continues to cause much excitement."

Whittaker had a bemused look on his face but wasn't ready to jump into this little soiree until he had a better feel how to not step on landmines.

"I'll let him fill you in later, but first," Villarreal asked, "you got anything going on right now?"

"Doctor, I just got here. My dance card is empty."

I decided I was going to like this man.

Villareal sprang up – no other way of describing it – and said, "Follow me."

Within minutes we were in the lab area of the ME's office. Three labs for autopsies, two with red lights lit over the doors, indicating the rooms were occupied. Villarreal pushed into the empty third, kicked on various lights, and punched the intercom. "Hector, my good man," he said into the speaker.

"'My good man, he says.'" came the voice on the other end. "Must mean our good Doctor Villarreal wants something."

"Hector, you are a candidate for MENSA."

"What the fuck is MENSA?"

"Never mind. Stuck up pricks, actually." He paused, reached into this lab coat's pocket, and pulled out a piece of paper. "Will you be so kind, my esteemed *amigo*, to bring us the contents of Drawer G351."

Chapter 13

Arturo Navarrete has some explaining to do

Guillermo Blanco, "Cantinflas," was pleased. Ciudad Acuña was now firmly in the hands of *los Zetas*. He didn't give a damn what the authorities in Del Rio thought about the massive killing and ensuing fires. What mattered was that *los Zetas* were back!

We sent those Jalisco puta madres packing. So, what if the border closes for a few days? The norteamericanos need their workers from Mexico. And their supervisors need to come to my side of the border to manage the maquila *factories. As long as the deaths of some pistoleros in Mexico don't interfere with profits. The border would re-open.*

It always had. In the meantime, the Acuña web of suppliers needed to be brought completely under control. Are you going to cooperate with *los Zetas? Si o no?* Anyone hesitating to give the correct answer would be "disappeared." The police? Made up mostly of poorly paid, poorly trained peasants, their bosses knew how to stay alive, and in business. *A few pesos here. A threat there. It always worked.*

Blanco's rumination was short. He had things to do, and he needed to ensure that Arturo Navarrete got them done. The two stood inside a deserted bar in downtown Ciudad Acuña. Blanco looked at the murals— poor copies of Diego Rivera's, glued to the walls. This had been a friendly watering hole for the *gringo* ranchers who visited on weekends. No more. No Americans in their right minds stepped onto Mexican soil here. Rows of various liquors, now coated with dust and grime, sat displayed behind a scarred oak bar. Several were broken, their contents stained the bullet-riddled mirror that had once reflected countless drinkers.

The Governor of Coahuila already had dispatched federal troops in a show of force. Two military Humvees with pedestal-mounted machine guns roared past the bar's open front door. The Mexican military looked capable, but its commanders, and the government officials overseeing the military were all in *los Zetas'* pockets, at least in this region. The poor soldiers, mostly indigenous and from poor rural Mexico, were usually directed to go where *los Zetas* weren't.

"We do what we've always done," Blanco said to Arturo Navarrete. "A week, or two, and the governor will find other concerns."

Navarrete, the "Cunning One," or "El Tramposo," shrugged. "Do you have something in mind?"

Blanco waved the suggestion off as if ridiculous. "No, my friend. Mark my words, the governor will send the troops go to another danger spot. *Los Zetas* have most of his staff on our payroll. They will whisper in the governor's ear." He paused again. "Besides, we are going to make other ways to get product to our customers."

Navarrete lit a cigarillo with a match, then tossed the match onto the linoleum floor. The idea of pushing drugs into remote areas like Kickapoo County seemed stupid to him. It would come back to bite *los Zetas*. He knew this in his heart. "Jefe, you need to hear something."

Cantinflas was immediately alert. "I always need to hear *everything*," he responded. He grabbed a flimsy metal chair adorned with Carta Blanca beer logos, turned it around, and sat. "What?"

"Of course, you remember when we took out Venustiano, using the *gringo* shooter?"

The only response was a brief nod, so Navarrete continued. "We cleaned up to make sure the killing did not come back to us."

"Fuck this! Get to the point!"

"Si, jefe. Things became quite bad on the American side with that shootout where Vasquez's *abuelos* lived."

"Yes. Yes. This is ancient history. What are you trying to tell me?" Blanco reached for Navarrete's vest and pulled the man partially across the small circular table. "Quit fucking with me."

"We sent two men to kill the *gringa* and the child of that *policia*, Kendricks. The woman killed one, *Quarenta-y-cinco*." He sped up his delivery.

Blanco pulled out a dirty handkerchief and wiped his reddened nose.

Hijole, Navarrete thought, *the cocaine makes this asshole look like a running faucet. His fucking eyes look like two lit coals. I'm on very shaky ground.*

Blowing his nose, Blanco honked loudly and then folded the handkerchief. "The *gringa* killed *Quarenta-y-cinco*. A goddamned woman! With a kid!" The killer named *Quarenta-y-cinco* had been Blanco's top man, nicknamed for the man's fancy .45 pistol. "I sent him to take care of business, and he fucked it up."

Navarrete leaned closer. "He killed the DEA agent for you. Didn't you entrust him with that?"

Blanco sensed immense anger coming from his second in command. It flowed toward him like a tsunami. He released Navarrete's clothing, patted it, and eased back into the chair. "He did," he acknowledged. "But he let Vasquez get away. Unforgivable." Another cough, then Blanco snorted loudly, and spat on the bar's floor.

"Vasquez is dead. The DEA man killed him." Navarrete's right hand, partially hidden under the table, touched the 9 mm automatic in his waistband.

"You aren't reaching for a gun, are you, *carnal?*"

Easy. Easy. Navarrete barked a laugh. "Never. *Tu eres el jefe.* You are the boss. But please, *Quarenta-y-cinco* was my brother, he was a good man..."

"And you wouldn't be my segundo if he hadn't got himself killed by that *gringa*, that Kendricks woman!" Again, Blanco wore that Cantinflas smile, as if it were glued forever on his face. "Well, it is certain that your brother was trusted, and..." He waved his arm in Navarrete's direction, as if in a peace offering. "I miss his counsel, and his ruthlessness. I even miss seeing his fancy-looking Colt .45," Blanco said, remembering how the killer got his nickname. "So, forgive me if I appeared disrespectful to his memory." Blanco lit and drew heavily on a cigarillo and continued. "We never learned what happened to his compadre, Jose Escarate. Well, a body in the river with a bullet to his head. Knife wounds, some. But no, we don't know who dared to do that."

"But we do, *jefe*, or at least who one was."

Blanco grunted an acknowledgement, then yelled at a waiter wearing a dirty white apron. "*Traiganos cervezas. Pacíficos! Apurate!*"

The waiter scurried behind a kitchen door, and returned with limes, salt, and four cold bottles of the light pilsner.

Blanco shooed him away and turned his attention back to his segundo. "You were saying?"

"Three weeks ago, a *gringo* passed along a message from Santa Rosa. The one we have on the payroll. He was at the courthouse at Santa Rosa. He has good ears and overheard something a *gringo* said. He let us know he had information that could lead us to the *cabrones* that killed our man. I sent Paco Carrizales, just to check. You understand?"

Blanco did not understand. Nothing happened without his consent. His face became taut, so much so that his eyes were hidden by the squint. "Why wasn't I told?"

"Jefe, everyone, but especially you, have been involved in taking back the plaza here in Acuña. This was supposed to be a small thing. A minor inconvenience." Beads of sweat broke on Navarrete's forehead. *Christ, I've got to keep his confidence.* "Carrizales found out who was involved."

"Who?"

"A janitor at that very courthouse in Santa Rosa."

Navarrete had Blanco's full attention now. Blanco took a swig of beer, burped, and then gently set the bottle back on the table. "What is his name?"

"Israel Sifuentes. Paco confirmed he'd been somehow involved, but that Sifuentes was a tough character. Carrizales tried to 'convince' this janitor to give him names. He never did. And now..."

"And now what?"

"Paco left Sifuentes' head on a post." He shook his head. "Paco did not return from *los estados unidos*."

"What happened to him?"

"I haven't heard from Paco in days. Nothing from the *policia*, nothing in the American press, no rumors on the streets," Navarrete said. *And Paco is either dead or locked up. Hopefully, dead. And now is not the time to mention the two men I sent with him.*

Blanco looked at his lieutenant. "Are you *not* telling me something? Why would some lowly janitor be involved in killing one of my *soldados*? It makes no sense that a *pulga* — a flea — would take it upon himself to kill a *Zeta*. There must be more to this."

"As far as we know, Sifuentes was just that — a janitor. Living in a small house. He drove an old truck. There were no signs of wealth. But Sifuentes may have had family in Mexico. Or friends."

"The last thing we need is for the *gringo* cops to pay too much attention to Kickapoo County," interjected Blanco.

"I made a mistake, *jefe*. It's just —." Navarrete looked down at the ground, hoping the anguish in his voice would be accepted as real. "—my brother's death and that of Jose, they needed to be paid for." Navarrete looked directly at the sun, hoping the pain would cause at least one tear to fall.

Blanco waved a hand dismissively. "Don't do anything like that again without clearing it directly with me, you understand?"

Navarrete stood stoically. *I will show you, Cantinflas, you smiling bastard, that your plans are shit. Then los Zetas will give me the privilege of killing you.*

Chapter 14

Baseball, a family outing, and nightmares

Hector Garcia, Dr. Villarreal's "good man," wheeled in a gurney containing the contents of Drawer G351. Instead of a body under a sheet or in a body bag, I saw a black garbage bag I'd last seen in Abner Selman's vehicle before he left Santa Rosa.

I glanced at Harris Whittaker to see his reaction. He lifted an eyebrow. Villarreal thanked Garcia, who disappeared.

"Mr. Whittaker, if you would be so kind as to assist?"

Whittaker nodded, and the two robed and gloved up. Villarreal activated exhaust fans and additional lighting and turned on a voice-activated microphone on a long flexible cable extending down over the table. Whittaker removed the lab's digital camera from a drawer, and checked its battery level, then took a surgical gown and a paper mask from a closet and tossed them to me. He and Villarreal rubbed some Vicks VapoRub under their noses, then donned plastic safety shields.

"You sure you want to be in here for this, Purdy?" the doctor asked when he tossed the odor masking gel bottle in my direction.

Good question. I felt like the assistant medical examiner had called my bluff in a poker game.

"No, doc, I don't want to be in here, but I'm not leaving."

"I'm sure this isn't your first rodeo, so you're welcome to stand closer. Take a seat if you get woozy, I don't want you fainting on me."

Why am I here, for God's sake? I ran through the reasons to convince myself I wanted to know if Israel had been put out of his misery with a bullet to the head before his body had suffered the horrific indignities Abner and I had seen.

When they opened the plastic garbage bag, both Villarreal and Whittaker winced, but said nothing. The gorge rose in my throat and I fought to keep it down.

For the next hour, the click of the camera, the whir of a bone saw, the snip of toothed forceps and scissors, and the clinical observations of Villarreal proved the autopsy was performed by an experienced professional. Occasionally, Villarreal would speak into the mic or point something out to Whittaker and me. The doctor's commentary was terse.

In an emotionless tone, the assistant ME called out the time. And it was over.

Israel's brain and tissue samples were placed in containers for later toxicology analysis, and the dead man's genitals went into a sealed plastic bowl.

I'd attended autopsies before, mostly in Houston when I worked with the Houston Police Department, and others from deaths in Kickapoo County, performed by the Bexar County ME on a contract basis. I'd become inured to them, able to separate the science from the sadness. But Israel's body, or what there was of it, and the abuse he'd suffered rapidly tore through this mental protection. The thought of a dead man's gonads plopped into a plastic container at an ME's office seemed like the ultimate desecration.

"Let's go back to my office," Doctor Villarreal said. "I'll give you the shorthand of what's going to be on the report, barring surprises from toxicology."

After we removed our gowns and masks, we strolled down the hallway. The other two chatted as if just returning from a grocery store outing. I couldn't overhear. I didn't care.

"Take a seat." Villarreal gestured when we arrived. I plopped down.

"Not pleasant, Doc. Not pleasant." It was trite but the best I could come up with.

Villarreal glanced at his new wife's photograph, as if to remind himself there was a world of the living outside his building. "Okay, Purdy, your John Doe died badly. But for what it's worth, I can tell you that—" He pulled up his dictation, already roughly transcribed on a computer program. "—the severance of his head occurred after he was killed with a single bullet to the brain."

He pointed to the back of his own head to show the entry wound location. "We've recovered what's probably an unjacketed 9mm slug, found in the nasal cavity. John Doe was likely dead before things were stuffed.... Well before everything else happened. My educated guess is that he didn't experience the defilement. The removal of the head was done postmortem."

I stood, shook hands with him and Whittaker, muttered thanks, and left. Anticipated relief had not come. Israel Sifuentes, a good man, a brave man, had been slaughtered. Whether he'd suffered obscene indignities before or after his death now seemed unimportant.

I unlocked the car door and crawled inside. The smell of formalin clung to my clothing, so I turned the air conditioner full blast, and pointed the sedan toward Austin and home. Forrest was expecting his mother and father to be at his T-ball game.

I called Abner. "Just got back from the ME in San Antonio," I said.

He seemed taken aback. "What? They've already started cutting on the three bodies 'found' on the Bar LJ?"

I'd forgotten all about the *sicarios* we'd left strewn near the earthen tank and entrance to Lowell Johnson's Bar LJ Ranch. "No, went to meet Harris Whittaker, who, by the way, I'm impressed with. While I was there, Assistant ME Villarreal decided he'd work on Israel Sifuentes."

Abner sounded confused. "What did you expect to gain from attending that autopsy?"

"Hell, Ranger, I don't know. I mentioned something to Tim Villarreal, and after meeting Whittaker, I found myself watching Israel's head coming apart in an autopsy."

"Aw, Jesus, Purdy. What were you trying to do? Beat yourself up some more?"

I had no good answer, but the ranger was getting close to the mark. "Just wanted to see if they could tell if he'd, you know…"

"Purdy, you're a hell of a law enforcement officer, but you are going to eat yourself alive if you don't put down this guilt you're carrying."

"Thanks. I guess you're right." I disconnected and thought about Abner's advice before calling Betty while driving up IH 35. When she answered, I said, "Heading home, Honey."

"We'll be at the ballpark. Forrest's got his Little League game in an hour, and I've volunteered for the concession stand. Uggghh. I'll be covered in goopy snow cone and pickle juice."

I swung by the house, changed clothes, and made it to our son's game. I crawled into the bleachers, surprising Betty from behind. I needed to see and feel the smiles and warmth of my family.

"Didn't see you at the concession stand."

"Finished early. Another mom volunteered to finish my shift. Said she didn't want to sit next to her husband at their son's game. He pisses off the umps."

I asked. "Is Forrest starting tonight?"

She shook her head. "Don't know, but he sure wants to."

"He has to practice more if he wants that to happen. I'll spend some time with him this weekend. We'll work on a few things."

Betty put her arm around me. "You're a good dad, Purdy Kendricks. That boy of ours thinks you walk on water."

"Hard to live up to that."

The Wildcats lost, 11-2. Forrest struck out, walked, and played three innings at first base. A mixed bag, but he seemed unfazed as he left the team meeting. "Can we go to Dairy Queen?"

We did.

"Booth or table, Forrest?" I asked as I pretended to cut in front of him at the counter.

"Booth! And I get the inside."

Our son licked on an ice cream cone that dripped on the table while he carried on about what the boys on his team talked about in the dugout. I didn't detect much sadness over the score. Betty and I caught each other smiling. For a few moments, all seemed right with the world.

When I walked through our front door, the difference between good and bad, tragedy and happiness, and how I'd gone from one extreme to the other hit me like a hammer blow. After I read a few more pages of Horatio Hornblower's adventures, I kissed Forrest goodnight and crawled into my bed, falling asleep almost immediately.

Suddenly, I woke to someone shaking me hard.

"Purdy! Hey, babe. Wake up!"

I slowly crawled into consciousness. Realizing I was in our home in Austin, I jumped up in alarm. "What? Is someone in the house?" Instinctively, I reached for the nightstand and my 9 mm automatic, forgetting it was locked in a gun safe in the closet.

"Purdy, you were talking in your sleep. Quite loudly. No one's here, but you'll wake Forrest."

I was soaked in sweat. "What was I saying?" I sounded mush mouthed.

Betty flipped on a lamp. "Something about a head, then some other gibberish. What's going on?"

The nightmare's tentacles reached out. "Oh, yeah. Just a weird dream, about a sea monster, I think." I laid back down. "Sorry, Hon."

"First time I've seen you have one on those since we moved from Santa Rosa. Something tells me you were back in your old stomping grounds, reliving something unpleasant." She clicked off her light, rolled over on her side away from me. "It's three in the morning. Get some sleep, Babe. I wish you wouldn't bring home whatever you're involved with – again."

She was asleep before I could respond.

I woke before Betty. Quietly, I pulled eggs, biscuits and bacon from the refrigerator and started breakfast. A quick hug from Forrest at his school, and my workday began at the Drug Interdiction Support Department. Alicia Trejo nodded, then handed me a handful of message slips, and reminded me of several appointments and a meeting.

"Oh, Ranger Selman called. He said he and a Mr. Whittaker will take you to lunch today."

Normally, I looked forward to Abner's company. Today, it reminded me of too much unfinished business in Kickapoo County.

Chapter 15
Who's been talking?

Three bullet-riddled bodies on Lowell's ranch got everyone in the county's attention. With Abner's connivance, Harris Whittaker was being seconded, as needed, to assist Kickapoo County's efforts to figure out what happened to the heavily tattooed Mexican *sicarios*.

Abner and I agreed Whittaker would take a Bexar County ME vehicle to Santa Rosa and meet me at the Sheriff's Office. Just before noon, I parked in the shade of the courthouse's east side and walked across the street to my old employer's office. Nothing seemed to have changed, at least on the outside.

Pushing open the door, I was glad to see a friendly face. Jake swung his office chair around and gave me a huge grin. "Purdy, welcome back."

Bless him, Jake was long on forgiveness. "You too, my friend."

As we shook hands, Kickapoo County Sheriff TJ Johnson lumbered out of his office and up the corridor toward the dispatcher's area and front entryway. He gave a sour look to Jake. TJ didn't trust Jake but remained blissfully unaware of his best dispatcher's hatred toward him.

"Can we visit, Purdy?" the Sheriff asked.

"Sure, but I'm waiting on someone."

TJ didn't ask who, but insisted I walk with him back to his office. "Send 'em back when they come, will you, Jake?"

When TJ turned, Jake shot a finger at his back, then responded with, "Sure thing, Sheriff."

I gave Jake a "naughty" finger wag and hid a smile.

We walked past the cubbyhole that was once my office. Its door was closed. I'd heard it was nothing more than a storage room now. Past the squad room, we reached the Sheriff's personal office. Nothing had changed there either. Trophy mounts from his many whitetail and mule deer hunts extended from the walls like cancerous polyps.

"Sit down, Purdy, will you?"

Careful to avoid getting an eye gouged by a low-hanging antler on the wall, I maneuvered into a chair. For a moment, the Sheriff and I stared at each other in uncomfortable silence.

I broke the ice. "I understand EMS trussed up the three dead guys from the Bar LJ and took the bodies to the Bexar County ME's office."

TJ nodded. "I'd like to know what in hell they were doing at Lowell's place. Makes no sense at all. And who shot them all to pieces."

So far, nothing made sense, and I told TJ that, without revealing anything about Abner's and my involvement.

After chitchat about our families, TJ broached the ever-present problems of border security. "Gotten worse since you left, Purdy, if that's possible. So many wets sneaking across that the border patrol can't catch them all."

Illegal border crossers, long ago dubbed "wetbacks" or "wets," were a hot topic in the national news, but I somehow doubted that Kickapoo County, with its nearness to the desolate emptiness of northern Mexico, posed a serious migrant problem. "Sheriff, Mexicans have been crossing the border before it was a border. My dad's water well drilling crew was made up of at least half Mexicans. No one gave a rat's ass about nationalities if they could hire someone who'd do a day's work. I don't think that's changed around these parts, has it?"

TJ, momentarily rebuffed, leaned forward in his creaky office chair. "When you got three dead ones on somebody's ranch, it's a problem, dammit."

He had a point, but TJ had a penchant for pissing me off. "Agreed, Sheriff. I guess I'm still remembering a simpler time."

Mollified, TJ eased back, his chair creaking. "Speaking of simpler times, it's been a while since you've been back in the county, hasn't it?"

"Just to check on the Griffin place, and not often."

TJ grunted at the mention of my newly obtained acreage. He'd pissed in his pants during the gun battle two years ago. Lowell Johnson had witnessed it and TJ's less than brave participation. Lowell had stopped TJ's badmouthing me when I was being considered for the position I now held.

Jake's booming voice in the front announced a new arrival.

"Can I help you, sir?"

The reply confirmed Harris Whittaker's presence.

"Sheriff, that's who I've been waiting for," I said.

Seconds later, Jake escorted Whittaker into TJ's office. As I introduced the investigator, I watched TJ's facial expressions. It was obvious he was as surprised as I had been by the man's behemoth proportions.

"Mr. Whittaker's here to help, on loan from the Bexar County ME's Office," I said.

Harris Whittaker perused the trophies, then took a seat. "Nice collection, Sheriff. Shot any elk?"

TJ winced. Unknowingly, Harris had hit TJ's sore spot. The Sheriff had made only one elk hunt to Colorado, had a chance at shooting a huge bull elk, and missed. I was beginning to like Whittaker more and more.

Abner arrived thirty minutes later. The sheriff, a deputy, Abner, Whittaker, and I traveled to Lowell Johnson's Bar LJ Ranch. The weather had remained dry since Abner and I had surprised the would-be ambushers. Blackened, dried blood and gore were still present on the ground near the gate and the dam. Whittaker walked the area with the deputy and TJ and photographed areas where the bodies had lain. He made few comments and asked fewer questions. TJ led us to where the first two men had died from Abner and my gunfire. We watched Whittaker walk around the earthen tank dam. The truck had been removed, but a deep brown spot indicated where the third man had been struck down.

TJ said, "They found one of them face down next to his truck. I'll email you all the photos."

"Actually, he was on his back," I interrupted.

Abner bumped me and I shut up. I hadn't read the reports yet to know this. TJ missed my comment. Whittaker noticed Abner's movement, glanced into my eyes, then turned away. *This man doesn't miss much.*

After returning to Santa Rosa, Whittaker expressed his intention of looking over scene photos. Abner and I said our goodbyes.

I told Abner of my visit with Jake. "I wouldn't know where to start. Even thought of our illustrious District Attorney, Josh Hinton."

Abner shook his head. "We've checked out most elected officials along the border. He's clean. He's fat and sassy with his title company, and besides, how many times does he even take a case to trial in any of the three counties he's responsible for? He hardly ever comes to Kickapoo County, leaving its dockets to a couple of ADAs, while he plays golf." He paused and shook his head. "He's too lazy. Like you said, it could have been anyone in or near that room, or someone who heard from someone."

Reluctantly, I agreed with him.

Chapter 16

DEA's new information and Zeta doubts

The two mysterious aircraft, dubbed Tango 1 and Tango 2 by the Americans, lifted off at two a.m. Central time, and flew south, disappearing from radar somewhere in the Sierra Madres Orientales.

EPIC passed the information to the DEA in time for a weekly intel meeting, Jack Eddleman and Leroy Breaux walked into the DEA San Antonio office's conference room, now filling with other agents. Soon, everyone was poring over the drone sightings and radar reports.

"Weird," Eddleman muttered. "No doubt those are doper planes. Why land miles from Texas, stay on the ground for a few days, then head south?"

Drug running aircraft functioned to bring narcotics *into* the United States. Whoever was controlling these expensive conveyances had stayed away from the border.

Breaux walked to the front and pulled down an old-styled roll-up map of Mexico and Central America. It reminded Eddleman of high school geography class. The agents stared at the familiar shapes and names.

"Which cartel controls which plazas right now?" asked Breaux. A babble of voices listed Mexican cities and states and their cartel overlords. Acronyms of the many competing groups rattled around the room. While the group talked, Eddleman went to the whiteboard and began writing.

An agent tossed out a question. "Where are the cartels' demarcation lines? In other words, where are the cartels' areas in flux?"

"Well, duh," muttered another agent. "How about everywhere in the goddamned country? Those fuckers are killing each other from Tapachula to Tijuana."

"And from Tehachapi to Tonopah," shouted another, producing peals of laughter at the similarity to Little Feat's classic song, *Willin.'* A falsetto imitation of Linda Ronstadt's version echoed, with several badly tuned voices adding bits and pieces of the lyrics.

"*Heart Like a Wheel*, 1974. Greatest album ever made," opined one of the singing agents.

"Christ almighty." Eddleman couldn't help but smile. "That song was written before any of you fuckers were thought of. Lowell George wrote the lyrics when he was still with Mothers of Invention."

Where in hell did Jack come up with that piece of rock'n'roll trivia? Leroy Breaux wondered. Eddleman said, "Cut the shit for a minute, please. I've got an idea."

"Harumph, harumph, harumph," one more agent called out.

More laughter.

Finally, everyone settled down, and Breaux pointed to Eddleman's list on the whiteboard. "Latest flashpoint – Ciudad Acuña. *Los Zetas,* pushing out *La Familia Norteña,* which didn't get as much help as it needed from Jalisco New Generation, or CJNC, A few days ago, they littered that wonderful town with burned or otherwise dispatched bodies of around twenty or so God-fearing men."

Several agents snickered at his sarcasm.

"*Los Zetas* and LFN had the same issues in Nuevo Laredo a couple of years back. Then, LFN's head honcho gets his head shot off at a place near...ta-da-...El Mosco!" Breaux tapped an unmarked spot in Mexico's northern desert. "Anyone see any similarities here? Because I think I'm having a brain fart or something, but these aircraft going the wrong way has me wondering."

"What if—" muttered an agent in the back of the room. "What if the airplanes are bringing dope to that marshaling point to transport it overland, because closer than El Mosco is too risky?"

"It's a stretch," suggested Eddleman. "But maybe not. Maybe *los Zetas* aren't sure of what territory they hold, and what they don't."

Another DEA agent chimed in. "So why don't the Zetas just route their drugs through any one of a number of places where they *do* control the plaza?"

The question had no satisfactory answer. "Kickapoo and these other counties..." Eddleman pointed to the barren expanse west of Del Rio, Texas. "...don't have legal crossing points. Don't have highways running north-south for quick movement out of the area. All have low population densities. Why would anyone in the drug business take a chance taking their business there?"

"Unless..." responded Breaux.

"Yeah," said another agent. "Unless they think they've figured out a way to increase their chances of success."

The meeting broke up. Eddleman stared at his whiteboard scribblings as Breaux released the catch on the map and it began its upward roll.

"All this is interesting, Leroy, but who's in charge of ferreting out details about this idea of yours?"

"Let's talk."

Breaux sat on the edge of his desk, his height advantage irritating Eddleman.

He thought, *Dammit, it's like he's trying to show me he's in charge now, the son of a bitch.*

Breaux ignored the scowl. "When *los Zetas* took out *La Familia Norteña's* Venustiano Huerta, it was at an old, fortified hacienda about sixty miles west of El Mosco."

"Yeah," said Eddleman. "He flew into that airstrip at El Mosco and then convoyed to the place. Which is where *los Zetas'* sniper took him out." He paused, then added, "I know where you're going with this. That hired sniper was later killed in Kickapoo County on the Griffin Ranch by subjects unknown.

This is old history, Breaux." Eddleman was using Leroy's last name now, his anger and frustration becoming more evident.

"Jack, you wanted back on the border. You wanted to be where the action is. I think this may be worth looking into."

Eddleman eased back in his chair and conceded, "I do. Suggestions?"

"Special Agent in Charge Fleming is interested, too, Jack." Breaux handed Eddleman an interoffice memo. "Along with my other duties, she expects I won't let whatever is going on in one of the most remote areas in Northern Mexico bite the Agency in the ass."

Eddleman bridled as he read the short memo. "Breaux, I used to be the one who got these memos. Now, I've gotta get this info from you?"

"Christ, Jack. I didn't go looking for this but think about it. Did you really think Fleming would give you the assignment after what you faced years ago? It's not in the memo, but she's given me the okay to use you in Kickapoo County, which is a big win. She's saying she trusts us not to fuck up; that despite the bullshit stirred up about you, we're free to work with local law enforcement."

Breaux leaned forward. "For God's sake, you're not just riding a desk here in San Antonio. You're back in the game all the way. Hell, let's go kick some ass and take some names!"

Despite his anger, Eddleman laughed. "Okay, Leroy. I'll be a team player. I just hope whatever is going on in El Mosco turns into something interesting." *I've got better satellite photos than anything Google Earth can provide. I've memorized every bump and bush on the seven thousand acres of the Griffin ranch. I've already made one trip and spotted some of Pete Vasquez' likely hidey-holes. If Kickapoo County is the focus of the cartel's smuggling plan, I'll have many more opportunities to find out where that dead bastard hid over seventeen million dollars.*

*****

Guillermo Blanco was riding high. Ciudad Acuña was back solidly under the control of *los Zetas*. The American side of the border swarmed with all sorts of law enforcement, and the town's traffic on its sole bridge backed up for miles as the *pinche norteamericanos* reacted to the slaughter by inspecting every vehicle crossing into Texas. That would change. It always did. In the meantime, Blanco's actions were not entirely his own. He dispatched the two aircraft from El Mosco south into the interior of Mexico where the cartel's labs cooked another load. All this took time. The Chinese were taking their sweet time providing precursors. Their slow-walking of clandestine shipments of *benzyl-fentanyl* and *4-anilinopiperidine* jacked the drugs' prices up, and the labs in China knew they had a captive market.

After listening to a satellite phone call from an associate explaining the supply chain issues, Blanco muttered, "problems, problems, problems." He sat in the large dining room of a Spanish tiled house tucked into the tree-less mountains south of Nuevo Laredo. "Those fucking *chinos*. I know they want to bring down the *norteamericanos*, but they're dragging their feet. Send the drugs faster and they'll all kill themselves."

It would be at least two weeks before the next fentanyl-laced heroin would be ready to move northward.

In the meantime, he was having to justify keeping thirty to forty armed men fed and supplied in El Mosco, a place he considered the asshole of the world.

Blanco turned to Navarrete. "Delays, delays. But once the next loads are flown in there, we control the territory north to the border and can start staging product to cross in places the gringos aren't watching."

Navarrete grimaced, pretending he was concerned. "*Jefe*, you sure this is a good idea? We move a big shipment of product, and if it gets taken down, it'll be hard to explain."

Blanco puffed on a small cigar, then spit a small bit of tobacco leaf onto the terrazzo floor. "This business is one of risk taking. Right now, we've got the LFN and their motherfucking allies away from our plazas. Any sign of weakness and they, or shall I say, the Jalisco New Generation, will be on us like jackals." He threw the cigar's remains out an unscreened window and looked at his lieutenant. "How long have you been with *loss Zetas*?"

Navarrete thought for a second. "I was fifteen, I think, when I was recruited in Tampico. Twenty years?"

"And you are still asking why I try new things? New ways to move product? We are like sharks. If we don't move forward, we die."

Navarrete nodded. *Yes, but if we do stupid things, we die sooner.*

Blanco looked at his frowning lieutenant and slapped him on the shoulder. "Relax, *carnal*. I know more about the *gringos* and who can be controlled than do you. My plan will work. You'll see."

Navarrete smiled. "We have a friend on the other side of the Rio Bravo, *sí?*"

"We always have friends on the other side. It's just a matter of where they are placed and how much they can help us."

"¿Pues quien son estos amigos, jefe?"

Blanco laughed. "If I tell you who our amigos are, I'll have to kill you."

Navarrete dared not ask again. Though not showing it in his face, anger filled his thoughts. *I'll find out who it is. I'm going to fuck your plan up, Cantinflas, one way or the other. I will control los Zetas. Your plans are too risky. I will prevent our territory from being taken over by the men from Jalisco. You are too old school. I, El Tramposo, the Trickster, will see you dead.*

Chapter 17

Two unhappy women and a night in Paradise

Abner and I shook hands and parted company after returning to Santa Rosa.

Now it was time to deal with Beulah Jackson at the Cenizo Diner. The few cars and trucks in its gravel parking lot told me I'd arrived during the afternoon lull before the early supper crowd hit. The eatery's front doorbell jingled when I stepped inside, while my eyes adjusted to its fluorescent lighting. I made a beeline toward a booth away from the diner's one large round table periodically occupied by the Brain Trust, as the morning and afternoon coffee break group was dubbed. I knew everyone in the Brain Trust and was friends with most of them. No doubt by now, news of my presence in Santa Rosa had filtered into the group, and I wasn't interested in any prying questions.

A waitress took my order for coffee. Before it arrived, Beulah took her seat on the opposite bench. "Where's Lilly? I miss her. She's my best waitress." I expected her directness, but Beulah's face showed more concern than anger.

"I don't know."

My coffee came, and the two of us paused our discussions while I added cream and sugar.

Beulah stared at my cup as I swirled the spoon around. "Quit stirring, dammit. The coffee'll get cold before you drink it."

I took a sip and put the cup down. "Beulah, I truly don't know and don't want to know right now. She's away from Santa Rosa, with her mother, and I feel like she's safe."

"Not if she's having to deal with that cranky mother of hers," she retorted.

I almost spit out a mouthful of hot coffee.

Her lips curled into a tiny smile.

Whew. I'd been on the receiving end of Beulah's anger before and was relieved that for now she'd signaled a truce of sorts.

"I promised you'd pay her for the time she takes off," I said.

"Boy, you don't know when it's time to quit." Beulah shook her head, and suddenly lowered her voice. "Purdy, just make sure she doesn't get hurt. I trust you to do right by her."

I drained the cup and walked with her to the cafe's door. The Cenizo Diner's dingy curtains, cracked linoleum floor, and ancient Bunn coffeemaker were part of Beulah's empire. She ruled it like a czar. Anyone who tried to harm her waitresses would suffer a grim fate.

My face felt beet red. The compliment, such as it was, was rare coming from this tough woman. "I will," I said. "I'll keep you posted." She squeezed my arm so hard it hurt. Not sure whether it was meant as a sign of affection, or a signal that she'd beat the hell out of me if I screwed up, I unlocked my vehicle.

It was time to head to Austin. But first, a quick visit to my sister-in-law. Paula Richardson, owner of CutNCurl.

The Brain Trust's denizens thought of themselves as the neural center of Kickapoo County. Paula and her hairdressers knew better. CutNCurl's customers, exclusively women, had neural ganglia mysteriously reaching into all parts of the county.

I parked next to a dually ranch truck taking up the one handicap parking spot. There was no handicap tag dangling in the windshield. The small shop's air conditioning competed with the blast from a pedestal mounted hair bonnet dryer. I couldn't tell whose head it encapsulated, but guessed it was the dually driver. She didn't look like she needed any medical assistance while she studiously ignored me and pored over a ragged *People* magazine.

Paula stepped out of her office, a little heavier, with a pageboy cut. She was almost as beautiful as her sister. "Hey."

"Hey, yourself," I replied. Paula gave me a thin smile and motioned me back.

"Wondered when you'd grace us with your presence. The kids were hoping you'd bring Forrest with you. Haven't seen their cousin in a while."

She gave me a quick hug before I sat down. Damn, I was two for two– so far. First, Beulah, now Betty's fiercely protective older sister. I said a silent prayer asking God to keep me from messing things up. "Knew you'd hear about me, so I wanted to stop by."

"Three dead Mexicans shot to hell on Lowell's ranch. You must be here on that," she said.

"Yup."

"Well, I talked to your wife. She's been pretty circuitous when asked about your whereabouts. Then the big hoo-hah about dead men. I put things together and expected you'd be involved."

She gave me the once-over. "You being back in Kickapoo County investigating killers doesn't bode well for your health and safety, if history is any indication. Nor is it good for my sister's peace of mind."

"Not going to pretend different, Paula. But others are handling most of the heavy lifting," I assured her. Maybe I *wasn't* going to go two for two.

"Un huh." The doubt in her voice was palpable. "Relax, brother-in-law. I'd pay a million dollars if I had it to get you away from law enforcement. But I don't have it, never will, and can't. So, I'll live with it. Betty and you, despite your mule-headed behavior at times, are meant to be together."

I gave a half-hearted smile.

I hugged Paula, pulled my hat down over my eyes and tromped out of CutNCurl. Paula's customer stared at me as I walked by.

"Shit," I muttered as I drove off. Paula had a way of quickly getting under my skin.

I reached for the MP3 player, jammed earbuds in, and pushed play without looking at the track. I just needed some music. A slight hissing indicated an old recording. A short blues intro, then Dinah Shore's cover of "Blues in the Night" flooded my senses. I thought, *Sorry, Ella, you're the best, but Dinah owns this song.* I replayed the song three times before my cell phone flashed with an incoming call.

I recognized Bexar County ME's number calling. I killed the music and answered. "Kendricks."

"Tim Villarreal here. You got a second?"

"More than a second. I'm somewhere between Del Rio and Uvalde with miles to go."

"You headed to Austin? If so, swing by here. Got something to show you."

"Doc, it'll be damned near eight o'clock when I hit San Antonio. Can it wait?"

"It can, but I think you'll be interested in what I've got to show you. I'll be here. Ring the buzzer and they'll let you in."

San Antonio traffic pushed my arrival to eight thirty, but Villarreal seemed unfazed and waved off my apology. "Come on back. Got three things I want to show you." He headed toward the autopsy area.

Flicking on additional lighting when he entered the chilly room, Villarreal motioned toward three bodies under sheets. "Your Mexicans. All autopsied today. Printed, photos taken, and so on." He pulled each sheet off. I was expecting entrails on the tables or worse but was relieved to see the chest and brain cavities were crudely stitched up.

"Prints scanned digitally to the FBI. These two —" He pointed at two tables. "— ID'ed quickly as illegals with some re-entry issues and a few US crimes on their rap sheets." He drew himself up dramatically. "But this one is a doozy."

Villarreal motioned me closer to a corpse with a pock-marked face. "Name is Paco Carrizales. Known hitman for *los Zetas.* Did a twenty-year stretch at TDC for manslaughter."

He handed me a criminal report with several pages of printouts.

"He only did ten of twenty," I noted. "Pled down from a murder here in Bexar County. Looks like paroled to INS for deportation three years ago."

The doctor walked to a file drawer and removed a manila envelope. "We found some stuff in his pockets at the beginning of the autopsy. I guess no one bothered to check the body very well before they loaded him on a gurney." He handed me the envelope. "Open it."

I carefully poured the contents onto an empty desk. Pesos, paperclips, and, inside a transparent plastic evidence bag, a nine-millimeter shell casing.

"John Doe, your John Doe. He was shot with a nine."

I thought of the slug Abner and I had seen on Israel's floor. "Because the entry wound on the gentleman's skull looked about that size. Of course, we can't be sure without a slug."

I thought of the pictures we had taken in Israel's house.

The assistant ME kept talking as if he knew he wasn't going to get an answer out of me. "But I've got something else for you, as well."

He reached into his lab coat pocket. "This hasn't gone into the manila envelope yet, but it will, of course." He extended another small transparent plastic bag.

Israel Sifuentes' Texas driver's license. "Jesus, Doc. Where did you find this? The son of a bitch swallow it?"

"In Paco's bloody, jean jacket's inside pocket. The photo on that ID sure looks like your John Doe?" He finished the sentence as a question.

I thought back. Israel's wallet was sitting on his kitchen table when Abner and I searched his house. We'd left it after finding nearly a hundred dollars in small bills and surmised nothing had been taken. I'd made dozens of photographs and but now wondered if I recalled seeing Israel's Texas license in the wallet "What the hell?"

Tim Villarreal cocked his prematurely gray head. "You're the cop. I'm just a sawbones. But you may want to give ME Investigator Harris Whittaker a call. He's still in your fair county. Claims he's holed up at a motel that reeks of curry."

I burst into laughter. "I know exactly where he is. Thanks. Going to make that call when I leave here."

"Commander Kendricks, if I got your title right.... I can't just ignore the correlation between our severed head and what was found on bad guy Paco's body. And if I was wanting to confirm this dead human garbage killed John Doe, or Israel Sifuentes, I'd make a request to type and check DNA on Paco's jean jacket. I'd bet some of that blood'll match your John Doe's."

"You'd make a damned good cop, Tim," I said as he escorted me out of the building.

"No way, Jose. I guarantee you, Purdy, I make a lot more money than you do, and I'm not risking getting shot."

I shook his hand and thanked him again. Once on IH 35, I punched in Harris Whittaker's number.

"Jeez, sir," he started off.

I interrupted. "Curry smell bad? You don't like Indian food?"

"I love the stuff, but this motel is suffused with the smell. What's the story?"

This had been a crazy day, and I caught my shit-eating grin in my rear-view mirror. "Welcome to Santa Ana. You are staying in the only motel in town. Mesa Tourist Court, owned by Jagir Patel."

"You know this guy?"

"Of course. I only have one question?"

"What?"

"How many of his kinfolk did you see around the motel or next door at the Stop Inn?"

"Quite a few. Why?"

"Because I gave up trying to keep up with how many he brought over from South Asia to work for him. It's a big family. I just don't know how big."

After a hearty laugh, I told him of my visit to the ME, and with what I'd been presented.

"Doctor Villarreal called me," he said, "and I suggested to my boss that you'd appreciate being brought into the loop."

"I did. A question to you. Why did Paco Carrizales have a photo ID of Israel Sifuentes on him?"

"So, you're saying that your John Doe is Mr. Sifuentes?"

"Yes, but I'm not sure when we need to let that information out."

"Your call. Now, about that ID," he said. "I think he took that ID to show his employer that he'd taken care of business."

I agreed with him. I disconnected. I was suddenly mad as hell. There'd be no "justice" in the courts for Israel's killer. Not once in the next fifty miles did the court system enter my thinking. I wanted to exact revenge on anyone involved.

Chapter 18

Alicia Trejo and the DEA grab Purdy's attention

I sat in my office, reviewing paperwork, intent on devoting time and energy to anything that didn't involve Kickapoo County.

Alicia Trejo tapped on my door. "You busy?"

"For you? Never. Come on in."

Something in Alicia's voice told me she had something I needed to hear.

She closed my office door and sat. Leaning forward, she put her elbows on my desk and pushed her reading glasses into her salt-and-pepper hair. Crow's feet betrayed her age as being older than her otherwise smooth complexion showed.

"Commander, how are you doing?"

"I'm doing okay, Ms. Trejo. Why?" I squirmed in my seat, already beginning to feel like I was being addressed by a counselor or psychologist.

"Commander, what in the world is going on?"

It seemed as if this woman was peering into my psyche. "Just the usual stuff, I guess. Why?"

She took her elbows off my desk. I could feel my face turning red.

"Commander," she began, "before my husband was killed, he sometimes tried to keep things about his work away from me. And when he did, he was hell to live with."

Alicia's husband, a highway patrol trooper, had been murdered on a lonely stretch of South Texas highway. He'd stopped a car on a traffic violation and was shot in the head as he approached the driver's side window. The car was traced to a drug dealer who'd slipped into Mexico and was never caught. She had been hired as a secretary with the Texas Department of Public Safety, raised three children by herself, and was now a grandmother six times over.

"Am I hiding something? Is that what you want to know?" The question sounded stupid as hell, but I felt myself digging in my heels.

"Commander, my husband wouldn't tell me about horrible accidents he'd worked as a trooper. Or about the children who'd died when some drunk plowed into a car they were riding in. When I'd asked about his work, he clammed up, but in the process became jumpy as a green-broke horse." She paused. "That's what's going on with you right now."

I apologized, hoping to end the conversation. It didn't.

"You've been back and forth to Kickapoo County at least twice, and you're huddled up with Ranger Selman, as if the two of you are planning a bank robbery. You're a good boss — one of the best men I've worked for — and you've got a good soul, with a good wife and precious child." She picked up the small, framed photograph of Betty and Forrest. "But if you're not careful, you're going to let whatever is going on in that place eat you alive. It'll play hell with you."

Flabbergasted at her confrontation, I said, "I didn't know I was acting badly."

"You're not 'acting badly.' You just seem to be in over your head." She pointed at a small disc embedded in plastic sitting on my desk. "That's a 24-hour chip, isn't it?"

I picked up the clear paperweight embedded with an Alcoholics Anonymous coin, awarded to someone who'd survived his or her first day without a drink.

"Yes," I replied.

I remembered that day. Like a kindergartner fashioning an ashtray for his parents, I'd made the crude block months after drying out.

She leaned forward. "I've been around drunks and recovering drunks for as long as I've worked with law enforcement. There was a time after I was widowed that I went down that road myself."

I had not known that, and I told her so.

"It wasn't pretty, and I thank God that I got through it somewhat intact." She stood and walked to the door. "I don't know when the last time you made a meeting. I figure you need some support you can't get from your wife, or from Forrest, or from the ranger. If you don't go, you might slip, and that first drink..."

She left the sentence dangling and closed the door behind her.

It was nearly noon. I skipped lunch and drove to a nearby church. The smell of stale coffee hit me the moment I stepped down the stairs into a basement room. It reminded me that I hadn't made a meeting in months.

"I'm Purdy, and I'm an alcoholic," I muttered to the three women and seven men sitting around a table. I put a dollar in the donation basket, listened to their stories of recovery, and endured the hour quietly. I didn't feel any better afterward. I returned to the office, nodding at Alicia Trejo as I passed her desk. She didn't comment, but I could swear I detected a slight smile developing, quickly suppressed.

I left early for home. I wanted to see Betty and Forrest and hoped their presence would shake me out of my dark mood.

Betty wasn't home from work, so I called to tell her I'd pick up Forrest from school. It went to voicemail. I phoned our realtor friend, hoping that, by some miracle, she'd found a house we could afford in Austin's hot market. It went to voicemail. I sat in the gloom of the curtained living room, with two hours to brood before the school pick up time.

Joining the line of cars outside Forrest's elementary school, I put in my earbuds and listened to a stream of 1940's big band tunes while waiting. A bell clanged, and children poured out of the nearby door. The kids were accompanied by teachers who handed them off to their parents. I spotted Forrest waving around a piece of paper and talking excitedly to another boy. He spotted me, and, after a go-ahead nod from a teacher, he raced to my car.

"Hey, Daddy. I didn't know you were picking me up today."

I pushed open the passenger front door, he slid inside, and buckled himself in.

"What were you talking about with your buddy?" I asked.

He handed me the piece of paper. "We had to draw a picture of something we'd like to do when we grow up," he said excitedly. "Look."

A little boy's penciled attempt at drawing a police car filled the paper. A stick figure with a cowboy hat appeared on the driver's side. "I want to be just like you, Dad."

Oh boy. "Thanks, son," I managed. "Your daddy's job can be dangerous sometimes. What about being a doctor or an astronaut?"

"Nah." Forrest grabbed the drawing. "I want to show Mom, so don't crumple it."

At home, we tossed a baseball back and forth for the next thirty minutes. The rhythmic back and forth, and Forrest's constant chatter pushed away my thoughts of Israel Sifuentes. The world consisted of only a father and his son, in the timeless ritual of a game of catch.

Our realtor hadn't called back— a bad sign, so Betty, Forrest, and I ate supper at a pizza parlor. After putting Forrest to bed, I told my wife that I went to an AA meeting.

"It's been a while, hasn't it?

"Too long," I replied.

"What prompted that?"

I told her of Alicia Trejo's warning.

Betty smiled. "I'm liking this lady more and more." She hugged me. "Let's go to bed."

We did, but sleep was the farthest thing from her mind.

*****

"You've got a call from the DEA."

It was eight-thirty the following day, and I had just walked into my office.

"Thanks, Ms. Trejo." I picked up the handset. "Purdy Kendricks here."

"David Sanchez here. I'm a supervisory agent at DEA headquarters in Virginia. This is a courtesy call to you, sir."

"Okay. Why do I need a courtesy call?"

"You are familiar with Jack Eddleman, I presume."

I could only nod, afraid that anything that came out of my mouth would be unpleasant, and probably an expletive.

"I take it from your silence that you do know him, Commander, so I'll continue. Eddleman's now in our San Antonio office."

"Why?"

"Personnel decision, sir. We need experienced agents on the Mexican border."

"Jesus Christ, Sanchez, that bastard killed one of his own snitches."

Sanchez seemed unfazed by my outburst. "We know the two of you have a history."

"What in hell does that have to do with anything?" I wanted to scream. "You are shitting me. The only reason Eddleman didn't get indicted..."

Sanchez interrupted. "Was because there was no evidence."

I was being informed that Jack Eddleman was back in the area. And being given the choice of graciously accepting his presence or not. Sanchez' demeanor made it clear that all he was doing was checking the boxes. I was powerless to object.

I choked out, "I appreciate the phone call, Agent Sanchez."

"Commander," Sanchez replied, "your office must know we've got some interesting activity in Northern Mexico, indicating cartels are moving drugs in and through some of Texas' remotest, least populated counties. That includes Kickapoo, your old home place. The DEA can't afford to not pay attention to what's going on." He paused. "And I'm sure you don't want us to, either."

Patronizing shit. "Of course not."

Sanchez' tone changed. "Commander, I don't know you, but by all accounts, you are a stand-up guy. Our agency is shorthanded, and like most, we've got more than we can say grace over. Our special agent in charge ordered that you'd be personally notified if Eddleman was transferred back to this area."

I thanked Sanchez again. He said his call was a courtesy call. I sensed it was also a warning.

Chapter 19
Los Zetas begin their move

The two planes recently dubbed Tango 1 and Tango 2 by the American DEA were rugged high-wing Cessna 180 taildraggers. Their transponders were inoperative, anti-collision lights, extinguished. The single-engine aircraft flew low and slow. Their pilots used the rugged terrain to shield their northward movement from tracking by United States agencies, trusting in GPS and radar until they picked up low power non-directional beacons sending a single Morse coded letter.

The airplane neared the tiny hamlet of El Mosco at three a.m. Two trucks, parked at either end of the narrow dirt runway, turned on their headlights when a man with a hand-held Garmin radio confirmed the aircraft's arrival. The two planes, purchased in the United States and quietly slipped into Mexico, were retrofitted with larger engines and top-of-the-line instrumentation packages. Relatively cheap, the venerable aircraft no longer had passenger seats, that area now refitted for storage.

Tango 1 overflew the strip once, banked, turned on its wing mounted landing lights, gently bounced once, took two-thirds of the strip to come to a stop, then back-taxied. The pilot cut the engine, and men from the trucks quickly offloaded its cargo. A stepladder appeared, and the plane's wing tanks were refueled from twenty-five-liter metal containers.

As Tango 2's pilot announced his approach, Tango 1, now lightened, took off, banked sharply, and disappeared toward the south. Tango 2 repeated the process.

The entire operation took twenty-nine minutes.

The two trucks, lights out, followed a Humvee to a crumbling hacienda once controlled by *la Familia Norteña*. The first driver beeped his horn, and two large doors swung open into the walled compound's courtyard. Arturo Navarrete jumped out of the Humvee and whistled.

"Apurate, muchachos. Get the merchandise unloaded and the trucks under cover." He figured the *gringos'* reconnaissance satellite, three hundred kilometers above the Earth, would soon sweep the area. "Those *pinche* cameras can count the fleas on your head."

When secured, Navarrete placed a call on an encrypted cell phone.

"Sí?" An unrecognizable voice, probably that of Blanco, he thought.

"Secured."

"Bien. Be safe." The line went dead.

The American satellite swept the area seconds later. Apart from tire tracks, there was nothing for its surveillance cameras to see.

*****

Breaux met with Eddleman and several other DEA agents for an intelligence update on the El Mosco landing strip.

"Any action since the two aircraft headed south?" asked one.

As others scanned the latest satellite images, Breaux responded. "Well, yes, and no." He invited the agents to sit. "The area's Tethered Aerostat Radar System balloon was down for a day for maintenance. It's back up now, but lightning storms played hell with some of its electronics. Wasn't monitoring for about twelve hours." He paused, then added, "Look at the reconnaissance pics, however."

The time-stamped printouts showed a six-hour difference in the photography. Eddleman compared the two. "Tire tracks."

"Yep," Breaux confirmed. "In six hours, something came into the El Mosco strip area."

Another agent chimed in. "At least two vehicles. Maybe three."

Eddleman walked to the front of the room and began posting photos of the bleak terrain around the tiny Mexican hamlet. Printouts were compared, then set in a mosaic of photos taken during two different passes.

"Hard to get a good comparison because of the darkness on the last pass," an agent commented, "but take a look at one end of that runway."

Breaux nodded. "Could be."

"Could be what?" Eddleman asked. "Oh, ho. Smaller tires, maybe a tail wheel. An airplane came off the landing strip?" He pointed to the faint arc of three impressions in the sand and gravel adjacent to the strip's more tightly packed surface.

Others joined in. "And maybe pushed back on the landing strip for a quick takeoff?"

Soon, all agreed that at least one aircraft had landed, been offloaded, and returned to the runway.

"I'm new to this area of the world," an agent said. "That piece of northern Mexico looks like all it's doing is holding the world's surface together. Are there any structures anywhere near that strip, besides that tiny bunch of adobes?"

Eddleman grinned. "Not nearby, but..." He turned to Breaux. "How do we get a look about forty miles west of there?"

Breaux opened the conference room door and yelled a name. Soon, the office's IT specialist, a woman with short-cropped, jet-black hair, came in and pulled up reconnaissance photographs of a walled enclosure on the desk-top computer's monitor and projected it onto the white screen in the front of the room.

"Ta da," Eddleman said, adding, "you are looking at one of *la Familia Norteña's* strongholds. Or it was, until *los Zetas* hired a sniper, ex-U.S. military, to put a bullet through Venustiano Huerta's head a couple of years back. Then disabled a helicopter by shooting out the tail rotor." He pointed to the aircraft's scattered wreckage strewn about inside the compound. "It's now under the controls of *los Zetas*, on the western edge of some territory it's contesting with the scum from Jalisco."

Eddleman checked the time stamp on the photograph that captured the hacienda and asked the IT specialist, "This the latest from that area?"

"Yes," the woman answered. She checked the monitor's readout. "Six days ago."

The IT specialist left, closing the conference door behind her.

Breaux asked, "Is it possible that someone is again using that old structure as a staging point for smuggling?"

Eddleman said, "Yep. It's in the middle of nowhere, but if information from Agent Fleming is correct, *los Zetas* may be running dope across the border from some really remote places."

An agent held a yardstick against the wall map. "Due north forty or fifty miles is Kickapoo County, Jack."

With approval from the Houston district office, Breaux contacted EPIC, which in turn sent a request to Vandenburg Air Force Base in California. The reconnaissance satellite's military users agreed to adjust the satellite's next pass over northern Mexico so its cameras would sweep an old hacienda.

At five p.m., Eddleman and Breaux left the office and walked to Angela's. Loud *conjunto tejano* music blasted them as they stepped into the gloom. The usual crowd of cops, defense lawyers, and court personnel were beginning to show, so they quickly found a booth in the back.

Two beers later, the refurbished, antique jukebox changed to a country western waltz, and the decibel level dropped.

"You thinking what I'm thinking?" Breaux asked.

"What are you thinking?" responded Eddleman.

"Don't play cute with me," laughed Breaux. "I saw you salivating during that presentation."

Eddleman grunted. "Yeah, you're right. I can't wait to see what a satellite shows of that hacienda. Maybe Huerta's brains and blood will show up on the images."

"Cold." Breaux waved for two more beers. "Those birds aren't *that* good. That sniper, what was his name? Shivelli?" He didn't wait for an answer. "Hell of a shot over that outside wall and through the glass to nail that bastard inside the house."

Eddleman interrupted. "I've always wanted to see the inside of that place. Just to see how much money was spent on making it habitable." He took a swig. "That isn't gonna happen, but..."

Breaux checked the time on his cellphone. "That satellite is scheduled to swing through that area in about four and a half hours. Let's hope we get some good shots of the place."

An off-duty cop punched selections into the juke box. A Ray Price two-step started, and Breaux leaned closer to Eddleman. "If *los Zetas* are coming through Kickapoo County, I don't see any way not to include local law enforcement, Jack. Suggestions?"

Eddleman shook his head. "None." *Purdy Kendricks isn't there now, thank God.*

Breaux said, "I bet I know you think Kendricks is out of the way is a good thing. But I'm wondering who else familiar with the county we can trust to be a straight shooter." He leaned back in the booth.

Eddleman drained his beer glass. "That little shit damn near got me fired and indicted," he muttered. "I'm not dealing with that bastard. I wouldn't piss on him if he was on fire."

Breaux waved off the waitress. "Jack, he's working for the State of Texas. 'Drug Interdiction Support Agency.' You know that. We are *all* going to have to deal with him again. He's been back to Kickapoo County at least twice that we know of. There've been three cartel killings down there and rumors of more. He and that ranger are already involved in some way."

"What are you suggesting?"

"Word is that as a 'courtesy' to Kendricks, our people at Headquarters in Virginia reached out to let him know you're back working the San Antonio office."

Eddleman couldn't conceal his surprise. "I knew that drunken bastard when he worked in Harris County," he blurted. "Saved his ass from an indictment."

Breaux picked up a beer coaster and idly moved it around in the table's wet spots. "He hasn't had a drink in years."

Eddleman ignored Breaux's comment. "Kendricks is weak. He'll eventually fold under pressure." He launched into a re-telling of leading a joint task force which included DEA and Houston PD officers, which had set to take down a big-time drug dealer. The dealer was gone, so most of the police officers and agents decided to hit a strip joint for a few drinks or more. A call came in. The dealer was returning to his neighborhood in a bad part of Houston. The stakeout crew, bailed out of the club and set up at the drug dealer's house. The suspect almost ran Kendricks down in an alleyway. Kendricks said he'd come under fire, then returned fire and killed the drug dealer. Eddleman, first on the scene, aware Kendricks was drunk as a skunk, used a 'throw down' gun to cover when, as Eddleman told Kendricks, no firearm was found near the dead dealer's body. Self-defense had been Kendricks' unwavering claim, but the plan had been to arrest and flip the bastard, then work up to even higher-level suppliers.

Kendricks had quit to avoid being fired, gone into rehab, and landed a poorly paid sheriff's deputy job in his old county. Probably destined for anonymity and a ruined marriage, or worse. Then somehow, Kendricks had redeemed himself, much of it at the expense of Jack Eddleman.

This wasn't the first time Eddleman had regaled Breaux with Purdy Kendricks' misadventures.

Breaux thought, *Jack, you forget I was there in Kickapoo County when all hell broke loose and saw Purdy Kendricks when he showed more courage than I've ever seen from anyone.*

Glancing up from the table, Breaux spotted something in Eddleman's expression that made him suddenly wonder whether, years before, his fellow DEA agent had found the drug dealer's weapon but had hidden that fact and used a thrown-down gun, so he'd have control over a drunken police officer.

He looked back down at the table, his face pensive. Two years ago, the DEA exiled Eddleman to North Dakota. Breaux, who vouched for his DEA friend's conduct, had come under uncomfortable scrutiny himself. He wasn't going to put himself in that position again.

Chapter 20
Ramirez seeks revenge

My cellphone buzzed when I entered the outer office. I glanced at the screen – Harris Whittaker. Alicia Trejo handed me a cup of coffee, and I mouthed a thank you. Arriving at my desk, I set the coffee down and answered. "Howdy."

Whittaker laughed. "Howdy? What kind of greeting is that? Is that a Texas thing?"

"Actually, it's an important friendly gesture. If you'd been smart enough to attend Texas A&M, you'd understand it. But since you probably didn't have a high enough GPA...."

"Whoa. Just kidding."

"Me too. Whatcha got?"

"They've given me a cubby hole of sorts at the sheriff's office. Probably a broom closet."

"Is it the first office on the right down the hall toward TJ's office?"

"Yeah."

"Once was my office."

"Anyway, about twenty minutes ago, someone from the courthouse, I think one of the ladies in the district clerk's office, came in and told Jake that Israel Sifuentes hadn't shown up for work in a couple of days. Was asking if the SO would send someone to check on him." I figured you and the ranger would want to know."

My mind raced. *Has anyone gone to his house yet?*

"Mr. Kendricks, or Officer Kendricks." He paused. "What do you want me to call you?"

"How about just plain Purdy?"

"Okay, Purdy. Let me guess: this Sifuentes, did he live in Santa Rosa? And is he the ME's John Doe? You haven't disclosed his particulars as I recall."

"No, I haven't, but I guess now's the time to tell you a bit more." I checked to ensure my office door was closed. "Israel's house lies about a mile south of Santa Rosa. After we recovered his head, Abner Selman and I went to his house and did a preliminary investigation."

"Geez, uh, Purdy. This is, as they say in the movies, 'highly irregular.'"

"We only took photos. I gave a thumb drive of them to Ranger Selman. He's got them locked up." I cleared my throat. "I prefer that no one in the SO knows we've been there, at least for now. My photos will show how Israel's living area looked when we were there. Compare them with what you see. Hopefully, no one else has been in the place since we left."

Whittaker made a fluttering noise with his lips. My suggestion wasn't being met with enthusiasm.

"Here's the deal..." I began. "Damn, I sound like a used car salesman."

Whittaker coughed out a laugh.

"No one in law enforcement in Kickapoo County knows anything about Israel's detached head in the Bexar County ME Office. No one at the Sheriff's Office knows he's dead. No one, so far, knows a cartel killer had Israel's Texas driver's license in his jeans pocket when he was shot dead."

Whittaker interrupted. "Let me guess. You think someone's dirty, or compromised, or talks too much, and you're holding your cards close to your vest."

"I'm calling it 'information management.'"

"Hell, I was looking for a job when I got this one," he said. "What's the plan?"

I felt my stomach unclench. "Volunteer to go with whoever TJ sends out there. You're trained in forensics and crime scene investigation. Do what you have to do."

"Purdy, what am I going to find out there? Did you or Abner tinker with the crime scene?"

"We took some pictures. Even missed that Israel's driver's license was missing from his wallet, which we saw on the kitchen table. We didn't touch anything and locked the place up. Unless someone else has been in there, nothing's been disturbed."

Somewhat placated, Whittaker agreed to volunteer on one condition: that I share this information with Abner Selman immediately.

I speed-dialed Abner and filled him in on my intention to have Whittaker go with Kickapoo County sheriff's deputies out to Israel's place.

"Son," Abner began, "this is getting weirder by the day. How long do you think we can keep the lid on? We've got a newspaper man, an ME, his investigator, a DPS trooper, a café owner, and a waitress, and probably your wife, who know all or at least part of Israel's story. And I'm not even mentioning the three dead Mexicans in Lowell's front pasture."

"Abner, I think Lowell Johnson will keep his mouth shut. The only thing he loves more than his Balvenie scotch is a good mystery. Two years ago, he got the story of his life because of my snooping around. I think he'll ride this out until we can piece this together."

"What's this 'we' shit again? I told you, I'm about to retire."

I snickered. "Hell, don't bail on me now. I may need a cellmate."

Selman grunted. "Not funny. Your suspicions about corruption on this side of the border could bite us both in the ass."

I changed the subject. "Got a call from the DEA."

"And?"

"Eddleman is back in Texas."

"That bastard? What hath God wrought?"

"Yep. One of the big cheeses in Virginia at headquarters called me. 'As a courtesy,' he said. I wasn't very polite. But Abner, the more I think about it, the more I want to call the guy back and thank him. I think he was warning me. I don't know why, but I got the impression that at least someone in the DEA may not be all that impressed Eddleman is still in its employ."

"Purdy, that outfit is full of snakes. Eddleman is just one of the more obvious ones. Where is Eddleman now?"

"San Antonio office."

"Shit. The Rangers didn't get that same courtesy. The fact that you are running the Drug Interdiction Support Agency warranted the call. No one in state law enforcement is going to be happy. Did whoever called you tell you if he'd be working Kickapoo County?"

"Not directly," I replied, "but it makes sense that he'll be somewhere close. He knows the area. He's worked in Laredo, as you recall. And I'm sure he still has contacts up and down the Rio Grande. Abner, I despise the man. He's capable of anything, including murder. I need to change the subject before I blow a gasket."

I looked up at the ceiling to calm myself, then said, "I sure enjoyed visiting with Whittaker. He's a straight shooter. How'd you say you knew him?"

There was silence on the other end of the conversation. Then, "Why?"

"He seems to think highly of you. Insisted I call, tell you what the plan is. Not that I wasn't going to anyway, but I was a little surprised at how adamant he was. Sounded like you fellows have more history together than an elk hunt." I paused, hoping the Ranger would shed more light on their relationship. I was disappointed.

"I guess we do," was all he said before disconnecting.

I spent lunchtime in my office, working on the Agency's budget proposal. Boring work, but for a while it kept my mind off the riddle of activity in Kickapoo County. At one p.m., my cell phone vibrated. Lilly Pardo was calling.

I kept my voice light. "Hey, Lilly, how are you?

"My mother is driving me crazy. My family is tired of me and my bitching. I'm running out of money. When can I go back to Santa Rosa and my own bed? Is it safe yet?" She sounded frantic.

I calmed her down, promising her exile from Kickapoo County would only last another week, at most.

"How do you know that?" she asked.

I didn't have a good answer, but Lilly didn't need to be anywhere near Kickapoo County. "How much money do you need? I've cleared it with Beulah to pay you for your time off."

"I need money *now*."

"How much?

The figure she gave me was something I could manage, but Betty and I weren't flush with cash, and eventually I'd have to 'fess up. While we talked, I looked up her nearest Western Union office. She wrote down the address, sounding calmer. The wiring fee was exorbitant, but it was the only way I felt assured she'd safely receive the cash.

Another idea struck me, and I almost cursed out loud. "Lilly, your cell phone. Do you subscribe to a service, like AT&T, or T-Mobile?

"No, I go to a store and buy time on it. Why?"

When I'd rushed Lilly and her aging mother out of town, I forgot that she could be traced through a phone service subscription. Relieved that my oversight hadn't further endangered her, I replied, "Good. Keep doing that. And, you haven't called anyone in Santa Rosa, have you?"

There was a pause.

"Lilly, shoot straight with me. Have you?"

"No, *pendejo*." Then another pause. "But I got a call from my cousin."

"Which cousin, Lilly? You've got millions of them."

Alicia Trejo tapped on the office door, her signal that I was getting loud. I took a breath, lowered my voice, and asked again. "Which cousin?"

"Just a sec. Momma's turned down the TV and is looking at me. Going outside."

I heard the slap of a screen door.

"Teofilo."

The name got my immediate attention. The headman of the tiny hamlet of Parrita, in the wastelands of Northern Mexico. The man whose grandson was involved with the cartels and died as a result. Teofilo Ramirez, the wizened, mostly indigenous grandfather, filled with anger, who had helped capture the *sicario* after the killer tried to kidnap Betty and Forrest. The Mexican who'd been at Lagrimas with Israel and Lilly, who had helped to snuff out the life of the *sicario* with a single pistol shot to the head.

My voice grew louder. "I thought you told me he never used his cell phone, Lilly. That there wasn't any coverage in his village."

"No, dammit. I said he *almost* never uses his cell phone. And I told you the government doctor sent him to someplace to get medicine. I didn't call him. He called me."

Another tap on my door. I walked over, opened it, muted my phone's mouthpiece, and muttered another apology to Alicia Trejo.

Without turning, she quietly said, "God, grant me the serenity to ..."

I closed the door, took a deep breath, apologized to Lilly, and began again. "Is it common for him to call you?"

"Almost never, but he said he'd lit a candle to the Virgin Mary at some church in Acuña, which I guess is where the doctor sent him. He told me he was worried about me, because, you know..."

"Did you tell him anything about Israel?"

"I told him to please be careful. He wanted to know why. I had to tell him something, Deputy."

Shit. "And then..."

"Teofilo is sick. The doctor told him he has cancer." Lilly's voice cracked and she began to cry. "A doctor came to Parrita, did check-ups, ran some blood tests on him, found something. Told him to get to a clinic in Acuña to get some medicine. Some other stuff...I don't know."

"Is he still in Acuña?"

"I...guess so. Or somewhere there's cell coverage in the area."

I'd just finished reading detailed intelligence reports on *los Zetas'* bloody takeover of that border city's plaza. "How's he getting back to Parrita?"

"He didn't say. He usually gets someone to take him. He doesn't have a truck or anything. He left Lupita..."

"Who's Lupita?"

"His wife. She's back in the *ejido*. They've got goats to take care of." Lilly's voice trailed off.

I thought back to the *sicario* who'd tried to kidnap my wife and child, and how Lilly, Israel and Teofilo had captured and killed him. Now, one of the three was dead, one was in hiding, and one was sick with cancer.

"Lilly, I know you've told me this, probably at least twice now. But, if you know, has Teofilo told anyone about that night in Lagrimas?"

"He says no." She sobbed. "I'm so sad, Deputy."

I looked out my office window at some of Austin's skyline. "I'm sorry, Lilly. I only met him that one time. But what he did means a great deal to me."

Lilly cleared her throat and interrupted, "You remember that Mexican you and the ranger and the other policemen pulled out of the Rio Grande? The one everyone at the café said had his guts hanging out. The one with part of his head gone?"

How could I forget that gruesome discovery? "Yes, downriver from Lagrimas. The one whose family had moved to Laredo from Mexico and who gotten tangled up with the cartels. What was his name?" *El Vaquerito* – the Little Cowboy, wasn't it? Last name was Sosa?"

"That boy was Teofilo's grandson, Deputy. He was involved with *los Zetas*, like that man who tried to kidnap your wife and kid. Teofilo, he helped us, and yes, he did it for you because we all respected you. But he also did it to take revenge on *esos putos carteles* that ruined that boy's life."

Wheels within wheels, I thought. "Has Teofilo told anyone? Is he safe? *Los Zetas* run Acuña now, Lilly."

"I saw on the news about *la matanza*. Those killings – *hijole*. So damned many. I know about that piece of shit town. No, *mi primo* hasn't told anyone, even Lupita. No one will know about him in Acuña. He's just a little bitty *campesino* with broken-down huaraches, and a sickness in his insides. He is worried about me, but I told him that the deputy he met that night in Lagrimas would make sure I'm okay, and he said that was good."

"I promise I will," I said, wondering once again whether my word was worth relying on. "I'll call when I get the money wired, Lilly. I'll do it this evening. Be safe."

I reached up to disconnect when she yelled my name. "Deputy, just a minute."

What now? "Yes?" I quit trying to get Lilly to quit calling me 'Deputy.'

"Teofilo, he's very upset about Israel, you know?"

"And?" My concern grew.

"He said to tell you that if you need any help in finding out who killed his *compadre*, you just need to get ahold of him, and he will help."

We said goodbye, and I flopped into my chair, suddenly exhausted, remembering Teofilo when he'd stabbed the *sicario* who refused to talk to me. Then, after the *sicario* admitted he'd tried to kidnap my wife and child, he'd put a bullet into the outlaw's head. Teofilo, a small man with great courage and even greater rage.

I wondered if the cancer was killing him, and if Teofilo would decide to exact revenge on another of *los Zetas*. He'd not hesitate to blow the brains out of anyone who posed a danger to Lilly.

Chapter 21

An ancient hacienda, a deadly product

The fortified hacienda came alive at five a.m. The cook, up since shortly after midnight, had laid out bowls and plates on tables in the enclosed patio adjacent to the main house what was once a rich Mexican landholder's home. *Los Zetas* soldiers crawled out of the compound's many bunkbeds and began moving toward the tables.

Some laughed, some grumbled, but all the men ate greedily of tortillas, huevos rancheros, and frijoles. Today would be long and hard. The pitchers of coffee passed up and down the tables were soon emptied.

After the meal, the cook and his helpers, three boys in their early teens, washed down the tables, banked the cookfires, and cleared the patio. In the meantime, Arturo Navarrete, nursing a blinding headache from a night of mescal drinking, called together his lieutenants. The five men, none older than thirty, trudged through the gloom of the once palatial hacienda to a hallway on the east side, where bullet-shattered glass lay on one side, and blackened blood and viscera, now resembling exploded tar, decorated the opposite wall.

Guillermo Blanco, "Cantinflas," had often bragged about the bullet fired by a gringo sniper that had blown the head off Venustiano Huerta, the jefe of *la Familia Norteña*, two years before. "No one," the local *los Zetas* chief said, "crosses *los Zetas*," and made a pistol with his finger and fist. He'd walked up to several of his *soldados* shouting "Boom" as he shoved his index finger into each one's temple. Blanco demanded loyalty, and the lieutenants remembered their fear of the *jefe*. For these five men, this was their first visit to the actual site of the killing, and the physical evidence was a strong reminder of his power. Yes, Arturo Navarrete was their immediate boss, but Blanco would be the devil incarnate if disobeyed.

They stood around, the room that brightened with the rising sun. Navarrete walked in and shook his head. "*Me siento crudo, cabrones.*"

The others burst into laughter. A mescal hangover was a bitch. Most of them were feeling just as lousy. Last night's festivities, at least for those who weren't standing guard, had turned into another celebration of *los Zetas'* success in Ciudad Acuña. *La Familia Norteña* had been vanquished – again, and, this time, many *sicarios* from the Jalisco interlopers had gone to the devil with the *Norteñas*.

Navarrete raised a hand, and the room quieted. "We move product today. Not across the Rio Bravo, but close enough." He observed his lieutenants, woolen balaclavas stuffed in their pockets, and all armed with military automatics. He pointed at three. "Take your men, and once they've stashed the product, they stay there. Rotate them on twenty-four-hour guard duty. You'll have encrypted cell phones and radios. No *federales* are in the area, but those *putos* from Jalisco, *pues, quien sabe?*"

"How long do we sit on the product?" asked the oldest of the five lieutenants.

"Until I tell you not to," Navarrete snapped. "You'll bring food and drink. *El jefe* wants to try new routes north."

Another asked, "We're going to cross dope in the middle of the desert? *Hijole! Esos pinches* Border Patrol have planted ground sensors all over the *norteamericano* ranch lands and along the river. Has *el jefe* thought of that?"

Navarrete had asked himself the same question, but he wasn't going to tolerate underlings demanding answers. He made note of the man asking the question. "You do as you're told. You don't like your assignment?" he spit. "I fucking don't have to explain anything to any of you. Understand?"

When Navarrete spit on the floor, an early morning cloud darkened the sun momentarily. The mood in the meeting room darkened with it.

Navarrete's men looked down as he tried to make eye contact with any single one. None of them, including the questioning lieutenant, dared meet his gaze.

With small acknowledgements and nods, the men filed out. The one with the questions, turned back.

"Sorry, boss. I meant no disrespect," he said, fear in his eyes.

Navarrete smiled and slapped the man on the back. "*No problema, compadre.* Just do as you are told. Much rides on our success here."

Visibly relieved, the man grinned.

Navarrete watched as he sped up to join the others. He smirked and thought, *When I am* jefe, *if you question me like that, I will put a bullet in your head.*

The fentanyl had come off the two aircraft in two-kilo plastic bags, sealed securely inside more plastic, and heavily taped. Wearing gas masks to avoid inhaling possible deadly dust in case of a rupture, several men divided the nearly seven-hundred kilos into two equal stacks, which were then carefully loaded into camouflaged Humvees parked nearby under a large open steel shed.

At one-hour intervals, the two crews drove out the hacienda's main gate, heading for GPS coordinates that Navarrete provided. The Humvees all boasted pedestal mounted .50 caliber machineguns. Each Humvee was accompanied by two pickup trucks carrying eight heavily armed men in their beds.

As each group departed, Navarrete ensured that the trackers attached to the drug-ladened Humvees continued to transmit. His instructions to the groups were all the same: conceal the vehicles, use cookstoves provided and not open fires, and report any humans spotted.

The wasteland of this part of the Mexican state of Coahuila was on the western edge of *los Zetas'* control. Navarrete wondered if the drugs would fall victim to another cartel even before the kilos were moved into the United States. The Jalisco cartel was increasingly powerful. He knew that, at some point, it would respond to *los Zeta's* slaughter of its men.

After the second Humvee and accompanying trucks left, Navarrete punched numbers into an encrypted satellite telephone.

"Si?" answered Blanco.

"Both have left. The tracking devices are working."

"Good. We are taking a chance on this. Santa Muerte deliver me if this doesn't work."

Navarrete thought *Santa Muerte won't help you, Cantinflas, if this fails. Others higher up will cut your balls off before they kill you. And I want to be there only if it is as a spectator. Your idea is dangerous and stupid, and I don't want to die with you.* "I will call you back when the crews arrive," Navarrete responded.

Nearing the tiny village of Parrita, the eastern-tracked crew enjoyed the relative luxury of a north-south dirt road. Once the vehicles passed its few jacals, the small adobe huts, and the goat pens near every home, there were few human markings apart from tracks left by herds of goats and faint tracings of roads that led to and from long-abandoned rhyolite or fluorspar mines.

At dusk, both crews checked in, confirming the locations on Navarrete's tracking devices.

"Did anyone see you? Did you see others along the routes?"

One crew chief replied, "Some old women and a few children at Parrita. One old goat herder, who stayed at least a kilometer away, *jefe*. Mostly we saw *arroyos secos* and rocks. Our asses are sore."

Navarrete reported to Blanco as wordlessly, a teen helper for the cook placed a plate of *carne asada* and tortillas in front of him. Only the cook and his young helpers would remain at the hacienda. It was time to return to Ciudad Acuña. Navarrete's head still throbbed from last night's mescal. The arid emptiness of El Mosco and the hacienda could go to hell. He was ready for a bath, a shave, and a woman. Idly, he wondered if the *norteamericanos* had been able to track *los Zetas'* movements.

*****

They had.

"Take a look at these stills," Breaux said, speaking to Eddleman and other agents who met again in the San Antonio office's conference room. Photographs from the military reconnaissance satellite passed around the group. The photos had time stamps, based on Greenwich Mean Time.

"First photos were taken a few hours after the request was made to Vandenburg," Eddleman said.

"Looks almost like daytime," an agent remarked.

Breaux responded. "Full moon, if you can believe it, no cloud cover, and the optics on those birds are amazing."

The hacienda's enclosure and various buildings appeared clearly in the stills. None showed any vehicular traffic, but a bright smudge caught Eddleman's eye. "What's this?"

After scanning the various photos, an agent said, "Huh."

"What?" asked another agent.

"Dollars to donuts, it's a cookfire, or campfire," Eddleman responded. He turned to Breaux. "Any video?"

The monitor lit up with video of the same scene. Eddleman walked closer to the large display. "Look." He pointed. "Tiny dots are moving. Some stop." He paused the video, backed it up and ran the same few seconds. "Lots of little dots. People walking toward the big house, some walking to and from outbuildings."

The agents moved closer to the monitor. The number of cartel members was unclear, as figures were seen going in and out of buildings. The officers agreed that at least forty persons now occupied the hacienda.

"Where are the people movers?" someone added. 'I don't see any trucks."

"Or a Humvee," added Breaux. "That compound must house some big-assed garages."

Breaux produced more stills and brought up another video on a desktop computer. "Daylight, taken yesterday. Same bird, same track, better lighting."

The time stamp on the handful of stills showed a GMT that translated to early morning in Northern Coahuila. The photos showed a Humvee and a balaclava-clad gunner at its pedestal-mounted machine gun. Breaux brought up a video. "Watch this."

When the Humvee moved toward the hacienda's large wooden gate, two pickups appeared from under a steel-roofed structure.

"Aha," someone said. "There's the parking area, at least for some."

The three vehicles headed east toward El Mosco, then turned north.

"No roads to speak of," Eddleman murmured. He'd opened his laptop and accessed Google Earth. "Rough terrain means slow going." Excitement gripped him, but he tried to dampen it. "Those boys are heading toward the border."

The video faded. The optics lost their acuity as the satellite continued its orbit. Eddleman pointed to the stills produced by the video.

"Look," he said, "here's that garage. The bird wasn't at enough of an angle to get a peek underneath it, but..."

He displayed another still. "The sun's coming up from the east, and its rays have bounced off of something." He reached into a cabinet drawer and retrieved a marking pen. Drawing a circle around light spots on west facing windows, he said, "Windshields. And lots of them. Their windshield glass is catching rays and bouncing onto the windows."

Breaux let out a low whistle. "Damned, if you aren't right." The window glass of several main house windows reflected a row of concealed vehicles. "Wonder why so many?"

Breaux called up video from the satellite's cameras as it tracked toward the Rio Grande. "Look. Humvee in the lead, two pickups loaded with gun toters behind it."

Someone threw up a smaller scale view of the border region. "They keep moving north. No road to speak of. Other than a tiny village or two nothing between them and the U.S. but arroyos, rough terrain, and lots of cactus and scrub."

After confirming radar from the Tethered Aerostat Radar System had not picked up aircraft traffic, the DEA agents re-convened. The satellite had made another pass of the hacienda. The stills were ignored momentarily. Everyone was interested in seeing the video.

GMT showed the overhead surveillance of the area as late afternoon in northern Mexico. The video showed nothing except a man in an apron, presumably a cook, scrubbing pots.

"Where is everyone?" Eddleman asked.

Breaux grabbed the stills and passed them around. Eddleman asked for the earlier stills to compare. Breaux ran his finger over one photo. "Look, more tracks. Several vehicles must have gone out of the gate. Not just the three from that first pass." The toothpick he had stuck in his mouth wagged up and down as he spoke. He grabbed another still, taken at a slightly different angle and pointed. "Areas disturbed from more than the Humvee and two pickups we first saw. All come out of the portal, then break north, but in slightly different directions."

"Nothing more around that hacienda," Breaux continued. "We've got to scour a few thousand square miles of Coahuila and hope that satellite caught a glimpse of something." He looked around. "Any volunteers for some late-night work?"

Eddleman sensed something. Perhaps the intel was right. The cartels were trying new and more difficult routes for their drugs. One thing was for sure, the satellite cameras had caught many vehicles heading north. And that meant toward Kickapoo County.

"Damn," an agent exclaimed. "There aren't many ways to move drugs in that border region. Only one highway, U.S. 90. A natural chokepoint. Doesn't seem that smart."

"Maybe they know something we don't. And maybe they're expecting us to think it's dumb, and won't pay attention to it," Eddleman said. *But we will, and in the process, unless someone beats me to it, I'll find some or all of Vasquez' cash, stashed on the Griffin ranch.*

Chapter 22
Promise kept

As expected, Israel Sifuentes' absence from his job and evidence of a violent encounter at his home stirred up Santa Rosa. Israel's as the Kickapoo County Courthouse janitor belied his status in the community. He had no immediate family in the county, but he had a passel of cousins of varying degrees and quietly had done many favors for the Hispanic community over the years. He also served as a pipeline into the court system and wasn't afraid to go to bat with judges, prosecutors, and law enforcement for someone on the wrong side of the law.

Israel had sought me out on occasion, always quietly, to express his concerns about an arrest and its consequences to a so-called cousin. The times it happened, I always agreed to a second look. He had an instinct for what was right and wrong, or mitigating circumstances ignored or overlooked. Kickapoo County's Hispanics were "his people." His fierce loyalty to that overwhelmingly poor part of the community was evident.

Not for the first, second, or third time, did I wonder whether Abner Selman and I should have just let Lowell call the Sheriff's Office with his macabre discovery. Israel's severed head, now rested in a cooler at the Bexar County ME's Office. The head had to be connected to the crime scene inside his house. It wouldn't take a rocket scientist to compare the dates.

"Fat's in the fire," I said to Abner over a quick lunch at a deli near his office. "Not sure what we did was the best idea I've ever had."

"Maybe," he countered. "But, for sure there'd have been more dead people scattered near Lowell Johnson's front gate if you hadn't acted on it. Those three Mexicans would have killed some unsuspecting deputies, and best guess, might have gotten away with it." He took a bite out of a kosher pickle and chewed on it thoughtfully. "Us being the incredibly competent lawmen we are, we did everyone a favor by killing those bastards."

"Yeah, but concealing that we were out there? And taking Israel's head..."

Abner interrupted me. "What's done is done, amigo. The less anyone knows about how Mr. Sifuentes' head ended up on Lowell's gate, and why those *sicarios* thought it'd be clever to kill Texas lawmen, the better. I still think your hunch is valid that someone on this side of the border is in cahoots with one of the cartels. At least worth looking into. I've backed your play, Purdy." Another chomp on a pickle, then, "Now shut up and finish your reuben."

Mollified, I took a bite. Abner's pep talk made the sandwich taste better.

*****

Two years earlier, Lowell had been lauded nationally and awarded the James Foley Medill Medal for "Courage in Journalism" and the Worth Bingham Prize for "Investigative Journalism" because of his reporting on Los Zetas' assassination of Venustiano Huerta, the murders of Otabiano and Raquel Vasquez, the ensuing investigation into their grandson Pete's involvement with the cartels and his serving as a confidential informant for the DEA.

Lowell had been present at the Griffin Ranch when a gunbattle between cartel gunmen and law enforcement broke out, and I'd crossed into Mexico to save Laura Griffin and Pete Vasquez. Lowell had witnessed the bloody melee and had praised my conduct. He'd also accused Jack Eddleman in print. of lying in wait and killing Pete Vasquez as Laura Griffin, Pete, and I were crossing back into Texas. The DEA closed ranks, and officially, Pete had died of a bullet through the heart from an "unknown assailant." I was treated like a hero, and Eddleman was quietly transferred to North Dakota.

Now, the *Kickapoo County Courier* was reporting Israel's disappearance, and making general references to an ongoing investigation, Lowell had kept his promise, and no mention was made of his discovery of Israel's severed head. I wondered whether the two awards, now hanging proudly in the *Courier's* front office, could be revoked if the organizations got wind of how Lowell was playing fast and loose with the facts now. I hoped not.

As I approached Santa Rosa, I punched in Beulah Jackson's cellphone number.

"Hello, Purdy. I *know* you're calling to give me the good news that Lilly will be back to work tomorrow."

"Actually, I'm just calling to tell you I'm headed to Santa Rosa."

I pulled into the parking lot of the Cenizo Diner. Only a few trucks were in the parking lot. I walked in and eyed the afternoon "brain trust," mostly retired postal workers and ranchers, seated at a round table in the back, opining about the woes of the county. A few recognized me and finger waved.

Beulah eyed me suspiciously. "Little late for lunch, Purdy. Little early for dinner."

She reluctantly honored the promise I'd made to Lilly Pardo and ponied up some cash for her. Lilly'd found family to look after her mother for a few weeks. When I called her at noon, Lilly answered groggily.

"You okay?" I asked.

"Just sleeping is all, Deputy Kendricks." She yawned loudly.

"Lilly, it's two o'clock."

"Mama's with one of her sisters for a while – it's been okay. I never get to sleep much, so now I am," she pronounced.

I wasn't sure her mood would last but was relieved she was safe.

"I'm still trying to get you back home soon."

Another, longer yawn. "Take your time, Deputy. I could get used to this. Just keep sending money. Bye."

"Lilly, dammit, don't..." *Shit.* She'd disconnected before I could give her some weak-assed lecture. I had to laugh.

I backed out of the Cenizo Diner's gravel parking lot, enveloped in a cloud of dust. Texas was in a drought, and there'd been nothing to tamp down the dust. The temperature was climbing into the nineties, and I cursed myself for taking my truck with its fickle air conditioning instead of the state sedan. I pulled up to US 90, intending to drop in on the Kickapoo County Sheriff's Office. My cell vibrated. I braked and checked my rearview mirror. No one was behind me, so I took the call instead of pulling onto the tarmac.

"Purdy Kendricks?" a vaguely familiar voice asked.

"Yes. Who's this?"

"DEA Agent Breaux. I think we've met."

"No shit." Not a particularly intelligent retort, but Breaux had been Jack Eddleman's cohort two years previously. I wasn't inclined to courtesy.

"Mr. Kendricks, I have no doubt you're delighted to hear from the DEA and especially me. We need to talk."

"I'm busy. So, talk." A rancher pulled up behind me and tapped his horn. I pulled onto US 90 and then onto the shoulder.

"You're in Santa Rosa, aren't you?"

"Either you've got a tracker on my vehicle, or you called my office. Given that you're DEA, I'm not sure which is easier for you."

Breaux coughed a small laugh. "For someone in law enforcement, you sure take a dim view of us. I called your secretary, who said you'd be in Kickapoo County. Come to think of it, I've got a sack of GPS trackers, and it'd been just as easy to use one of those, instead of extending the courtesy of calling your office."

"Nice come back, Breaux. Now that we've compared dick sizes, what do you want?"

"Look across US 90."

I moved the phone from my ear and looked north. A Walmart tractor trailer obstructed my view as it headed east. The rig cleared, and I peered into the parking lot of a Family Dollar store. A dusty black SUV sat idling, the driver's window down. An arm appeared and waved.

"You shopping?" I asked.

"You got a place, away from Santa Rosa, where we can talk?"

I thought about it. "The Shell natural gas processing plant, past Lagrimas, near the county line. Except it isn't Shell anymore. Don't know who bought it, but it's still there. You know it?"

The window rolled up, and the SUV pulled out, heading west. I guessed that meant "yes." I inserted earbuds, hit play, and followed. Madeleine Peyroux's solo version of *La vie en rose* began. I knew about four words in the French language, and I didn't hear any of them in the song. But for a few minutes the dry Texas countryside disappeared, and I imagined a smoke-filled Paris nightclub.

I didn't try to keep up with Breaux, and soon lost him in the increasingly hilly west end of the county. An abandoned service station at the junction with a dirt county road announced the existence of Lagrimas. Toward the south, I spotted a few bedraggled adobes and single-wides. In seconds they disappeared, leaving fences and telephone lines the only evidence of civilization.

Six miles further loomed the automated collectors, fracturing towers, and pipelines of a facility that, much to the consternation of Kickapoo County officials, scrubbed and processed natural gas from wells enriching adjoining counties. The chain link gate stood open, and a white pickup sat in front of the facility's small office. Breaux's SUV was nowhere to be seen. I slowed, then spotted him behind the plant parked against the perimeter fence. Breaux waved. I slowed, then turned onto the rough terrain.

I pulled out my earbuds and stepped out of the truck. "Odd place to be meeting, Agent. Phone calls are cheap these days."

Breaux leaned against his SUV and wiped the dust off a Tony Lama boot with the back of his pants leg. He reached into the breast pocket of a western-cut shirt, pulled out a toothpick, and stuck it in his mouth. "Been awhile since we've seen each other, Mr. Kendricks. Congratulations. A big jump from a pissant county deputy to a high mucketymuck in Austin," he said, a slight inflection showing his Cajun heritage. His tone was friendly, and I felt myself wanting to like the man.

A tractor trailer with a load of drill stem roared by on US 90, a blast of stifling air and grit washing over us.

"It's Leroy, isn't it? I said. "I remember when we met. You and Eddleman had lost track of Pete Vasquez and Laura Griffin and came asking for help."

Breaux nodded. "And all of us damned near got shot up on that woman's ranch." He paused. "I'm not here to walk down memory lane with you." He looked around. "This is one godforsaken place. Let's at least sit in the AC. Yours work?"

"Barely," I said and stepped into the passenger side on his black SUV. Breaux started the engine, pushed a button, and the vehicle's AC blasted chilled air. Another heavily loaded diesel went by, its roar muffled by the closed windows. "What's going on that you've tracked me to Santa Rosa?"

"Trust, or the lack of it, I guess." He turned toward me. "You know about the shootout in Acuña."

I nodded.

"*Los Zetas* solidified their hold on that plaza and are looking for new ways to run drugs across the border."

"No surprise there. But in Kickapoo County? They sure haven't been too subtle. DEA must know three *Zetas* were killed on a ranch nearby two weeks ago."

"That's a puzzlement," Breaux added, "and now I hear your courthouse janitor is missing and probably dead. I agree it's odd. Any ideas if they're connected?"

If you only knew, I thought. I looked out the passenger window. "Nope."

Breaux seemed to accept my response. "You mind if call you Purdy?"

I nodded. "Okay, but that doesn't mean I'll go out with you."

He chortled, and I smiled. "Leroy, how in hell did you get hooked up with Jack Eddleman?"

"Long story. He's back, you know."

"Oh yeah, I know. Doesn't sound like there's anything I can do about it either." Curiosity was killing me, but I didn't want to get sidetracked regarding Eddleman. I changed the subject. "You said 'trust.' What do you mean?"

Breaux coughed, rolled his window down and spat, then rolled the window back up. "We don't know who to trust. Whatever you think of us, the agency — apart from Jack Eddleman — says you're our 'go to' guy for now. I agree with that assessment. Don't forget. I saw you in action. We need your intel. We need to know who it's safe to work with. This border region is its own world." He described two possible shipments positioned to cross the Rio

Grande disturbingly close to Kickapoo County. "I'd like to keep at least some of the fentanyl from killing more Americans."

"You want something from me," I responded. "I want something from you."

"What?"

"Yep. Keep Eddleman away from me."

Breaux shook his head. "That one I can't promise. He's already involved in trying to guess where *los Zetas* will cross drugs into Kickapoo County. You want to know where he thinks two of them are?"

"Best bet is one's going to be at the low water crossing at Lagrimas," I responded. "What about the second one?"

"The ranch you inherited from Laura Griffin."

I thought of the additional lock on the property's front gate, and tire tracks I'd followed and wondered if there was a connection. *Oh shit.*

Chapter 23

A coin toss resolves nothing

Breaux shook my hand, got back in his truck, and pulled out onto US 90, heading west. I returned to mine, sat with the engine off, my door open, and let the heat wash over me. The compressor plant's machinery hummed, and, occasionally, a passing car sent dust particles into the cab.

I needed to be in Austin. Betty was meeting with our real estate agent who'd found some properties we might be able to afford. This afternoon, I missed another of my son's T-ball games. Alicia Trejo was sending me not-so-veiled warnings that I was neglecting my duties at the Interdiction Support Department.

Instead, I sat there, squinting at the sun's last rays filling my windshield. I pushed the seat back, tilted my hat, and closed my eyes. What in God's name had I got myself into – again?

"Hey, mister. You okay?"

Startled, I sat up and turned toward the voice. A compressor station employee in a khaki uniform and hardhat stood inside the chain link fence, staring at me.

"I'm good," I said. "Just taking a nap."

The worker looked at the sun, then at me, and shook his head. "Facing the wrong way to be comfortable taking a nap."

Embarrassed, I thanked him, started the engine, adjusted my seat, and backed my pickup toward the highway. The worker disappeared into the compressor station's tangle of tubing and machinery. A mile later down the road, as I crested a rise, my phone vibrated. I didn't recognize the number. Too many digits were showing. I dropped into a low spot, lost the signal, but the next rise, the cell buzzed again. I pulled onto the shoulder. I had a feeling it was a Mexican phone number.

"Hello?"

"*Estoy hablando con el sherif que se llama* Purdy?"

The voice sounded vaguely familiar. I switched into Spanish. I said, "Yes. My name is Purdy. I was a sheriff. Who's this?"

"I am Teofilo Ramirez."

"How did you get my number?"

"My cousin, Lilly."

I made a mental note to give Lilly hell. "What can I do for you?"

"It is what I can do for you, *señor*."

Lilly had said Teo, as she called him, had contacted her from Ciudad Acuña, where he was receiving cancer treatment. "Where are you?" I interrupted. "How are you? Lilly says you have cancer. Are you safe?"

"Many questions. Lilly says you are no longer an *ayudante del sherif*. That you and your family no longer live near the Rio Bravo. But she says, you still take care of problems there. I am afraid for my cousin. I am afraid for my people."

It was stated as fact, so I said nothing, hoping not to lose cell coverage.

"You know I am from Parrita," he continued. "The narcos came near our village four days ago."

"Where are they now? Is the village safe?" The last question was a stupid one. No one in Mexico was safe from the cartels.

Teo coughed several times. I wondered if it was a symptom of his cancer. "Are you in Acuña?" There was no cell coverage in Parrita.

"I am near Lagrimas," he responded. "But on the other side of the Rio Bravo. I wish to talk with you."

"Where? When?"

"Someone says you were in Santa Rosa today. Do you remember the old adobe in Lagrimas?"

There were several old adobes in Lagrimas, but I knew instantly which one he was referring to. "When?"

"When can you be there?"

I was ten minutes away and told him so.

"*Si puedes*, now." He paused. "I cannot stay on your side of the river very long. I'll be waiting for you, but only for twenty minutes. *Comprendes*?"

"*Claro.*"

"You are in a white truck, yes?"

How in hell did a cancer-ridden village elder with no transportation get from Ciudad Acuña to Lagrimas, Texas, and then track me down? And know I was in my truck? The border region's mysterious telegraph always amazed me.

"Yes."

"*Entonces.*" He disconnected.

I was raised in Lagrimas, one of two Anglo kids in the community, the other being Jake Nichols. Dad's water well business had been located there until Mom sold the equipment after he died. I'd fished at the low water crossing for years. There'd been some happy times then. But now what went through my mind was the number of violent deaths there, all cartel related. Teofilo Ramirez, along with Lilly and Israel Sifuentes, executed a *Zeta* gunman in the adobe I was nearing. Did I trust this man? Was I willing to take a chance he wasn't setting me up to be killed or kidnapped? I speed-dialed Abner Selman's cell, but the call went to voicemail. I didn't leave a message. I called Betty.

"Purdy, where are you? I'm looking at a house I think you'll like. I tried calling you. It went to voicemail."

I glanced down. A message popped up that I'd missed. *Uh oh.* "Just saw it. I'm still in Santa Rosa," I said. A small lie to be sure, but still uncomfortable to say it. "Got stuck out here."

"I'm with our real estate agent, and I want us to make an offer on this house. I love it, and I was hoping you would too. It's near a great school for Forrest. I think it's one we can afford." Her voice was chilly, so much so I could feel her icy breath over the phone. "Why didn't you let me know you couldn't make it?"

"Can I talk to the agent?" Anything to mitigate the trouble I was in.

"I guess," she said, clearly exasperated.

There was a pause, then another female voice. "Mr. Kendricks?"

"What's the asking price?"

She told me. I winced, then took a deep breath. "I'm asking Betty to put a contract on the house. I trust her judgment. I'll be back in Austin, and I'll sign the contract in the morning."

"Are you sure, sir? You haven't seen the house or the neighborhood."

Right now, all that mattered was avoiding disappointing my wife. Fortunately, the listing agent had uploaded two videos and over fifty stills of the property, which Betty and I had reviewed together. I wasn't shooting entirely in the dark. "Absolutely."

I could hear her hand the phone to Betty and say, "He says he wants you to put in an offer."

"Purdy," Betty said, sounding confused. "You did what? What if you don't like it?"

"I will, Honey. Don't forget. I saw the internet listing photos and video. I liked what I saw."

"Are you saying this because you trust me that you'll like the house, or because you're guilt tripping?"

"I trust you implicitly, Betty. If you love the house, you know I will, too." In my mind I said, *I'm guilt tripping, but I'm not about to admit it.*

"Thank you, Purdy," she said in a warmer tone. I glanced at the time. I had seven minutes to make it to an abandoned adobe in Lagrimas.

"I love you, Betty. I'm excited. I'll be home later tonight." I disconnected.

My mind suddenly panicked, I thought, *If I'm still alive.*

I pulled off US 90 at an abandoned service station and remembered the miserable childhood of my friend Jake Nichols. His father was a drunk, and Jake's mother had struggled to keep the business going with Jake's help.

A gravel road led to a low water crossing into Mexico. Fifty yards past the service station, I turned left and off the road and into the ruts of the tiny village, the remains of adobes melting back into the earth, scattered among ratty-looking mobile homes. Trucks without wheels sat in front of several dilapidated single-wides that would soon be no better off than the older native structures. Clothes dried on a line and a few chickens pecked at seed someone had strewn in front of another home. They were the only signs of life.

I pulled up to an adobe. More of its roof had collapsed since my last time there two years ago. I killed the engine, checked, and took my pistol out of the holster. I wondered what value it would be if someone was intent on killing me by ambush.

I stepped out of the truck and called to make sure he was there. *"Teofilo, estás aqui?"*

The soft crunch of someone stepping on a dirt floor. *"Si."*

Relieved, I shut the truck's door and walked around to the house's doorway, the wooden door long gone. Inside, a jumble of trash, broken pieces of wood, and an old cast iron stove shown through a filter of dusk's light and newly disturbed dust. Teofilo stood in the corner near the one window. The one time I'd seen him by flashlight was imprinted firmly in my memory. Now, he seemed smaller. His dark indigenous features were more pronounced by weight loss, a gauntness in his face I didn't recall.

"Thank you for coming, *señor.*"

I stepped over the threshold, dust covering my boots. I shook Teo's hand which was still callused and as tough as a turtle shell.

"It's many kilometers from Parrita to this place, Teo. Did someone with a truck give you a ride?"

"Pues, I walked." He pointed at a wicker-encased water bottle. "Not so far." He broke into a bark-like cough, spitting bubbly phlegm onto the floor near his huarache-clad feet. In the gloom, I wasn't sure, but thought I saw blood in the spit.

Teo reflected the reserved dignity of a *campesino.* I waited for him to begin but twitched when a truck rattled into town. The vehicle drove past the adobe, its radio blaring a *corrido tumbado,* through the truck's open windows, *a* song which extolled a cartel gun battle. It pulled up to a single-wide mobile home. Six pack in hand, the driver got out and climbed up the rickety steps and went inside. The door slammed. Silence resumed.

"Do not worry, *señor*. We are safe here...for now." Teo extracted a broken-backed chair from the debris and sat. "There are *narcotraficantes* very near *los estados unidos*."

Aren't there always? I thought and nodded.

"They are camped two hours' walk from here. There are men and bundles of drugs." He described a Humvee and a pickup, and at least six heavily armed *sicarios*.

In the increasing darkness, Teo's cough seemed to envelop his small frame.

"How do you know this?" I asked.

"They passed near Parrita. My woman saw them. She told me. I followed their tracks..."

I thought of the many eyes in the sky, the airplanes, drones, and satellites. I pointed upward. "But—"

"They cannot be seen from above. They have hidden under *afloramientos rocosos*."

I struggled with the expression, then realized he was talking about rocky outcroppings. "Where, exactly?"

Teo described the terrain, using landmarks I was unfamiliar with. Desperately, I punched in Google Earth on my cell phone, but it refused to load. I turned my attention back to the small man. "You have cancer. You have taken a big risk trailing these men. Why are you telling me this, Teofilo?"

"I am dying, señor. I have killed only one of those *putos*. They ruined my grandson. They killed him. They killed Israel, a cousin. They could harm Liliana, another of my family. I intend to kill many of that scum before I go to be with God." He reached into a small bag and stepped to the window. The last light silhouetted a revolver.

"Christ," I said. "They will kill you before you get close to them."

He coughed again, stood, and walked toward me. Barely five feet tall, he stared at me in the gloom. "Then, you must help me kill them first."

"I can't do that," I said with quiet reserve. "I can't go into your country."

"Why, *señor*? I came into yours two years ago."

Teofilo's suggestion was nuts. He'd never hinted that a repayment would be sought for exacting justice for what had happened to Betty and Forrest. But that was exactly what was happening. As indebted as I was to him, I had no intention of being part of his madness. Desperately, I thought of things that might stop his suicidal plan. "I need to think about this, Teofilo. When do you plan to do this?"

He coughed. "I am hiding in the brush on the other side. I will wait one day. If you wish to help me, come back here. If you do not come by tomorrow night, I will understand. But I will get my revenge, with or without your help."

He stepped into the sunlight and was quickly gone.

*****

In Santa Rosa, I pulled behind the *Kickapoo County Courier* office, relieved not to see Lowell Johnson's truck. I needed some privacy. I called Abner's number. This time he answered.

"You got a few minutes?" I asked, keeping my tone neutral.

"Of course. What's on your mind?"

I told him of Teofilo's meeting and his demand.

"Let me get this straight. A Mexican you hardly know calls out of the blue, and, without any backup, you drive to the most godforsaken part of a godforsaken county and meet with him, and he wants you to go into Mexico with him and get yourself killed. And this is for a debt he claims you owe him. How am I doing so far?"

"Pretty accurate."

"Let's see now. This is right after a DEA agent meets you in the middle of nowhere and sweet-talks you by saying you're indispensable to their noble efforts at stopping drugs being smuggled through Kickapoo County."

"Abner, I know it's crazy. But I've got to stop Teofilo from getting himself killed..."

"Hell's fire, he's dying of cancer, Purdy. You aren't going to save him from a damned thing."

Another thought came to me. "If he goes John Wayne into that camp he's talking about, they'll kill him, and for sure they'll change their route into the states. Can we agree that's a bad thing?"

Abner was breathing heavily into the phone. "I'm pissed as hell at you, Purdy. This call is fucking up an otherwise pleasant evening." He paused. "But your point about Teofilo scaring off the drug shipment to somewhere unknown is valid. I'll get back to you."

He'd ended the call. I wondered whether I wanted Teo to fail. It was wrong and crazy, but at that moment, I wanted to sneak into Mexico and kill every one of the bastards hiding under rocks. I wanted payback for Israel. I wanted payback, hell, just for my own shitty situation, too.

I pulled a coin out of my pocket. "Tails I go. Heads I stay." I flipped the coin. In the darkness, it fell onto the floorboard, and then rolled under my seat.

Chapter 24

A phone call and a provocation

Arturo Navarrete stepped out of the shower and wrapped himself in a large terrycloth towel. "Maria," he yelled, "take these filthy clothes."

The small-statured maid scurried into the bathroom, snatched the pile up from the floor and disappeared. Navarrete reached for a bottle of *El Amo* tequila, poured two fingers into a tumbler, swallowed it, and burped.

"Aiii, clean again. Now for a siesta."

His cell phone buzzed. The incoming call's sender was blocking identification. Curious, he punched the line open. "*Sí?*"

"*Estoy hablando con* Arturo Navarrete, the one they call *El Tramposo*?"

"Who is this?" Navarrete answered.

The caller ignored the question. "Your boss thinks he and *los Zetas* can move into our territory, kill our men, take our plaza, and nothing will happen to him and his *pinche jotos.*"

Navarrete dropped the towel. Naked, he sat heavily on the edge of an oversized bed. "Is this some kind of fucking joke?" he asked, eyes narrowing as he stared at the terrazzo floor. He knew what the answer would be.

"*Cabrón.* Do you think we are joking? We are the Jalisco New Generation. We are coming after that *puto* called Cantinflas. We are going to cut off his balls and stuff them in his mouth. We will do the same to you."

Sweat appeared on Navarrete's forehead, and he had a sudden urge to move his bowels. His phone still to his ear, he scuttled toward the toilet. The stench of the release of his feces almost gagged him.

"Not saying anything? Are you a coward as well as a *puto*?"

Relieved to have escaped fouling the bed sheets, Navarrete looked around to confirm that the maid had closed the door to the suite. "I don't listen to silly threats. I don't talk to little shits like you. Whoever this is, don't waste my time with this cheap bullshit." He disconnected, flushed the toilet, and sniffed his armpits. The smell of fear seemed to seep from his pores. He'd need to bathe again.

He thought, *Hijo! How did those fuckers get my phone number? Were they recording everything?* Navarrete had toyed with the idea of betraying Blanco and *los Zetas*, but it was secondary to his wish to succeed Blanco and remain within this cartel. And now? Someone had found him, threatened him and *los Zetas*.

Oh shit. Does the Jalisco group know I might be available if the right people contact me? He stared at his image in the bathroom mirror. *Have I put a target on my back?*

Shaking his head, he dressed and reached for the tequila bottle. It was time to meet with *el jefe* and tell him about this new threat. He had to do it in person, and not over the phone.

*****

"Jefe," we need to talk.

"Arturo, I'm busy right now. Can it wait?"

"I don't think so. Have you been contacted?"

"By whom?" Blanco's voice turned suspicious.

"Jalisco, I think."

"*Mierda*! When? How?"

"Just now. By phone. Those bastards have my cell number. I thought everything about the phone was encrypted."

Blanco paused, then asked, "You know where I am?"

"Of course."

"Come."

An hour later, Navarrete's three-vehicle convoy pulled off Mexican Federal Highway 29 into non-descript hills one hundred kilometers south of Ciudad Acuña. A kilometer off the paved highway, the road was blocked by a barricade comprised of oil drums and heavy timbers. Two balaclava-wearing *sicarios* stepped from the heavy brush on both sides and almost casually, pointed automatic weapons at the vehicles. One walked to Navarrete's SUV.

Navarrete's driver rolled down all the vehicle's windows. The road guard, who looked no older than fifteen, leaned in, staring intently. He stepped out of earshot and spoke into the hand-held radio clipped to Velcroed body armor.

"What the fuck, Chief," Navarrete's driver muttered. "What's going on?"

"Don't know, but stay calm, my friend. This kid looks twitchy. I don't want to get shot up." *Did that phone call condemn me?*

The young road guard returned to the SUV and pointed to Navarrete. "You only from this point on. And only after we search the *camioneta*. No weapons go up the road." He turned and shouted something, and four more *sicarios,* faces hidden, joined them from the concealment of heavy shrubs lining the road.

"Please, *señor.* Step out of the vehicle."

Navarrete carefully reached for the door handle and stepped out. Arms above his head, he turned and yelled to his bodyguards. "Everyone out. Do what he says."

One of the guards stepped into the lead vehicle, started the engine, and pulled it to the side of the road, then let the engine die.

Navarrete made a show of slowly reaching to his shoulder holster and withdrawing his 10 mm Glock automatic.

"Gracias."

This fucking kid is scared as shit, Navarrete thought.

The barricade was disassembled, and the barrels and timbers set to the side of the road. A radio crackled, and the young gunman pointed at Navarrete.

"Please, *señor.* Only you go further. The rest stay down here with us."

Navarrete nodded, walked to the driver's side of the SUV. Turning to his driver and four bodyguards, he said, "It's all good, *muchachos.* Stay in the shade."

He pointed to a small oak tree. "It's hot out here. I'll be back soon," hoping his voice showed more assurance than he felt.

The disarmed men stood aside, and Navarrete slowly drove forward past the barricade. In the rearview mirror, he watched the guards re-establish the barricade.

Navarrete rolled up the windows and set the air conditioning on high. Sweat poured off his face, and his shirt showed rings of moisture under his arms. At the crest of a small hill, the road made a sharp right turn. He slowed, then gently accelerated to a wide-open area near a large Spanish-tiled house.

Three more *sicarios* waited at the foot of a wide staircase leading to the veranda, their automatic weapons at the ready. Navarrete squinted toward the bougainvillea-shrouded veranda and spied several more armed men.

What the fuck? Slowly, he opened the SUV door and placed his foot on the ground. "*Cálmate, muchachos. Cálmate.* I don't want to get shot."

One man stepped forward. "*Disculpe*, but I have to pat you down for weapons."

Navarrete turned and put his hands on the SUV roof.

"Again? *Tu compañero* searched me at the entrance," Navarrete felt hands roaming from his shoulders to his waist to his crotch, then down to his knees.

"You can go up now," the *sicario* said as he stepped away.

"Not so fast, *joven*." Navarrete pulled up his right pant leg, exposing an ankle holster with a small automatic. "Both you dumbasses missed this one." He carefully unsnapped the holster's gun strap and handed over the weapon, butt-first.

The balaclava covering the sicario's face couldn't conceal the raw fear in the eyes. "*Gracias, señor.* Please, do not tell *el jefe.*"

"I won't. I could have killed your boss, kid." Navarrete turned toward the house. "I'm not the enemy." As he reached the veranda steps, Navarrete had two thoughts: *One: that was a good move that shows I'm loyal, Two: I've just surrendered my only weapon to someone who might put a bullet through my brain.*

Navarrete got no read from the taciturn men on the veranda. Their casual behavior was belied by eyes that bore holes into him. Navarrete stepped to a front door with a large cross carved into it, no doubt once an entry to some church. A gunman unlatched it. Navarrete nodded his thanks, felt the door's ancient surface, then stepped inside. *I hope I'm not about to do penance for my sins.*

"Come on back, my friend." The familiar voice echoed from inside the cavernous house.

Not relieved by the apparent friendliness in the tone, Navarrete glanced at the thick stucco walls as he moved toward an open shaded central courtyard. He hoped no one was waiting to attack him.

If I get it, I hope it's a bullet, and not a machete or chainsaw. He'd personally used all three.

Instead, Guillermo Blanco slumped in a straight-back chair at a small table under a lime tree.

"Come here." He motioned toward a bottle of mescal and two heavy glass *caballitos*. "Have a drink with me."

Relieved, Navarrete affected annoyance. "Are you sure you trust me to get near you?" His sweat had begun to dry. It was time to show indignation at the affront. "What does it mean that those *cabrones* would not allow my men to accompany me? Those *pinche culeros* out front fondled me!"

Blanco waved the bottle in a conciliatory gesture. "I trust you." He handed the mescal-filled glass to his lieutenant. "Just not too much." He belched, then suddenly, he leaned forward, colliding with the metal table and rocking it. Navarrete grabbed the bottle that almost spilled.

Blanco squinted and glared at Navarrete. "You don't get to tell me that Jalisco scum calls you, out of nowhere, and threatens *me*, and expect that you can waltz into my home, without me taking precautions. Do you? Do you?" Blanco's face darkened. He snatched the bottle from Navarrete. "Answer me, goddamit!"

Navarrete thought, *I've pushed him too far. A drunk Cantinflas is a dangerous Cantinflas.* Navarrete spoke to sooth him. "Of course, you are right, *jefe*. Please accept my apologies. It's just that I'm worried."

"I am worried as well. Worried that my *lieutenant* would get phone calls from another cartel, threatening me. That those *pendejos* choose to reach out with a threat to you, El Tramposo. That is your name, isn't it? 'The tricky one'?"

Navarrete sat quietly, thinking *I would kill you now if I thought I could get away with it, you bastard.* As Blanco eased back into his chair, Navarrete said. "I don't know who called me. I am afraid that someone in *los Zetas* is working for the competition. I've tried to imagine how, with all we pay for electronic security, those animals from Jalisco dug up my cell number."

"Who, then?" asked Blanco.

Navarrete shook his head. "Not our *soldados.* They are uneducated. We need to find out."

"And quickly, Arturo."

Arturo? I'm now Arturo again? A good sign. But not something to be taken for granted. "*Jefe,* if this is really a warning from the Jalisco scum, we can expect a war. We need to be prepared. We must find out where they plan to hit us."

Blanco nodded. "We need to get those shipments across the river. If someone knows how to find you, they may already know where the drugs are being staged to cross into Texas."

*****

A chilly, electronics-ladened room at DEA San Antonio was full of servers, screens, and monitoring equipment. DEA Agent Art Reyes, fluent in Spanish, played back the recording of his call to Arturo Navarrete, aka El Tramposo.

Breaux kept his head down, as he leaned his elbows on his knees. Eddleman spit Kodiak snuff into a Styrofoam cup. He and Breaux listened to Navarrete's response.

"Any word yet on whether that phone call spooked anyone?" Breaux asked.

Reyes said, "Some phone traffic from another source, a hundred or so kilometers south of Acuña, then EPIC says it got satellite photos of three vehicles turning off Mexico 29 and into some hills toward what we think is one of the *Zeta* safe houses."

Breaux turned to Eddleman, grinning. "This may scare them into moving those caches of dope before they're ready to."

"Hope so." Eddleman dribbled more spit into the cup.

Breaux's phone buzzed. "Hey, what's up?"

After a minute, he disconnected, a worried look on his face.

"That was Purdy Kendricks," Breaux announced. "Says it's important. Says an old man is going to kill a bunch of *Zetas* before he dies of cancer."

Shit, Eddleman thought. *Any time Kendricks is involved, it can be guaranteed our plans will go to shit.*

Breaux said, "We need to see him, before someone goes off the reservation and fucks with our plans."

While Breaux spoke with Reyes, Eddleman reached into his pocket and pulled out a heavily creased slip of paper and read it to himself.

Hackamore tree - 375k

Diablo chico - 1.2

Oto's bench - 823k

East vega notch - 228k

Sunset Y - 1.7

And many more caches. He smiled and said to Breaux, "I guess we need to head toward Kickapoo County, partner.

Chapter 25

Jagir provides a meal, and Purdy hatches a plan

"**A**re you sure?" Breaux asked of my question.

"Trust me," I replied. "If the man says he's going to kill *Zetas*, he means it."

Breaux's hesitancy was pissing me off, but I didn't have the time or inclination to get into Teofilo's background. "You remember the Mexican several of us fished out of the Rio Grande, head blown off, guts hanging out, just downriver from Lagrimas?"

"Sure," Breaux replied. "As I recall, we tied his death in with the killings on the Griffin Ranch."

"We sure did. The dead man in the river was Teo's grandson."

"You're kidding. So, this indigenous guy from somewhere in Mexico is using the grandson's death as a reason to kill people? Sounds like a stretch to me."

"I don't give a shit what you think, Breaux." I sat on the bed in Room Four of the Paradise Inn, the barely adequate space suffused with the sound of a rattling window air conditioner, hoping no one was in adjoining rooms to overhear my end of the conversation through the motel's paper-thin walls. I tried to explain. "He's going into Mexico, with or without me. You just told me that the DEA is trying to determine where some big loads are crossing. If you want Teo to fuck things up, then, hell, I'll come home. I'm in deep shit with my wife and kid right now, anyway." I paused. "But someone's got to figure out how to stop Teo."

"You want to go with him?"

I couldn't believe what I was hearing. "You are shitting me, aren't you?"

Breaux spat a laugh. "Of course, but I bet you've thought about it."

"Honestly? It's crossed my mind." *Did I just admit to that?*

Breaux muttered something, and I realized he wasn't talking to me.

"Eddleman with you?" I asked.

"Yep. We're on our way to you. We'll meet you someplace. Sheriff's Office?"

I thought about it, then said, "No. I'll call you back." I disconnected, then called Lowell Johnson. "I need your office for a few minutes later tonight."

"Sure. What's going on?"

"Can't say. Leave the key under the doormat in the back, okay? Stay gone for a couple of hours."

"Christ, Purdy. This cloak and dagger shit is getting out of hand."

I thanked him, disconnected, then called Breaux. *"Courier*. Back door. Park behind the building."

In the motel office, Jagir Patel was holding court with several kinfolk, speaking in an Indian dialect. I wondered if he understood the irony of his modest motel's name – Paradise.

When the door shut, the group quieted. "How do you like your room, Purdy?" Jagir asked.

"Just great, Jagir." The smell of curry was overwhelming. Despite my stress, I was salivating.

"Some more folks coming," I said. "I'm going to need another room."

In his lilting accent, Jagir assured me that my business was appreciated. He handed me a key to Room Five and yelled a string of words I didn't understand at the rear part of the office. Soon, a large plate of chicken and rice appeared on the counter.

"Eat. Eat. You look worried, my friend. Food is good for you. I know you are a busy man, but you must take sustenance."

Where did he learn 'sustenance'? This ten-cent word wasn't something commonly used in Santa Rosa.

His eyes, deep set in the folds of dark, chiseled features, showed genuine concern. I wanted to hug him. Instead, I took the proffered plastic fork, realizing I hadn't eaten all day. A woman appeared in the doorway and joined Jagir and the others. They said nothing and merely stared while I wolfed down the food.

The woman, of indeterminate age, wore a sari and her forehead showed the *bindi*, or dot, signifying she was a married Hindu. I realized I was looking at Jagir's wife, who I had only seen once, right after I'd moved back to Kickapoo County. Embarrassed by my lack of manners, I wiped my mouth on the back of my sleeve and introduced myself, apologizing as I did so.

"No need, Purdy. No need." Jagir translated, and his wife shyly extended her ring encrusted hand for me to shake.

I gently took it and thanked her and Jagir. Waving goodbye, I walked to my truck. I told myself, *Purdy, you're wound too tight. Take a breath. Calm down.*

From a block south of US 90, I watched Lowell exit the back door of the *Kickapoo County Courier*, climb into his pickup, and drive off. I moved into his vacant parking spot, retrieved the key, and unlocked the door.

Now all I had to do was fret. No way could I keep my promise to get home. I called Betty who was still at the real estate agent's office.

"Something has come up," I said. "I'll make it up to you, but I'm stuck here." Fortunately, the agent agreed to email me the contract for my signature.

I sat in Lowell's desk chair. He'd left on his computer. I opened my email, downloaded the document to the desktop, then glanced through the several pages, wincing at the price and the expected down payment "If I want to keep a family, I'd better sign this," I said aloud. I did so electronically and punched *send*.

I still had an hour to kill, so I put in the earbuds, punched *play*, and eased back as Helen Humes' 1948 cover of *Today I Sing the Blues* washed over me. "...my lonely room. I didn't know why..." The lyrics hit me hard. My family was waiting for me in Austin, and I was sitting in the dark in someone's rundown office. Tears welled in my eyes.

The song ended, and for a few seconds, I heard the *chuk shee chuk shee chuk shee* of the needle tracing the grooves. A newer digital recording hadn't completely erased scratches on the old 78 rpm vinyl record. "I'm feeling mighty lonesome," Sarah Vaughn began in *Black Coffee*. Two late- night blues downers were more than I could manage, so I pulled the earbuds out, and shut my eyes. Just a few minutes of rest, I thought. Just to unwind.

*****

"Hey! You in here?"

Breaux's voice startled me. It was inky black outside. I checked the time on my cell phone. I'd been asleep for over two hours.

"I'm here. Come on in." I stood, tucking in my shirt, and slicking back my hair with my hands.

The office's backroom light clicked on, and the heavy thump of boots sounded on the *Courier*'s wooden floor. For the first time in over two years, I stood face to face with DEA Agent Jack Eddleman. He didn't offer a hand to shake, and I didn't make any attempt either, instead aiming a curt nod in his direction.

I detected a slight smirk from Eddleman who stepped back so Breaux and I could shake hands.

After a few uncomfortable moments, Breaux plopped down on Lowell's ratty sofa. Eddleman stepped toward the coffee bar, reappearing with an empty Styrofoam cup. After tapping his snuff tin, he shoved a large pinch of Kodiak under his lip.

Breaux initiated the conversation. "We'd been stirring up some shit with *los Zetas* when you called."

"Why?" I asked.

"Hoping we might make them do something to show us what they're up to," he explained. "Pretending to be some of the Jalisco cartel."

I was confused and said so.

"They've got two loads hidden somewhere near the border. We don't know which load will cross over first, or if they'll send all at the same time. Nothing recently on satellite."

"We were hoping to spook them," Eddleman added, startling me.

I walked to the coffee bar, poured fresh grounds into the Bunn, and added water from the sink faucet. I needed a jolt of caffeine. "So, what are we going to do about Teofilo?" I asked.

Eddleman started to respond, and I cut him off. "And don't say we need to kill the old man," I yelled.

"Easy. Easy," Breaux cautioned. "We're on the same side here, remember." He raised both palms in surrender.

I rinsed three ceramic cups and filled them with coffee. Handing out the cups, I said, "I'm not going to go too much into it, but Teofilo had something to do with saving my wife and child from being kidnapped." I looked at the two DEA agents. "You fellows remember when *los Zetas* nearly grabbed Betty and Forrest, don't you?"

Breaux nodded. "I remember the incident, and your wife's good shooting, but don't remember anything about this Teofilo fellow."

I'd said too much, and I didn't offer any more. "Anyway, any ideas on how to keep him from upsetting whatever the DEA's got planned?"

Breaux nodded. "Can you get him over on this side of the border again?"

"I'm supposed to meet him tomorrow about dusk if I'm going to help him kill *sicarios*," I said. "We're meeting in Lagrimas."

Breaux and Eddleman glanced at each other, and I realized I'd hit on a plan that might keep Teofilo from getting killed.

"You guys too fancy to hide in a filthy, run-down adobe hut?" I asked.

"Why?" Eddleman asked, snuff bulging under his lower lip. He raised the Styrofoam cup and spit snuff into it.

"How about we kidnap a Mexican citizen and put him under wraps?" I responded.

"Jesus. Are you serious? Who's going to take care of the man if we do this?" Breaux asked.

I thought of my old friend, Jake Nichols. He owed me a favor. "I know just the *hombre*."

The Paradise Inn was hardly that, but it was the only motel in town, the rooms were clean, and Jagir appreciated the new business I brought him. I handed the Room 5 key to Breaux and told him I was going to get some sleep.

But first, I needed to recruit Jake Nichols. His phone rang seven times before he answered.

"You still awake?" I asked.

Groggily, Jake assured me he was.

"I'm heading to your house. Be there in a short."

"Where are you?"

"Paradise." Five minutes later, I pulled up to Jake's house. Darkness helped hide some of the place's shabbiness. For a moment, a wave of sadness enveloped me. If Jake had been given a fair shake growing up, he wouldn't be holed up in Santa Rosa, Texas. He had the brains to complete any course of study at a university. I remember urging him to enroll at Texas A&M. "We could be roommates," I told him, although Jake's sloppiness was already evident. "You've got the brains, and Momma and I will help you fill out scholarship and grant applications."

Jake's mother was still alive then, and she'd shielded him from his drunken father until the old man's death. My pleading fell on deaf ears.

"I'll just work for a little while, Purdy, and join you next year," he'd said.

It never happened.

Now, I was a lawman, and I was going to ask Jake to commit a crime.

The front door opened, and the porch light came on.

"Come on in, Purdy. What's up?"

I sat at the kitchen table and gave him a half-cocked smile. "I need you to help me kidnap someone."

Jake plopped onto the sofa. Instead of an expression of incredulity, he merely nodded. "Okay, who?"

"A Mexican gentleman who is brave as a lion but will get himself killed unless I stop him." I then filled in the details. I hoped he'd kick up a fuss. All I got was an expression of doubt.

"Gee, Purdy, sounds possible, but once you've trussed him up and handed this Teofilo fellow over to me, what do I do with him? And for how long?"

"We can use old man Griffin's place," I said, handing Jake a key to the ranch's front gate.

"The Vasquez house is shot to hell," he countered.

"No, the old headquarters. The house still has electricity, and I'll be sure there's food in the refrigerator."

Jake broke into an uneasy grin. "You're not going to make us stay in the bedroom where that sniper got blown to pieces, are you?"

"We cleaned up the place." I grimaced, remembering the viscera and blood from the shotgun blasts that ripped apart the body of a contract sniper. "There's a fold out couch in the living room."

"I can do it," Jake replied. "As long as I don't have to go in that bedroom. You forget, I saw all those pictures of the body." He shivered. "That room's gotta be spooked, for sure."

Chapter 26

The abandoned adobe house. The unexpected truck

We decided the DEA agents would leave the truck they came in parked at the Paradise Inn. The fewer unfamiliar vehicles at Lagrimas and the US 90 approaches to the low water crossing, the better. With weapons and gear stowed in my pickup's toolbox, we squeezed into the seat, and I headed west. I dropped off Breaux and Eddleman, along with their gear, at the crumbling adobe structure and drove my pickup down to the— illegal since 9/11— low water crossing. The murky river gurgled, running about a foot over its rocky bottom. It'd be easy to cross right now, then hunt for Teofilo. But I was worried that maneuver would scare him off.

Instead, I sat in the truck, the engine off and windows rolled down, listening to the pings of the hot hood's metal contracting. The Rio Grande's susurrations were hardly audible. The cane near the riverbank suddenly stirred with gusts of cool air. I turned toward the sun's setting rays. They announced the formidable beauty of a looming thunderhead. Idly, I wondered if its rain would bless the parched land.

It was time to call Abner. Cell coverage this close to the river at Lagrimas was spotty. I considered backing up to US 90, a few hundred feet higher in elevation, but was pleasantly surprised when I got two bars on my phone.

I punched in the ranger's cell.

"Please tell me you aren't in Mexico right now," he said.

"Close. Lagrimas."

"Why?"

I told Abner I intended to grab Teofilo and, with Jakes' help, keep him under wraps for a while. "Maybe he'll cool off. But in the meantime..."

"Grab him? How?"

"Well—"

Abner interrupted. "Are you by yourself?"

I explained that there were two DEA agents hidden, waiting to help me pull off the kidnapping. I also shared that the DEA was stirring up *los Zetas* with faked phone threats, wanting to see if the cartel exposed any of its crossing points.

"You're there with Breaux — who I can tolerate, and Eddleman — who is lower than a snake's belly. And no other backup?"

It wasn't framed as a question, so I didn't respond.

"What's Jake gonna do with Teofilo?" he demanded. "Point a gun at the Mexican's head? How's he getting off work for this little fiasco? 'Hey, Sheriff, I'm just a pissant dispatcher, but I need time off so I can kidnap an old man dying of cancer?'"

Abner's sarcasm felt like a blast of hot air exploding through the cell phone. Trying to justify the plan wasn't going to do any good. Besides, I was having second thoughts about it anyway.

"I'm about thirty minutes out. Let me know where to meet so I don't scare off Teofilo," Abner said. He sounded resigned to the situation.

"I've barely got coverage down in this hole," I reminded him. "The cell gods are cooperating for the moment. I'm going to pull back up the hill now that Teo's had time to spot my truck. He knows I'm in the area. You'll see my truck at the old service station just off US 90. Park next to mine and we'll walk down toward Lagrimas together. I'll tell Breaux you're coming."

"Good idea. I don't want either of those bastards shooting me and then saying it was an accident." He disconnected.

When I started the engine, my phone vibrated. Breaux.

"We've got more agents heading this way," he said.

I thought that was a damned good idea and said so. "At some point, Breaux, we've got to let local law enforcement in on some of this."

He agreed. "If we have time. Seems the phone threats to the *Zeta* second-in-command, Arturo Navarrete, is paying dividends. Satellite photos may have picked up where one of the drug stashes is located. Sending a big drone as close as we can get away with to confirm it." He paused. "The location is ten miles south of the border. An area with some huge boulders and overhangs. We may not have time to ask for local help."

Grabbing Teo would require physical force only, but Breaux had insisted he and Eddleman take all their weaponry with them. I was now thankful they had. I tried Google Earth again. Surprisingly, it loaded, and I two-fingered to enlarge its satellite map.

"Got it on Google Earth. It matches the terrain Teo was telling me about. Just so you know," I said, "Texas Ranger Abner Selman is on his way here. He'll park next to my truck at the abandoned service station and walk down with me to the adobe. Don't shoot us."

Breaux grunted.

"Grunt all you want, but I trust him with my life. Don't know anyone in the DEA I can say that about," I retorted.

"Calm down," Breaux said, backing off. "Is the ranger bringing anyone else?"

I doubted it. "But if *los Zetas* is actually moving a load across, who do they have on this side?"

Suddenly, I heard a tractor trailer rig enter both the phone's speaker and through my pickup's open window. I couldn't see over the lip of the hill in the road to the north. "What the hell is that?" I asked.

Breaux's volume dropped. "Cattle truck pulled off 90 from the west. Turned toward the river, then east and into this burg's open space. Moving up to one of the mobile homes about a football field east of us."

The truck made a hissing noise when its air brakes released and the truck idled.

"Anyone in Lagrimas a long-distance cattle hauler?" Breaux asked.

"Hell, if I know." I'd once known everyone in the town, but not anymore. "The trailer's full of cattle."

Stamping of hooves, a slight waft of manure, and loud bawling confirmed the statement.

"Sign on the cab says *Lopez Cattle Company*, and Canutillo, Texas, as its location," Breaux said. "Came by too fast with too much dust to get any license or permit information, dammit." Then, "Driver's out, taking a piss. You coming up from the river?"

"Right now. See you in a sec." I did a three point turn on the road's narrow surface, and, avoiding raising dust, drove slowly past the cut-off into Lagrimas toward US 90, glancing at the adobe ruin where the two DEA agents were hiding. In the distance, I spied the back end of the cattle trailer. I did a one-eighty just off US 90, then pulled onto the cracked concrete of the abandoned service station once owned by Jake's mom and dad. Two mechanics' bays yawned open, the lifts and overhead doors long gone. I backed in as far as I could go, stopping when I heard the metal bumper crunch into an old, rotting workbench.

Unlocking the cargo box, I retrieved and pulled on a ballistic vest, gathered my shotgun and the M-16. I could faintly hear the cattle-hauler's diesel rumbling in a low idle. My phone buzzed.

Selman was calling. "I'm five out," he said.

"We've got a new development," I replied, and quickly told him of the cattle truck now parked some hundred yards from where Breaux and Eddleman waited for me.

I watched Abner's pickup pull off US 90 from the west and stop next to the raised concrete islands that once held two gas pumps. No doubt he'd come from his fishing camp on the Pecos River, three hours' drive away.

The mountains now partially blocked the sun's rays. The sweet and acrid smell of rain reached my nose. The thunderhead was beginning to collapse. The sunlight contrasted starkly with clouds, almost black with their fullness of moisture.

Abner, pulling on his vest, didn't appear too happy to see me.

"I don't want Teofilo showing up at that 'dobe and getting spooked by the two DEA agents," I said. "If he shows."

My phone buzzed. Breaux again. "There's a Lopez Cattle Company in Canutillo. Probably a legitimate business, but whoever's the owner can make a hell of lot more money running drugs. Where are you?"

"The ranger and I are parked at the old service station. It won't take more than two minutes. I'll call you when we head your way. Please tell me you have it on 'silent.'"

A car zoomed west on US 90, a child in its back seat staring at us. There was little traffic on US 90, but no sense being more obvious than necessary. We strode through crunching shards of broken glass that once was the station's front window, then over the rotten threshold and onto the tiled floor of what had been its office. Dirt daubers buzzed overhead, and a cast-off, molted, snake-skin bore witness to the place's abandonment. Even the graffiti looked tired. I dialed Jake. "Where are you?"

"At my house. Thanks for the food," he said, acknowledging that I had restocked his refrigerator and freezer, and provided a new ice chest. I hadn't had time to make a run to the Griffin place, so I told Jake he'd have to lug groceries and water with him, if we grabbed Teofilo.

I'd forgotten to provide Jake with handcuffs to manacle Teo to a bed if necessary. "No problem." Jake had thought of it and had 'borrowed' a pair from the Sheriff's Office inventory. Satisfied that I was as ready as I could be, I told Jake to head toward Lagrimas, then disconnected.

The day's heat slowly relented. Suddenly, the idling tractor's engine changed tone as its rpms ramped up. I called Breaux.

"What?" he whispered, as if anyone could hear his voice over the diesel engine.

"Is the truck leaving?" I asked.

"Wait one," he said. "Looks like the rig is turning around."

It would take the truck several drives forwards and backs, even in the desert and Lagrimas' sparsity of houses. The gravel road to the river crossing sat in a depression which would allow Abner and me to reach the abandoned adobe without being seen, but we agreed to hang tight until we knew the intentions of the cattle truck's driver.

Five minutes later, the diesel rig's engine quieted.

Breaux again. I put him on the speaker. "Driver's killed the engine. He's turned on an inside light." A pause. "Looks like he's climbing into the sleeper. This may be the American side contact."

A possibility hit me. "*Los Zetas.* You say you stirred them up. Could this rig be used to haul a load of drugs?" I knew the answer before Breaux spoke.

"Fucking a, it could."

"Aw shit," I said. "This is turning into a nine-line bind." I wanted to save Teofilo's life and, at the same time make sure he didn't screw up the DEA's attempt at scoring what could be a huge drug bust. "If Teo shows up, just grab him," I barked.

Abner leaned toward the phone. "Would the DEA grab these guys at the border, or follow the dope and take it down somewhere else?"

Breaux responded. "We don't have a snitch to protect on this one, at least as far as I know. That said, it'd make a whole lot more sense to take the load down away from the border. Too high a possibility of a shoot-out here."

I nodded. "If we don't get Teo out, and fast, he'll blow your plans to hell and back, and get himself killed." Cold sweat trickled down the center of my back. Abner and I nodded at the same time.

I prayed silently as the sunlight waned. If a load of drugs was moving toward Lagrimas, the reasonable thing to do, if you were a Mexican, was to get the hell out of the way. Teofilo wasn't reasonable.

The crunch of tires on gravel announced Jake's arrival. He exited his tired looking pickup quietly, then entered the station's old office. A strange expression crossed his face. "It's been years since Momma and I ran this place, Purdy. You know enough to know why I've made it a point of never coming in this godforsaken building." He took a deep breath, let it out, and shook his head. "But here I am."

I gave him a bone crusher of a hug, whispering "Thanks. I'm going to head toward the adobe. Abner, why don't you stay here with Jake? It'll get crowded in that adobe if more than one of us goes."

Two minutes later, I stepped into the adobe hut's darkness. The wintergreen scent of Eddleman's snuff filled the air. "Any sign?" I asked.

"Nothing," Breaux responded.

"Damn," was the best I could come up with. "When does the cavalry show up?"

Breaux said, "Don't know. Maybe fifteen minutes. Maybe half an hour."

The three of us stood quietly looking out a frameless window. Darkness brought with it cooler air. Then, we heard the soft padding of sandals.

"Señor Purdy, *'stas aqui?*"

Careful to keep the adobe between me and the diesel's cab, I stepped out, responding in Spanish. "I'm here."

Teofilo's eyes darted suspiciously to the adobe's entrance. "Are you alone, my friend?"

I stepped toward him, gave him a hug, and assured him I was alone. Together, we turned toward the south, and I said, "I'm here to help you."

Teofilo's head drooped. "I was afraid I was going to have to go against those *pinches* alone," he answered.

As he said this, the two DEA agents tackled him. The three of us were barely able to pull him inside the adobe, where Eddleman turned on a flashlight, and I handcuffed him.

He raised his head from the dirt floor. "You deceived me," was all he said.

"That wiry son of a bitch may have cancer," Breaux muttered, "but he's still a tough one. Kicked me in the balls."

There was no time to explain why I'd done what I'd done. No time to justify the shame I felt. I lifted Teofilo to his feet, and the three of us hustled him out of the adobe to the gravel road and then up toward the service station. Teo didn't resist, but he didn't help either.

We half-carried Teo, his huaraches barely scraping the caliche. When we left the dusty road's surface and stepped into the creosote near the service station, the sound of vehicle suspensions rattling on a rough surface overcame the gentle burble of the Rio Grande.

I handed Teofilo to Jake. "Get him the hell out of here, and fast."

Abner Selman and the two DEA agents stared into the distance. In the twilight, we could just make out three vehicles silhouetted on the ridgeline in Mexico. The vehicles crept toward the river.

I prayed *God help us.*

Chapter 27
Odds turn, and sicarios show up

A bolt of lightning flashed, and, before I could say "One Mississippi," an immense crack of thunder assaulted my ears.

Huge drops of rain followed, pelting the ground, creating smoke-like puffs as they agitated the dust. Seconds later, rain roared, overawing any lesser sounds. The lead and tail vehicles approaching over the slight hill were pickup trucks. In the middle, a Humvee with a pedestal mounted machine gun. The three vehicles slowly descended toward the river crossing, then disappeared into a gray sameness.

Oh, Lord. I nervously thumbed the M16 selector switch.

As Breaux, Eddleman, Abner, and I pushed into the shelter afforded by the old service station, I saw the dim headlights of Jake's Ford F150 come on. When he backed onto US 90, I hoped he had a handcuffed Teofilo secured by seatbelt in the front seat. The truck yawed back and forth as Jake overaccelerated on the newly slicked highway. He regained control, and the pickup's taillights disappeared into the maw of darkness.

Within seconds, US 90's shallow bar ditches filled, and rain, discovering the many holes in the station's long-neglected roof, began dripping, then pouring onto our heads. I moved my firearms further into the building but was completely soaked and shivering from the icy water and from the other unknowns.

"Can they cross the river in this?" Breaux asked, almost shouting. "Will the river be too high?"

I shook my head. "Not sure. Unless there's rain upriver, there won't be a rise. It'll all be downriver from here." I reached for my cell phone and punched the weather app. Nothing. The thunderstorm's fierce electrical activity had wiped out Lagrimas' intermittent cell coverage.

I remembered the uncomplicated design of the service station from my childhood – office with storage room, two-bay garage, bathrooms with exterior doors around the back side. The Nichols family had made do with an old single-wide mobile home set to one side. It had long ago disappeared. I shoved open the rotten door into the storage area. By my cell phone light, I confirmed my memory: a small window faced toward Lagrimas.

"Hey, I need some help," I bellowed, and others appeared. I tore at the wood nailed over the window. "We need someplace we can see from," I explained, clawing at a one-by-four nailed tight to the walls on either side of the window.

Breaux brushed me aside. "Found an old tire iron," he shouted. He levered off chunks of wood. Seconds later, the window covering was in pieces, which I helped push out into the rain. Now we had an aperture facing the right direction. But in the downpour, our visibility was only as far as the greasewood clumps just past the old waste oil pit.

"Dammit! We still can't see a damned thing," Breaux said.

Abner disappeared into the deluge, then reappeared carrying a slicker.

"What the hell, Ranger? We're already soaked to the bone," Breaux shouted.

Eddleman wiped the wetness off his Kodiak can, removed the lid, and tongued a glob under his lower lip, seemingly undisturbed. For a moment, I admired the bastard's calm demeanor.

"Someone's got to see what's going on," Abner said, putting on the slicker. I grabbed it out of his hands. "You're not going out in this, Abner. Remember, it's six months 'til your retirement."

That got a guffaw from Breaux. I slid the gray slicker on over my wet clothes.

Eddleman shouted above the storm's roar, "What's your plan?"

The crash of rain slackened for a second, and I thought that, like most West Texas gully washers, this one had run its course. To prove me wrong, the downpour increased, and heavy gusts of wind buffeted the building.

"Unless you guys know where your reinforcements are, it's us against a shitload of *Zetas*, is what I'm betting." I half-racked the slide on my 9mm Glock. Water hadn't gotten into the workings, so it was okay. I cradled the M-16 close to my body.

Abner had untucked his undershirt and was futilely searching for dry cloth. "I don't want Purdy or me to get shot to hell. Breaux, do you have any information on who'd mule the dope out of here?"

Both DEA agents shook their heads. "No idea," Breaux said. "If this rain abates, we can find out quick enough. None of us needs to get shot. We can track the tractor-trailer and pull it over somewhere on US 90. Use the Border Patrol. They don't need a search warrant."

"I'll sneak through the greasewood and see if the Mexicans have crossed," I said, sounding much braver than I felt. "If we're lucky, this rain has spooked them. Maybe they'll wait to cross. Buy us some time. At least we'll have an idea of what to expect."

Nods all around. I was hoping someone would have a better idea.

"Stay low," Abner said, "Don't try to be a hero. We'll cover you best we can from the window. You should be okay for a look-see. But if the rain slacks off, you may stick out like a sore thumb." He squeezed my shoulder, a small assurance that I appreciated.

I eased into the rain, avoiding the dirt road, heading in the general direction of the tractor-trailer. There was no letup to the downpour, and I skittered between clumps of creosote. In seconds, my boots had filled with water.

Vague shapes — three single-wide mobile homes I recalled north and east of the adobe where we'd just taken Teo captive. I veered thirty degrees and spotted the propane tank adjacent to the first trailer. Where was everyone who lived in Lagrimas? Then I remembered that most of the residents worked on ranches or in Santa Rosa. Returning home was problematic. No way would they chance US 90 until the rain stopped.

My mental map of Lagrimas told me I was at the furthest mobile home from the diesel rig. I skirted the ratty structure's wooden steps and moved to the edge of the metal structure. Suddenly, the rig's diesel engine began a low rumble. I squatted down, then peeked. Through sheets of rain appeared a pickup, then another, and then the Humvee, with the pedestal mounted machine gun.

They huddled like suckling pigs around the cattle trailer. Several dark forms, men, moved from the smaller vehicles, carrying plastic-wrapped bundles toward the trailer's lowered rear ramp.

"Huuh! Huuh! Muevete!" one of the *Zetas* hollered.

The stamp of panicked hooved feet said someone was moving inside the transport, shoving cattle out of the way. I crawled underneath the mobile home, thankful no one had bothered to put skirting around the bottom, and hoping some rattlesnake hadn't decided to shelter there as well. I started counting bundles disappearing up the ramp, unsure of how many had already been loaded.

A tiny sliver of open sky widened off to the north.

Time to get the hell out of there. I shoved backward, and stood up, the mobile home between me and the men guarding the rig. I turned and scampered toward the brush line a trailer-length away.

Someone yelled. I didn't know whether to run, fall prone, or freeze. The rain slowed. As the voices continued to yell, and at least one of the smaller vehicles' engines fired up, I realized I hadn't been spotted.

A *sicario* was gesturing toward one of his compadres. *"Necesito cagar, cabrones! Espérame!"*

Now in the scanty concealment of brush, I edged backward as the *sicario*, assured he would not be left in Texas, dropped his trousers and began to take a crap beside the nearest mobile home.

No toilet paper and a wet butt. An odd thought, but everything about the scene was weird. I reached the service station just as a rifle disappeared from the recently re-opened window. I'd made it.

"They're moving stuff in the big transport." I said, breathless with fear and adrenalin. "Two pickups and a Humvee with a machinegun mount. They *did* cross, dammit to hell. They've loaded dope into the back with the cattle."

"That rig'll be heading out onto 90," Eddleman said, laconically. "The driver will see two pickups parked here. He may figure it's just folks waiting for the rain to stop. At the very least, he'll call someone to come check them out."

In an instant, the rain stopped. Eddleman's last words, said loudly to overcome the downpour's roar, reverberated inside the service station. "Damn," he muttered.

"Do you young studs want to tangle with heavily armed cartel members?" Abner asked. "I sure as hell don't."

Breaux glanced out the back window. "Let's get out of here."

I shucked Abner's slicker and reached for my keys. It was time for all of us to let someone else take over. "Hope the cartel's three vehicles go back across the river," I muttered. One cattle hauler from Canutillo, Texas, wouldn't want to tangle with the law, if it came to that.

But for the three loads of *sicarios*? All bets were off.

Chapter 28
Firefight

The summer heat had been replaced by cool, crisp air. Any other time, I'd have savored the rain quickly soaking into the sands and the smell of citrusy oils from the creosote, and I might even have crushed the wet leaves between my palms. Now, I just wished the wispy desert plants were trees large enough to shield our trucks and us from view and Mexican bullets.

The crystalline air carried the sound of the rig's driver shifting it out of neutral. Once out of Lagrimas' muck, the cattle hauler would be on gravel, then at the junction with US 90 in less than a minute.

"Let's move," Abner ordered "Eddleman, you with me. Breaux with Kendricks," We grabbed our firearms and ran.

I'd left my truck's driver's side window down. The seat was soaked. As if that mattered now, but it's funny what went through my mind. I stabbed the key in the ignition switch and started the engine, praying the wind would blow the engine noise away from our unwelcome visitors.

I pulled out of the service station bay. Just a few seconds to US 90's solid surface. Breaux fiddled with his cell phone. "Got coverage," he said.

Three bullets punched through the passenger side window, then exploded the Chevy's windshield. "Holy shit!" I screamed. *How did the rounds miss me?*

Thunk, thunk, thunk. More rounds punched through the Chevy hood's thin sheet metal.

A surge of panic gripped me. I tried to will my truck to leap across the shallow bar ditch and onto the asphalt highway. As the tires spun, I caught a glimpse of Abner's truck. He'd accelerated so hard his vehicle had jumped onto the highway, then slid into the swale on its north side.

I screamed, "Oh, shit! Oh, shit! Oh, shit!"

I cleared the mud-slogged shoulder and bounced onto the highway. But Abner's truck wasn't moving. The rear tires whirred uselessly in the muck. Eddleman had exited the truck, slogged through the mud and somehow made it around to its driver's side. He was dragging the ranger out of the cab. I spun to a stop, my vehicle across both lanes, blocking the highway, I threw open my door and ran to the cover of its passenger side. Breaux appeared next to me. *No way I can leave now.* I flipped the M-16 safety switch and crouched near the front bumper, wondering if I'd lost a dear friend.

In my mind, I was trying to tell where had the shots come from.

Leaning forward near my passenger side headlight. I saw the tractor trailer was nowhere in sight, but a *sicario* pickup now sat at the river road's junction with US 90, shielding several armed men.

"They beat us to the punch, setting up to make sure the rig's driver got that big diesel onto US 90," Breaux yelled.

Relieved that he was still alive, I said, "No shit, Sherlock." I aimed at the *sicarios.* Six quick pulls of the trigger, and I felt immense satisfaction when a scream erupted from one of the armed men. Before I could savor it, my right headlight shattered, sending glass into my face. Leaning back behind a front tire, I palmed embedded glass off my cheeks, my hand now red with blood. *Nothing in my eyes, thank God.*

Breaux screamed into his cell phone. "Get here now. These bastards have us pinned down!"

Lying next to the front tire, I moved the M-16's selector switch to 'automatic' and sank the magazine's remaining rounds into the *sicarios'* vehicle. Rather than return fire, four men bolted from behind its cover. Eddleman raised up from behind Abner's pickup and cut loose a round, and one runner fell, clutching his leg. The remaining three disappeared down the road toward the

Rio Grande. The wounded man tried to stand, then began to hobble after his compadres. I jammed in another magazine, pulled the charging rod, then shot. I missed. Eddleman didn't. The *sicario* appeared to melt into the wet desert sand, then began to crawl back to the cover of the pickup sitting just off the US 90 tarmac.

"Abner!" I yelled as Breaux and I ran the thirty yards to the ranger's truck. "Are you hit?" He sat slumped against the side of his truck.

"Thought I was, Purdy," he called. "Bullet went between my fingers and broke the goddamned steering wheel." He displayed two bloody fingers. "But I almost shit in my pants."

Relief washed over me like a cold shower. I laughed and said a silent prayer of thanks.

Suddenly woozy, I leaned onto Abner's truck. Taking several deep breaths, I glanced at Breaux. He was helping Abner to a standing position. "Where are your goddamned backups?" I asked.

"Coming, but not fast enough." Then, "Where's the cattle truck with the dope?"

Good question. Nearly deaf from gunfire, I couldn't detect the rig's diesel. Where was it?

Eddleman raced toward the *sicarios'* abandoned pickup, then carefully moved to its driver's side. Now blocked from our view, I jumped as a pistol shot echoed. Eddleman reappeared, signaling all clear. I wondered who he had shot.

Gunfire erupted and a volley of rounds flew toward him. Eddleman dove into the wet caliche. Unhurt, he scrambled to his feet in the lee of the now shot-up pickup, pointed toward the river. Bullets pierced the pickup, and smacked the soaked earth around him, throwing chunks of wet dirt into the air.

Eddleman made frantic hand gestures, then ducked as another burst of gunfire erupted from the second set of sicarios. "He's wanting us to help him out," I said.

Breaux chuckled. "We could let him stew for a while, Purdy."

"Love to, for old time's sake," I said, hoping that a bullet would clip off Eddleman's lower lip. We spread out and moved across the highway, using the service station as cover. "What's going on?" I yelled at Eddleman.

"I think they're going to make a run for the river," he yelled back. "I hope they get away, and fast."

Abner wheezed. "I'm getting too old for this nonsense."

"Let 'em go," Breaux added. "We've got the dope."

"That's what I'm trying to tell you," Eddleman yelled. "The Humvee's at the road's entrance into Lagrimas. Like it's standing guard. It's sideways on the gravel. They're trying to take the dope back with them."

A burst of automatic gunfire growled from the heavier weapon on the Humvee. In the dusk, small sparks of lights from the machine gun were followed by howls and whines of ricochets. We crouched below terrain level to keep from getting shot.

I'd watch the loading process. It had appeared time consuming and arduous. "That dope is in with the cattle!" I yelled. "What're they going to do with the cows?"

Hooves scrambling on rock announced the *sicarios'* intentions. Spooked, bug-eyed bovines frantically scattered through the desert in all directions.

I saw an opportunity and Abner and I cut cross-country on the same path I'd followed earlier into Lagrimas, heading toward the diesel rig, now parked next to the abandoned adobe where we'd grabbed Teofilo. At least seven *sicarios* swarmed the now-empty trailer and humped the bundled drugs out and into the bed of the cartel's remaining pickup.

The pedestaled machine gun opened up from the Humvee. Abner and I were shielded from the gunner's view by a mobile home and several old adobe structures. Occasional pops from Eddleman's firearm were keeping that crew occupied, focusing fire on the vehicle he stooped behind.

We crouched, much too close to the human feces left by the *sicario* who'd relieved himself. Abner looked at me and shrugged his shoulders, as if to say, "What now?"

Before I could formulate a plan, a *sicario* yelled at the pickup driver. *"Ya! Es todo!"* They'd succeeded in reloading the bundles into the back of the pickup.

Three Mexicans ran down the cattle trailer's ramp, then climbed on top of the bundles of drugs in the pickup. Its wheels hurling gravel and mud, the pickup sped toward the road leading to the low water crossing.

I ran toward the rig, pushing back fear of an ambush. The rig's owner/driver or whoever he was, late of Canutillo, Texas, lay sprawled next to the cab. The recently soaked ground seemed reluctant to absorb the blood and brain matter splattered on it. The price of his suspected betrayal had been a bullet between the eyes.

Eddleman appeared, out of breath. "The *Zetas* are at the river. Looks like it's come up at least three feet, but they're trying to cross."

Suddenly spent, I replied, "I don't care. We're alive. And that's a miracle."

Breaux had other plans. He shouted wildly. "I don't give a shit about those Mexicans, but by God, I'm not going to let them get that poison back into Mexico! Who'll help me stop them?"

"You must be out of your fucking mind!" I yelled back.

He trotted toward the crossing.

"Shit," I muttered. "Let's help."

The four of us edged toward the gravel road where the anxious chatter of the *sicarios* crept over the roar of the Rio Grande on a rise. I hit the ground, crawled like a snake, and peered down at the crossing. The Humvee had abandoned its defensive position and made it through the rising waters to the safety of Mexico. Its driver had gotten it turned around, and it now faced north, perched at the water's edge. The reason was obvious. The pickup with the dope in its bed had stalled, water to the top of its front tires.

Two *sicarios* crouched on top of the pickup's bundles of drugs, warily clutching automatic weapons, eyes scanning for targets. Someone had flung a rope from the Humvee, and three men, two in water to their waists, and the other kneeling on the hood, were desperately trying to tie the rope so the Humvee could pull the truck through the water. The pickup's driver remained in his seat, screaming orders to the three who were trying to secure the rope without being swept downriver.

Losing millions of dollars in drugs would result in slow and painful deaths for those men. They had a strong motivation to retrieve the packages.

I took aim at the back window of the pickup, took a deep breath, then released it. Tap, tap, tap. The M-16's kick was comforting. The driver's head exploded into a fine mist. The *sicario* on the pickup hood looked our way and screamed. He handed the tow rope to two others who ducked, either to avoid getting shot, or searching for somewhere to lash the rope's end.

Breaux calmly shot the man on the hood, who fell and disappeared into the river.

Two down, four to go on this side of the river.

Abandoning the pickup's bed, two jumped from the bundled drugs onto the ground, and began firing wildly.

The Humvee boiled with activity. The machine gun began a deadly chatter, spraying dirt and caliche near us. As the big gun swept away, both *sicarios* working with the tow rope were furiously signaling to the Humvee. They'd succeeded in affixing the tow rope. They quickly climbed through the pickup's open windows. One pushed the driver's door open, and the dead driver's headless body fell into the boiling current.

Abner tapped me on the shoulder. "Take out the machine gun. We'll try to kill the Humvee's driver."

I moved a few yards to my left and onto a mound of soaked earth. A horrible idea, as it erupted with angry red ants. Ignoring their bites, I took a breath, let it out, and fired. The machine gunner, as if pulled by an invisible rope, flew backwards, and disappeared inside the Humvee. Another *sicario*, more ant bites, and another shot. That Mexican went down. No one else tried to man the gun.

Breaux, Eddleman, and Abner poured round after round into the Humvee. Its driver, seemingly protected by the bulletproof windshield, began backing, taking up slack in the rope, and gently pulling the disabled truck further into the river.

The Humvee suddenly stalled. The windshield's protection failed under the hail of bullets. The Mexicans near the pickup's hood dove into the angry water, reaching for the tow rope. One grabbed and missed, screamed in panic, and disappeared under the roiling water. The other pulled himself toward Mexico. Oblivious to my danger, I stood and screamed, and I put two bursts of 5.56 mm rounds in his direction. The river frothed as my bullets tattooed its waters. Another spray of blood and viscera floated on the surface, and he was gone.

A *sicario* yanked the Humvee door open, and its driver's body flopped out, as if unsupported by bones. The *sicario* screamed something, and he and another man bolted up the embankment and over its rise, into a most uncertain future.

The river gulped at the partly submerged pickup. Steam rose from the Humvee's hood, the coolant system perforated. Were there any more *Zetas*?

"Get down, Purdy!" Abner yelled. "You've been screaming like a banshee. You'll get yourself shot like that."

As if to confirm my stupidity, gunshots from this side of the Rio Grande erupted, simultaneously with the gentle whipping sound of bullets narrowly missing my head. I threw myself into the wet ground.

"The two near the pickup," I remembered. I chanced a glance and let loose another flurry of automatic gunfire.

I heard a gentle oomph. The sound seemed of no consequence, and I ignored it as I tried to get an idea where the sicarios were hiding.

"They're running," Breaux said. He stood and unloaded his pistol's clip. His targets were untouched as they threw down their automatic weapons and splashed into the Rio Grande.

And suddenly, the battle was over. The Rio Grande, ignoring humanity's foibles, continued to push its waters toward the Gulf of Mexico, hardly hindered by a pickup foundering in its course.

Grinning, I saw that the truck's huge trove of drugs would be easily recoverable. We'd won.

"Purdy," Breaux yelled. "I've called 911, and also alerted Austin to get here quick."

Puzzled, I turned. Breaux was kneeling in the mud, cradling Abner's head in his lap. Foaming blood spilled from the ranger's mouth.

Chapter 29

Back-up arrives, but is it too late?

The distant whomp, whomp, whomp signaling a helicopter's approach somehow made its way through the buzz that reechoed in my gunfire-deafened ears. I'd left Abner lying in Breaux's arms and ran toward my pickup that was still blocking US 90.

When I neared my pickup, two cars sat on US 90 facing east, their occupants standing outside and staring slack-jawed at the bullet riddled pickups.

"Hey, mister! Can we help?" yelled a balding, heavy-set man wearing a I ♥ Texas t-shirt.

Ignoring the Samaritan, I shoved open my Chevy's cargo box and furiously pawed through camping gear and tools until I found my first aid kit. I grabbed it and turned to run back to where Abner lay.

A sedan braked furiously, swerving to miss me. I barely noticed. "DEA," yelled its driver. She stepped from the driver's seat, an Uzi-like automatic pistol hanging from a shoulder strap. "Where's everyone?"

Ignoring her, I ran, praying my tiny amount of first aid equipment would somehow save my dear friend's life.

A massive downdraft from the helicopter's rotating blades blew water out of the recent rain puddles. It flared and began its vertical descent, four DEA camouflaged and helmeted DEA agents perched in its open side entrances. Ducking instinctively, I turned and screamed, "Where were you fuckers when we needed you?" Blade noise and the whine of the bird's turbine ensured that I wasn't heard.

Breaux had Abner partly propped up, and I tried futilely to open the kit 's plastic top. When the helicopter's skids squatted in the mud, its engine began to unspool. and the wind died. I still managed to spill half the first aid kit's contents onto the mud next to Abner.

"I'll be okay," he muttered, his mouth frothing bright with blood as he tried to assure us. One of the last rounds, fired blindly by panicking, fleeing *sicarios*, had found a way to avoid Abner's protective vest. Blood-soaked Breaux's pants legs and the ground beneath the two men. My guess was Abner was lung-shot.

We were in the middle of nowhere and needed to get Abner to a hospital before he died. Abner's face became almost translucent. His body began to shiver. For a second, I thought he was having a seizure, then realized he'd gone into shock and his body temperature had dropped. He was freezing to death in the early dusk of a Texas summer.

Oh God, I prayed. *Please let this man live*. I'd heard them said by victims' families in Houston. I'd listened to the anguished pleas of family members as a son bled out after a gang shooting in the barrio. I'd waited for ambulances at highway collisions when I was a deputy with Kickapoo County Sheriff's Office and seen the life ebb from mangled bodies.

"Get out of the way!" came a voice behind me.

I was pushed aside, and almost fell on my face. A tough-looking man knelt beside Abner, a large paramedic's kit next to him. "Are you a Texas Ranger?" he asked.

I stood up, way too fast. I blacked out and stumbled, but consciousness returned, and I remained erect. No one was paying any attention to me. The twilight was almost gone and the strobing of white lights from emergency vehicles seemed to fill the spaces around the melting adobes of Lagrimas. Several persons crowding around Ranger Selman, nearly obscured him. One brawny fellow furiously pulled off Abner's vest and applied pressure to the bleeding wound while another held an IV bag aloft, its clear line extending into Abner's arm. A third listened with a stethoscope to Abner's chest. Numerous flashlights wielded by a host of officers created a macabre scene of lights and darks — some darks with the reflective shine of fresh blood.

Two more figures appeared, rolling a gurney. The helicopter turbine suddenly howled. As its rotor blades turned, lights from the many cars and trucks that had appeared bounced off the surrounding land and vehicles like a kaleidoscope.

"We've got a pulse! Quick. On the stretcher and into the bird." This from the paramedic who'd shoved me out of the way. I somehow got close enough to the scrum to lift Abner's left leg as it fell off the stretcher, now being hoisted by four individuals.

"Go. Go. Go!" a medic hollered.

Seemingly hours later —but only long enough to secure him inside the aircraft — the chopper lifted and banked toward the north.

"They're taking him to San Antonio. One of the trauma centers there." Breaux stood next to me.

I began to sob uncontrollably, then slumped to the ground. *Get ahold of yourself, Purdy.* I finally stood and walked to the edge of the cut to Lagrimas' low water crossing. A commercial wrecker from Santa Rosa was parked uphill from the *Zetas'* pickup. The pickup bed was empty. *Where were the bundles of drugs?* I wondered.

As it slowly backed, the wrecker's taillights bounced off Eddleman, the DEA agent's face appeared as an evil glow that seemed fitting. The wrecker driver said something, Eddleman nodded, and a steel cable was attached. Slowly, the waterlogged pickup emerged out of the Rio Grande.

"Hey, Purdy Kendricks."

I recognized the voice but couldn't see who had spoken until the man turned on a small electric lantern. Sheriff Thomas Jefferson Johnson, Kickapoo County's elected sheriff, stalked toward me, two deputies in tow.

"You want to tell me what's been going on in my county, Kendricks?" In the brightness of the lantern, TJ's face was florid with anger. "A goddamned DEA operation, a Texas Ranger maybe dying, and Mex drug runners all over the damned place. And no one bothered to tell me shit! Who in hell do you bastards think you are?"

I was too worried for Abner, and too tired to argue. "Talk to the DEA boys," I said, and pointed toward a gaggle of men and women, all wearing distinctive windbreakers. "I've gotta go."

US 90 was a confusing mess. Abner's truck was half-cocked in the bar ditch, mine blocking both lanes of traffic. Deputies with flashlights waved traffic onto the eastbound shoulder. Rubbernecking drivers stared at the bullet-riddled metal carcasses.

I needed to get out of there. I needed to get to San Antonio. I needed to call my wife and assure her I was alive. No way was that going to happen in my pickup. It was part of a crime scene investigation.

"Shit, where's my cell phone?" I muttered, patting pants and shirt pockets until I felt its rectangular shape. As I pulled it free, the screen lit up. Betty was calling.

"Hey, Hon," It sounded as stupid as it felt. "How are you and Forrest?"

"Dear God in heaven, Purdy. Where are you? What's happening?" Betty's voice quivered with fear. "Kickapoo County's all over the news. A San Antonio news station is showing iPhone videos sent in from folks on US 90. The station says there's been a huge shoot-out. They can't even pronounce Lagrimas right." She went on and on, then finally winding down. "Were you involved in that?" Her question sounded like an accusation.

"Somewhat," I said.

"Are you okay? Was anyone hurt?"

"I'm fine. Just tired." I paused. "But Abner Selman..." I couldn't finish. My chin began to quiver uncontrollably. "He's ..."

"Dead?" Betty asked, quietly.

"Mom, when's Daddy coming home?" Forrest's voice from the background.

"Hush, honey. I'm talking to him now." She returned to me. "Is he?"

"He's hurt bad, Betty. I'm praying he'll make it. He was shot through the lung, I think. He's being medevacked to San Antonio now."

"Oh, dear God. Oh, dear God. Your son needs a father. I need a husband. This isn't the time, I know, for me to rant and rave. But we moved out of Kickapoo County because of what's going on there right now. You almost died there. I don't need to remind you what Forrest and I went through." She hesitated a long moment, then asked, "When will you be home?"

My night was just beginning. "As soon as I get cut loose here, I'll be home," I promised, and wondered what to expect when I arrived.

Chapter 30

Purdy makes two unpleasant visits

It was six in the morning before the Lagrimas crime scene was cleared. Bleary-eyed from exhaustion, and jittery from too many cups of brackish coffee, I climbed into Lowell Johnson's pickup.

"Thanks for coming," I mumbled, suddenly chilled by the desert's dry morning air.

"Wouldn't have missed it," Lowell cackled. "Give me an exclusive, and I'll make you famous again."

I shook my head.

"Sorry, Purdy. You've been through the wringer. What can I do for you?"

"Fix my truck," I said. "And my marriage, and somehow keep Abner alive."

Bright oranges dappled the low hills to the north, announcing another hot Texas day. The dawn's beauty was a stark contrast to my dark mood.

Lowell grabbed his Walgreens-bought, cataract-patient sunglasses from the pickup's center console and shoved on the oversized lenses, just as the eastern sky lit up. He looked like a bug. "Can't do much for any of those things," he said. Then, "Hey!"

"Huh?"

"You'd drifted off. You hear what I said?"

"Something about letting me borrow a truck," I responded, pretending I hadn't fallen asleep. "Thanks. I've got to get to San Antonio, and fast."

Lowell shook his head. "This may not be the best time, but I've got to ask you – did that killing of Israel on my ranch lead to that clusterfuck in Lagrimas?"

I shook my head. "Maybe, but I'm not sure. Still trying to connect the dots on why someone would draw attention with what was done to Israel, then try to run dope through the same county it happened in."

Lowell pulled into the gravel parking lot of the Cenizo Diner. "You're going to get something to eat before I let you go anywhere," he announced, shutting off the engine and climbing out.

My phone buzzed. Harris Whittaker was on the line I almost ignored the call, thought better of it, and connected. "What?"

"I know it's been a rough night, but I'm in San Antonio. Abner's through his surgery, and it looks like he's going to make it."

"Oh, thank God. I'll be there as soon as I can," I replied.

"Thought you'd like to hear that," Whittaker responded. "Take your time. Get some rest."

"Okay," I said, "but I'll be there to check on him."

"Drink some coffee first," Whittaker said, and disconnected.

Once again, I was puzzled by Abner's relationship with this huge man from Colorado, and once again, I'd forgotten to ask him about it.

Relieved, I followed Lowell into the diner, the smell of its hot griddle mixing with the pungent aroma of countertop cleansers. I was still too groggy to worry about Beulah Jackson. I'd been avoiding her because of Lilly Pardo, and I idly wondered if Beulah's waitress would ever return to Santa Rosa. I wondered if she was aware of Teofilo's appearance on the American side of the border. Remembering her worries about his health, I doubted it, sure she would have called me had she known. The gossipers' table was full, and its occupants paused their discussions when we walked in, then started back up in hushed tones.

Steering me toward a booth, Lowell said, "Well, you sure make folks speechless when you hit Kickapoo County."

"Think any of these folks remember me as a meek, God-fearing youth, respectful and full of promise?"

"Nah. You've pretty much blurred that image as your body count has risen."

The diner's tinny bell rang, announcing two women in suits, followed by two scruffy-looking men. All wore plastic IDs. Through the open door, I spotted a van sporting a sophisticated antenna, and WOAI stenciled on its side.

"Surprised WOAI took so long," Lowell muttered. "Two other stations already have crews here. Spotted one bunch heading west on 90 when you nodded off to sleep."

Beulah waved from the kitchen, but otherwise ignored me. Relieved, I ate my bacon and eggs in silence, hoping I wouldn't get noticed by the news crew. No luck. A beautiful Hispanic woman, with heavy makeup for television, stood and walked to our booth.

"Aren't you Purdy Kendricks?"

Lowell jumped up with a toothy smile and introduced himself and his newspaper. "Lowell Johnson, at your service. Perhaps you've heard of me. I'm the publisher of the *Kickapoo County Courier*." He flashed a smile fit for a door-to-door vacuum cleaner salesman. "This isn't Purdy. It's his younger brother, ma'am."

The woman showed her media badge. It read Sylvia Rincon. She smiled back. "Do I look that stupid, Mr. Johnson? I may be young and the most beautiful Chicana you'll ever see in your life, but I've been in the business for a few years. I know Purdy Kendricks. My station covered the big shoot-out down here in Kickapoo County two years ago."

The woman had grit. I caught myself grinning. Wearily, I reached up and shook her hand. "Purdy Kendricks. What can I do for you?"

"May I?" Sylvia Rincon motioned toward Lowell's vacated seat. It wasn't so much a request as a command for Lowell to get out of the way. She slid into the booth. She oozed sensuality and knew it. "Just looking for a story. Were you involved with the big shootout and drug bust?" Her dark eyes were captivating.

"No," I shook my head. "Down here, heading to my ranch," I lied. "Mr. Johnson's got a prize bull he's willing to sell me."

Showing perfect white teeth, the reporter threw back her head and gave a throaty laugh. "That's bull-*shit*, of course." She leaned forward, her breasts nestling comfortably on top of her crossed arms. "Coincidence, Mr. Kendricks?"

"Probably, Ms. Rincon. What I hear is that drug bust in Lagrimas was a DEA operation." I glanced nervously at the news crew who were standing a few feet back. At least none had lugged a camera or microphone into the café.

Lowell made a face at the woman.

She laughed and laid a perfectly manicured hand on my arm. "And no, we're not going to ambush you two with cameras and mics when you come out the door." She handed me a business card. "But if you have something worth telling, my station will be glad to air it."

She stood sinuously and walked to a table and sat, her crew joining her. I held up her business card. Even it smelled of temptation.

"Get the shit-eating grin off your face," Lowell said. "Everyone in here knows who you are, and that you're married. By noon, your sister-in-law, Paula, will know everything that happened here, through the filter of all the hens at the CutNCurl."

The air conditioner worked in Lowell's ranch truck that he loaned me. The diner's food, or the disturbing memory of the beautiful reporter, kept me awake long enough to reach San Antonio. Traffic on Loop 1604 was heavy, and I caught my head bobbing. I turned on the truck's radio and tuned to a talk station.

"...and the Drug Enforcement Administration is saying that the seized drugs, believed to be fentanyl, has a street value of at least twenty million dollars, making it one of the largest drug busts of its kind. There are reports of as many as six cartel members killed." Then somberly, "And a Texas Ranger was critically injured. He was airlifted to San Antonio's Level One Trauma Center, University Hospital, but there is no word on his condition. The DPS has not announced the injured ranger's name. We'll stay on top of this breaking story and, as always, bringing you the latest. Now, a word from our sponsors—"

I punched the *Off* button and pulled into University Hospital's parking garage. I stepped out of the truck and saw myself in its wide side mirror. "You look like shit, Purdy," I muttered. Two nurses walked by and stared at me as I furiously brushed dirt from my pants and shirt. The skybridge led me to a reception desk. The female hospital volunteer checked her computer screen then pointed me toward ICU. "Lots of prayers for your friend," she smiled.

I turned away quickly, my eyes tearing up. Stepping into a bathroom, I rinsed my face and ran a comb through my hair. Looking in the mirror, my eyes looked like fried eggs slathered in pepper sauce. The waiting room in ICU was packed with law enforcement. Texas Rangers, DPS troopers, DEA agents, and cops from several counties. Everyone's faces displayed quiet concern.

Looking out a wide window of the waiting room toward the portico, I saw three television remote transmission trailers parked. A cameraman aimed a shoulder-held camera at a male reporter wearing a dress shirt, necktie, and blue blazer, but also shorts and sandals. I guessed his reporting wouldn't require the TV viewers to see anything below the waist. He was speaking earnestly into a mic.

I had no idea what I was doing there and didn't know whom to ask.

Someone tapped on my shoulder. I turned and was face to face with Harris Whittaker. "He's been calling for you," he said quietly.

"How's he doing?"

Harris ignored the question, walked to a house telephone, said something, then returned and put his arm on my shoulder and led me toward the locked doors into the ICU. The automatic door swung open. A nurse waited in the corridor. "You'll have to suit up first," she said, and led us to a small room. I left my sodden boots in the room and donned paper booties, hair covering, gown, gloves, and mask.

At least he's still alive.

The endless beeps of monitors followed us to a glassed-in room, a view inside blocked by a dark blue curtain. Whittaker thanked the nurse and tapped on the door frame.

"Can we come in?"

A small, worried-looking woman stepped out of the room and removed her mask. "He's not doing so good, Harris."

This must be Abner's wife, I thought, as the two hugged. He turned to me. "This is Purdy Kendricks."

Like someone greeting a new neighbor, the woman took both my hands. "I'm Doris. Doris Selman," she said calmly.

I stammered a response, awed by her poise.

"Come on in," she said, and masked up as she pushed open the curtains.

Abner Selman's eyes were covered with gauze, affixed with surgical tape. Tubes and electrical leads seemed attached to every part of his body. A sheet only partially covered his bare torso, his chest swathed in bandages. A tube from his lung moved a frothy red liquid into a small bottle dangling from the hospital bed.

My friend appeared to have shrunk and aged in mere hours. The airy cough of oxygen pulsed through the endotracheal intubation and Abner's chest moved with the pulse. I glanced at the pedestalled heart monitor and wondered whether the heart waves I was watching were good or bad.

I wanted to take Abner's hand and tell him it was going to be all right. Instead, I stood and stared. Whittaker whispered, "They removed chunks of two ribs. Bullet splintered on its way through his left lung. Six hours in surgery. They think they got all the fragments."

Doris Selman took her husband's hand and squeezed it. "You stay with us, old man, you hear me?" She bent and kissed his forehead, then said, "Thank you for being here, Purdy. My husband thinks the world of you."

I began to cry silently. "I'm so sorry," I said, once, then again.

Doris Selman rounded the bed and put an arm around my waist. She couldn't have been over five feet, two inches tall. "You stay strong, Purdy. Abner needs you right now. Like he needs me. Like he needs Harris."

I stepped to the bed. "Abner, Purdy here. You're in good hands here in San Antonio. We need you to get well."

Heavily sedated, I could only hope that he heard me. I looked for some sign, but nothing came. As I stood there, the monitor began a quickening beep. A nurse rushed into the room. "You need to leave now." She pushed me out just when two nurses maneuvered a crash cart into the room.

Doris Selman began to cry when the intercom bayed "Code blue. Code blue. ICU. Room Three."

Chapter 31

A scare in the ICU. Teofilo escapes

I was hustled out of the ICU and back into the waiting room, still in clean garb. Several Texas Rangers, evidenced by white hats and badges shaped from Mexican five-peso silver coins, surrounded me.

"How's he doing?" one asked in a loud voice.

Still taking in what I'd just witnessed, all I could say was, "I don't know."

Not satisfied, his voice got louder. "Goddammit! You were just in there. How bad is it?"

The crowd around me had grown. I spoke to the floor. "He'd come out of surgery. His wife's with him. Crash cart just headed toward his room. I think he was coding."

I knew most of the Rangers, some well, others by reputation. Their faces showed grim determination and concern. I read into some of the looks a resentment that someone not of their fraternity had been allowed back to see their compadre and was now returning from the inner sanctum with unwanted news. Several muttered curse words, some lifted prayers. I stepped out of the circle, suddenly woozy. I found a chair and sank into it, taking deep breaths to keep from blacking out.

An arm went around my shoulder. "Mr. Kendricks, you okay?"

I put my head between my legs, and my vision started to clear. "I think so." Everything I'd eaten at the Cenizo Diner acted as if it were about to vomit onto the hospital's linoleum floor. Waves of nausea swept through me as I stood. "Bathroom. Quick!" I managed, shivering with sudden chills.

"Let's go." My helper was Harris Whittaker. I stumbled into the toilet stall and managed to get the toilet seat up before spewing food and bile into the bowl. I caught my breath, then the gorge built up again. It seemed never to end. Then it did, and I managed a small, "whew," and I pushed open the stall's door.

"Who are you?" I asked. "In relation to Abner?"

"Abner is my stepfather," he said as he waved his hand trying to chase away my rancid odor. He handed me a dampened paper towel. "You've got tears and gunk all over your face."

"I'm confused," I said.

"Sorry about that, but I figured if Abner wanted you to know, he'd have told you. Grace Selman, his first wife, died; then he married Doris. I'm her son and his stepson."

It was starting to make sense, or at least some of it. "So, are you really working for Bexar County because of problems with altitude? Or have I missed something?"

Whittaker smiled. "No. That's legit. Used to smoke years ago. Some onset of COPD, and not helped by mountains. Abner knew about it, and when the position opened up here in San Antonio, he put in a good word for me."

"Huh. How long's he been married to your mom?"

Whittaker got a quizzical look. "I thought you and he were tight." He paused. "But he does keep things close to the chest. He married Mom about twenty-five years ago. After his first wife and small son were killed in a car wreck."

"Jesus. I had no idea. All I know about Abner you could put it a teacup. He's got a fishing camp on the Pecos, south of Ozona. I guess you know that, though."

"I was a rebellious teenager when he and Mom first married, but yeah, I've been there. Abner tried to teach me to fish, but I didn't have the patience. Anyway...."

I wiped my face, then went to the sink, rinsed my mouth, and looked in the mirror. "I look like something the cats dragged in." I turned. "Your momma needs you right now, a lot more than I do."

"They ran me out too," he said, as his phone vibrated. He picked it up, then smiled. "Thanks, Mom. I'm out here with Purdy Kendricks. We'll keep praying." He disconnected. "They got him back, so the crisis has passed...until the next one, God forbid."

We walked out of the men's restroom and back into the ICU waiting room. Whittaker smiled. "Mom just buzzed me," he announced to the officers in the room. "They have Abner stabilized again. She says the crisis may have passed, but your prayers are still needed. He's got a long way to go."

Several in the room began clapping. Others wiped away tears. A few came up to offer comfort to Whittaker.

Adrift, I wondered whether it was time to head to Austin. Then my cell phone vibrated. Jake Nichols.

"Yeah, Jake."

"When can I let the Mexican go?"

I'd totally forgotten all about Jake's assignment.

"Where are you?" Cell coverage at the Griffin ranch was spotty, at best. I doubted Jake was calling from there.

"Actually, Teofilo and I have gotten to be good friends. He and I are eating breakfast at the Cenizo Diner right now. He's eating migas. I've just finished off some pancakes."

"What the hell?"

"Gotcha," Jake said. "I'm about six miles up the county road from the Griffin place in my truck. I've got Teo with me. I couldn't get coverage closer to the river, so I loaded him back up and headed toward US 90 until I got two bars. He's not feeling well enough to run. I'm worried about him, Purdy. He looks like shit. He's tough as nails but I think the cancer is working on him big time. I don't think he's in any condition to hurt anyone."

"Just keep an eye..."

"Hey, what the fuck?" Jake hadn't directed that at me.

"What's going on?"

"Gotta go! I'll be back." The sound of Luke's cell phone being dropped, then "Come back, dammit," in a voice fading in the distance.

Minutes later, Luke was back. "Lost him," he wheezed. "Jeez, he's off in the brush somewhere out here, Purdy."

"You cuffed him to make sure he wouldn't leave?" I knew the answer before I asked it.

"No. But he promised..."

"Aw, jeez!"

******

I reached Kickapoo County in three hours, apologizing to Lowell's truck for the mistreatment I put it through. I pulled off US 90, churning up a huge cloud of dust as I fishtailed down the county road to the Griffin place. This end of the county hadn't caught a drop of the downpour that had washed through Lagrimas.

My gate was open, and the truck clattered over the cattle guard. Minutes later, I pulled up to the old headquarters. Jake's truck stood by the back screened porch door, looking like a dejected sentry. I tapped my horn, and Jake appeared, confirming what I'd suspected. Teofilo was gone.

"Purdy, I'm sorry—"

"Forget it," I said, getting out of the pickup. "Have you looked for him?"

"I tried looking for tracks, but hell, I'm no good at that."

"Let's take your truck, Jake," I said and crawled into its passenger seat. "I've abused Lowell's truck enough."

"Where to?"

"Let's start at wherever you were when you made that phone call and he skedaddled. Then we'll work south toward the river. Drive slow. Maybe we'll get lucky and spot him."

Jake crept along at ten miles an hour while I leaned out the window, hoping to spot the old Mexican. No luck. The ranch road ended at Otabiano's and Raquel's house, perched on a bluff overlooking the Rio Grande.

"Place looks a little better, Purdy. Not as shot up to hell as the last time I saw," Jake said nervously.

"Quit pretending you're impressed. All I've done is replace the front door, and patched bullet holes in the roof. Haven't even replaced most of the busted windows." I told Jake to turn off the truck ignition, wishing he would shut up. I'd cooled off. I got out and walked under Raquel's old clothesline and stood on the bluff staring at Mexico. In the midafternoon sun, I couldn't sense any malignancy in its dry features, but knew better.

"River's on a rise," Jake said, as he stepped next to me.

"Crazy place, isn't it, Jake? You and I, we grew up next to this ribbon of water. Not a drop of rain here, but that storm upriver has got the old Rio Grande boiling. Never know what to expect."

Jake nodded, perhaps remembering the countless times he and I had fished or played in the muddy flow.

"Jake, I'm not mad. To be honest, I'm not sure what the hell we'd have done with Teofilo anyway. What we did was illegal as hell, but if that rascal wanted to leave, eventually, we were going to have to let him. I'm scared the cartels will get him. He needs to die peacefully." I squeezed Jake's arm. Let's see if we can see any evidence he's crossed into Mexico."

We walked on the sand and powder between stands of salt cedar, cane, and huisache.

"Purdy. Look!" Jake pointed to a soft footprint. Bermuda grass concealed any further markings, but closer to the river, marks showed where some two-legged beast had slid in the soft muck and into the river.

Teofilo had made it to the Rio Grande, which was impressive. He'd covered over ten miles on foot. I wondered if he'd drown, almost hoping so. It was a better death than what awaited him with the cancer or the cartels.

"Time to head back,' I said. "When do you need to be back at work?"

Jake apologized again for Teofilo and said, "Be a good idea if I show up for work. TJ needs me, but no doubt he's pissed as hell about being excluded from the Lagrimas drug bust. He knows you and I are friends, and I'm not sure I want to chance my indispensability with that stupid bag of wind."

"Indispensability? That's a ten-dollar word, Jake." I patted him on the back. "Let's get you back to Santa Rosa." I lowered my voice. "Besides, I've got some peace talks I've got to attend to with Betty when I get back to Austin."

Chapter 32

There are consequences to failure and crossing a line

"How many men did we lose?" Guillermo Blanco's voice cracked, his face unnaturally ashen. The response threw him into a paroxysm of coughing, and he threw his cigar over the low railing of the bedroom patio. Distractedly, he watched it be rekindled by its sudden trajectory and impact onto a garden's concrete divider, showering carefully tended flowers with its glowing embers.

"*Jefe*, what should we do?" The *sicario's* plaintive voice faded out on the encrypted cellphone. "We have another load waiting for orders to cross, and ..."

Blanco almost felt sympathy for the man Navarrete had left at the hacienda west of El Mosco. "Keep the men supplied, but no movement across the river until I tell you." He ended the call, wondering why he'd allowed Navarrete to return to Ciudad Acuña, instead of remaining to ensure flawless crossings. "Are you sure the attack wasn't by those scum from Jalisco?"

"*¿Pues, quién sabe? Pero me dijeron que era puras yanquis y DEA.*"

He thought *the Jalisco New Generation I could deal with. But DEA? How did those bastards know? And now I break this news to my bosses.* Blanco made the sign of the cross, as if God would somehow protect him from others of his kind, or perhaps Santa Muerte the patroness of the cartels. He punched in another number on the encrypted cellphone.

When the man on the other end of the encrypted conversation heard Blanco's telling of the event, his reply had a gravelly quality to it. *"Escúchame bien, Cantinflas*. Listen well to me. Just because you are the fucking boss of a section of the border with *los estados unidos* doesn't mean there won't be consequences when something like this happens. You fucking understand me, *cabrón?"*

Blanco wiped his sweat-drenched forehead as he spoke. "Of course, I understand. Don't you trust me?" He cursed silently at the whine in his voice.

"You are *jefe* because *los Zetas* made you a *jefe,* but what you allowed to happen.... You make sure the other shipment of *las pastillas* — the pills the Americans love so much — don't get lost. You cut off the balls of the *puto* who fucked up that crossing. Then find out what *pinche maricón* fucked us. We want proof that you've taken care of business. You send us a picture of whoever is responsible for that fuckup of *millones de dolares,* and you make sure that picture has the *puto's* dick in his mouth, and that he is still alive when you take the picture. *Entiendes?"*

"Claro." He clearly understood. "I have been a *Zeta* for years. You know that. Have I ever given you one second of doubt? I've just recovered the plaza in Ciudad Acuña for *los Zetas*. My *soldados* have pushed the bastards from Jalisco, and..."

The man on the other end of the conversation interrupted. *"Mi amigo,* I know you are a man of your word. I know that you are *un hombre fuerte y de honor."*

Blanco did not feel his *jefe* really meant he was strong and had honor.

The gravelly voice went on, "It was your idea that we move product by this new route of yours. It was your assurance to *los Zetas* that moving the product across the border in this godforsaken area was possible. My word will be worth little or nothing if you don't make sure the remaining fentanyl is successfully moved, and that there is *justicia* for *los Zetas* for what happened to us and our product at that shithole, Lagrimas. *Comprendes?"*

"Sí." Blanco's response went unheard by his boss. The man had disconnected.

*****

Arturo Navarrete pulled up to the roadblock off Mexico 29. Blanco's summons had been expected. He'd denied a request from his men to accompany him. "No," he said resignedly to them. "There is no reason for anyone besides me to be killed." As if he could protect anyone from death if his gambit didn't work.

Navarrete carefully stepped from his SUV, raised his arms, and allowed two stony-faced *sicarios* to search him thoroughly. "Check around my *huevos*," Navarrete joked. "I may not have them the next time you see me."

The macabre attempt at humor was ignored by Blanco's road guards, who then drove him to the hacienda, where he was escorted into its cool interior.

Blanco sat in the same flimsy metal chair, at the same small table as his last visit. His eyes were the red of fiery coals, but there was no booze on the table. This time, four *sicarios* stood like compass points at each corner of the courtyard.

"Sit."

Navarrete sat.

"You and me," began Blanco. "We go back a long way. We've fought some good battles together."

Navarrete nodded. *This sounds like the beginning of my obituary*, he thought, but remained mute.

"Six *soldados* dead on the other side of the Rio Bravo," Blanco continued, his voice almost too soft to be heard. "And two more on our side." He rolled his shoulders, as if to unkink the muscles in his neck. "More importantly, we have lost product — millions of *dólares* of product. And, I have no one to blame. The truckdriver, they say we killed him, which I am sure is true. But now, there is one less person for me to question about how..." Blanco suddenly screamed, "how my plan was fucked up!"

Wiping the spray of spit off his face, Navarrete leaned forward, his face an inch from Blanco. He spoke in a low voice. Blanco's gunmen did not need to hear what came next. "Your plan was fucked up from the beginning, *jefe*. It was a stupid plan, *jefe*. I warned you that trying to push product across too far away from where *los Zetas* could guarantee protection was a stupid idea. And now—"

Navarrete leaned back and pointed at the four gunmen who had inched forward toward the two men. "Now, Blanco, you are looking for someone to blame. And you have only me. You can break all my bones, gouge my eyes out, pull out my tongue. I will scream. I will admit anything the torturers ask of me. But as Santa Muerte is my witness, I have not betrayed you." *I would have, you son of a whore, if I could turn it to my advantage. But the fucking americanos ruined that opportunity.*

Blanco wiped the spittle from his lips, shaking his finger at his underling. "Very good. Very good indeed. You are indeed *El Tramposo* — the tricky one, the sneaky one. I could have you killed, you know. I could have them break all the bones in your legs and feet. Smash them with pieces of wood."

Navarrete stood. "Then do it, *jefe*. But don't accuse me of disloyalty." *Christ, I am playing with fire!* he thought.

Blanco waved the gunmen back.

Navarrete then whispered, "There is the other load of drugs, and much larger than the first, kilometers from the Rio Bravo. *My* men, they are loyal to me, and they don't know who to trust right now. They know their brothers were surprised and killed. They wonder if someone in *los Zetas* has betrayed *them*. I have not betrayed them. I have told them they are to trust no one unless they hear from me."

"And if they don't hear from you?"

"They will destroy the product."

Blanco's eyes widened. He made a dismissive sign gesture with his hands to the four killers. "Leave us alone." As the men left the courtyard, he asked, "How do we get our product across without another disaster? If we cannot, then my bosses will come for both of our necks."

Navarrete thought, *My plan has worked. I have bought time to make the other crossing a success for los Zetas. But I have challenged Cantinflas. This could cost me my life unless I can neutralize him.*

*****

"We are encouraged by this seizure of narcotics," intoned DEA Special Agent Victoria Fleming. "As always, we are deeply appreciative of our partners in law enforcement, and their assistance in events in Kickapoo County. Any more questions?"

"Yes." Sylvia Rincon answered, then proceeded to talk over the other reporters who surrounded Fleming outside the San Antonio DEA office. "Is it true that Kickapoo County Sheriff's Office and other local agencies were not consulted because of the DEA's distrust? What involvement did the Texas Rangers have? Did Purdy Kendricks have help in this interdiction? We understand that he is now head of the Texas State Drug Interdiction Support Department, with his only office in Austin, Texas."

"Whoa. That's several questions." Fleming feigned a smile. "I'm not sure where some of this is coming from, Miss...?"

"Rincon."

"Miss Rincon. We have always had a great working relationship with the fine men and women of Kickapoo County law enforcement, as with others on the border with Mexico. Mr. Kendricks, as you know, is a heroic law enforcement officer, who, because of his efforts two years ago, is now the head of a state agency. While I can't comment on any individual officers involved, the Drug Enforcement Administration has and continues to work with the Texas State Drug Interdiction Support Department. It goes without saying that our partnership with the Texas Department of Public Safety and the Texas Rangers is a long and cherished one." She paused for effect. "I hope you and your audience will join with all of us as we keep Ranger Abner Selman in our thoughts and prayers."

Fleming stepped away into the San Antonio DEA office foyer, pretending to ignore the TV reporter's continued questions. As the inner door closed, Fleming muttered "Jesus Christ," and disappeared into an empty office. "Get me Breaux," she barked. "Now!"

Fleming removed her suit jacket and draped it over the back of a chair. A secretary tapped on the office door. "Agent Breaux is on his way. I brought you some bottled water. Figured after the press conference, you'd need it."

Fleming smiled. "I need more than water after that, but I'll wait 'til five for a single malt." Breaux arrived, and the secretary disappeared.

"Close the door and grab a chair."

As Breaux pulled up a desk chair, Fleming sat behind the bare desk. "What the hell happened in Lagrimas?"

"What do you mean, chief?" Fleming had attended the de-briefing via encrypted video conferencing before driving to San Antonio from Houston this morning. "Did we miss something?"

"We've got eight dead bodies, two that we brought over in boats from the Mexican side. Over the usual protests from the Mexican government over an intrusion onto the sanctity of its soil, I might add. All of them are in the ME's coolers. Not that I give a damn, but why does one of those sicarios have a close-contact gunshot wound to the back of his head?"

The question seemed to come out of left field. Breaux shook his head. "I don't know, but we just came from a goddamned gun fight with a bunch of Mexican gangsters. Why does it matter?"

"It may not, Agent Breaux." Fleming took a small sip from the water bottle. "But someone may get curious as to why every other dead Mexican has wounds consistent with a goddamned gun fight and one, well, he died of a close-in head shot." She paused, swiveling her chair back and forth. "Not that I care, of course, but there may be questions, and I'm just covering all the bases."

"The cattle truck driver? Shit, they capped that guy before they lit out for the river."

"No. One of the gunmen."

Breaux tried but failed to conceal a memory.

"You won't make a good poker player, Agent," Fleming said. "That's a 'tell.'"

You're fishing. Breaux shook his head, remembering the pistol report when Eddleman stepped behind the *sicarios'* pickup truck near US 90. "I'm not aware of anything There were so many bullets flying, it was a fucking circus. Maybe they capped one of their own. I have no idea."

"Bullshit. You know. And I know you know." She took another sip of water. "Want to tell me about it?"

Breaux looked toward the office door, as if hoping for an escape route. *Holy hell, I know why. My partner may have executed a Mexican cartel member.*

Fleming leaned forward. "I'm going to be in this office for the rest of the week. If a bullet is found inside the *sicario's* skull, questions may be asked. I'm assuming you had nothing to do with something like that. We didn't have this discussion. Understand? We'd better hope no slug is recovered that is matched to an agent's firearm."

Breaux simply nodded. Not for the first time, Breaux wondered if he was going to catch blowback for something Jack Eddleman had done. *I'll be damned if I let it happen again.*

Chapter 33
An ultimatum and a promise

I called Betty and told her I'd be home soon, but first I needed to check in at my office — if I still had one.

"Well, well. Lookee what the cat dragged in." Alicia Trejo's greeting didn't seem to bode well.

"I'm back, Ms. Trejo. Hopefully for a good long while." I walked down the carpeted hallway to my underused office.

She followed me inside and shut the door. "Commander, you may have a problem."

I pulled at a wad of spiked pink phone messages, knocking the desk tool over in the process. "Okay." What else could I say? I rounded the desk hoping to gain distance and cover, then sat in the desk's large rolling chair. My manipulation didn't seem to work. Alicia pulled up another chair, as she'd done in the past, took a seat, and leaned her elbows on my desk.

"You want this job or not, boss?"

Uh oh.

I hoped to distract her, but she unfolded a sheet of paper I immediately recognized as the statutory enabling act creating the Texas State Drug Interdiction Support Department. "Be it enacted," she began, pushing her readers higher up on the bridge of her nose, "that there is hereby created dot, dot, dot." She paused, ran a finger down the paper. "Aha! Here's what it says about the Texas State Drug Interdiction Support Department's function."

I squirmed and tried to cut her off.

All I got was a glare. "Article 12, subparagraph C states that 'said department's duties *shall*" she leaned on the shall – "provide research, intelligence and logistical support to other law enforcement and related agencies whose missions are the interdiction of illegal and harmful controlled substances from entering the State of Texas."

I was being lectured by my secretary, and her presentation made it clear I could not leave my chair and avoid her.

"Shall I continue, Commander?" My head wagged a distinct "no," but Alicia waved the copy of the enabling statute a bit, then, acting as if discovering a new land, read more. "Aha! Subparagraph E paragraph one is under what the law says are your office's limitations. I'm sure you want that clarified, right? 'The creation of this Department shall in *no way* be construed as empowering it to supplant the duties of city, county, or federal law enforcement efforts.' Shall I go on?"

"Ms. Trejo, you've made your point in spades." I needed to show some righteous anger at being talked to like Peck's Bad Boy; someone whose bad behavior is a source of embarrassment or annoyance. I was failing badly.

"I'm just the secretary at this place," she said, leaning back, more timid now than her earlier performance as a mama grizzly bear. "I'm not getting paid nearly enough to take questions from the press, and legislators' staffers about what my boss is doing in the middle of a gun battle in his old stomping grounds on the border."

For a second, I thought this was my indispensable secretary's valedictory speech, and said so. "You're not thinking of..."

"You're not getting off that easy. No, I'm not leaving." Alicia's diminutive stature seemed to grow at least a foot when she stood. "But, boss, you are good at this job, and you make others look good too. Running around the border and doing shoot 'em ups with drug dealers isn't your job." She trudged to the door, shaking her head. "All I can say is that I'm glad the legislature's not in session right now, or you might find yourself and this department de-funded."

"Ouch." I stood and looked out my window, watching traffic thicken with after school and late afternoon commuters. "You're right, of course, Ms. Trejo. Thank you."

"Hell, Commander. I know I'm right. That's why you hired me – to keep you organized and on target."

I grinned. That wasn't why she'd been hired. I had only known her by reputation as being a crackerjack secretary and a cop's widow. But now, she was attempting to save my ass. All I could do was thank her and begin returning phone calls waiting in the wad of pink message slips.

*****

It was after six when I pulled Lowell's pickup into the driveway of our rented home. I killed the engine and sat there for a moment, feeling guilty and wondering how I was going to placate Betty. Finally, I pushed open the truck's door and muttered aloud, "Let's get this over with." As if I knew what "this" was, and as if I wanted anything involving my wife and child to be "over with."

"Daddy! Daddy!" Forrest burst out of the front door and leaped up, expecting me to catch him. His little boy strength and the love in his embrace swept over me like a gentle surf. For a moment, I just rocked the boy back and forth, repeating "I love you so much. I love you so much."

Excited that I was home, Forrest grabbed my hand when I set him down. "C'mon, Daddy. Mom's got me a new Lego set. This one has pirates and a ship. We've almost got it built, but we haven't put the sails on it yet!"

He pulled me inside, and I looked for his mother. We turned toward the kitchen table. There sat Betty, staring at instructions in a Lego pamphlet, one hand holding a plastic sail, and the other hand holding what looked to be a portion of the ship's mast.

She glanced up with a small smile. "Hey, hon. Come help. I can't make heads or tails out of this next step." She stood, giving me a quick kiss on the cheek, and motioned toward the chair she'd just vacated. "We ate on the way home from the baseball game. I'm going to run a bath for Forrest while you boys keep working."

Forrest scrambled into the adjacent chair. Within seconds I was immersed in Lego construction and Forrest's endless chatter, as his small hands occasionally found pieces I'd overlooked.

"Bath's ready," Betty's voice called from the bathroom.

"Let's go, champ." Over his protests, I carried him into the bathroom. Thirty minutes and two stories later, I closed his bedroom door.

"I love you, Daddy," he yelled when I clicked off his light. In the gloom of the small hallway, sudden tears filled my eyes. In the living room, I found Betty sitting on the sofa, idly flipping through channels with the remote. I plopped down next to her and watched as she finally settled on a PBS mini-series on British kings and queens.

"I love this show. Don't you, Purdy?" She muted the volume. "It's so important to know about your family, don't you agree?"

She turned off the television and set the control down. Still staring at the TV's empty screen, she asked, "Do you know who your family is, Purdy?"

"Just some of our old relatives, Betty." I played along, knowing she didn't give a damn about my genealogy. "Mostly poor whites drifting across the South, and ending up in Texas, at least on Daddy's side."

Betty turned to me. Despite the sadness I saw in her face, or maybe because of it, she was achingly beautiful. "Forrest and I are your family, Purdy Kendricks. We're all you've got. You don't have a brother or sister. Your daddy's long gone. Your momma's in a nursing home. We are your family." Her tears fell. "And you are ours. I've got my sister down there in Santa Rosa, and her good-hearted husband, and her kids. But what's important to me are you and our boy."

"I know that."

"Do you?" She dabbed at her cheeks with a paper napkin she'd produced from a jean pocket. "Do you? When you stopped drinking, I admired you so much, but figured it was too late. And then, when you couldn't find a job because of the bad-mouthing in Houston, and you ended up in Kickapoo County again, I was sure it wasn't going to work. That you'd go back to drinking. But you didn't."

Another juddering breath. "Instead, you almost got yourself killed. And, although I don't blame you, honestly, I don't, you almost got Forrest and me killed. But somehow, we *did* put it back together, and stronger."

I yearned to reach for her, to hold her, and promise that everything was going to be all right, but that wasn't going to happen. Betty held herself tense, sending me signals I was not to come near.

"And now this, Purdy. You're back involved in that county." She shook her head. Her disappointment in me cut to the quick.

"What do you want me to do?"

She inhaled. "I want you away from Kickapoo County. Whatever hold it has on you is tearing at my heart. You claim you can't stand the place, but it's as if there's some evil magnet drawing you back."

I nodded, searching for words to convince her that wasn't true. But I wasn't sure she was wrong.

We sat there in silence, and I reached for her hand. She didn't pull it away. Finally, Betty stood up. "I'm going to bed, now. If you want me to be a part of your life; more importantly if you want to remain in my life and in that of your son's, I want you to promise me two things."

"Anything." I was looking up at her helplessly.

"Don't go back there."

I tried for a smile. "But your sister and brother-in-law and their kids live there. What about them?"

She ignored me. "And two, she said firmly: sell that damned Griffin Ranch."

Betty disappeared down the hallway. I sat, staring at my hands, contemplating how I could live without Betty and Forrest, and deciding I couldn't. When I entered our bedroom, the lights were off, and Betty lay far on her side of our bed. I prayed I could honor her demands.

Within forty-eight hours, I had broken both promises.

Chapter 34

Navarrete takes a ride. Breaux confronts Eddleman

"Jefe," Navarrete pleaded, "we can pull back from that location west of El Mosco and push the drugs across somewhere else. It's not too late."

Blanco refused. "Time is money. We have dealers waiting for the product in *los estados unidos*. Our cartel has made a promise to deliver. If we don't, others will take our place. I'll be damned if Ciudad Acuña is our only gain. We can control much more of the border for *los Zetas*. Otherwise, the scum from Jalisco, or Sonora, or Tijuana will step in. You ought to know that. Despite your insistence that I am stupid, our cartel needs to expand its area of control. We will cross the product where I decide." Blanco pounded his fist against his stucco wall like a metronome keeping the beat as he shouted the last sentence "The next crossing is more than one hundred kilometers downriver from Lagrimas. And you, my friend, will ensure the crossing's success. You will be responsible for the product's delivery into San Antonio."

Navarrete knew he no longer held sway with his boss. He shook his head sadly as he was escorted back to the roadblock off Mexican Highway 29:

Navarrete understood the ramifications. *The bastard has staked his reputation in* los Zetas *on his ability to move drugs into the United States in the vast, sparsely populated area west of Ciudad Acuña. The bigger bosses don't look kindly on mistakes, so the remaining crossing will need to succeed, or it will be his life.*

Navarrete's future was now tied directly to the success or failure of another man's plan in a desolate stretch of Mexico adjacent to Kickapoo County, Texas. Navarrete was alive and in one piece, but that was subject to change if the next and much larger load of fentanyl wasn't moved successfully across the Rio Grande and into the markets of the drug-hungry *americanos*.

*****

Dust consumed the black SUV as it bounced and yawed through the barren wasteland along the rocky, dirt surface of the road. It was unpleasantly bumpy even in the best of times. Now, the *sicario* behind the wheel was driving at a perilously high speed.

"Cuidate, hombre! It won't do any of us any good to be killed before we get to the hacienda." Navarrete held onto his seat belt and door handle on the passenger side as the SUV slowed slightly for a rocky outcropping.

The vehicle hit a hump in the road and seemed to leap into the air. Navarrete's stomach lurched, and the two *sicarios* in the back seat began to curse their *compadre*. Their curses, or the fear of puncturing the SUV's oil pan, had more of an effect than Navarrete's warning.

These *sicarios* were *Zetas* hand-picked by Blanco, to "escort" and ensure Navarrete's appearance at the ancient hacienda west of El Mosco. Because, as Blanco had promised, Navarrete would now be personally responsible that the fentanyl crossed from Mexico. Navarrete would personally see that the drug was loaded onto transport once inside the United States, and Navarrete would personally ensure the fentanyl transport safely left from US 90 and arrived at distribution points in San Antonio.

Navarrete had tortured and killed traitors, snitches, and enemy cartel members. Recalling the eyes gouged out, leg and foot bones smashed with hammers, and electric shocks from car batteries, he thought: *A quick death will be welcome if I fail.*

At the ancient fortified hacienda, the SUV roared through the open portal and swung under the covered parking area, once filled with pickups and Humvees. Navarrete stretched his legs while looking around, wondering if the *gringos'* satellites had observed his arrival.

An older man, crippled from street battles with other cartels, who was also the hacienda's majordomo and cook, appeared from an outbuilding.

Navarrete shook the man's gnarled hand. "Where is what's left of the crew that tried to cross at Lagrimas."

Wordlessly, the cripple motioned for him and the escorting *sicarios* to follow him. When he entered the main house, Navarrete paused so his eyes could adjust to the gloom. He followed a stream of low groans into an interior room. Two men sat on low cots, one cradling his arm in a bloody sling.

"What happened?" Navarrete demanded.

The wounded *sicario* shook his head. "We had the product completely loaded, *jefe*. The cattle truck was ready to roll." He grunted in pain, and Navarrete got a whiff of a wound going septic. "One pickup with a few of the boys left the cattle hauler to make sure the way was clear for the semi to get onto the highway. I heard shots. Lots of gunfire. Next, we are fighting for our lives as we try to re-load *las drogas* onto the other pickup and get it and us the hell back across the river."

Navarrete turned to the uninjured man. "You are the one who called Blanco?"

"*Si*. The cripple gave us a cell phone."

Immediately suspicious, Navarrete leaned forward. "How did you get back here? Walk? Who gave you a ride? The Jalisco scum?"

Whimpering, the man replied, "No, *jefe*. You know both groups had a phone. We called the other group. One of their men took a truck from the other location and met us walking in the desert. We had walked at least ten kilometers before he got to us." He motioned to his wounded companion. "He had caught a bullet when we swam back across the *rio*."

"Where is that phone now?"

"*Aqui*." The cripple reached forward with a grimy encrypted phone. "Its batteries are dead now." He quietly confirmed the gunman's story.

Placated, Navarrete turned to leave.

"*Jefe*, my arm. I think it's infected with the filthy water. What do I do?" Rising unsteadily from the cot, the wounded man's eyes showed an unhealthy gleam of high fever.

Navarrete nodded. "We'll get you back to Acuña and a doctor." He stepped out of the room and, out of hearing of the others, punched in an encoded number on his personal cell phone.

Blanco answered after the first tone. "What?"

"Two are here." He didn't describe where 'here' was, for fear that even with encryption, the conversation could be detected and understood. "One hurt, badly. The one who made the call, not. The cripple confirms their stories."

"What about the others? When are you going there?"

Christ, Navarrete thought. *I just got here.* He rubbed a hand over his eyes, feeling the left socket's badly knit orbital bones. "Soon. After dark. No sense in helping the *gringos* with their satellites and drones."

Blanco disconnected with a grunt.

Navarrete called for the cripple. "We'll get the *soldado* to a doctor, but only after we are finished here." He motioned northward toward the border.

"And if he can't wait that long for a doctor?"

"Then he dies. I'll take the other *soldado* with us."

The cripple had seen too much death to show concern. "I have little here to care for him. His wound is already putrid. How much time before I can get the man moved?"

"Two days. Perhaps three. *Quien sabe*?" Navarrete had sympathy for the wounded man, a good soldier for the cartel, but that concern was blunted by the immediacy of the task at hand.

*****

"Hey, amigo, you got a sec?"

Eddleman nodded absently while he held the cell phone to his ear. "Sure. What's up?"

"We need to talk," Breaux said, his Cajun accent more obvious than usual.

"About what?" Eddleman's voice already held a hint of suspicion.

"Can't say."

"C'mon, partner. Don't feed me shit and ask me to enjoy it. What's going on?"

Breaux said, "Meet me downstairs."

Eddleman stared at his cell phone, then slipped on boots and a hat, closed and locked his apartment, and descended a flight of metal and concrete stairs. He stepped outside the apartment complex breezeway, peering into the dimly lit parking lot. Nothing but crickets and distant road noise.

"Hey." Breaux waited in the shadows of crepe myrtles surrounding the complex's first floor units.

"Christ! Scared me," Eddleman muttered. "What's with the cloak and dagger?"

"Let's go for a ride." Breaux walked back through the crepe myrtle toward a parking area well away from Eddleman's unit.

Eddleman followed, and, moments later, sat in the passenger seat of Breaux's pickup truck. "Okay. You've got me here. What's up?"

"Jack, Special Agent in Charge Victoria Fleming wants to have a chat with you."

"So?"

"You haven't heard this from me." Breaux started the truck engine, then turned off the radio as the tuned station's steel petal guitar began to whine on a Buck Owens song. As he backed out of the parking lot, he said, "It's about the Lagrimas thing."

Eddleman reacted testily. "What Lagrimas 'thing' do you mean? Do you mean the fucking gun battle we just survived? You mean the fucking dumpster load of fentanyl we kept off the streets?"

Breaux's nod was visible in the dash lights. "Save the righteous indignation. She's asking about a *sicario's* close contact head wound."

"What's that got to do with me?"

"Jack, one of the *sicarios* was, in her words, 'executed.'"

Eddleman reached for the tin of Kodiak. "Humph. Beats hell out of me." He pushed a large glob inside his lower lip.

"Jack, we aren't having this conversation, you get me?" Eddleman's casual attitude was pissing Breaux off.

Eddleman shrugged. "Okay. We aren't having this conversation. But I don't know what you're talking about anyway."

Breaux pulled up to a stop light, turned, and drove into a quiet neighborhood. He slowed, pulled into a driveway, rolled down the windows, and turned off the ignition. For a second, he sat staring at the brick exterior of a house.

"Better back out of here, partner," Eddleman laughed. "Neighbors might call the cops."

Breaux slammed the steering wheel with the palm of his hand. "Goddammit, you stupid fuck. Fleming finds out the bullet is still inside that fucker's head, and they can match the slug to someone's gun…. By any chance, could that be your pistol?"

"Don't know what you're talking about." Eddleman said spitting his dip out the window. "It's after my bedtime, *amigo*." Eddleman leaned hard into the Spanish word for friend. "Take me home, will you?"

Breaux's mouth straightened into an angry line. "I'm trying to warn you. You need to look out. Get rid of the gun. Do whatever you need to do." He rolled the windows up and backed out of the driveway.

Breaux pulled into the remote apartment lot again, and Eddleman wordlessly exited and walked into the dark.

Inside his apartment, Eddleman kicked off his boots, splashed three fingers of Glenfarclas into a glass, and walked to a small desk. He sat, woke up his computer, and, for the umpteenth time, opened Google Earth's satellite view of Kickapoo County's eastern edge. Zooming in, he recognized the Griffin Ranch's structures. He isolated the screen shot and punched *print*. He accessed a thumb drive, found a folder holding a one-page document, and printed that. While the printer churned, Eddleman unrolled a United States Geological Survey 7.5-minute map. From a drawer, he pulled prints from the many digital photos he'd taken of various geographic and man- made structures on the desolate seven thousand acres.

When the copier finished printing, he took the stack of photos, the USGS map, and the satellite's image, along with push pins, and walked to the apartment's single bedroom. Moving the dresser to bare a wall, he mounted the map and satellite image. The one-page document was the only item on the thumb drive, recovered from the dead hand of a murdered DEA agent, head blown off as he lay on a South Texas highway. It held the key to finding the money Pete Vasquez had stashed on land now owned by Purdy Kendricks.

Hackamore tree - 375k

Diablo chico - 1.2

Oto's bench - 823k

East vega notch - 228k

Sunset Y - 1.7

Once again, he compared terrain on the maps and photos, pinning his digital photo prints, taken on another quick search of the ranch, into the sheetrock wall. He drew lines from several of them to the points on the USGS and Google features, again hoping he'd reached the correct conclusion of what locations Pete Vasquez' cryptic notes meant.

It's time for me to take some vacation time. I may not have as much time or as many opportunities to search for that money on the Griffin Ranch as I thought I would have.

Chapter 35
A warning and an informed guess

Leroy Breaux glanced at the San Antonio Channel Four ten o'clock news, relieved to see something besides the Lagrimas drug shootout as the lead story. Six minutes and two commercial breaks into the program, the huge fentanyl haul was already replaced by two drive-by shootings, a city councilmember's DWI arrest, and a puppy mill animal cruelty allegation. He drained a bottle of Yuengling and tossed the empty bottle into a small recycling bin.

Just then, the station's talking head announced: "Tomorrow at five o'clock, we bring you more interesting developments arising from the huge gun battle on the Rio Grande, when we ask the question: Were all the Mexicans involved in the shootout with local and federal law enforcement shot in the heat of battle? Be sure to tune in. And now, WOAI will be right back with the weather."

Breaux started to call Jack Eddleman, then thought about it. Any phone contact they had could easily be discovered by DEA Agent in Charge Victoria Fleming. "Shit fire," he muttered. "I hope Jack is watching the news." He walked to his bedroom, pulled a burner phone from his nightstand, and punched in a number.

"What?"

"We made the news again."

Eddleman grunted. "I guess that's why you aren't calling me, and I'm not hearing you tell me anything."

"Something like that. Channel Four had a teaser. Something about how one of the *sicarios* died, I think." When Eddleman didn't respond, Breaux continued, "This fucking town is like a sieve. No telling where WOAI got its information, but as far as I know, no autopsies have even been performed."

"This place is more like Mexico than anywhere else. Everything leaks like a sieve, or an off brand of baby diapers. You ought to know that."

"Well, Jack. I warned you. Are you okay?"

"What do you mean?"

"You know damned well what I'm talking about. Are you okay?"

Eddleman walked back into his apartment bedroom and flipped on the overhead light. "Uh huh. I'm just fine." *I don't know if I even can trust Breaux,* he thought. *He could be recording this conversation.* "No problems at all on this end."

"Okay, just checking. See you tomorrow." Breaux disconnected.

In the bedroom, Eddleman looked at the Google Earth satellite photo, comparing it with the 7.5-minute USGS map. He unpinned three ground-level photographs from the wall and walked back to his desk. He sat and woke up his laptop.

He grinned as he again stared at the cryptic printout from Pete Vasquez' thumb drive. *Sure glad I didn't get caught the last time I snuck onto the Griffin Ranch.* The first digital photo print showed Otabiano Vasquez' house, or what was left of it, looking from the northwest. In the background, salt cedars and cane blocked a view to the bluff overlooking the Rio Grande. Downriver from the house, the distance from a pitcher's mound to home plate, perched a wooden bench. *Oto's bench - 823k.*

"'Vega,'" he muttered, "is 'a large plain or valley, typically a fertile and grassy one,' according to the dictionary. That godforsaken ranch doesn't have a large, fertile anything. Damned place is dry as a bone." He tapped another ground-level photo he'd taken. It was labeled 'looking south. East side near fence line.' Yellowed grass in a pasture stood knee high, a sharp contrast to the rocks and sands on most of the Griffin Ranch's seven thousand acres.

"Holy shit." Eddleman walked back into the bedroom and, pulling a push pin out of the sheetrock, removed another photo, then carried it back to the apartment's small desk, but he didn't sit. The second print was labeled 'East side, near fence line, looking south.'

"Hot damn! How did I miss it?" In the grassy area's background stood the horns of two eroded sedimentary rock towers, or hoodoos. *East vega notch - 228k.* "Dollars to donuts, that's the notch."

Hackamore tree – 375k Eddleman wasn't a horseman but he'd googled 'hackamore.' "There's no such thing as a hackamore tree," he muttered. "A hackamore is a 'bitless bridle for a horse.'" This time, he unpinned a photo of the large outbuilding next to the Griffin Ranch main house. "What the hell?"

He took the photo, returned to his computer, and googled 'hackamore' again. Pulling up an image, he compared it to something dangling tiredly from a nail on the north side of the weathered structure. "Wish I'd known what a hackamore was earlier," he muttered. The photo revealed the dangling object as a worn bit of rope and leather, with the characteristic nose and chin pieces of a hackamore bridle. Two paces from the outbuilding's north wall stood a tired mesquite tree. "Hackamore. Tree. I'll bet three hundred and seventy-five thousand dollars there's one of Pete Vasquez' stashes somewhere in that six-foot area."

Eddleman closed his laptop, set the maps and prints down. He stretched and walked to the kitchen. He reached inside a cabinet for a two-hundred-dollar bottle of twenty-five-year-old Glenfarclas and unwrapped the stopper. "I'm looking at almost one-and-a-half million dollars, in just those three places. I think I can afford a nip of this good stuff."

*****

A contingency of DEA agents sat around the San Antonio office's conference table. "Any suggestions as to where those other sets of tracks went?" Fleming asked.

"No idea," an agent responded. "Satellite hasn't picked up anything."

Breaux shined an image onto a screen, and someone dimmed the light. "Here's what we saw at that hacienda west of El Mosco. Two distinct travel patterns."

A female agent raised her hand. "Question: have we given any thought to the possibility that the Lagrimas load might be the only load? That the other tracks were to confuse us?"

Fleming answered, "I'd give it a fifty-fifty chance you are right about that, considering the amount of fentanyl scarfed up at Lagrimas." She turned to Breaux. "Your thoughts?"

"No way to know right now. But drones haven't spotted anything in the last few days, and satellite coverage of that area..." He pointed at the sinuous winding thin line of the Rio Grande south of Kickapoo County. "...didn't show anything."

Agent Art Reyes leaned back in a swivel chair. "We've got drones all over the damned border. If *los Zetas* have another cache of dope, they're not going to leave it untended. That whole border area is up for grabs. *Los Zetas* may have Acuña right now, but intel has picked up a lot of chatter from the CGNC. That cartel is gunning for the *Zetas*. The fact that *los Zetas* took over the plaza in Acuña, and then tried that massive dope transfer west of there, in the middle of nowhere was audacious. It has their competition riled up."

He paused. "If I was a *Zeta*, I wouldn't dare leave a bunch of drugs anywhere in an any area west of Acuña." He gestured toward another wall map of the Texas-Mexico border that included the Rio Grande's southern border of Kickapoo County.

Fleming walked to the front of the room. "Mexican military has moved a few troops out of some of their barracks." She smirked. "Not that I expect anything worthwhile from that bunch, but some soldiers stirring around is not something either cartel wants to bother with. Bad for business."

She turned to Reyes. "Agent Reyes gets an attaboy for the phone call. We won't know for sure, but I'm betting that little ploy, calling Navarrete on his personal cell phone, pushed *los Zetas* into panic mode."

Reyes made an exaggerated bow, and the agents gave desultory applause and cheers. Someone made kissing sounds, then whispered, "ass kisser." Everyone, including Fleming, burst into laughter.

When the room quieted, Fleming asked, "What's the latest on the ranger?"

"Hanging in there, chief," Breaux responded. "But he's not out of the woods by a long shot."

"I know we have a lot of trust issues with some of the cops along the border," Fleming said, "so I'm reaching out to the Texas State Drug Interdiction Support Department. That's Purdy Kendricks. I'm going to ask him, as a courtesy if nothing else, for some assistance. He knows the area. He's proven more than once a considerable skill set." She turned to Breaux. "You've had contact with him. You saw him in action. Any objections?"

"Not at all. He'll do."

"His agency is supposed to be providing intel and coordination support. I'm hearing that his personal involvement in Kickapoo County may not have been the sharpest thing he's done lately, but he knows the territory and he knows the players."

Maybe he knows too *much about some of the players,* Breaux thought.

The meeting broke up. "A word with you, Agent Breaux, please." Fleming was stuffing files in a computer case. "Walk out with me."

The two rode the elevator to the basement parking area.

"Where was Eddleman this morning?"

Breaux shrugged. "He called me. Said he's sick with the flu. Going to try to get a doctor's appointment."

"Hmm."

The two walked to her sedan. Fleming unlocked the vehicle then turned to Breaux. "The DEA doesn't need liabilities. I'm not accusing you of anything, but I'm not stupid either. If an agent does something stupid, it can be forgiven, usually. But like it or not, my sources brought up the *Zeta* with the close contact bullet in his head, and I've been told to look into it."

"What the hell, Chief?" Breaux retorted angrily. "You haven't said his name, but I'm not stupid. I know who you're talking about. If you don't trust Eddleman, get rid of him, but don't come after me."

Fleming opened the car door and sat in the driver's seat. "You're your brother's keeper, my friend. See you later." She backed out, and Breaux stood to one side. Fleming never made eye contact, looking straight ahead.

Chapter 36
An unexpected visit and bad news

"D on't forget," Betty shouted. "The sellers have cleared out of our new home, and they're letting us in before the closing. We need to pick out colors, Purdy. I have the key." She grinned and waved a lone key and a fan-shaped collection of paint samples in front of my face. "If you can get off a little early, we'll go by our new home-to-be. Those colors in the bedrooms and living room have to be changed."

I thought about the hefty mortgage payments, and suddenly had thoughts of untold amounts of money Pete Vasquez may have stashed on land I now owned. *It'd be nice to have some of that cash.*

Forrest and I gave her hugs, and I hustled him into Betty's car. I got in the driver's seat and started the engine.

"Mom sure is excited," Forrest said, snapping on his seatbelt.

"Indeed, she is. We're going to fix up our new house." I took a chance on what color a young boy would pick for his room. "Maybe we'll let you pick out the colors for your bedroom. Okay with you?"

Forrest nodded. "I want my room to look like the inside of a pirate ship."

"And what color would that be?"

"Oh, Dad. You know. Lots of brown. Like the wood they made ships out of."

Uh oh.

When I pulled to a stop in the drop-off lane, Forrest yelled "I love you, Daddy," and got out of the car. I watched him make his way to the entrance, mesmerized by how fast he was growing up. A polite honk reminded me other parents were letting off children too, so I waved an apology to the driver behind me and turned toward my office.

Walking in the door of my office, Ms. Trejo gave me a hand wave, then went back to her phone conversation. I turned toward the office's small kitchen. I heard fingers snapping. Still cradling the telephone, she showed me a notepad.

"Don't forget your meeting with Fleming," it read.

I mouthed a silent: thank you." Once at my desk, I called Harris Whittaker and left a message. Five minutes later, my phone beeped. He was calling back.

"How's Abner doing?" I asked.

"Not so good, Purdy. His physical condition is somewhat stable, but the doctors haven't been able to bring him out of the coma. My mom is worn out but refuses to leave him by himself."

"Damn. I'm sorry. Is there anything I can do?"

"No." Harris paused. "Well, yes, there is, come to think about it. I don't have any vacation or sick leave since I just started here at the M.E.'s office. I can't take as much time off as I want. Can you make a run down to University Hospital and sit with her for a few hours? I'm not sure what Abner told her, but she seems quite taken by you."

There was a sudden catch in my throat. "Sure," I managed. "Let me clear it with Betty," I said, then remembered the paint swatches. "Give me your mom's phone number too." I'd find the time but didn't know when.

Two East Texas sheriffs had requested my department's assistance in obtaining cooperation from a large municipality's police department's drug task force. They were getting stonewalled, the city claiming a lack of funds, which was partly true, plus a bit of 'look-down-our-noses at the country goobers,' assuming that rural folks' problems couldn't approximate the woes of a big city. I had been trying to coax some sort of help to underfunded and understaffed counties. They deserved it, but it was taking some arm- twisting and assurances to the city police that, as part of the state bureaucracy, I'd speak kindly about their gestures of brotherly love at the next legislative session.

Ms. Trejo's voice came on the intercom, "Commander, your visitor has arrived."

"Thanks, Ms. Trejo. I'll step out." I minimized the computer screen, relieved for the break in answering another email, and turned off my portable recorder, stuffing my earbuds in my breast pocket. There'd be time to savor Sarah Vaughn's cover of "Black Coffee" later.

In the foyer, Ms. Trejo stood next to a woman with an attractive cropped white-gray hairdo, dressed in a conservative skirt, blouse and double-breasted suit jacket. They seemed deep in conversation. Although we'd not met, I knew DEA Special Agent in Charge Victoria Fleming by reputation. We shook hands. My attempt at formally introducing Alicia was cut short.

"Oh, we've already introduced ourselves," Fleming said in a deep contralto. I invited her back to my office, but she turned to my secretary and shook her hand. "So good to meet you, Ms. Trejo. I've heard so much about you."

Alicia beamed, and she never beamed. Hell, she rarely smiled. Agent Fleming's effect on her was impressive.

In my office, Fleming took a seat. After I made an offer of coffee, which she politely refused, and we shared the usual pleasantries, she said, "I want to thank you for what you helped pull off down on the border."

I thanked her but expressed my concern about Abner Selman.

"That, too, Commander. But I'm talking about two years ago."

"I appreciate that," I said, wondering where this visit was going.

Fleming stood and walked to the window behind my desk. "I'm here to formally request your department's assistance," she said while her back was turned.

"Not to minimize our ability to 'assist' the DEA," I offered, "but what can a small Texas department offer that your people don't already have?"

Fleming stepped back from the window and gave me a hard stare. "Nice view from here. Lot nicer than the one from my office in Houston." She retook her seat, then sat quietly for a few minutes, as if contemplating the best way to approach me.

"Are you checking my suit for lint?" I began to feel like a bug under a microscope and hoped the question would lessen my tension.

Fleming's stern demeanor eased a bit with the beginnings of a smile, then her face quickly recovered its no-nonsense countenance. "Maybe what I'm doing is trying to figure out why you're sitting behind that desk, and not out taking down the bad guys." Her expression softened. "You're good at that."

Having the Special Agent in Charge of DEA operations in a wide swath of Texas compliment me felt downright awkward. And this severely dressed agent was also a beautiful woman. "I've got a family," was the best I could come out with.

Fleming said, "I don't. Two marriages, two divorces. No kids. Cops generally don't make good spouses." She suddenly laughed. "If you ever decide you'd like to get back out on the street again, come see me. My agency needs some straight shooters."

"Are you here to offer me a job?" I asked. My tension hadn't eased one bit.

"It's there if you are ever interested," she said. "But, no. I just put that out there."

"I'm deeply flattered." And I was. "But—"

Fleming stood. "We don't know if *los Zetas* are going to try another crossing in Kickapoo County. I'm going to have Agent Breaux fully brief you on everything – and I mean everything – we have in the way of intel. There may be another attempt in or near Kickapoo County, but we don't know for sure." She stepped to the office's door. "I've done some homework on you, Commander, as you might expect that I would. And the DEA needs all the help we can get right now. What I'm saying is, I personally trust you. I trust that any information we provide you and your department will be used in the right way." Fleming paused and the intensity of her focus on me lessened "And I would appreciate that trust being reciprocated."

"I'm flattered," I repeated and gestured at my meager office. "But what is it you are asking of me? This conversation isn't just about the Texas State Drug

Interdiction Support Department, is it?" This conversation was getting stranger and stranger.

"No."

"Then what?"

"I've got good agents. They need to know that the DEA has friends who are willing and able to help them. One is Leroy Breaux."

I couldn't resist. "What about Jack Eddleman?"

Without answering, she extended her hand, and I shook it.

"I'll see myself out. You have my phone number, and I can be contacted any time you feel your department can be of assistance. I would appreciate it if you have something important that you call me personally before sharing that information with anyone else."

She turned and exited my office, exchanged pleasantries with Ms. Trejo, then disappeared out the front door.

I stood still, wondering exactly what was being asked of me.

"Commander, can I come in?" Ms. Trejo rapped on the door.

Her eyes widened when she saw me looking somewhat dumbstruck.

"I like that woman," she said. "Not much nonsense." She cocked her head. "You look stunned. Are you okay?"

"I think so." I shook my head, remembering Fleming's non-response when asked about Eddleman. "I'd hate to be on her bad side."

I returned to my desk chair and Alicia followed me in.

"If you don't mind my asking, Commander, what does she want our department to do for the DEA?"

I turned and gazed out the window. "I'm not sure. She's making a request for assistance, which is pretty standard. She says she's sending an agent to give me a briefing." To myself, I conjectured, *Or she just signaled that she doesn't trust one of her own agents and wants me to be her eyes and ears.*

*****

Betty and Forrest were in the living room when I opened the front door. I thought of my offer to come sit with Doris and reached for my cellphone to call.

The anticipation on Betty's face made me put the phone back in my pocket. I'd call later.

"Let's go, Dad," Forrest yelled. "We're going out to eat before I pick out the paint I want."

Walking to the car, Betty muttered, "What's this about it being okay with his room looking like the inside of a pirate ship?"

After a meal of chicken tenders and French fries, and a child's impatience with his parents' endless comparisons of different shades of off-white, Forrest fell asleep on the way home. I gently carried him into his bedroom, and Betty and I undressed him and tucked him in.

In the kitchen, Betty pulled out a container of Blue Bell chocolate ice cream. She handed me a bowl and we sat at the kitchen table.

"I enjoyed our time together as a family, Purdy."

"I did too," I replied, "but I must tell you 'ancient Persian alabaster' isn't going to cut it in our new bedroom."

She feigned shock. "What? And you want what? 'Chantilly lace?' Ridiculous."

We broke into laughter. The colors were virtually identical.

My phone rang. Harris Whittaker. I'd forgotten to call Abner's wife, Doris. I'd forgotten my offer to come sit with her. "Harris, I was just going to call. Sorry."

"Purdy, it isn't necessary. Don't worry about it." His voice cracked.

"What?"

"Abner's gone. He went into arrest about an hour ago. They couldn't get a heartbeat back. He's dead."

Chapter 37

An unpleasant truth and a long, lonely ride

Betty carried my overnight bag and we walked to Lowell's four-door pickup. He'd said he wasn't in any hurry to get it back, and I'd kept putting off doing something about securing another vehicle.

"I'll miss you, big boy," she said.

"I'm not planning on an overnighter, hon," I replied, "but you never know."

Abner Selman was dead, and Abner's wife, Doris, wanted me to serve as a pall bearer at his funeral. I was driving to San Antonio to visit with Doris to provide some support and learn about the arrangements. Victoria Fleming's not-so-veiled suggestion that I assist her with issues within the DEA was gnawing on me, but I put a smile on my face.

As promised, Breaux had arranged a meeting with me. "I'm going by the ME's office," he had said. "Picking up some evidence recovered off the bodies of those *sicarios*. It's near the ranger's home."

When my cell phone vibrated, I distractedly reached into my pocket and glanced at the screen: Lilly Pardo, the last person I needed to deal with. I mouthed an "I'm sorry" to Betty, and reluctantly, answered. "Lilly, how are things?" I kept my tone light and breezy, like asking someone, "Hey, how'd it go at Disneyworld?"

"What did you do with Teofilo?" Lilly shouted, loud enough I had to pull the phone away from my ear.

Betty looked at me quizzically. I hung up and gave a sheepish look.

"What was that all about?" she asked.

"Nothing."

"Uh huh." She reached her arms around me and rested her head against my chest. "Be careful, Purdy. Please be careful."

I felt myself drawing strength from that amazing woman. "I will," I responded, not very reassuringly. I kissed her forehead and stepped up into truck, but a familiar gray Toyota pulled to the curb, and blocked me. Instinctively, I got out, pulled Betty around behind me, and reached for my pistol.

Long salt and pepper hair flying, a female exited the car. As I was trying to piece together where I had seen the primer-spotted car, the driver yelled. "What did you do to Teofilo?"

Holy shit! Lilly Pardo, I thought. Her black hair was showing grayer than the last time we'd met. She slammed her car door and stomped up the driveway, hands on her hips. "What did you fucking do with Teo, Deputy?"

I glimpsed the retired couple next door and worried what they would think. My face must have turned beet red. I knew I had to get Lilly out of the public eye, and not so much for her safety, which at the moment I didn't give a damn about. I was ashamed I had allowed Lilly to embarrass my wife. I was also afraid of what she might reveal to Betty. I had never talked about the *sicario's* killing at the hands of Lilly, Teofilo and Israel Sifuentes. It was a necessary act, I knew. Had the killer been turned over to the police, or turned loose, their lives, and no doubt those of any family members would have ended brutally at the hands of a Mexican cartel. Its dark reality was not something I wanted Betty to be involved in.

"Calm down, Lilly. Let's talk somewhere." I said, thankful Forrest was in school. "How did you know where I live?"

"I found out where your office is and was going to go there, then I saw you leave that big building, so I followed you." Her shoulders sagged. "I'll lock my car and be right back." She turned toward the street.

"You want to tell me what's going on?" Betty asked.

"That's Lilly Pardo," I said.

"Well, duh. I've eaten a few dozen times at the Cenizo Diner. But why is she raising hell with you in front of our neighbors?" Betty squinted. She was pissed.

Lilly returned and gave Betty a hug. "You are still as beautiful as ever," Lilly said. "How do you put up with this guy?" She lowered her head. "Sorry for making so much noise."

I had not shared Teofilo's involvement in the recent Lagrimas shootout with anyone except law enforcement. Nor had I shared his semi-illegal kidnapping that I instituted. I wracked my brain figuring out how much Lilly knew. I didn't want her in the house.

"Leave your car here, Lilly. Let's get a cup of coffee."

"You all can come inside," Betty offered, glancing at the neighbors who seemed reluctant to leave the show. "Or if not, at least keep your voices down."

I said, "C'mon, Lilly. Let's go talk."

She walked past me and right through the garage and into the kitchen. She took the chair Betty offered and pulled it up to the table. *Shit.*

I caught Betty's eye when I closed the door and quickly shook my head. She took the hint and excused herself. I breathed a sigh of relief.

Once I heard the door to our bedroom close, I turned to Lilly and, in a low voice, demanded. "What are you talking about?"

"You know goddamned well what I'm talking about, Deputy."

I dissembled. "I still have no idea what you're talking about."

"Fuck you! My cousin said you kidnapped him!"

Oh shit. I motioned for her to talk softly. "Teo's alive? Where is he?" *And how in hell did he get ahold of you?*

"Purdy, Teo's dying of cancer. You shouldn't have treated him that way." Lilly began crying. "I gotta take care of him. He's family."

I was now *Purdy*, instead of *Deputy*. I wasn't sure that was a good thing.

"Where are you staying now? San Antonio? Seguin?" I got no response. "You watch TV?"

"*Pues*, yes," she said in a tone showing how stupid she thought the question.

"Then you've seen all the coverage on the drug bust at Lagrimas." I paused.

"Jesus, Purdy. Teo was there?" She sounded incredulous, her eyes flashing.

I reached into a cupboard, took a glass, and poured Lilly a glass of water from a pitcher in the refrigerator. She looked like she needed it. I leaned toward her after she had taken a drink. "Hell yes, Teo was there. He wanted me to cross into Mexico and help him kill *sicarios*. I couldn't do that. When he crossed the river, we grabbed him to keep him from getting himself killed." I thought through the whole scene when Lilly, Teofilo, and Israel Sifuentes killed the *sicario* in that deserted adobe structure two years ago. Now the whole incident had landed smack dab on my table. "You remember that 'dobe with the missing door, and the roof caving in?"

She blanched, pushed away some hair that had covered her face, then sat quietly. "You mean the same one we had the *sicario* tied up, before we...."

I stopped her. She'd said too much.

"Jeezus, of course I do."

I took a deep breath, catching a glimpse of my image in the reflection off a window above the sink. My face was flushed. "We got him out just before the cartel showed up with a load of drugs, and all hell broke loose. The Lagrimas shoot-out all over the news. Last time we talked, you told me he was at a doctor's office in Acuña, hitching a ride back to Parrita. Then he shows up in Texas, promising to kill as many cartel members as he can before he dies. Had he told you those plans?"

"Well..."

"Well, what?" I took a deep breath. I wanted to pull my hair out and scream.

"That silly bastard," she laughed. "He didn't tell me all of this. Just that he met with you about something and then, a little bit later, you and some other *pinches* grabbed him."

Teo had told her the truth— as far as it went. "Where is he now? And how'd he get in touch with you?"

"Like I said, he didn't *before* all this. *Mi primo* kept his cell phone. He told me he jumped out of a truck. He said a *bolillo*— a fat, bald one who sounds like it was *tu amigo,* Jake, the dispatcher handcuffed him and took him somewhere. Is that right?"

"Doesn't matter. What matters is where he is now. Is he in Mexico?"

"No," Lilly smacked the kitchen table hard with the palm of her hand. "He's sick, Deputy. I could barely hear him." She whimpered. "Teo's a good man. He doesn't need to die away from his family."

"Lilly, when did he call you?"

"He said the driver got distracted. The driver got out of his pickup truck, to *hacer pis*, and Teo jumped out and ran into the bushes and started walking toward Mexico, but he got tired."

I shook my head. Jake was supposed to hide Teo at the Griffin ranch house, but when I failed to check on him, he had loaded Teo into his truck and driven back toward US 90 where he could get cell coverage. I imagined Jake, standing next to his F150 taking a leak as his prisoner hightailed it. "Where is Teo now?"

Lilly jutted her chin out indignantly. "I don't want to tell you. I trusted you. You might call *la migra* on him." She took out a handkerchief to wipe her sniffles.

"Christ Almighty, Lilly, you know me better than that." With the many illegals crossing the border these days the chances of interesting the Border Patrol in picking up a dying Mexican in the middle of nowhere was unlikely, and she knew it. "Did Teo go back to Parrita?"

Reluctantly, Lilly said, "No, he never crossed."

I had seen the huarache prints in the mud at the Rio Grande's edge, but I said nothing. "Well, where is he now?"

"He said the water was too high and he was afraid he would drown. He's hiding at your old girlfriend's — I mean that ranch you own."

"Holy shit, Lilly. Are you saying your cousin is at the Griffin Ranch?" There was no cell coverage at the Griffin Ranch. I knew that as a certainty. "Where did he call you from?" I persisted.

"He said he wasn't feeling strong enough to swim across, so he climbed up on some small mountain and that's where he got a phone signal. He called me."

It made sense. Teo may have been uneducated, but he wasn't stupid. If Jake could search for cell phone coverage, so could he.

I was afraid to ask again but did anyway. "When was this? Please, Lilly, where is Teo?"

"He's in a barn next to that big ole house at Laura's— oops, sorry — Mr. Griffin's, I guess now it's your place. He broke in. He's hiding out. I want to go help him, Deputy, but I'm not sure how to get there. I only know more or less where it is."

The dying village elder was in an outbuilding on my ranch close to the Rio Grande. *What else could go wrong?* I thought.

I secured a promise from Lilly to go back to her cousin's house, wherever that was, and assured her I'd be responsible for Teofilo's wellbeing. I escorted her to her car. I couldn't erase the mental image of Israel Sifuentes' head impaled on a fence post. I didn't want what happened to him to happen to Lilly or Teo.

Betty came out of the bedroom when I walked back into the house. "Purdy, I wasn't trying to listen in. I even started to turn on the television to drown out you two. But I didn't. And now I'm wondering how much you've kept from me."

The fat was in the fire now, and I groped for the right thing to say. "I've always been truthful with you, Betty. But some things have happened that you don't need to know about. So, I left some stuff out."

"To protect me?" Her voice rose.

"Believe it or not, definitely yes." The pistol shot that dispatched the *sicario* echoed in my memory.

Betty's face was telling me a story I had heard before: The trust I had won back had been lost again.

"Sounds like you're going to go to Kickapoo County. Are you?"

"Yes, I guess I am."

I tried to hug her, but she turned away and walked toward the bedroom.

*****

I called Lowell Johnson at his office. He, like probably everyone in the state of Texas with a television, had heard about Abner's death.

"Sorry, amigo. I know you and he were close," Lowell said.

"Didn't know how close 'til it was too late," I said, remembering how Abner had saved my life more than once. We had seen human brutality up close. The ranger had been instrumental in me getting the new job in Austin. Yet, as many experiences as we'd weathered, he had never told me anything about his family. I learned Harris Whittaker was Abner's stepson while Abner lay unconscious, near death.

"I was going to get your truck to you, but I need it just a little bit longer, if that's okay."

"Just don't get it shot up."

I knew he was joking but the comment jolted me, remembering the damage done to mine in the gun battle at Lagrimas.

I got in the pickup and I started it up to drive to Kickapoo County. We were still connected on the phone, but neither of us was speaking. My thoughts encompassed me.

Lowell broke into my thoughts. "When's the funeral?"

"Not sure."

"When are you coming back to Santa Rosa?"

"That's what I wanted to talk to you about." And for the next ten minutes, I unloaded on Lowell. I heard the *clack* of ice as he worked on his early afternoon scotch. His drinking bothered me. No telling what it was doing to his liver. But right now, I needed an ear to bend, and he was willing to provide it.

I slowed as I entered Hondo, not so much because I was worried about a speeding ticket, but out of respect for any town that had the *cojones* to greet motorists at the city limits with a sign loudly proclaiming "This is God's Country. Please Don't Drive Through It Like Hell."

I crossed the bridge over the northern reaches of Lake Amistad. US 90 wended north through the tiny town of Comstock, and then generally west, following the Rio Grande's course to its south. The headlights caught fewer and fewer images of vegetation.

I kept my foot pinned to the accelerator. I passed the historical markers pointing toward Judge Roy Bean's Jersey Lilly saloon. Soon, I'd be back in Kickapoo County, and Lowell and I were still talking.

As my headlights reflected off the Kickapoo County highway marker, the newspaper editor yawned. "You've kept me up yakking so long I've damned near drained a good bottle of scotch. I need to head to the house."

"Don't drive drunk, Lowell," I cautioned, knowing he often did.

He ignored me. "You're always welcome to sleep on the sofa here at the office. Key's under the mat if you don't want to rent a room in Patel's luxury motel. Sounds like you've put yourself between a rock and a hard spot, Purdy."

"Yes, I have," I acknowledged.

"I have full confidence in you." Lowell's vowels were starting to elongate. "You'll figure something out."

I hoped he was right.

Chapter 38
Zetas await orders, avoiding surveillance

This waiting is for shit. Navarrete thought and pulled a bandana from his hip pocket to wipe his forehead, hoping his panicky thoughts couldn't be sensed by the three *sicarios* who had accompanied him to the hideout north of the Mexican village of Parrita.

The three, selected by Blanco, had escorted him and the unwounded survivor from the Lagrimas battle. The group, its number swollen to fifteen, sat somnolent in the late afternoon sun under a rocky overhang that did little to ease the stifling heat.

For the fourth time since dawn, Navarrete counted the bundles of fentanyl lashed down in the bed of a pickup, as if his life depended on each one's continued existence. Sweat dripped from his face when he leaned over the truck's side. Suddenly, a wave of nausea swept through him.

Fighting against the sudden urge to vomit, he glanced around. One of his "keepers," as he had dubbed the three *sicarios* assigned to him, wore a baseball cap pulled low, which concealed his face. That one sat in the sand whittling on a small stick. The knife's stroke paused just long enough to confirm he'd seen Navarrete's furtive glance. Navarrete stepped away from the truck and reached for a water bottle.

My keepers look like the yanqui *characters I once saw on television,* he thought. He tried to remember the names. The one carving with the knife had a full head of hair, chopped off abruptly at ear level. He thought, *I'll call that evil-eyed bastard Moe.*

Deeper under the overhang, he spotted the other two keepers. The stockier of the two wore no hat and kept his hair cropped short, looking almost bald. That bald-looking thug he called *Curly.* His thoughts ranged facetiously. *And the taller one with the lighter, curly hair and look of innocence? I think the gringos named him Larry, but he'll be Lorenzo. Yes, Lorenzo with the curls, Curly the* melonhead, *and Moe, the evil looking little shit with a mop of hair. My keepers.*

A quiet buzz broke the group's lethargy. Navarrete answered the satellite phone. *Si?"*

A heavily modified voice answered. "You go tonight. The crossing is safe."

No way to know, but Navarrete felt sure that he was talking to Blanco. "Time?"

"Get the product across before dawn. There, someone will meet you."

"How do I know who to look for?"

"There'll be a boat. There was rain to the west. The water's up in the river, so you may need to make two or three trips. Get the product across the river. Someone will take delivery there."

"I need more information."

A grunt followed, or what seemed like one, although with the encryption it was hard to tell. "What?"

"You say someone will meet us. How much time will I have to leave the area once the loads are across? What is my window? Sunset? Last light? Sunrise? Moonrise?"

"I'll give you the specifics when I call the next time." The contact disconnected.

Several in the group now stood, looking at Navarrete. He nodded at them. "We go tonight."

A few smiled, relieved to have something to do to break the boredom of the last few days. Navarrete checked his watch: Two p.m. At least six hours until it would be dark enough to chance movement. With only twenty or so kilometers to the Rio Bravo, it will take less than an hour to reach the crossing.

US border guards usually underestimated *los Zetas'* ability to penetrate their empire's fragile border. But why go now so soon after the disaster at the first crossing?

Navarette knew *los Zetas* gathered intelligence like a warring nation. Likewise, *los Zetas* did its best to keep track of *los yanquis* and their drone schedules, the coverage obtained by the tethered balloons, and the *norteamericanos'* military satellites on their polar circuits. If there was any question that trafficking drugs into the United States could result in disastrous consequences, one only had to look at what had just occurred at Lagrimas.

And now, Navarrete thought, *I am being told to ensure a successful crossing into the same fucking part of Texas and at a location where two years ago, there was a huge gun battle with the* gringos.

Navarrete eyed Lorenzo, Curly, and Moe, who had intermingled with the others. He announced, "Time to get something to eat. No more mescal or tequila. Check your weapons. Start the engines and let them idle for a few minutes. I don't want any surprises like dead batteries at the last minute."

An hour later, the phone chirped again. "Do you have something to write on?"

"Yes." Listening, he wrote down the specific times for sunset, moonrise, and total darkness.

"Anything else?" the voice asked.

"And what are my instructions for San Antonio? I am responsible to ensure the delivery."

A pause. "You'll get those instructions once the product is crossed." The phone connection ended.

Bile rose in Navarrete's throat, and a sudden cold sweat made him involuntarily shiver.

"*Que pasa, jefe*?" one of the *Zetas* asked.

"*Nada,*" Navarrete responded. He swallowed, once, twice, then reached to steady himself on a rocky protrusion of the overhang wall. "All is well. We have our times for darkness. There will only be a sliver of moon tonight." Feeling less likely to faint, he took a deep breath. His three keepers eyed him closely. Finally, he steadied his hand, and drank from a water bottle. His mind raced as reality hit. *Santa Muerte, there won't be any instructions for me once the drugs are across. Cantinflas, that rotten bastard! He's going to have me killed!*

Navarrete walked to Lorenzo, the nearest of the three keepers. "Let me inspect your weapons."

"Why?"

Navarrete grabbed the man's AK-47 and pulled back the charging handle far enough to see a round in the chamber. "Because I want to come back from this job alive, *pendejo.* And, because I said so." He checked the safety, then tossed the weapon back. "Now your *pistola.*"

Lorenzo cut his eyes toward Moe, then grudgingly handed Navarrete his holstered automatic. Navarrete repeated the procedure, then handed the weapon back.

As I suspected, the little mop-headed bastard is calling the shots for you three, he thought.

Seeing Navarrete's sudden anger, the other men lined up to be inspected. He went down the ragged line, eyeing each weapon, pretending that he cared.

Navarrete finished the inspection and squinted his eyes against the harshness of the northern Mexican desert. There was no one he could trust, no one with whom he dared share the realization of his own impending death. Probably, his killer would be one or more of his 'keepers' Blanco had ordered to accompany him. But it could easily be any of the men, despite his claim to Blanco that this crew of killers were loyal to him personally. His eyes scanned the entire group while he wondered, *which one of you has the instruction to put a bullet in my head? When will you do it?*

*****

Blanco disconnected the encrypted link and settled back into a wicker chair on his hacienda's wide veranda. He reached for a bottle of mescal and poured just enough to fill the slender glass container called a *caballito.* Honeybees flew about the nearby bougainvillea's pollen-ladened blooms. A slight, dark-skinned gardener slowly hacked at shrubbery with a machete, his slices syncopating to the drone of the insects. Blanco took a sip and set the liquor gently on the table next to him. This was no time to allow the liquid to affect his judgment.

He rose and strode to his armored SUV. "It's time to go," he said to a burly *sicario*, who immediately stepped into the driver's seat. "It's going to be a long drive."

With lead and tail vehicles ensuring his safety, Blanco drove toward Ciudad Acuña, then onto the dirt road that, in five grinding hours of dust, led to the ancient, fortified hacienda west of the hamlet of El Mosco. He was going to be certain that Navarrete, once his trusted lieutenant, would not return alive once the drugs were successfully moved into Texas.

You sent a sicario *into Texas to kill some pissant named Israel Sifuentes without my permission because you wanted revenge. You insulted me – called my plans stupid. Well, Señor Navarrete,* El Tramposo, *your cunning can no longer be trusted. You will not live to see tomorrow's dawn.*

Chapter 39

Teofilo found and someone prowling the ranch

T he moment I arrived at the Griffin Ranch, I realized I had forgotten my appointment with Agent Breaux at the Bexar County ME's office. My phone showed no cell coverage. Should I retrace my steps to US 90, call and re-schedule, or blow it off and try to find Teofilo?

I decided Breaux deserved the courtesy of a phone call. I turned around and headed north on County Road 106, eyeing my cell phone screen. I finally got a signal halfway to US 90 and punched in Breaux's number. It went to voicemail. I checked the time: 8:45. Some orange sky was still visible in the west.

"Agent Breaux, Purdy Kendricks here. I can't make it to the ME's office. Had to make a run to Kickapoo County. Personal emergency. I'll get with you asap. I apologize. We'll need to reschedule. I'm losing coverage in a mile or so, so if you call and don't get me, I'll call you back."

I disconnected, then drove to the ranch. Approaching the front gate, I wondered if I would ever think of the acreage as anything other than "the Griffin Ranch." It was mine and had been for two years. Recently, I'd thought of its possible uses. Return it to a working ranch or just a place to take family and friends hunting. Those ideas were all academic now. I promised Betty I would sell the place.

The front gate chain was secure, but now that someone had inserted another lock in the links, whoever it was could have easily entered and re-secured the opening. I opened my lock, unhooked the chain, and pushed the gate open. I killed the truck headlights and drove onto the property then got out of the truck and re-hooked the lock in the chain but didn't secure it.

I reached in the back seat for the loaded M16, its extra two 30-round magazines, and the assault shotgun loaded with double aught buckshot. I set the firearms barrel down to the floor on the front passenger side and set the extra magazines on the seat.

A quarter of a mile from the house and smaller structures, I pulled a football length off the road, tucking the truck in behind a small rock outcropping. From my vantage point, the dim shapes of the place's old headquarters, which included the workshop that Lilly had called the barn, and the lone live oak tree, formed gray shapes against the lighter background of caliche and sand. Turning the engine off, I grabbed a flashlight from the glovebox, stepped out, and gently pushed the driver's door closed. After hearing the door's soft click, I moved away from the truck and into the sparse brush and waited.

The caress of a gentle north breeze magnified the emptiness of this part of Texas. A few grasshoppers flitted by in the gloom, their legs sawing the air. Miles away, a pack of coyotes yipped and were soon answered by another pack. The sweep of the Milky Way, and its billions of stars, burnt a hole through the darkness, casting an eerie collection of shadows as it lit greasewood, huisache and mesquite spread across the ranch.

Lilly had said Teofilo was hiding on the property. Even if she hadn't told the village elder, Teo would know I'd be the one who'd come looking for him. He wouldn't hurt me. Anyone else lurking on the ranch wouldn't be so inclined.

I stood quietly, listening. Several minutes passed, and I wondered if a trespasser was even anywhere nearby. I clicked on the flashlight, shielding most of its light with the palm of my hand. I stooped and moved to where the road's hard caliche base dipped for several yards into soft sand. The surface showed several tire tracks, but the edges of the tracks had crumbled into the impressions. There was no way for me to tell when the road had last been disturbed. The vague outlines might show Jake's coming and going, and nothing more.

I touched my cellphone: 9:05. I walked back to the passenger side of Lowell's truck. Reaching through its window so the interior light wouldn't come on, I grabbed the M16 and slung it on my back, stuffed the extra magazine in my pants pockets and, carrying the shotgun, began walking toward the ranch's old headquarters. Boots weren't the best footwear for creeping up on someone, so I kept scanning the buildings and charted a zigzag course around loose pebbles as the structures loomed closer.

Clayton Griffin's ranch house was a rambling structure, added on to haphazardly over its life. As originally planned, its main entrance faced me. However, in all the years I had worked at the ranch and known the man, I could not remember a soul who ever used the house's front door. Its cement walkway, cracked in several places and covered with the creep of desert sand and weeds, was a testament to its disuse. Everyone used the screened patio's entrance on the back side of the house.

The front windows, covered with thin, metal venetian blinds, appeared closed. About half a football field away, I squatted and listened long and hard. All I could hear was blood pulsing in my ears.

Willing my heart to stop racing, it dawned on me — I'd left my body armor in the truck.

Shit! Stupid. Stupid. Stupid. Well, Purdy, what are you worried about? I thought. *If someone's going to kill you, it'll probably be with a headshot.*

I took a deep breath, then raced to the corner of the house. No gunshot. No sounds but me gulping air. Why was I doing this? I stepped around from the side of the house and looked south. The lone live oak tree had provided respite from the Texas sun in the open parking area. It stood sentry about a hundred feet from the back of the house. There was no sign of any vehicle in the triangle formed by the tree, the workshop, and the Griffin screened-in porch. Staying close to the walls and ducking under the windows, I made it to the screen door and pulled it open.

The wooden door's long spring moaned as it stretched. I moved through the porch to the exterior wooden door that opened into the kitchen, and gently turned the knob. Its mechanism squealed. I was sweating and suddenly wished

I'd brought a can of WD40. I pushed open the door and it banged against an interior wall that separated the kitchen from a bedroom. The only sound was the ancient refrigerator's uneven hum. I remained on the porch, propped the shotgun against the outside wall, and, shielding the beam, turned on the flashlight. I knelt and rolled the flashlight inside across the worn linoleum floor, I ducked back outside. I checked the window adjacent to the door and directly above the kitchen sink. My heavy metal flashlight tracked an arced course, its light showing the kitchen and adjacent living room were unoccupied.

Checking behind me, I grabbed the shotgun and entered the house. The flashlight's beam noiselessly yawed back and forth. Nothing. Another heart-pounding minute confirmed there was no one in the house. Inside the refrigerator, some of the edibles I'd bought for Jake and Teo were missing. The half-gallon of milk was almost empty, and sandwich meat containers were almost depleted.

Still leery about turning on any lights, I closed the refrigerator and stepped back onto the screened porch. Lilly had described a barn. The workshop that she had called a barn stood a stone's throw away. The building had mostly sat unused for years. The workshop's two oversized wooden doors drooped tiredly on their massive strap hinges, and the crude iron latch dangled from its pivot point instead of securing the other door in its drop bar.

A shadowy figure swooped down, scaring the hell out of me. A giant barn owl made quick work of a small rodent which had lost its race along the ground to the safety of some low bushes. If that predator felt comfortable enough to have supper nearby, I figured there was no one lurking in the shadows.

The owl swiveled its head toward me in that eerie owl fashion, When I neared the workshop, it took two hops, and holding its victim in its beak, flapped its huge wings, and disappeared into the foliage of the live oak. I turned the flashlight on the shop doors and spoke softly in Spanish. "Teofilo, are you in there?"

I heard a soft rustling, then a low moan. Pulling up on one door to keep it from dragging the ground and swung it open, aiming my flashlight inside. The beam swept past walls adorned with old fan belts and benches holding oil cans and dusty tools, then onto a small figure, prone on the ground.

Teofilo shielded his eyes from the light. I aimed the light away from him, ensured he was alone. He had spread a yellow sheet he'd retrieved from the house on the dusty floor and now lay on his side, his ribcage showing the heavy breathing of someone in pain.

"Por qué estás tirado en la tierra y no dentro de la casa?" I asked. *Why are you lying in the dirt and not inside the house?* I propped the shotgun up against the back wall and knelt and felt his forehead. He was burning with fever. "Let's get you in the house."

The disease seemed to have whittled on Teo's small stature. I clicked off the flashlight and stuck it in a back pocket, then scooped my hands under him. When I stood, he groaned in pain.

"Just a few minutes, *viejo.* We're going into the house and put you in a real bed." My mind raced. *Do I dare take him into Santa Rosa for medical help, and if I do, will it make any difference?*

He reached up and pulled on my shirt. *"Espérate, por favor."*

I kept walking and his tugging became violent, or as violent as a dying man's tug could be.

"No sales de aquí. Hay otro hombre en tu rancho. Cuidado." He was telling me another man was on the ranch and to be careful.

"Mejicano o gringo? ¿Dónde está ahora? Where is this hombre now?" I peered into the starlit terrain. A thin crescent of moon crept over the horizon.

"Creo que es un bolillo. I did not hear the *camioneta* leave."

Deep worry filling my mind. I was about to drop Teo. I shifted him gently, took a breath, and started toward the house's screened porch door. I wondered, *Who is this "white man" he said was here.*

Teo pulled on me again and pointed at something to my left. "Look," he said. "The white man was digging there."

I turned. A small mound of dirt lay piled between the building's north wall and a mesquite tree. *What in hell? An Anglo digging a hole, driving a pickup, and still on the ranch?* I grunted and continued into the house, clicked on an overhead light, thankful I'd paid the electricity bill, and placed Teo on top of a double bed in the nearest bedroom. I covered him with a quilt. Two years before, a sniper had been brutally snuffed out in this room. The repainting job didn't erase the memory of the gore that had been splattered over the room's walls.

"Please, Señor Purdy, cover me up," he replied. "*Tengo frio.*"

Despite the fever, he shivered. First, I got him a drink of water, filling a glass from the kitchen sink. He guzzled it down. Then I grabbed another quilt and tucked it around him. "I'll be back in a minute."

Teo's eyes closed, and his withered hands appeared from under the quilt, pulling it up further toward his chin. I clicked off the light.

"I'm going to get my truck," I told Teo. "We're going to see about getting you to a doctor."

I took the half step from the screened porch to the dirt and checked the cell phone. It was now 9:30. Only twenty-five minutes since I'd checked, but it seemed like an eternity. I went inside the workshop to retrieve my shotgun, all the while wondering what I was supposed to do with a dying man on the wrong side of the border. I dragged the two doors closed, flopped the wooden latch into its holder, and jogged up the road. Adjacent to the ranch's road, a pasture fence was anchored by a string of ancient mesquite fence posts. Something caught my eye. It was a faint light reflecting off the greyness of the fence posts.

Headlights seesawed up the Griffin Ranch road. No way could I make it to Lowell Johnson's truck. I turned and raced to the house. The vehicle, maybe a mile away, was coming from the direction of the river.

Chapter 40

Breaux's unlawful entry yields an important clue

Leroy Breaux squeezed into a booth for supper at the Jim's Restaurant on Broadway and Loop 410. He was due to be meeting Kendricks at nine p.m. There were other Jim's nearer the Bexar County Medical Examiner's office, but he'd still have fifteen minutes to get there, and he liked this location.

His waitress, Dottie by her nametag, sported a beehive hairdo with more than a touch of henna. She plunked down a large plate, and then topped off his tea glass. He thanked her, which was all that was needed to get her talking.

"What's your name, honey?" she asked.

"Breaux. Leroy Breaux." He extended his hand. She shook it, nodding. "Thought you sounded like a Breaux, with that accent of yours. What part of Louisiana?"

He told her Vinton, which drew a cackle from the waitress. "Good Lord, I'm from Sulphur." He glanced at his chicken fried steak, hoping it wouldn't get cold, but soon was trading stories about growing up in Calcasieu Parish.

Breaux's cellphone, tucked into a light jacket wadded up next to him, buzzed. He didn't notice it.

He left a generous tip on the table and donned his jacket. Time to meet with Purdy Kendricks. When he pulled the cellphone out of the jacket's pocket, he noticed the missed call. After listening to Purdy's message, he muttered "Damn it." He glanced at his briefcase. "I spent a shit load of time putting together this intel package for you, and you blow off our meeting." He got in his truck and started the engine. *And my boss made it clear I was to brief you as if you were one of ours.*

Breaux punched in Purdy's phone number, and it went to voicemail. He started to leave a message but disconnected instead. Where was Kendricks going in Kickapoo County that he was about to lose cell coverage? Breaux wasn't as familiar with the area as Kendricks, but he'd spent enough time there to know where some of the dead spots were. He turned off the engine and considered a mental map of the border county. Coverage near Lagrimas was spotty. So was the western edge of the county near the old Shell gas plant. So was the Griffin Ranch.

Breaux tried Kendrick's cellphone. Voicemail again. "Hey, you stood me up, Purdy. Where are you?" He scrolled through his phone's contact list until he came to Special Agent Victoria Fleming's personal phone number. He was tempted to call it but didn't. He didn't have enough information and he'd just piss off his boss.

Instead, he called Jack Eddleman. The phone went to voicemail. "Hey, just calling to check on you. Seeing if you're feeling better." Breaux disconnected.

While he backed out of the parking lot, his cellphone buzzed. Eddleman. Breaux pulled off the Loop 410 access road and into a service station and said, "Hey, just called to see if you were doing okay."

Eddleman laughed, then coughed. "Sorry, yeah, I'm doing better but still have a nasty cough. I'll try to make it in to work in a couple of days. If something interesting comes up, call me, but I don't want to pass a bug around the office."

They talked for a few moments. Breaux, remembering Fleming's warning, decided not to tell Eddleman about sharing information with Kendricks. Instead, he offered to stop by a Walgreens and buy some cough medicine. The Vasquez killing almost got Eddleman fired. Now, Fleming was asking more questions about Eddleman's conduct. Breaux felt he had been put in the middle, and it felt extremely uncomfortable.

"I'm okay. Thanks, but I just need to ride this out," Eddleman responded, ending the call with a sneezing attack.

What am I going to do now? thought Breaux. *Go home and twiddle my thumbs?* Whatever was bothering him hadn't gone away. He pulled out of the service station and drove toward Eddleman's apartment complex.

From where he parked, he could see Eddleman's second story apartment. From a distance, it looked as if the lights were out, and the balcony drapes were closed. Odd, or maybe not. Eddleman could be in bed in a bedroom with its door shut. Breaux parked at the far end of the parking lot and searched for Eddleman's truck. The complex had numbered slots for its tenants. Empty. To be sure, Breaux made two more passes through the complex's parking lot.

Satisfied Eddleman's vehicle was absent, Breaux climbed the concrete and steel staircase to Eddleman's apartment and knocked on the door. No response. He kept knocking even louder, then the door to an adjoining apartment opened.

A skinny, nose-ringed, young woman, probably a college student, said, "I don't think he's here."

Breaux feigned indifference. "Okay, thanks. Just wanted to say hi to an old friend. I'll catch him later. Any idea when he'll be back?"

"No. I think he just moved in, didn't he? I saw him leave earlier today. Doesn't he have a pickup truck?"

Breaux paused and opted to answer the second question. "I think so, yes."

"Yeah, it was him. I was coming back from an early class and saw him driving off."

Breaux thanked her and walked down the stairs, paused, and then returned to Eddleman's apartment. *If he's sick, why isn't he here?* He wondered. *And where's he been since the nose-ringed kid saw him this morning?* He looked at the door with its Schlage deadbolt and keyed lockset. He returned to his truck, opened the truck's console, and removed a small toolkit pouch.

Back at Eddleman's door, he caught a whiff of marijuana from the student's apartment. Then female and male voices and laughter. He pulled on latex gloves and opened the toolkit. Inside lay a lock pick, rake pick, wafer pick, round pick, and hook pick. "The results of a misspent youth," he said to himself. The complex hadn't splurged on expensive door protection. The question was whether Eddleman had a security camera or some sort of tell awaiting uninvited visitors inside his apartment.

Using the lock picks, in less than a minute he was inside, softly closing the apartment door. Breaux breathed a sigh of relief. There was no unobtrusive piece of paper stuck in a crack of the door, or anything else to detect entry. He switched on a small penlight and held it in his mouth, sweeping the apartment for cameras. Nothing seemed out of the ordinary. The kitchen appeared hardly used. The small living room desk was bare. No briefcases, no computers. No shredder. He stepped toward the only bedroom. The double bed sheets and a quilt were pulled up and over a single pillow.

The walls were bare, except for dozens of pinholes that measled the wall between the bedroom and the living area. A single pushpin lay abandoned next to the baseboard. Something had been tacked up, then taken down. But what?

Eddleman could return at any minute. Breaux checked the waste baskets. Empty. Eddleman was too savvy to not see if someone had rifled through his clothing, so Breaux stayed away from the chest of drawers, feeling guiltier by the minute. Had he misjudged his fellow agent?

Ten minutes passed. Time to get out. His penlight beam swept across the bedroom floor. A piece of torn paper lay behind the door. It appeared to be a small fragment of a copied photograph. He slipped it in his pocket, checked the peephole to ensure no one was on the landing, stepped out, re-locked both the keyed entry and the deadbolt, and scurried down the stairs.

Slipping off the gloves, he hurried to his truck and stashed his lockpick set. If Breaux had left any evidence of his entry, Eddleman would figure the intrusion had been committed by someone close to him, or at the behest of the DEA. Not wanting to think about the potential consequences, he pushed it out of his mind. At a convenience store a few miles away, he sat in his truck trying to make sense of the lone scrap of paper.

The piece had been torn horizontally from standard width copier-quality paper. The imprinted side appeared to contain the base of a wood framed building, and, perhaps, the base of a tree.

"Hard to tell," Breaux muttered. He turned the strip over. He recognized Eddleman's printing: *Hackamore*. "What the hell does a horse halter have to do with this sliver of a photograph?" he muttered. He'd ridden horses while growing up. He looked at the scrap again. Something about the wooden structure and the dirt and caliche around its base rang a distant bell. It appeared to be a barn. "I've seen this," he mumbled. *But where?*

Breaux grew seething mad. Eddleman had lied to him and was nowhere to be found. Kendricks had begged off on a meeting at which he was supposed to receive all the DEA intel on potential drug smuggling attempts in Kickapoo County.

He wracked his brain, wondering whom he trusted to call to find out what was going on. His first thought was to contact Kendrick's friend, Jake, but he didn't have his cell number and didn't want to chance calling the Sheriff's Office number. Any calls in or out on that line were probably recorded.

"Lowell Johnson," he said out loud. Johnson had gone after Eddleman in print two years before, doing everything but accusing the DEA agent of murdering Pete Vasquez. Maybe not the best idea to reach out to this person, but Breaux admired the scrappy editor's personal courage, and was aware of the man's loyalty to Kendricks. He thumbed through his phone contacts and found the editor's number.

Lowell's voice was slurred when he answered, and Breaux wondered if he'd been drinking. He identified himself, then asked, "Have you heard from Purdy Kendricks lately?"

"Depends. Aren't you yoked at the hip with Eddleman? Why should I tell you a damned thing?"

"Eddleman's not with me, Mr. Johnson. I'm trying to find Kendricks. I'm concerned about him. I'd appreciate your cooperation."

Johnson belched. "Let me turn on the light. I fell asleep in front of the TV.

There was a click and shuffling noises. "Better. Yes, I've talked with Purdy. What time is it?" He didn't pause. "Yeah, we talked quite a bit. He was on his way here."

"Where's 'here'?"

"I assume Santa Rosa. He still has my truck. He said he'd had a row with his wife. She wants him as far away from Santa Rosa as one man can get, but he said he needed to get back to Kickapoo County. It didn't set well with her. I offered to put him up at my place, but he turned me down. I doubt he'd bother Paula, his sister-in-law. She's usually not a fan of his. I'm guessing he's at Patel's motel." He gave Breaux the phone number. "Is everything okay?"

Breaux didn't know enough to say otherwise, so he told the editor to go back to bed and hung up. He called Jagir Patel's motel office phone. Kendricks had not rented a room at the Paradise Inn.

Finally, Breaux checked in with the San Antonio DEA office. "Anything going on south of Kickapoo County since I left work?" he asked the duty agent.

"Nothing's changed. We've got a bird up with infrared tracking, but nothing spotted. No reports from the balloons, or from EPIC," the agent replied. "The Marfa balloon is down for maintenance but should be up tomorrow."

Something isn't right. "I'm heading to Kickapoo County now," Breaux said. "Show me checked out that way." Turning his truck toward US 90, he felt sure he'd find Kendricks at the Griffin Ranch. He worried that Eddleman might be there too.

Chaper 41

Navarrete awaits orders. Where is Eddleman?

Navarrete moved back and forth from men to equipment to men, repeating the process until his obvious stress evoked snickers from several *sicarios* hiding beneath the rock overhang. Navarrete realized he was looking foolish when he noticed eye rolling by several men who had been instructed for the third time to check the bindings on the drug bundles.

The sun's arc tracked west and south, the late afternoon shadows lengthening. Not trusting the deep shadows to protect his movements from snooping satellites — or worse — drones, Navarrete glanced overhead repeatedly. The simple truth was that he desperately needed to shit. No doubt the group had constructed some crude privy system before his arrival. Doubtful it would provide him much, if any privacy, Navarrete didn't ask about it.

Right now, I feel my keepers will look at my shit and try to read it like tea leaves. From a truck, he gathered a roll of toilet paper and a small shovel, and then found a place between two boulders. He lowered his pants and wedged himself into a squatting position. As his bowels relaxed, their watery contents confirmed nerves — and fear — were the primary causes for the sudden need to shit.

He scuffed a trough with his boot to allow his urine to drain away, adjusted his clothing to ensure he wouldn't soil them, and stared at the satellite phone he'd set on a nearby rock ledge. In the distance, a mockingbird kept up an endless squawking alarm, as if defending its nest or food supply. The occasional low laughter of the *Zetas* broke through the buzzing noise of grasshoppers. Vultures wheeled on updrafts in the distance, searching for carrion.

I need to think. Navarrete's mantra. *I need to think.* He had played out several scenarios so far and had not been able to find an ending in which he survived. The best he could come up with was to ensure the product got to the river and watching his back as best he could. He had challenged Blanco's authority and his intelligence. He'd even boasted he was indispensable. He had crossed the line. Blanco would kill him at some point. But when? The idea of vultures plucking his eyes from his corpse caused another shudder.

His phone beeped. Wedged into his basalt throne, he struggled quietly to finish his business and reach for it. The sound had carried far enough that the camp's low murmur of activity suddenly halted. He zipped up his trousers and stepped gingerly from the waste, then opened the phone's line with a curt, *"Aqui estoy."*

The strange, scrambled voice again: "Reach the water by ten. You'll be guided from there."

Navarrete had formed a question about finding another crossing point in the eastern end of the Texas county, but there was no chance to ask it. The connection ended as abruptly as it had opened.

Pura mierda, he muttered. Pure crap. Rejoining the men, he passed the word, "Tonight, we cross." He checked his wristwatch. His instructions were clear: Reach the river by ten p.m. Full darkness occurred around nine, and it would take less than an hour to cover the twenty kilometers. He checked the time. By that reckoning, it was three hours until the small convoy should move north.

Navarrete considered his chances of surviving Guillermo Blanco's wrath were slim, at best. If a complication entered his boss's plan, percentages might go higher. "We leave in an hour," he said.

"That's before dark," Lorenzo, one of the Three Stooges, said, making it sound like a question.

"I have to rely on what I'm told," Navarrete snapped. "That the balloon near Marfa is down for maintenance, and drones and the satellites are off somewhere else." Navarrete hoped his keepers would not survive whatever happened, so they could not relay this falsehood to Blanco, or anyone else in *los Zetas*. A long shot, but his time for choices were diminishing like the light in the western sky.

*****

Victoria Fleming's phone buzzed while she idled in a traffic jam eastbound on Interstate 10. She recognized the number and answered.

"Tim Villarreal here, Agent Fleming. I'm the Assistant ME in Bexar County assigned to the autopsies on all those dead guys from your agency's confrontation at Lagrimas."

"What do you have for me?"

"My boss said you wanted a verbal report on something before this office signs off in writing."

Fleming said nothing, unsure of exactly what the chief medical examiner had told her assistant.

After a pause, Villarreal continued. "I just finished the autopsy on John Doe Number Five, an unidentified Hispanic male, described in the submission report as being one of those killed in Kickapoo County."

"And?"

"And this fine specimen of humanity suffered three gunshot wounds. First one went through the right calf. Second was to the upper right arm, splintering the bone, before exiting. Neither of those wounds were fatal."

"And the third?"

"John Doe Number Five's cause of death was a close contact gunshot wound to the cranium. The bullet entered the parietal portion of the head. That's the top..."

"I know basic anatomy, doctor," Fleming interrupted.

"Anyway, penetration through the parietal bone, just left of center, angling downward. There appears to be a muzzle imprint at the point of entry. Little stippling however..."

"Which means that whoever pulled the trigger on this guy had the gun jammed against his head."

Villarreal laughed. "Clinically speaking, no, but in layman's terms, exactly."

"Any suggestion of bullet size, doctor?"

"No suggestion, ma'am."

Fleming momentarily felt relief. "Why's that?"

"I'm looking at the round right now. I'm not qualified to testify to this, and we'll submit the round to Bexar County Criminal Investigation Lab, for those wonks to say, but it looks like either a nine or a forty."

"Wait. Unless it was a .22, that bullet should have blown completely through someone's head. You recovered a jacketed hollow point that went through? How is that possible?"

"Yep. Don't see this often. But whoever pulled the trigger on John Doe Number Five shot at a downward angle, back to front at about ten degrees from vertical, and I found the round inside the thoracic cavity. Round traveled downward. No exit. In surprisingly decent shape, given how much damage it did to the recipient." Villarreal couldn't resist emphasizing the last two words in jest. "Just wanted to give you the *head's up.*"

"Thanks, doc." Fleming groaned and disconnected. She thought, *Eddleman, you stupid son of a bitch. You skated on killing Vasquez two years ago. Now, it looks as if you executed a wounded* sicario. *And Bexar County has the round they can match with your service gun. Damn. Damn. Damn!*

*****

After a long day of meetings, DEA Agent Art Reyes was ready to head for home when an analyst at EPIC in El Paso called. Now, he sat staring at the computer screen while EPIC streamed real-time satellite transmissions to the San Antonio DEA office.

"Holy hell," Reyes muttered and called Victoria Fleming's number.

She answered on the first ring. "I'm on Interstate 10 with traffic backed up for four miles, and I haven't even made it to the Buc-ee's in Luling. I'm pissed off. Tell me something interesting."

"Looks like we need to call in the troops."

"We always need to call in the troops. Explain."

"Remember the group of *Zetas* that went to ground somewhere east of Lagrimas? We thought it might be nothing more than a ruse. A Humvee and pickups just appeared on satellite. They'd been hiding under bodacious rock outcroppings, so, we couldn't find them."

"It's not dark yet. Are they just stupid?" She didn't wait for a response. "Where exactly are they headed?" Fleming was already eyeing the grassy median swale, hoping it was dry enough for her sedan to make the tortuous turn to the west-bound side of the Interstate.

"East end of Kickapoo County is a direct shot." By this time, Reyes had summoned several nearby agents into his office. "If you don't mind, I'm putting you on the speaker. I've got other agents watching the same thing with me."

"Just a sec." Fleming sounded distracted.

The gathered agents heard bangs and clangs, then, she announced, "I jumped the median and am heading back to San Antonio. Don't think I lost a fender or tailpipe, but there was water in the damned ditch and thought I might have to be towed."

One of the agents in the room said, "That took balls."

"I heard that, whoever you are. And thank you. It did. I'm about an hour out, but let's talk."

Within second, she muttered, "Dammit, a county Mountie just lit up his overheads."

The *wah wah* of a siren came over the phone speaker. Reyes and his men tried to suppress their laughter, but it echoed in the small office.

"I'll be back with you shortly." Fleming disconnected.

"Well, I'd hate to be in that cop's situation. She'll blister him."

"Or her," opined another agent.

"Women are smart enough not to give speeding tickets to DEA Special Agents in Charge," retorted the lone woman in the room, raising a hand for a high five which was ignored by the males.

Minutes later, Reyes' phone rang again.

"Quick question before we get serious here, chief," Reyes responded. "Was the cop a man or a woman."

"Guadalupe County constable— man. Why?"

"Told you, you numb-nuts. Women are smarter," pronounced the female agent, her arms crossed.

Fleming turned all-business. "Who do we have in Kickapoo County?"

"Breaux called in and said he was heading there. Asked me to log him out," Reyes responded. "Didn't say why."

"Where's Eddleman, for Christ's sake?"

"Called in sick."

"Start assembling a team and be prepared to give me a head's up on whether there's anyone in that county we trust besides Purdy Kendricks. Oh, and see where the hell he is. I'll call you back." Fleming disconnected. "Siri, call Leroy Breaux."

A pause, then Siri responded. "Just to confirm, you wish to call Larry Brown."

"Fuck!"

Fleming spotted an exit ramp and crossed two lanes to get at it. She narrowly avoided getting sideswiped by a school bus, whose driver shot her the bird and leaned on the horn.

Fleming parked in a convenience store parking lot. "Finally," she exclaimed when she found Breaux's phone number. Three rings. "Pick up, dammit, I think something's about to go to shit."

"Chief? What's up?" Breaux's asked.

"Where are you?"

"About twenty miles from Santa Rosa. Just thought I'd make a run down here."

"Leroy, you've got about two seconds to come clean. Why are you going to Kickapoo County?"

A pause. "Eddleman's playing hooky, Chief. He's not in his apartment. I think I know where he is."

"And?"

"Not sure, but it's got something to do with the Vasquez killing two years ago. I found stuff..."

"You were in his apartment?" Fleming was incredulous.

"Well, not officially."

Fleming said nothing for several seconds. "Christ. I didn't hear that. What did you find?"

"Not sure. A piece of paper. Maybe nothing. Maybe something. I think it's a torn copy of a photograph. It might be of something on the ranch property that Kendricks inherited."

"Why would he be there?" Fleming wondered aloud.

"Rumors, only, chief, but..."

"But what?"

"Vasquez was rumored to have stashed a butt-load of cash somewhere. We debriefed him. He made a deal with the government contingent on, along with upping the names of his cartel contacts and working as a CI, he surrender any ill-gotten gains from the drug business. You know how pissed Eddleman was with Vasquez. He's always blamed Vasquez for Luke's death. You know the story. He was convinced that Vasquez hid money somewhere."

"He ever tell you where?"

"Nope. He hasn't brought the subject up to me in quite a while."

"Uh huh." Fleming sounded doubtful.

"I'm shooting straight with you," Breaux said. "Kendricks is down here on the border somewhere for some unknown reason. I'm trying to find him. And I've got an uneasy feeling about Eddleman."

"What? That he'll do something to Kendricks? What are you talking about?""I don't know," Breaux admitted. "Just a bad feeling."

"We've got bigger fish to fry right now, agent. The birds spotted movement in Mexico. Looks like another shipment headed directly your way."

"Where exactly?"

"Oh, you'll recognize it. The Griffin place. Kendrick's place now. I'm sending support but you're the only man on the ground. Find Kendricks. Find Eddleman. We've got to stop the drug runners."

Chapter 42

A trespasser and his intentions revealed

Who in the name of God was on my ranch at this time of night? Whoever it was heading my way. For a second, I hoped it was some game warden, checking for a hunter spotlighting game, or perhaps a fisherman without a license. I pushed that innocuous thought out of my mind. The local game warden had keys to damned near every ranch property in Kickapoo County, but he probably wouldn't be out here after dark.

As I watched the seesawing headlights going up and down in the swales, I wondered if I was watching a cartel's drug run, or someone smuggling illegals across the border. Both were possible. Either way, alone and tending to a dying man, I wasn't in a position to confront anyone. I hoped I'd turned off the ranch house's lights. If I didn't, at the very least, the trespasser would know someone else had entered the property. At the worst, Teofilo was in even more danger.

I desperately checked my cell phone. No surprise — no coverage. Lowell's truck was partially concealed in the mottle of a cholla-covered outcropping, but a casual scan by whoever was coming this way would easily spot it. I reached the relative safety of the house, its lights extinguished.

The headlights disappeared, then reappeared as the pickup truck bobbed on the dirt track leading from the river toward me. I made it inside the back porch just as the headlights swept across the ranch house, too quickly for whoever was in the truck to make out my shape through the porch screen. I ducked inside the kitchen. Teo lay under the quilts in a bedroom, sound asleep. I wouldn't disturb him. *He can't help, and the trauma might kill him.*

My cellphone read 9:42. Still no coverage, but as a precaution, I put it on silent mode. My luck would be that the damned thing would miraculously get service and ring while I was in hiding.

Another dipsy-doodle of the headlights reflected off nearby bushes. *A Chevy, or a GMC? Fairly new. Maybe white or tan.* I leaned the shotgun in the corner next to the kitchen door opening onto the porch, and the M16 on the other side against the sink cabinet. Then I waited.

The truck cleared the rougher terrain a third of a mile from the house. I knew every inch of that soft sandy stretch of road, and imagined sitting in the cab, feeling the slight tugs of sand pulling against the steering. The intruder would be at the house in less than a minute.

Finally, engine noise. *Probably a half-ton and not a diesel.* Carefully, I pushed open the sliding glass window over the kitchen sink. The screen in that window was long gone. I tried to see inside the pickup. No luck. *Maybe he'll keep going, but I would like to know who the hell is on my land at night.*

The pickup neared the unfenced beaten dirt parking area around the ranch headquarters and slowed to a crawl, its headlights washing over the giant oak tree in its center. There was a sudden flutter in the upper branches and a flash of white. The tree's resident owl was having no part of this latest intrusion. Three wing sweeps in the darkness and the hunter flew out of sight. *I wish you'd stay, old owl. I could use some company, or a witness.*

Instead of passing by the house and proceeding northward toward the ranch entrance, the driver pulled the vehicle up to the old workshop, parked, cut the engine, but left the headlights on, focused on the structure's north side and the adjacent mesquite.

The driver stepped out, walked to the truck bed, and reached down. I heard a slight metallic scrape, and the rustle of plastic. Then footsteps. Whoever it was wore a cowboy hat and denim jacket. In the headlight beams I could tell the driver was a male who was in good shape. He carried a shovel.

Who the hell are you? And what are you doing? I thought.

I didn't have long to wonder. He set his hat on the truck's hood, then, shovel in hand, walked to the dirt mound between the mesquite and the barn's wooden siding.

I recognized him. *Jesus Christ! Jack Eddleman,* I thought, the words almost spilling from my mouth. He stabbed the shovel deeper, then grunted with each stroke. Headlight beams revealed motes of dust as each shovelful landed on the disturbed ground. I wondered, *Maybe the stories of Pete Vasquez's hidden drug money are true.*

I suddenly remembered locals seeing Laura Griffin Saenz, shortly after Pete's death, in a Santa Rosa hardware store, buying a shovel and wheelbarrow, then driving around town in a borrowed pickup truck. And the questions about where the money had come from to remodel her Alamo Heights home. Despite my warnings to her that she was an easy target for cartel vengeance near the border, she'd returned to the area at least twice.

All these memories came flooding back to me. Pete Vasquez' grandparents had run the ranch for Mr. Griffin, and later for Laura, after the old man died. Pete had been Laura's lover off and on for years. After Pete avoided getting killed by the *Zetas* on the highway north of Laredo, he'd summoned Laura to help him. She'd been spending her time in Alamo Heights, pretending she was financially solvent, but desperate for money.

I'd always wondered what drew Vasquez to this ranch, and how he'd convinced Laura to bring him here, instead of to a hospital. When I found them hiding in his murdered grandparents' house, Pete and Laura displayed raw hatred for each other. Yet, there they were— co-conspirators.

After her death, I'd had my own issues, like saving my marriage, and didn't give it any more thought. Seven thousand acres of land is a lot of area to play guessing games on, if one is looking for buried money. Even if the stories were true, I wouldn't have had any idea of where to look. *Maybe Eddleman got a heads up from Vasquez on where to search. But how?*

I quietly opened the kitchen back door, the M16 slung across my chest, carrying the 12-gauge shotgun. I glanced over my right shoulder as I gently pushed open the screen door, again cursing myself for not spraying its long rusty spring with WD40. I slipped outside and prevented the door from slapping shut.

Eddleman stopped and looked around as if he'd heard something, and I froze, partially blocked from his view by the porch uprights. He stepped away from the headlight beams and for a second, I lost sight of him in the contrasting darkness. He made no noise, and I crouched down, hoping he hadn't detected my movement.

In the distance, a brace of coyotes began their yips, answered almost immediately by a pack nearer to the house. Eddleman let go a laugh and reappeared in his headlights. When he bent to enlarge the hole, I raced the ten steps through soft, noiseless sand to his truck. At the back bumper, I laid in the dirt, trying to recover my breath, and then peered under the truck's body. Eddleman continued to shovel dirt. He hadn't noticed the noise of my footsteps. I raised up to be sure no one was in the truck bed. Leaning the pump action shotgun against the right rear tire, I cupped a hand over my flashlight and turned it on, aiming its muted beam into the pickup bed.

Nobody. Just two large black garbage bags lay pooled on the bed liner, each loosely tied in a knot at their necks. I killed the flashlight, stuck it in my hip pocket, grabbed the shotgun and confirmed its safety was off. Moving as quietly as I could toward Eddleman, I shifted the shotgun to my left hand and felt for the contents of the nearest bag. Several rectangular blocks, each pliable and about an inch thick. They felt like bundled paper money.

I gripped the shotgun in both hands, aiming at the back of Eddleman's head. As if sensing me, he turned.

"Don't move. What are you doing on my property, Eddleman?"

He tossed the shovel onto the ground and faced me, bare hands at his sides. "Kendricks, I must say I'm surprised to see you, this time of night," he said almost casually. "Just doing a little prospecting, you might say."

"Move over toward the front of the barn, then take a seat."

"Or what? You going to shoot me? I'm the guy that saved your ass in Houston." He started to move toward me. "You're not stupid enough to kill a federal agent."

I wondered if he was right. I pointed the shotgun at the ground near his feet and fired. The buckshot smashed into the ground inches ahead of his right foot, spattering his pants leg with dirt and gravel.

He lunged at me, bridging the six-foot gap in an instant. I fired again, but Eddleman had swept an arm against the barrel and the pellets blew by him harmlessly. His fist smashed into my right cheek, causing me to stagger backwards. I raised the shotgun, but now Eddleman was holding an automatic against my nose.

"Drop the shotgun, drunk, or I'll blow your goddamned head off." Eddleman's face was contorted in anger.

In the lights from the headlights, he backed toward the barn, pulling me with him. My head clanged like a bell; my right eye was already swelling shut. He tossed the shotgun, M16, and my pistol against the workshop's closed doors, dust erupting where they landed. He pointed me toward the structure. "Stay in the lights, Kendricks. Don't want to shoot you. At least, not yet."

Ashamed and embarrassed, I squinted at Eddleman through my one good eye as he prodded me toward the hole near the edge of the building. He tossed the shovel to the ground in front of me. "Start digging."

"Can I ask a question?"

"Yeah, but make it quick."

I caught a whiff of wintergreen. Eddleman had managed to reload his Kodiak while holding a gun and flashlight on me. I wondered how that was possible.

I said, "This hole's supposed to hold money, I'll bet. It doesn't, so I'm guessing this was one of the hidey holes Laura found after you killed Vasquez."

Eddleman merely grunted.

"You've got two sacks with bundled cash in the back of your truck, so I'm guessing you've found at least some of Vasquez' money that she didn't get. How'm I doing?"

"Not bad for a loser. I should have let you take the fall for that Houston shooting instead of covering for you. Keep digging."

I filled the shovel and continued talking. "Wondered about that. That piece of shit gun you said you found on Bootsie Cardenas that night in the alleyway. That wasn't his, was it?"

"Of course not. That bastard had a G18 full auto. Too nice to turn in."

"When did you find that piece?"

"As soon as I got to his body."

"And you let me sweat about the missing firearm. You're a pure bastard, Eddleman."

He huffed a laugh. "Hey, I covered your drunken ass with the throw-down."

"You made sure that with the doubts raised by my alcohol content and the dubious firearm 'found' next to a big-time dealer, I'd be asked to resign from the Houston Police Department." I pushed the shovel harder into the dirt, wondering what path my life would have taken had I known the truth.

"Well, Eddleman," I continued, trying to show bravado I wasn't feeling, "you killed Vasquez not far from here. Do you think you can get away with killing someone with a badge? How many stashes are there? How many have you found so far? How are you going to keep the money hid? A Swiss bank account? Or maybe one in the Caymans? The DEA doesn't generally look kindly on bent agents." I was just fishing, buying time, but for what? There wasn't anyone out here except a dying Mexican too sick to get out of bed.

Eddleman stared at me as if I was a bug in a specimen jar. He wasn't deciding whether to kill me. He was deciding *when* to kill me.

"Folks know where I am, Jack. May I call you Jack?" I was babbling now. "You kill me, it's not going to be like when you killed Vasquez. Your boss doesn't even trust you anymore. You know that don't you? Do your keepers know where you are tonight?"

"Shut your fucking mouth. You were a lousy drunk in Houston, and I covered your ass. You'll always be a drunk, no matter how long you try to stay sober. You aren't worth a shit. You got lucky, but that luck is about to run out."

My heart was pounding. *When is he going to shoot me?*

The question was answered a fraction of a second later. He raised his automatic, standing six feet from me. I knew I was about to die.

"Señor Purdy!" Teofilo's cry startled both of us. Eddleman's head jerked toward the call. "Who's there?"

I thought, *How in God's name has the old man gotten out of bed?* "He's my witness, Eddleman."

Eddleman swung his weapon toward Teo's voice and fired three quick shots. I took my chance and charged at his midsection, driving him to the ground. The blast of the fourth and fifth round erupted next to my left ear. I slammed my left fist into his ribcage. He let out a grunt and skittered on his back out of the reach of the headlights. I grabbed his legs and pulled myself onto his torso. I was soon lying on top of him, trying to pin his shoulders to the ground. He still had his pistol. In the dark, I grappled for his gun hand, but he kept pulling loose from any grip I got. My main desire was to keep him from shooting me. He grasped my hair with his free hand, pulled my head to his mouth. I screamed as his teeth bit into my right ear.

His pistol fired and something smacked against my left leg. Whatever it was didn't come close to the pain of Eddleman's attempt to chew my ear off. I drove my right palm up and into the base of his nose. I instantly felt warm blood explode from his damaged face, and his teeth released me.

I lunged upwards and pinned him down with my knees on his shoulders. But where was his gun? Fleetingly, I recalled seeing Eddleman in the past with a Heckler and Koch, but which type? They held different size magazines. How many rounds had he already fired? Crazy things went through my mind while flailing away with one fist and trying not to get shot again with the other.

My left hand found his wrist and I pushed the gun barrel into the dirt as another round went off, clanging into his pickup. I had to get the gun away from him, so I grabbed it with both hands, allowing him to smash his left fist into the side of my head. Ignoring the pain, I held the pistol, then bit down on his thumb, gratified by the crunching sound as my teeth gnawed into his bones.

Eddleman screamed, his gun fell loose, and, suddenly, I was standing while he lay on the ground. He felt around for the gun he'd been forced to release. I dove toward the three firearms lying in the dirt in front of the work shed door and came up with the shotgun. I swung it under my arm with the barrel pointed behind me and, not looking at what it fired at, I pulled the trigger. The sound of the blast blended with my screaming. Metal clanged as some of the buckshot pierced Eddleman's pickup.

My sprint to the oak tree some forty feet away took no more than two or three seconds that seemed an eternity. I dived behind it, praying Eddleman wouldn't kill me.

Silence. Why hadn't he pulled the trigger? Then I heard a low moan. I peeked around the tree. Eddleman stood awkwardly against the driver's door, one leg akimbo. He jerked the door open, and the cab light came on. He was attempting to crawl onto the driver's seat, but couldn't, and sank into the dirt.

"Goddamit, help me!" he shouted.

Maybe I had hit him? Moving carefully from behind the tree, I found my flashlight and turned it on. The beam revealed Eddleman's pant leg sheeted crimson, a wound pumping out blood. "You're hit in an artery," I said.

Eddleman raised himself from the dirt, leaning on an elbow a moment, made a weak gesture with a hand, then let his body drop. He was bleeding out. I grabbed the M16 and slung it over my shoulder, stuffed my automatic back in its holster, then dragged him onto the porch. Teo, wrapped in a blanket, stood in the doorway, staring, but unhurt. Just to his right, three holes starred the window over the kitchen sink. Eddleman's quick shots had nearly found their mark.

"Turn on the lights, please," I said.

Tio complied, and the light flooded the living room.

I pulled Eddleman inside and heaved him onto the couch. It didn't take long to assess the damage just above his knee. I cinched my leather belt to make a tourniquet and tightened it as high as I could near his groin.

"*Guardalo*," I instructed Teo. "Watch him." I could barely hear my voice in my damaged ear.

He nodded. *"Pistola, por favor?"*

My hands were slick with Eddleman's blood, so I wiped them on the blanket over Teo's shoulder. I handed my Glock to the old man. He nodded and pointed the gun at the gravely wounded man. I limped to Eddleman's truck bed. Each garbage bag weighed at least fifty pounds. It took two trips, but I got the black bags inside the shed. I didn't know what I was going to do with the money, but the bags' contents didn't belong in the open. I grabbed the shovel off the ground, and Eddleman's pistol, and tossed them inside, then secured the door. I killed the truck headlights and made my way slowly toward the house. Feeling a squishiness, I shined my flashlight on my left leg. The lower half of my pants leg was red. A bullet had made a hole in my calf, and I was bleeding into my boot.

My ear screamed with pain, and my right eye was swollen closed. I was a mess.

What the hell am I going to do now?

Chapter 43
The Zetas show their hand

Fleming called Breaux.

"What?" He tried not to hide his exasperation.

"I'm taking a chance," she said, "but we need local help. I'm calling the sheriff."

"TJ Johnson and company? That dumbass? He can't find his way out of a paper bag."

"But no one's ever shown him to be on the take. We need numbers maybe more than expertise."

Breaux found himself nodding. "Probably right, chief. But you'll put some of the locals in harm's way if you do it."

"You call them, or I will. Your choice." Fleming's tone made it clear who she expected was to oversee the situation. "And once you make contact, let me know what kind of help we can expect. Oh, and if you can raise any DPS troopers working in that area, that'd help too. I'm heading your way. Two, two and a half hours away. We'll get a bird up too, but I don't want those bastards getting spooked. I'm guessing it's another load of fentanyl, and we need to snag it. If they turn and run, we'll get no help from the Mexican police or military."

She hung up.

Breaux then called the Kickapoo County Sheriff's Office.

"Sheriff's Office. Is this an emergency?"

Breaux immediately recognized the voice of the dispatcher, Jake Nichols. "Jake, Agent Breaux here. Is this on a recorded line?"

"No, only 911 calls are recorded. What's up?"

"Is your sheriff in county?"

"No," Jake replied. "I can raise him on the radio though. He's at a high school girls' volleyball game." He mentioned the other high school in a town ninety miles away. "Santa Rosa may make the playoffs this year."

"No, and no radio traffic either." Breaux demanded, then asked for the chief deputy.

"Out sick. He's been in the hospital on and off with long-term something or other." Jake paused. "You sound desperate, Agent. What in hell is going on?"

Remembering Jake's help in getting Teofilo Ramirez away from Lagrimas, Breaux asked, "Have you seen Kendricks?"

"No, is he supposed to be around here?" Jake's curiosity showed in his voice.

Breaux gave a vague response. "Drug activity near your county. DEA on the way, but we may need some help. Who's left at the department, the county animal control officer?"

Jake couldn't help but laugh. "That's funny. We don't have one of those. We've got a deputy patrolling right now, but he's past Lagrimas. You said no radio. I'll try calling, but you know cell coverage sucks out there." With the Sheriff not in the office, Jake chanced some humor. "Of course, as pissed off as TJ was when the DEA didn't ask for our help at Lagrimas, he may tell you guys to shove it."

Breaux checked his speed — Ninety-five miles per hour. He backed down to eighty, ignoring Jake's wisecrack. "Have you seen Agent Eddleman?"

"No, sir. But, as I said, I can start calling folks on cell phones. DPS Trooper Bonavita, you remember him, don't you? He's working this area, and he's at the café, eating a late supper."

Breaux felt like he was pulling teeth. "Just give me his phone number, and I'll try to catch him. But no reserves." He had little trust of TJ's abilities or his honesty and knew little or nothing about Kickapoo County's unpaid reserve deputies. This wasn't the time to bring in poorly trained part-timers. He thanked Jake, disconnected, and punched in the cell number for the highway patrolman. He'd witnessed Bonavita's coolness two years ago. He decided the DEA was going to need the young trooper.

When the trooper answered, Breaux said, "DEA Agent Breaux here. Trooper, you sitting with anyone right now?"

A pause, then, "How'd you know where I am?"

"Jake Nichols."

"Figures. I'm in a booth by myself. Why?"

Breaux checked his speed, and guessed he was about ten miles from the eastern edge of Kickapoo County. "We may have a situation."

*****

Jake sat in the dispatcher's chair. No radio traffic. He dialed the on-duty deputy's phone, and the call went directly to voicemail as he suspected it would. "Jake here. If you get this, call me on your cell. Don't radio." He disconnected, swiveled back and forth, peered at the Tupperware container holding some leftovers he'd brought to eat midway through his shift.

The large clock on the wall read 9:22. *Hell,* he thought, *I have almost three hours until midnight.* His stomach growled, and he opened the rubber lid of the container, sniffed the contents, then resealed it, his appetite suddenly gone. He knew something big was going on. *Sounds like some trusted men were needed. Breaux made it clear this wasn't the time to call in rookies.*

But where was Eddleman, that sneaky shit? And, more importantly, where was Purdy Kendricks, his best friend in the world? Jake knew he'd screwed it up when the old Mexican he was supposed to guard got away just before all hell broke loose in Lagrimas. *Man, I had to pee bad and stepped out of the truck to take a leak and the guy disappeared. I was outfoxed by a dying old man, who's probably back in Mexico, if he hadn't drowned in the Rio Grande.*

This wasn't the first time he'd let Purdy down. A few weeks ago, Purdy had braced him about a strange phone call Purdy had made two years earlier, about meeting with Israel Sifuentes in Lagrimas in the middle of the night. Purdy had sworn him to secrecy, but, he thought, *Hell, as always, I ran* my *mouth.* Long afterwards, he mentioned it to someone at the courthouse. When he'd remembered talking about the incident and called Purdy, his friend had sounded upset. *What was that all about?*

Now, there were whispers about how long Israel Sifuentes had been missing from work. Jake glanced out the glass door and across the street. The dim outline of the Kickapoo County Courthouse, Israel's workplace, lit by flood lamps, blocked the sky to the west. *Where has Israel gone? And what about Lilly Pardo? She's been long gone from the Cenizo Diner, and all I've got out of Beulah Jackson is that her favorite waitress is on vacation.*

Jake shook his head. There was too much going on that he didn't understand. For someone who tried to keep tabs on everything in Kickapoo County, it was embarrassing. *Something isn't right. But what, exactly?* Who would have any idea? Jake thought about it, then reached for his cell phone. If anyone knew more about what was going on in Kickapoo County, it was Lowell Johnson.

"Hello?" Lowell sounded groggy, and Jack wondered how much the newspaper editor had had to drink that evening.

"Mr. Johnson, it's me, Jake Nichols. You got a second?"

*****

A semi shifted gears when the traffic light changed on US 90 and moved eastward out of Santa Rosa. Jake heard a bell clang twice when a vehicle drove across Santa Rosa's only full-service gas station's signal hose and pulled up to the pumps. The air had cooled and there was little traffic tonight.

Jake scrolled through his phone contact list, then dialed the number of another dispatcher, due to come on duty at 4 a.m. "Buddy, it's me, Jake. Hey, I must have eaten something bad. I've got the shits really awful. Is there any way you can spell me tonight?" Buddy owed Jake some favors. He had two kids in Little League baseball, and Jake had pulled Buddy's shifts more than a few times so Buddy could help coach the kids' games.

When Buddy agreed to cover for him, Jake said, "Yeah, I'll wait, but c'mon. I need to get home and take some Pepto. No, I'll be all right, but I'm getting queasy. I'm afraid I'm going to stink up this place!"

He disconnected, pleased with the Buddy's loud reaction to the graphic description of what might await him if he didn't step on it. He stood, stretched, and walked down the hallway and into the classroom, switching on the overhead lights. Across the room, the gray reinforced steel door to the gun locker contrasted with the off-white of the surrounding walls. Jake touched the door keypad, then squinted his eyes shut, remembering a set of numbers to unlock the safe. Satisfied he'd remembered them correctly; he began punching in the six-number combination.

Now was time to find Purdy and figure out what was going on. *Maybe this time, I won't screw things up.*

Chapter 44

Zetas approach the Rio Grande. Jake Nichols is an unlikely reinforcement

N avarrete looked up in the sky. To the west, the sun was within thirty minutes of hiding behind the bleak northern Mexican hills. "We move, nice and slow, spread out," he announced to the men. "We'll stop far enough away from the river so we can't be seen from the other side, and we'll make sure that no *norteamericanos* are there."

The men said nothing, although several glanced overhead as if they would be able to spot an American spy satellite or drone.

No doubt they're wondering why we've moved this far in daylight, Navarrete thought. He climbed into the drug-loaded pickup cab. He wasn't surprised when his keepers, Lorenzo, Curly, and Moe clambered onto the bundles in the back.

The driver, a skinny, long-haired kid who looked about fifteen, started the engine. "*Jefe,* who are these three *pinches*? They came with you and are sticking together. Don't wanna share smokes. Don't wanna talk much. Just keep standing around, like they're watching you." He propped his left arm out the open window. When Navarrete didn't respond, the kid muttered an apology. "Sorry, *jefe.* None of my business."

Navarrete shook off his gloom, turned and asked, "What's your name, *hijo*?"

"Epifanio, *jefe*, but everyone calls me '*Chato*.'"

Navarrete grinned. The kid *did* have a pug nose, to be sure. "Well, Chato, don't you worry about those three. They're just extra hands to make sure we get this delivery done right, *entiendes*?"

Epifanio said, "*Si*, I understand," relieved Navarrete hadn't scolded him.

Navarrete patted the boy on the shoulder. *Good chance this poor bastard will be dead before the night's over,* he thought. *But then, probably so will I.*

The daylight faded rapidly, the low hills on the American side hazy in the distance. Navarrete, using his GPS, calculated his *Zetas* were eight kilometers from the Rio Grande. He had Chato tap the horn, then waved to the others to stop.

"Stretch your legs, compadres." The men gathered around him, and he showed them the GPS map, although he wondered whether some of the group could read it. "Take a piss, smoke your last cigarette, and get some water. No lights. when we get closer."

Ten minutes later, Navarrete had Chato move ahead of the Humvee, and the *Zetas* slowly continued the trek north, the trucks' speedometers rarely going over ten kilometers per hour. The sun's rays disappeared, and the desert was suffused with charcoal tones mixed with gray shadows. Navarrete called another stop at two kilometers from the Rio Bravo. He imagined the river and the land on the other side of it. *I hope we make it across and I am not killed, or at least killed easily, not with torture.*

The drivers of each vehicle disconnected the interior lights, and the men hunkered down beside their vehicles, their sweat from the day cooled by the night air.

Navarrete forced himself to stay seated in the pickup, holding the satellite phone below the dash, wondering when the call would come.

9:24. Almost completely dark, with the sliver of a waxing moon showing above the southeastern horizon. Then Venus.

The phone buzzed.

"Sí?"

The disguised voice made macabre by the dark desert setting came through the earpiece. "A boat will be there to transport the merchandise. Get it loaded. Make sure it gets reloaded on the trucks on the other side."

Navarrete wasn't so sure it was Guillermo Blanco on the other end of the line this time. *Was Cantinflas already divorcing himself from what his Keepers are going to do to me?* He bit his lip to keep from confronting his boss. There were so many things that could go wrong with his plan.

Instead, he calmly asked, "How will we know who this is?"

"He works for us," the voice said. "He'll flash a light three times, then twice, then once. He will be in a boat, or near one."

"Three times, then twice, then once," Navarrete repeated. "Does this man have a name?"

"He'll go by Lazarus."

Navarrete almost laughed. *Hell, I'll need that name if I'm going to rise from the dead tonight.*

The call ended. Navarrete took a deep breath, gathered his men, and gave them their instructions. In the distance, indistinct sounds, like coughs reached them.

"Gunfire, *jefe*?" one of the *sicarios* asked.

The group stood quietly. "I counted two," someone said. "Three, maybe," another replied.

Navarrete checked the time.

9:36.

"Maybe a shotgun, maybe not," he said. "I'm not worried about some *gringo* ranchers dumb enough to shoot in the dark. If it was the DEA, we wouldn't hear it until the bullets were cutting us to pieces. We have to be at the river ready to load at ten o'clock. He and Blanco had stood near where they were, just a few weeks before, surveying the proposed crossing point.

Some of the *Zetas* gave uncomfortable chuckles as they remounted the three vehicles.

Quietly, lights extinguished, the small convoy moved forward. Ten minutes later, another stop. The *Zetas* were perched on a rise. From there, only a gentle drop to the Rio Bravo lay ahead.

*****

Breaux pulled onto County Road 106, checked for cell coverage, and saw he had one bar. He called Jake Nichols on his cell. Jake answered, but Breaux couldn't understand anything over the crackling. Then the line dropped.

"Shit!" Sitting with the truck engine off, Breaux wondered why he'd charged off to Kickapoo County with no backup. Kendricks, so far, had been a stand-up guy. He hoped the Texas lawman continued to be. As far as his fellow DEA agent was concerned, he was convinced Eddleman was in the middle of something bad. "Jack, I hope you aren't tangled up with the cartels." He muttered. "I wish to hell I knew what it is."

*****

In Santa Rosa, Jake walked quickly to his truck, placed an M16 and three boxes of ammunition on the passenger side, then shut the door quickly. He scurried back inside the office and ran down to the classroom, afraid he'd some-how left the weapons vault open. Quickly switching on the lights, he breathed a sigh of relief. The steel door was shut. He flipped off the light switch and turned right. The front door's ding announced Buddy's arrival.

"Hey, where are you, Jake?"

In the darkened hallway, Jake stepped into the public restroom, reached, and flushed the toilet, slamming the door behind him. He walked toward the dispatch area. "Whoo, don't go in there for a little bit, Buddy. I almost had an accident." Jake waved a hand through the air for good effect. "Thanks for coming. I owe you."

Buddy flounced into the dispatcher's chair and checked the penciled entries on the call log. Breaux's conversation with Jake had not been entered.

"Nothing much going on, is there?"

"Nope. Thanks again. Gotta go. No pun intended." Jake ran to his truck and backed into the street. He'd pulled in facing north, so he'd have to loop the courthouse square to get back on US 90. His cell phone beeped. Breaux was calling again.

"Breaux, where are you? Anything going on I can help with?"

Whatever Breaux responded was lost in the atmosphere, and the call ended. Jake opened the screen, tapped the incoming call, and punched *send*, hoping to reconnect. Breaux didn't answer.

The screen read 9:15.

There was no time to waste.

Chapter 45
The river crossings begin

The light-skinned man wiped the sweat from his face and used his thumb and forefinger to nervously stroke a small mustache. *Lazarus. What kind of piece of shit name is that?* he thought as he unstapled the barbed wire fence from two weathered cedar posts, less than a mile from where they'd been parked under camouflage netting. He finished the lower strand and carefully put the staples in his pocket, then pushed the fence to the ground and laid wood planks over the barbs. There was no sense in rushing this, and a flat tire on his truck or boat trailer would be a disaster. On his return, he'd re-staple the wire to the posts.

He drove over the downed fence and onto the adjoining property. Reaching the ruins of the small bullet-riddled house, he turned, and carefully backed down a dim track through cane and salt cedar. *This could happen to me and mine,* he shuddered.

The green of cane and salt cedar rose from the blackened masses, and he wondered what fire had burned an extensive part of the riverfront foliage. At the lip of a sandy berm, he got out, and carefully pulled a light fifteen-foot aluminum boat off its rails. He slid it into the murky river and tied the bow line to a metal stake that had once secured someone else's boat.

Lazarus looked up at the sky. Already late afternoon. He carefully pushed the boat away from the shore and moved to the stern seat, hoping the electric powered outboard was powerful enough to buck the current. *I have so much to lose,* he thought. *If the* Zetas *don't kill me and my wife and my kids, I'll be set for life. I'll never come back to this godforsaken place again. I'll sell the crappy three-hundred acres to the first buyer. Maybe even Kendricks, the guy who wanted me to run cows on this place. As if I'd know which end is which on a cow.*

He drifted with the current past the abandoned house. High bluffs and the river's cut sped the current, and Lazarus used the motor to maneuver into the deep shadows of overhanding reeds and salt cedars directly under the bluffs of his small property. He'd move to the Mexican side later.

Now all he had to do was wait.

*****

Navarrete climbed onto the truck hood and raised a light-gathering monocular to his eye. The regular shapes of an abandoned house contrasted with the irregularities of the high bluffs overlooking the river, three hundred meters downriver.

The old couple who lived there had been slaughtered, Navarrete remembered. *Their worthless grandson hauled drugs for* la Familia Norteña, *and we flipped him. To avoid dying, Pete Vasquez arranged for us to stage from the ranch when we hired the American sniper to kill their worthless leader.* He snickered. *Of course, after he finished the job, we'd tried to kill the sniper when he'd done the job and succeeded in killing the sniper's guide at the low water crossing at Lagrimas. Never any sense in leaving witnesses. But the* Norteños *got to that dago first. What was his name? Shivelli? Somehow, the* Norteños *figured it out, and killed the sniper when he hid on the ranch. They'd killed the old couple too. There are no innocents in our business, I suppose.*

He moved the monocular back and forth, looking for any sign of danger and for the man called Lazarus. From his vantage point, the dark green smoothness of the Rio Bravo was only visible in short stretches. Then, a small disturbance in the eeriness of green revealed the low profile of a boat moving upriver, past the bluffs. Navarrete's expression changed, and a small smile passed across his face. It was 9:53. Lazarus was on time. If Blanco was telling the truth, Lazarus would stop upriver from the old couple's ruined home.

One more sweep of his monocular, and Navarrete saw nothing out of the ordinary.

"We go," he said softly. "We move slowly." He pointed to four men armed with automatic rifles. "You four. Walk ahead of us, one hundred meters. We'll follow. There should be one man, in a boat, on the river or pulled up on this side. That's all. If you see or hear anything that doesn't seem right, signal us."

The four nodded and crunched along the sand and caliche, winding their way through cactus and greasewood in the pale moonlight. After a minute, Navarrete whispered "Now," and Chato started the engine. The three vehicles crept forward. To Navarrete, the short distance to the Rio Bravo took what seemed like an eternity.

The rocky surface turned to sand a dozen yards from the meandering river's edge. The Humvee pulled around Chato's pickup as planned, and its driver killed the engine. A balaclava-clad sicario stood in the Humvee rear, hands at the ready on the pedestaled machine gun.

"Is this where the battle with *el DEA* was, two years ago?" whispered Chato.

"*Si*. Lucky for us that we weren't here," murmured Navarrete, remembering the stories of the earlier shootout with the American *policia*. "We shot down their fucking helicopter, but many *muchachos* were also killed. Wait here," he said. He gently closed the pickup door. "I'm going to make sure."

"We'll go with you," said Lorenzo.

"No," retorted Navarrete. His sharp tone carried authority and his nervous keepers backed down. *How much does Lazarus know? Is he a part of the plan to kill me?* There was no way to tell. "I'll confirm," he said, "when I'm sure, I'll signal you and everyone begins to move the bundles to the river and the boat."

He trudged toward where he'd last seen the boatman, and seconds later, carefully negotiated the sandy rim of the small drop to a sandbar. The river gulped and gurgled as currents grew and dissipated over unseen rocks.

"Lazarus?" he whispered in a harsh voice.

"Here," a voice responded, barely audible over the river's noise.

Before moving further, Navarrete turned to assure himself none of his keepers had followed. He stepped over and around pools of water.

A V-hulled boat with some sort of outboard engine waited, nose-in on the Mexican side. The vague shape of a man rose, his dark form contrasting with the pale of the gravel.

"Hurry up, please," said the man in slightly accented Spanish. "We don't have much time."

Navarrete touched the boat's gunnel. Aluminum, with a deep hull. Two trips, easily. Cupping his hand over the flashlight, he shined it into Lazarus' face. "You are a *gringo*," he pronounced, noticing large freckles spattered on fair skin above the thin mustache. "I don't trust *gringos.*"

"*Mitad-mitad,*" Lazarus replied. Half and half. As if to assure the *Zeta* of his credentials.

"What are you going to do when we load the boat?"

"We cross, and then I load a truck on the other side."

Navarrete had more questions. "Why are we crossing here? This place has a bad history."

"I own the land downriver. You can't cross there." Lazarus' gesture was barely noticeable in the dark. "All high bluffs. This place? No one comes here anymore. I'll drive the truck and product onto my land through the fence, after you've gone back into the interior."

Navarrete grunted his approval. "How do you want it loaded?"

"Are you going to do it yourself? I'm nervous enough, so let's get moving." Lazarus said. "Are any of the *muchachos* going to help?" Lazarus' voice belied any confidence in the gloom. "The sooner we get across the better. I don't want to get caught in some gunfight."

"Wait here." Navarrete climbed the sandbank and returned to the vehicles.

He gave a low whistle when he neared the huddle of *sicarios*. "Everyone, start a line and move the product down to the river." He located Lorenzo standing by the pickup and tapped him on the shoulder. "You, come with me. You will help load the boat."

Lorenzo had no choice but to obey, but clearly, the man wasn't happy. *With your hands busy at the river's edge, there'll be fewer chances for you to kill me, cabrón,* Navarrete though. As Lorenzo walked ahead, Navarrete reached into a front pocket to ensure his extra pistol's safety was off. *The one in my holster may not be enough.*

Seconds later, the *sicarios* began unloading the wrapped kilos carefully from the bed of the pickup, and an ant-like procession of men carrying bundles of the fentanyl reached the river.

Navarrete checked the time: 10:05. The moon was now higher in the sky, with Venus, Mars and Jupiter standing out against the background of the Milky Way. At the boat, Lazarus quietly instructed a reluctant Lorenzo where and how to stack the drugs, his directions accompanied by the slap of water and the dull sound of boots and bundles thumping against aluminum.

Ten minutes passed, and Lazarus said, "Stop. All for this run. How much is left?"

A *sicario* reported to Navarrete, "*Jefe*, not as much as what's in the boat now. We can get all the rest of the bundles here and the next load will only be about half of what's in the boat now."

Navarrete made a beckoning gesture to Lorenzo. "Bring everyone but the drivers and machine gunner down here."

When Lorenzo seemed to hesitate, Navarrete reached for the pistol in its holster.

Lorenzo put aside whatever he was thinking and passed the message up the human chain. Two minutes later, eight heavily armed *sicarios* stood beside the aluminum boat.

"How many of us can cross with you on this trip?" Navarrete asked.

"Four," Lazarus said. "The river's up, but we'll be okay I think, as long as no one does anything stupid." He pointed in the darkness toward the sand upriver from the ruined house. "We unload there. My truck is fifty yards away."

"What are you to do with the product once it's loaded?" Navarrete asked.

"Get it to San Antonio," Lazarus replied.

"And if you don't?" Navarrete asked.

Lazarus climbed into the boat and activated a button. The outboard propeller bit into the current. "Then my wife and children will be killed. You know that. You're a *Zeta*. You think I'm here because I want to be?" The bitter acid in his voice curdled in the night air.

Navarrete didn't pursue it. "We go with you to the American side." He looked at the boat, sitting low in the water, "I have my instructions. You'll need our help loading this product. You know that. And I'm to make sure you get away from the border."

Lazarus pointed in the darkness toward the embankment upriver from the ruined house. "We unload there. My truck is fifty yards away."

Navarrete had to think about the term "yards" but quickly converted it to meters to figure how far away the truck was hidden. He pointed to three *sicarios*, none of them his keepers. "You three. With me now. Sit quietly and don't rock this boat."

Sensing he was losing control, Lorenzo tried to insist on going, and Curly and Moe edged forward on the sandbar. Navarrete pulled his pistol and jammed it into the man's face. "You do as you're told, you piece of shit." There was no sign of law enforcement on the Texas side of the border. Any chance of the DEA interrupting the crossing was slipping away. Navarrete fleetingly thought of disappearing into the United States. He looked at the murky swirls of the river. *I'll have to kill all three keepers, ensure the product gets to San Antonio, then somehow convince that bastard Guillermo Blanco I am loyal and worthy of trust. Or I will die, and my death will not be a pleasant one.*

Chapter 46

A tourniquet, and an unlikely trio. Time runs out

Eddleman stared at me through half-opened eyes. He shifted his gaze to Teofilo when I spoke with the old man.

"Forget it, Eddleman," I threatened him in Spanish. The DEA agent was fluent in the language, and I wanted to be understood by Teofilo. "Your leg's got a tourniquet on it. You try to jump the Mexican, he'll shoot you dead. Better yet, he'll forget to loosen that binding. If you somehow survive, you'll lose your damned leg."

Teofilo shuffled over to the kitchen sink. He wet a towel and tried to squeeze water out of it. Not easy with the other hand holding a gun and holding the two ends of a blanket.

"*Aqui,*" he said, and handed me the dripping cloth. "You don't look so handsome, with that bloody face." The sick and taciturn man even managed a small cackle at my expense.

I dabbed at the side of my head. and my partially mangled left ear. Even the slightest touch hurt horribly. I tossed the stained cloth into the sink. I knew I kept a well-stocked first aid kit in the Lowell's toolbox. I would drive the truck back from where it was hidden to the house, try to patch myself up, and hopefully stabilize Eddleman so he could make it to a hospital. I was too addled to think of how many tasks I'd just committed to.

"Me voy a la troca. Regresare en diez." I assured Teofilo. I hoped it would only take ten minutes to return with Lowell's borrowed truck.

He pulled a chair close to Eddleman and gingerly sat down. "We'll be here." He pulled the blanket closer around his tiny frame, one hand keeping my Glock on display. "Please hurry. I'm very tired."

To make it back in ten minutes, as promised, I'd have to run. But I couldn't. My leg throbbed when I increased my pace, and every time a foot hit the ground, my face and ear pulsed with blinding pain. I settled for a quick limping stride, each pace accompanied by a grunt. As my eyes grew accustomed to the darkness again, I stepped off the road's dirt surface and headed toward my pickup. I eased into the seat and couldn't find the key to the ignition. I sat staring at the dash under the dim dome light, my heart pounding in panic.

"Son of a bitch!" My fist hit the dash. I was angry and wasn't thinking clearly. Grunting, I dug in my pocket for Lowell's truck key on my keyring. I stuck the key in the ignition and started the truck, backed out of the brush and away from the rocks, and aimed toward the ranch road, a football field away.

I shoved the accelerator down as I hit a mound of sand and caliche, and the truck bounced in the air, then slammed forward. My wounded face hit the steering wheel and I howled like a banshee. *What the hell else could happen?* I thought, as I eased off the accelerator and turned south.

I noticed small white lights dancing in the vibrating rearview mirror. Convinced I was losing it, I ignored them, and pulled around to the porch. Pushing open the truck door, I stepped out and almost fell as my left leg, now numb, gave way. I grabbed the truck door, recovered, thankful that Lowell's truck had a similar bed-mounted toolbox like mine. I felt for the first aid kit I'd recovered from my shot-up truck, my hand sweeping over rusty tools and assorted clothing Lowell had accumulated over the years. *Where in hell was the first aid kit?*

I hobbled around to the passenger side and unlatched the other side of the toolbox. One quick reach inside and I felt the kit's heft. Suddenly, headlights washed over me. Instinctively, I dropped the kit and reached for the passenger door. Locked, the dome light displaying my M16 on the seat. I took a step toward the porch screen door, hoping desperately to reach the relative safety of the house.

"Hey! Whoa, buddy."

Someone wrapped his arms around me as I fought to get through the door. In my panic, I kicked backward with my right leg and made hard contact with the assailant's groin. A temporary success but my leg cratered under the weight shift, and I fell halfway onto the concrete of the porch.

"Son of a bitch! You did it to me again!"

The voice sounded familiar. I rolled onto my back. DPS Trooper Bonavita, on one knee, clutched his crotch. "Goddamit, Kendricks! You kicked me in the balls, and it hurts like hell."

I pulled himself up. In my relief, tears welled up and spilled down my cheeks. "What are you doing here, trooper?" I managed. "I'm so sorry. I'm so glad to see you. I'm so glad it's you and not..." I was jabbering.

Bonavita dusted off his uniform pants. "I think I just became a landowner," he said. "I'm going to have two achers." He reached and pulled me to my feet. "Last time, you cold-cocked me and disappeared into Mexico. I forgave you then, but I'm not sure I can take many more punches and kicks." Bonavita eyed my damaged face.

I was still ashamed of slugging Bonavita two years before, and now I'd injured him again. I wanted to apologize, but this wasn't the time.

As if to confirm this, another truck pulled up next to Eddleman's pickup.

"What the hell is going on?" I said while Bonavita turned to look, still clutching his injured gonads. The truck engine died and two people sprang from the cab, moving quickly through the dust cloud they'd just stirred up.

DEA agent Breaux was first to the screen door. "Been looking for you, Mr. Kendricks," he said in his low Cajun drawl, "You look like shit." He sounded relieved. Pointing to Eddleman's truck, he continued. "Eddleman's truck confirms my guess was right. Where is he?"

Suddenly pulled back to reality, I pointed inside. "He's in a bad way. We need to get him to a hospital asap."

The floodlight over the porch provided Breaux enough light to give me a quick once-over, before disappearing inside. Trooper Bonavita followed in his footsteps. I started to go after them, my mind grasping for a sensible explanation for what they would find.

"Hey, Purdy." Standing at the edge of the floodlight's reach, partially in shadows, stood Jake Nichols, his pudgy hands wrapped around an M16.

"Jake, what are you doing here? And what are you doing with an M16?"

Jake stepped toward me. From inside the house, I heard Breaux and Bonavita exchange comments, their voices mixed with Teofilo's Spanish and murmurs from the wounded Eddleman.

"I came here to help you, Purdy," Jake said, apologetically. "I heard you might need it, and I guessed where you'd be."

Things were coming at me too fast. I waved Jake inside the porch while I desperately searched for a place to sit down. "Why are you three here?" I leaned forward and put my head between my legs, about to black out. How was I going to explain how I'd damned near killed a DEA agent? And two bags full of money stashed inside the old barn? Before I could dwell on the mess, Breaux stepped back onto the screened porch.

"My old partner doesn't look so good, Purdy. You shoot him?"

I nodded, too tired and hurt to explain. Besides, I wasn't sure my explanation would make any sense. "He tried to kill me, Leroy."

Breaux didn't pursue it. Instead, he squatted down next to my chair. "We've got help coming, Purdy, but right now I've got other things to deal with."

I looked up quizzically. "What?"

He pointed at me, then swept an arm as if to include Jake, and the occupants of the house. "Good intel. Drug crossing." He handed me a cold soda he'd retrieved from the old refrigerator.

I took a swig. The sugary drink seemed to restore my senses. "Coming here? You're shitting me."

"Maybe, but we've been tracking what can only be part of *Zetas* heading toward this end of Kickapoo County."

I glanced at Jake, who was awkwardly cradling the M16. "This is the best you can get?" I wanted to pull the words back as soon as they came out. Too late. Jake slumped as if he'd been smacked by a bullwhip. I tried to make it sound better. "I appreciate Jake. He proved his worth big time at Lagrimas. But where's the rest of the sheriff's office?"

I eyed the sad-eyed dispatcher, knowing I'd damaged what little self-pride he had. I felt like a total jerk, but Breaux wasn't aware of or interested in the slight I had given my friend.

"We need to get down to the river. If the *Zetas* cross, it won't take long for us to lose them. We're sure this is the follow up to their attempt at Lagrimas."

Feeling a little more cognizant, I rose, and we all made it inside the house, collecting around Eddleman, who still lay on the linoleum floor. Tio had found two pillows to prop him and an old jelly jar. Despite blood loss and shock, Eddleman had reloaded a mouthful of snuff, which he now dribbled into the glass.

My first aid kit was spread open around him, and Bonavita used the kit's surgical scissors to cut off his pant leg to expose the buckshot wound. The tourniquet's constriction had stopped the wound's flow of blood.

"When's the last time the tourniquet was loosened?" Breaux asked in English.

Teofilo responded in Spanish that he had done so about five minutes ago. The weathered old village elder knew more English than he'd been letting on.

Blood loss had taken the fight out of Eddleman. Teofilo, with dried blood on his hands, returned the Glock to me. *"No la necesitaba."*

I re-wet the towel at the sink and wiped my face. More of my facial blood turned the dingy cloth red. While I tried to clean myself up, Breaux, Bonavita, and Jake Nichols disappeared outside.

Teofilo patted me on the shoulder. "I am very tired, and you *norteameri-canos* are not helping me die in peace." He shuffled to the bedroom.

I took his place on the chair next to Eddleman. "Eddleman, you shot me," I said, and tried to pull my boot off. No luck. the wound began to bleed again. I decided to leave well enough alone. Another wave of darkness and nausea swept over me, so I decided I'd better stay put in the chair.

"You shot me better," he replied. He glanced toward the porch's open door. "What are you going to do with all that money?" he asked softly.

"I haven't given it much thought," I said, more worried about how we were going to get me, him and Tio to necessary medical facilities.

"Bullshit," he replied. "You're not as righteous as you let on, Kendricks." Eddleman dribbled more snuff, then shifted uncomfortably. "First thing you did was stash those bags in that old shed. You're no better than I am."

His accusation landed too close to home. I stayed busy applying a large bandage over my bloodied ear.

The porch door's spring squealed, and then it slapped shut. The three men returned to the kitchen.

"Problems at the river," Breaux said. "They are crossing drugs any time now. Just got some cell coverage, somehow. We need to try to stop them."

"Who?" I asked. It was the best I could manage before it dawned on me why Breaux and Bonavita looked so solemn. Even Jake, eternally clumsy and unprepared, seemed to grasp the seriousness of the soon-arriving event.

"You stay here, Purdy, while we'll see what we can do," Breaux said. "We've got backup coming."

"Like hell I will," I responded. I pointed toward the bedroom and joked, "As sick as he is, Teofilo could probably manage this shot-up bastard. I'm going with you." I rose unsteadily.

Jake reached out to stop me, but I pushed him aside, picked up my weapons, and staggered out to Lowell's abused truck.

Chapter 47

A double cross at the crossing

The aluminum boat scraped against the Texas shore, and a *sicario* leaped out to secure the line to the old sucker rod driven deep into the sand. Lazarus waited until Navarrete and the *sicarios* pulled the boat further up onto the shore before leaving his position by the electric motor.

"Where's the truck?" Navarrete asked.

Instead of answering, Lazarus led the men into the riverine foliage where the truck and boat trailer sat, facing away from them. He lowered the truck tailgate. "Load goes in here."

The five men returned to the boat, and, within ten minutes, the bundled fentanyl was stowed in Lazarus' truck bed.

"Now, for the rest of the load," Lazarus said while they walked back to the riverbank.

A *sicario* started to step into the boat with Lazarus, but Navarrete stopped him. "You stay here. We all stay on this side. No one else needs to cross." Lazarus opened his mouth to complain but Navarrete cut him short. "There are plenty of *muchachos* on the other side. Tell them to load the rest of the product and remain there. No reason to chance all of us getting caught on this side of the river." Navarrete pushed the boat off the sand, and Lazarus engaged the electric motor for the short crossing.

In the dim recess of the river's slopes, Navarrete could barely make out the keepers and two other *sicarios* awaiting the boat's return. *I'm not going to make it easy for you bastards to kill me,* he thought, pleased that, with his instructions, his keepers wouldn't be crossing to the American side. *I've bought some time. I'll make the run to San Antonio with this half-Mexican Lazarus. I may not need the DEA to save my ass.*

Ten minutes later, a low whistle signaled Lazarus was on his way back with the last of the fentanyl. The boat came into view and scraped into the sand on the American side.

Navarrete misjudged his keepers. Fewer drug bundles meant additional space in the aluminum craft for Lorenzo, Curly, and Moe and four others.

Lazarus spoke softly to Navarrete, his mustache crawling up and down on over his lip. "I gave them your instructions not to come. They said they were coming and pointed a gun at my face when I tried to stop them." Lazarus' voice cracked. "What in hell is going on?" The keepers helped unload the drugs and carry the bundles to the waiting truck.

Navarrete muttered a silent curse, then said, "What are your instructions about the boat?"

Lazarus cleared his throat. "I was to make sure the job was completed, drop the motor in a deep part of the river, then pull the drain plug and let the boat drift downriver and sink. How am I going to do that with almost everyone from your crew on the American side? I don't have any orders about someone staying on this side of the border once we get the truck through the fence and stashed on my property."

Moe appeared at the landing. "*Jefe,* the truck is loaded, and the product tied down. What now?"

Sicarios appeared from the cane brake and stood around Navarrete while he voiced his instructions. "Everyone, down to the river. Now!" Navarrete said. "I am to stay with the product along with the *norteamericano.*" He gestured to Lazarus. "You, take everyone else back across the river, come back, and I'll shove the trailer into the water too." He turned to the cartel members. "The rest of you get out of this area as soon as possible."

Navarrete stood, hand on his holstered handgun, anticipating some movement from the keepers. If they wanted to kill him, this was their last chance to do so, assuming they followed his orders and returned to Mexico. Only he and Lazarus would remain on the American side.

"*Perdoname, jefe.*" Someone, not one of his keepers, shoved the barrel of an automatic rifle against the back of Navarrete's head. "We cannot do it the way you said." The bastards had allies Navarrete hadn't known of. "We all go with the truck to where this half-breed *gabacho* says, and we unload it."

"There is no reason to unload the truck," Lazarus replied, seemingly oblivious to Navarrete's personal danger. "I'm to stash it. Another vehicle will move the drugs off my property and to San Antonio. My instructions were explicit."

A *sicario* relieved Navarrete of his revolver from its holster. "Sorry, *jefe*, but change of plans."

It was now clear to Navarrete. *I thought I had outthought those bastards. Instead, my keepers are here in Texas and at least one more sicario is in on their plan.* He turned to Lorenzo and the two other keepers. "So, I'm to die?"

"No, *jefe*, we were sent with you to ensure the product's safe delivery."

"Then why did you take my weapon? Does Cantinflas no longer trust me?"

Lorenzo shook his head. "I am a *Zeta, jefe*. I just do what I'm told."

Witnessing the exchange, Lazarus began to moan.

"What's *your* problem," Navarrete asked.

"Are you bastards going to kill *me*?" Lazarus asked.

Both of us, Navarrete thought, but only said, "Let's get this product onto your property."

Lorenzo pushed Navarrete toward the truck. Navarrete let out a low laugh. "You bastards are going to double-cross me, and you are also betraying our *norteamericano* landowner. Cantinflas will kill all of you."

Lorenzo said, "Ah, *jefe*, please don't insult me with your threats." Two other *sicarios* patted down Navarrete and Lazarus. They missed the small pistol in Navarrete's pocket.

Moe, the presumed stupid one, began to give orders. "Everyone get in the truck." He grabbed Lazarus' shirt collar and pushed him into the driver's seat. "Drive slowly, to where you intend to hide the truck."

Lazarus pleaded, "I have my own job to do. If I do it properly, I am to be let free, and my family won't be harmed. Please." He began to sob.

"Not our problem," Moe said. He climbed into the passenger side, his machine pistol pointing at the broken man. "Very slowly. Take us directly to where you were to hide this truck."

A tall *sicario* forced Navarrete on top of the bundles, where he sat. *At least when I die, it will be quick,* he thought. *No torture. It could be worse.* Through driver's side window, he heard Lazarus blubbering, pleading for Moe to spare him.

Another *sicario*, one from the first crossing, tapped Navarrete on the shoulder. "Sorry. We didn't know until just before we crossed. It wasn't our plan. Blanco has given us all orders. We mean no disrespect."

Navarrete said nothing. He looked up at the sky. No helicopter. No *gringo* DEA agents. Nothing to stop what was about to happen. He made the sign of the cross, something he never did, wondering how many minutes until a bullet shredded his brain.

Chapter 48
Redemption and battle

Eddleman's unintelligible noises reached me as I stepped out of the patio. Breaux turned, opening the kitchen door, then ducked as a jelly jar partly full of snuff-ladened spit shattered against the rear wall.

"Don't leave me here," Eddleman managed, totally spent from the angry effort. He coughed, then gagged. "Don't leave me here," he repeated.

I followed Breaux inside. He squatted on his heels next to the wounded man. "You're not in good shape. Help's on the way. There's a helicopter coming, just like at Lagrimas. They'll get you to a hospital."

Eddleman shook his head violently, then let his head fall back on the pillows. "Listen. I can help. Doesn't take a standing man to help you in a firefight."

Breaux shook his head, but Eddleman suddenly reached out and pulled him off balance.

"I need to go," Eddleman said, gritting his teeth. As he spoke, his clutched fist pushed and pulled on Breaux's shirt.

Bonavita, Jake, and I looked at each other uncomfortably. Dirty linoleum floor, yellowish overhead kitchen light, tattered furniture were all part of a badly prepared stage set for a family argument. Breaux looked at his phone again.

"No bars." He speed-dialed despite this. "No coverage again, dammit." Clearly conflicted, he looked at the three of us. "Can someone stay with Jack?"

All three of us offered. My offer was tepid. I couldn't help but wonder whether staying with Eddleman was truly the smartest thing to do. *This is going to be my, what? Fourth gun fight with Mexican cartels? The odds surely are gonna catch up with me.*

Breaux pulled Eddleman's hand away and turned to me. "Purdy, let's double check Jack's wound."

I bent down and confirmed that the tourniquet was working. The wound barely seeped. I rummaged in the first aid kit and found several trauma bandages — the type that could be tied.

"Time's running out, if there's a river crossing," Bonavita offered.

I packed the leg wound with a trauma bandage, then another. "We'll all get caught flatfooted in this house if the drug runners come this direction. I carefully released the tourniquet pressure. The bandaged area bloomed with fresh blood, but the flow was light. "Either the trauma bandage is holding without the tourniquet, or you're running out of blood," I said.

"Good. Load me up," Eddleman said, his ashen face belying the brave suggestion.

It sounded like a horrible idea to me, but it wasn't my decision. Breaux turned to Bonavita. "Help me carry him to my truck. We'll put him in the front seat."

"Geez," Jake muttered. He looked like he was seeing a ghost. He set his weapon against a wall, and, with Breaux and Bonavita, struggled with Eddleman out the door.

I followed, thinking that if that bastard was willing to bleed out in order to get into the fray with a bunch of bloodthirsty *sicarios*, I couldn't think of a good reason for him to not do it.

Breaux helped me into my truck. "What are you doing with Lowell's truck? Can you drive? Come to think of it, are you in any better shape than Jack?"

I ignored the questions and started the engine.

"We need all the ammo anyone brought." Breaux shouted.

"Wait!" I hobbled out of the truck. "Are we just going down there to get our asses shot off, or are we going to come up with some sort of plan?" I swept my hand as if to include all five of us. "Because I haven't heard anything about how this is going to go down."

A short interlude with lots of suggestions from all of us ensued. I don't remember any of us contemplating any exit from the river except through my property. Jake, rummaging around in Lowell's toolbox for more ammunition, pulled out a small black case.

"What's this, Purdy?"

Abner had gifted me a night vision monocular the night we shot up the *sicarios* on Lowell Johnson's ranch. I'd forgotten it was one of the things I'd pulled from my shot-up truck at the wrecking yard.

He handed the case to me. I unzipped it and removed the monocular, then checked its battery strength. "Son of a gun. Still has forty percent strength," I muttered.

Breaux immediately recognized it. "This could save our asses, Purdy."

I led in Lowell's pickup, lights doused, with Jake in the passenger seat, and Trooper Bonavita in the bed. It was less than two miles to the Rio Grande. Breaux, with Eddleman, followed in his vehicle. In the darkness it was almost impossible to tell how close a distance Breaux was keeping behind me. How far did we dare approach before risking an ambush?

The road's deep depression several football fields from Otabiano's and Raquel's old house gave us a perfect place to stop without the brake lights visible at the river.

I got out of the pickup, and the throbbing pain in my injured leg almost took me to the ground. Steadying myself, I grabbed the long guns and quietly shoved the truck door shut. Breaux came up from his vehicle and whispered, "I remember this place."

His remark got head nods from Jake and Bonavita. I glanced through his windshield to get a read on Eddleman, but the cab was swathed in darkness. We belly-crawled up to the lip of the swale. The cloudless sky with only the Milky Way gave nothing remotely close to light. The area and everything nearby was a pale gray. Beyond that was the black sky and the gurgling river.

Breaux nudged me. "I don't see anyone."

I'd turned off the monocular to save the battery. Once on again, nothing in its eerie greenish tint looked out of order. Sudden movement flashed to the left - a jackrabbit.

"Someone anywhere near the riverbank will hear our trucks coming. As crazy as it sounds, it's probably safer to spread out and go by foot," I whispered.

"It's what? Three hundred yards or so to the house?" Breaux asked. "Then what?"

I explained the layout. Vasquez's old house was situated on a small bluff just above the river. Upriver, the land elevation dipped down toward a large cane break, and a low sandy bank where Otabiano had kept his john boat. Downriver, heavy foliage, then steep cliffs on land just outside my property. "If they cross, it'll be toward that sandy area where Otabiano and Raquel were murdered."

They were all familiar with what had happened two years ago.

"What about Eddleman?"

Breaux scrambled down to his truck and opened the passenger door. With the cab light turned off, Eddleman looked more dead than alive but responded with a grunt when Breaux spoke to him. Breaux gave a low whistle, and Bonavita and Jake scrambled to help him. The three-half carried, half-dragged the wounded man up to the lip of the swale. They laid him on the sandy soil. He put his head on his arms.

"Here's a rifle, Jack," Breaux whispered. "Jack? Jack?" He shook his DEA partner. "You still with us?"

Eddleman raised his head and mumbled something. He grabbed the weapon and put his head back down, this time laying his cheek against the buttstock.

Breaux patted his shoulder, then moved to where I was hunched down behind a dense bush. After another minute of scanning the area, Breaux asked, "You think your leg is up to a quick move?"

I didn't have a choice. "Let's move." I stood, dealing as best I could with the throbbing in my leg, and we moved onto the brush and grass covered flat along the river.

"Spread out," Breaux whispered. Jake's eyes looked like saucers, and he panted from exertion and fear. But he was still with us, and not showing any signs of quitting.

The three football fields to cover stretched for miles. I trotted and limped, feeling my leg pulsing blood into an already soggy boot. I wondered if I'd lose the leg. The thought flickered just long enough for me to realize how absurd this whole damned situation was. *We're all going to get our asses shot off, and the leg wound isn't going to make a bit of difference.*

We reached the bullet-pocked stucco wall of the small house once happily lived in by Otabiano and Raquel Vasquez. Its solidness never felt so wonderful. Bonavita was already peering into the darkness past the east end of the house. Breaux crouched next to the low ornamental stacked rock wall that Otabiano had constructed outside the house years ago. *Jake?* I wondered, *Where the hell is he?*

Huffing and puffing, and nearly dragging the purloined M16, the over-weight dispatcher was still half a football field away.

My head seemed to be on a swivel. One moment watching Jake, the next peering into shades of gray and coal black landscape, trying to see the Rio Grande and its features. Over our heavy breathing, I didn't detect any unusual sounds. I powered on the NVS monocular and began to scan the terrain in Mexico. Three box-like shapes, the middle larger and more sinister, were silhouetted against the lighter green of the Mexican desert. "Holy shit," I muttered, mentally urging the monocular to draw in more details.

An engine started. The sound came from my right, upriver and on the American side - on my property. No road lay that way, only a path through the slowly recovering salt cedar and cane that had been burnt years ago. Headlights shone from inside the growth, splashing onto to the house's surface.

"Jesus Christ," Bonavita muttered. The cartel was already on this side of the border. Instinctively, Bonavita and I squatted, and Breaux spread prone, his weapon supported by the low wall's rocks.

A pickup truck shifted into gear and moved toward us. *Dear God*, I thought. The headlights encompassed Jake, still jogging along in his clumsy lope.

Jake was twenty yards from where we crouched when someone on the truck spotted him. Shots pierced the night air, and puffs of dirt exploded around him. In one desperate leap, he flopped behind the low rock wall.

The headlights continued to illuminate the house, but the truck abruptly stopped at the edge of the cane, less than forty yards away. Spanish words flew from several men around the pickup. *They found us.*

A hail of bullets splattered into the already abused structure. The muzzle blasts were blinding. We'd stirred up an ant's nest.

"I think we found our smugglers," Breaux shouted.

The gunfire suddenly stopped, and the night was filled with Jake's wheezing and Mexicans screaming instructions.

More shouting, then the pickup crept toward us, dismounted shooters followed behind, like infantry using a tank for cover.

"Stay down," My warning wasn't necessary. Everyone was in survival mode. The truck neared the house. It braked suddenly and muzzle flashes showed attackers breaking from the truck's cover, screaming and running toward us. Our once-protective wall was now a backdrop for an execution unless we moved quickly.

A Mexican raced toward me, his gun blasting lead. I dropped the monocular and dove through a broken window of the house into what had once been the bedroom. Scrambling to my knees, I stuck the M16 out the window and pulled the trigger five times. The attacker fell quickly. "Got you, you motherfucker," I screamed, my adrenalin overwhelming all other senses.

Someone, probably Bonavita, maybe Breaux, maybe both, opened up and splashed the truck cab with bullets. Whoever was inside screamed in pain. The passenger side door flew open, and a shape hurled out and, in a few steps, launched over the small rock wall and leapt onto Jake. Jake screamed as his attacker raised a knife. I swung the M16 around and emptied it. The attacker dropped his knife, and both men fell into the dirt. I climbed out of the window and pulled Jake from under the body. "Get your fucking gun and use it," I yelled, relieved my friend was still alive.

Breaux had disappeared into the darkness. Jake got to his knees. I pushed him down again and yelled. "You stay down. Just look for targets."

"Flashes have blinded me," he managed, then rolled toward me and emptied his magazine into the dark. "Someone moving! I think I got him."

I hoped so, but in the madness, there was no way to tell. I dropped lower on the ground and came up with the monoscope. Green suffused my vision. I swept it left. Right. Then toward the truck bed. Two legs showed a shooter using the truck for cover. Dropping the monocular again, I fired underneath the truck and heard the satisfying howl of pain. I raised the scope again. The legs were now part of a body, starting a crawl to safety. I fired four rounds, and then there was no movement from the lump on the ground.

Suddenly, five gunshots on the driver's side of the truck. Breaux, who'd come from somewhere, screamed, "Get out of the fucking truck, you bastard."

I couldn't see because of the truck's bulk and the covered load in the bed, but whatever had happened, the truck engine quit running and steam poured from under the hood. Jake lay still on the ground, but alive. I heard Bonavita around the east side of the house, taking deliberate shots toward someone or something just downriver from our position. *What the hell was I doing*? Lying there, so full of adrenaline, I felt I could take on the world.

The immediate danger seemed to have passed. Bonavita came around the edge of the house. "Maybe one, maybe two, went that way," he shouted, pointing downriver.

"Let's see what's in the truck bed," I said, and kicked Jake. "Get up, dammit. You're no good to us lying down."

We carefully moved around the truck. A quick count showed five dead. Breaux and Bonavita scurried around the shot-up bodies, grabbing weapons. Jake, for someone who'd witnessed a horrific fight, seemed to come out of it. "Hey, everyone. Look at this." We walked to the driver's side. The man Breaux had flung to the ground was dimly lit by the truck's interior light. He wore a thin mustache and a look of surprise at the holes in his chest where three rounds had exploded his heart and lungs. "He doesn't look like a *sicario*," Jake said.

"Holy shit," I said. "That's my new neighbor. Or, at least, was."

Breaux's next comment brought me back to the danger of our situation. "There were a lot more than five on that truck. "We need to find the others."

"Fat chance, in this darkness," Bonavita offered, as I turned the night vision scope on and began scanning the area. I saw nothing, until I looked across into Mexico. "Holy shit! Everyone get down," I screamed. We ducked just in time as the heavy bark of the Humvee pedestal-mounted machine gun began spitting bullets toward us. In the darkness, the deadly beauty of tracer arcs reached toward us. I squatted behind Otabiano's house as low as possible, hoping its concrete and rock walls were strong enough to withstand the punching power of the machine gun bullets.

Jake pushed around me to the edge of the house. "You all go look for the others. I can keep this guy busy."

I wondered *Where did that bravado come from*? I patted him on the shoulder.

"In a minute, Jake. Be careful. Aim toward the flashes." I yelled out, There are two other trucks, one on each side of the Humvee. Aim at them too," The night vision scope had help save us.

I knelt beside him and began putting rounds across the river. Bonavita and Breaux joined in.

Five minutes of unholy racket numbed my ears, and, suddenly, the Humvee backed up and drove away. The two pickups didn't move. The firing from Mexico stopped. The threat from the other side of the Rio Grande seemed to have ended.

"Let's wait for reinforcements to find any others," I said unenthusiastically. The idea of tromping in the bushes looking for armed *sicarios* in the pitch black with a bum leg was a non-starter. Jake had been shooting from a kneeling position. "C'mon, buddy. You've done real good." I slapped him on the shoulder. Jake didn't move. I reached down to pull him erect and jerked away as my right hand felt his blood.

Before I could fully grasp what had happened to my friend, gunfire erupted from the swale we'd just come from, clearly from at least two different caliber weapons.

"Oh shit," screamed Breaux. "Eddleman."

Chapter 49

A bloody aftermath, a funeral, and a parting gift

Breaux sprinted back toward Eddleman's location where we'd left the trucks. Bonavita yelled, "Wait!" and chased after him.

Not very smart, but I didn't give a damn. I found my flashlight, bent down, and shined it on Jake's face. His left eyelid drooped. His eyes were open, but he wasn't seeing anything. I pulled him away from the wall and jerked his jacket open, feeling his torso with my free hand. It was coated in his blood.

Not thinking, I screamed for help, then realized there were unaccounted-for *sicarios*. I grabbed the monocular and swept the area as best I could from a kneeling position, threw the device to the ground, and ripped at Jake's shirt. Buttons popped off, one smacking me in my right eye. I blinked away blurriness and looked for his wound.

"Aw, Jeezuz." A bullet had hit Jake in the abdomen, two inches below his bellybutton, probably fired from the machinegun mounted on the Humvee. Which meant a large caliber bullet with massive force. We were three hundred yards from our vehicles and a lot farther to the ranch headquarters where we'd left my first aid kit.

In the dark, I was helpless. Despite steam pouring from the *sicario's* truck radiator, I raced to its driver's side, stepping over a dead body half in and half out of the cab. I pushed and kicked the corpse out of the way and climbed onto the seat. I shoved the shifter into park and twisted the ignition key.

The bullet-ridden vehicle coughed and chugged, then started. I left the engine sputtering and ran to Jake, somehow getting his damaged body up and partially over my shoulder.

"Damn your fat ass." I grunted as his legs caught in the rocks of Otabiano's small wall. I pushed his limp body partially into the cab. Then from the driver's side, I pulled his shoulders until he was mostly inside. Ignoring Jake's legs draped nearly to the ground out the open passenger door, I feathered the engine, put it in gear and turned to the north, banging on the horn. The temperature gauge, amazingly intact, showed in the red, and the engine backfired.

A body lay in my path. No time to maneuver. No time for niceties. The truck bumped over the dead man. The body got entangled under the frame and scraped through the rocks and brush. It was suddenly released, and the rear wheels climbed up and over the mutilated corpse.

When I neared the shallow swale where we'd left Eddleman, it dawned on me that I was driving head-on into where the last gunshots had come from. The engine started to die. Too hyped, I feathered the accelerator and the truck spurted forward. Then the engine quit. Going too fast to negotiate the drop, the truck went airborne, then slammed down and stopped. My head smashed into the headliner, and Jake's body began a quick exit out the passenger side open door. I grabbed his jacket but was unable to stop his limp body from flowing out onto the ground.

"Shit. Oh, shit. Oh, shit," I screamed and clambered out of the truck, stepping around bundles that had been flung out of the bed and were strewn all over the ground, some broken open with a white powder around them.

Jake may have moaned when I reached him. I'm not sure, as all hell broke loose where Breaux and I had parked our trucks. Even with the sliver of the moon, now out from behind the cloud cover, all I could see were dark figures and muzzle flashes.

Suddenly, someone knocked me to the ground and yelled, "stay down," then disappeared into the darkness.

Three shots from a pistol went off. Then...nothing. *What had just happened?*

"Over here," Bonavita yelled.

Breaux responded with a cough, and then a weak "on my way."

I sensed that Jake's and my presence was of little importance to the two men at the moment.

Then, with unconcealed Cajun accent, Breaux screamed, "Goddammit, Jack, don't die on us now."

I crept toward Breaux's voice and tripped over a *sicario*. Taking a chance, I turned on my flashlight. The body was unmarked, arms crossed over its chest. I kicked the body's ribs hard to make sure he wasn't playing possum. No movement. I started to pass by, then noticed his hands: scarred and heavy. A memory flitted by, and I shined the light on the man's face. The cheeks showed old damage, and one eye orbital area was pushed in. This one had once been a boxer. Nothing more to see above the eyes. A bullet had exited his forehead, taking much of his head with it.

Breaux and Bonavita knelt around Eddleman. He lay on his back, arms splayed on each side. I knew immediately he was dead and wondered whether the buckshot wound had caused him to bleed out. I hoped not.

Breaux flashlight's beam confirmed the sightless eyes of the dead DEA agent. For some reason, I took note of the round shape of Eddleman's snuff tin, undisturbed in his shirt's left breast pocket.

"What happened?" I asked.

"He got one of them," Bonavita volunteered, "but he took two rounds through the chest." The young highway patrolman's voice cracked. "Didn't know the guy, but..."

"Chest?" We'd left Eddleman prone on his belly, barely able to hold his head up.

Breaux nodded and pointed toward a dark form lying in the bottom of the swale. "Looks like he managed to roll over and catch that Mexican coming up behind him before he died." Breaux was clearly distraught, tears in his eyes, not yet falling.

I changed the subject. "There's a dead one over there." I pointed. "He took a round through the back of his head. I can't tell, but I think I've seen pictures

of the guy before. Which means he was something more important than just a
gun toter."

In the distance, the eggbeater sound of helicopters increased in volume.
The cavalry had arrived. Just not in time.

******

First Methodist Church in Santa Rosa seats about one hundred worshipers,
which made Jake's funeral impossible to be held there. Father Joseph Levant,
priest in charge of the Most Pure Heart of Mary Catholic Church, graciously
offered its much larger facilities. Even then, the place was packed to overflowing.
Jake didn't have any close family, at least none that I knew of. But he was known
by everyone in the county. He'd coached Little League baseball, volunteered for
blood drives, and was often the smiling face of law enforcement. As expected, I
was asked to do the eulogy.

Earlier, I'd checked on Teofilo at the Golden Horizon Senior Services
Center outside of town, the same place where my mother was spending her
last days. Immigration authorities hadn't known what to do with him, so they
did nothing, and, with my promise that I'd pay for his no-doubt short stay, Teo
found himself well cared for in a safe place with clean sheets.

I drove back into Santa Rosa, and, using a crutch to steady my bad leg,
limped into my sister-in-law's house. Betty and I hung out with Paula and her
family as everyone dressed for the service. I'd written six single-spaced pages
about Jake but what I was going to say couldn't capture the essence of my
friend.

"I can't go through with this," I said to Betty, both of us sitting at the
kitchen table. "Fifteen minutes? It's like trying to fit fifty pounds of memories
into a two-pound paper bag."

Forrest ran past me, chasing one of his cousins. He stopped suddenly and
gave me the look that only a child can give. "Daddy, wasn't Jake your bestest
friend?"

I allowed that he was.

He tilted his head, reminding me for a second of a wise old man. "If
you want me to, I can go up and help you say the words." He reached up and

wrapped his arms around my neck. I caught a look from Betty before she turned away, eyes full with tears ready to fall.

"Forrest, you are a wise young man." I stroked his soft brown hair. "I want you to sit with your momma and Aunt Paula. They're going to need your strength. And do you know what? I'm going to feel your strong hands holding mine all the way from where you are sitting to where I'm talking. Deal?"

"I can't reach that far, Daddy."

I assured Forrest that, in a strange and wonderful way, he and I would be holding hands as I spoke about Uncle Jake.

Somehow, I got through the eulogy. Many in the audience wept through most of the service. There were some confused looks when the funeral director announced that Jake was to be buried in the Guadalupe Cemetery instead of the Kickapoo Settler's Cemetery where the county's Anglos were buried. Someone asked how Jake was going to end up "with all the Mexicans." I'd had a hand in that. He'd lived on the poor side of town most of his adult life, and before that, in Lagrimas. He would be buried with his people.

Lilly Pardo had returned, announcing she'd had all she could tolerate of her family, and that she was needed at the Cenizo Diner. Quietly, I'd enlisted her help in buying a cemetery plot near her family's. Jake would have loved it.

Rangers, members of law enforcement from all over the border region, and a good-sized contingent of DEA agents stood quietly as the VFW bugler pretended to blow Taps on a bugle with a recorder inside it. A color guard from a National Guard unit in Del Rio did their routine with the American flag, despite Jake never having served in the military. A captain, upon receiving the flag from his NCOs, presented the triangle of red, white, and blue to Betty, as Jake's representative. She wept quietly.

After the graveside service, people trickled out of the cemetery and into their cars. District Attorney Josh Hinton, checking his watch like he was late for his tee time, shook my hand and glad-handed Sheriff TJ Johnson and anyone he noticed wearing a star. As Abner once opined, our DA was just too dumb or lazy to get involved with Mexican cartels.

Betty walked to where I drooped on my crutch, and gently took my arm. Her eyes were red as coals from the crying. "What are we going to do with this flag?" she asked.

"How about we frame it and see if Forrest would like to hang it on his wall," I replied. Somehow, I thought it would be just fine there. She and Forrest left with Paula and her family, and I watched the gravediggers break down the tent and remove the fake grass covers over the mound of dirt that would fill the grave.

My leg throbbed, and I turned toward the chain link gate, hoping to catch a ride to the

VFW Hall where Lowell Johnson was hosting a barbecue for everyone. Special Agent in Charge

Victoria Fleming stood next to DEA Agent Leroy Breaux. She approached and shook my hand. "Thanks for everything you did."

I knew she didn't mean my shooting Eddleman with buckshot. The huge amount of fentanyl seized, and the *sicario* body count had helped the DEA gloss over the origins of Eddleman's initial wound.

"Rumor has it," Breaux said, "that parts and pieces of one of the *Zeta's* bigshots, Guillermo

Blanco, have been scattered all over Acuña."

Remembering the body of the former boxer and *Zeta segundo*, I said, "I'd still like to know what Navarrete was doing on this side of the border, and then with his head blown off."

Fleming suddenly gave me a hug. "That money Eddleman had? Thanks for turning it in."

"Only thing to do," I responded, but I knew Eddleman had only found a small part of Vasquez's stash.

Fleming, a stunner even in funeral garb, reached up and pecked my cheek. "You need to go find your family, Purdy. Again, thanks for everything." She turned and walked toward a government sedan.

Breaux lingered and I asked him for a ride to the VFW hall. "Sure," he responded. He opened his truck's passenger door and handed me my crutch after I sat. When he started the engine, Breaux reached into a pant pocket. "Here," he said. "This is yours."

He placed a non-descript flash drive in my hand.

"What's this?"

"Eddleman was rummaging around your property and found a shitload of money. So did Laura Griffin Saenz a couple of years ago. Purdy, you and I know Pete Vasquez buried a lot more money on your ranch than what's been uncovered so far."

Stunned, I stared at the flash drive.

"It was in Eddleman's pocket," Breaux said.

"What's on it?" I asked, still not grasping what I held.

"Purdy, don't be a dumbass. There'll come a time when you and Betty and Forrest will need some cushion. Just take it. There's some cryptic notations on the tiny amount of data there, but I suspect you'll know what it means." He pulled up to the VFW hall. "I erased any mention on Eddleman's computer. What's in your hand is for you and you alone. I give you my word that this conversation never happened."

"What about Victoria Fleming?"

"I liked Jack Eddleman, but he'd turned into a loose cannon. I didn't want to see him die, but it seemed inevitable that he'd put himself in a bad way, just like he did two years ago. Fleming, besides being a looker, is smart as hell. Let's just say that Agent Fleming knows a lot but doesn't know anything." Pulling up to the VFW hall, he smiled. "Now, hobble on in there, and make nice to Betty. She's your most valuable treasure."

And I did.

About the Author

Todd Blomerth is a retired district judge. He and his wife reside in Spring, Texas. He is the author of *Border Crossfire, Dalton's Run,* and *They Gave Their All: The Story Of The True Stories of the Brave Men and Women From Caldwell County, Texas Who Gave Their All In World War Two*. He can be reached at blomertht@gmail.com or his history blog at https://toddshistory.com.